Y

-3899

MAR 1 1

By Elizabeth Moon

The Deed of Paksenarrion

Sheepfarmer's Daughter
Divided Allegiance
Oath of Gold
Oath of Fealty*
Kings of the North*

The Legacy of Gird

Surrender None
Liar's Oath

Vatta's War

Trading in Danger*
Marque and Reprisal*
Engaging the Enemy*
Command Decision*
Victory Conditions*

Planet Pirates (with Anne McCaffrey)

Sassinak
Generation Warriors

Remnant Population*

The Serrano Legacy

Hunting Party
Sporting Chance
Winning Colors
Once a Hero
Rules of Engagement
Change of Command
Against the Odds

The Speed of Dark*

Short-Fiction Collections

Lunar Activity
Phases
Moon Flights

*Published by Ballantine Books

KĬΠGS
OF THE
ΠORTH

KINGS
OF THE
NORTH

ELIZABETH MOON

BALLANTINE BOOKS + NEW YORK

Copyright © 2011 by Elizabeth Moon

Published in the United States by Del Rey, an imprint of The Random House Publishing Group, a division of Random House, Inc., New York.

DEL REY is a registered trademark and the Del Rey colophon is a trademark of Random House, Inc.

LIBRARY OF CONGRESS CATALOGING-IN-PUBLICATION DATA
Moon, Elizabeth.
Kings of the north / Elizabeth Moon.
p. cm.
ISBN 978-0-345-50875-1 (alk. paper) —
ISBN 978-0-345-52479-9 (ebook)
1. Paksenarrion (Fictitious character)—Fiction.   I. Title.
PS3563.O557K56 2011
813'.54—dc22   2010041124

Printed in the United States of America on acid-free paper

www.delreybooks.com

2 4 6 8 9 7 5 3 1

First Edition

For Linda Varda, Master Sergeant, retired after thirty-four years in uniform (Army, Texas Army National Guard, Texas State Guard), senior NCO of her unit and First Sergeant. Served overseas in multiple areas, recipient of the Humanitarian Service Medal when, as part of the 92nd Aviation Company, she was involved in multiple rescues while supporting a high-altitude project on Mount Rainier.

And for Richard Dykstra, Lieutenant Colonel in the U.S. Army Inactive Reserve, after active-duty service in the Army and the Texas Army National Guard as Ordnance Officer, both here and abroad.

Both have served their country in many other ways as well, and it was my honor to sing with them in the choir of St. David's Episcopal Church in Austin, Texas.

Thank you for your service, and may the winds blow always at your back.

Acknowledgments

Thanks are due to the Thursday Evening Fencing Group (my title, not theirs) with whom I can work out the details of combat situations involving swords, daggers, polearms, crossbows, and so on. Access to the library at New World Arbalest was, and will continue to be, a great advantage to these books.

Thanks are also due to the community forming at the Paksworld blog, source of new alpha readers who were very helpful in pointing out problems with the first draft—and to existing alpha readers whose experience and ability to articulate what was wrong materially improved the book, especially David Watson and Karen Shull.

Once again, and every time, thanks are due my agent, Joshua Bilmes, my editor, Betsy Mitchell, and the "crew" at Del Rey for their fine work and their ability to keep me on track.

Errors, as always, are my responsibility.

Dramatis Personae

Fox Company (was Kieri Phelan's mercenary company)

Jandelir Arcolin, commander, Lord of the North Marches
Burek, junior captain of first cohort
    Stammel, senior sergeant of first cohort
    Devlin, junior sergeant of first cohort
    Arñe, corporal of first cohort
Selfer, captain of second (short-sword) cohort

Tsaia: senior noble families

Mikeli Vostan Kieriel Mahieran, king of Tsaia
    Camwyn, his younger brother
Sonder Mahieran, Duke Mahieran, king's uncle
    Beclan, a younger son and Duke Verrakia's squire
Selis Marrakai, Duke Marrakai
    Gwennothlin, his daughter and Duke Verrakai's squire
Galyan Serrostin, Duke Serrostin
    Daryan, youngest son and Duke Verrakai's squire
Dorrin Verrakai, Duke Verrakai, formerly a senior captain in Phelan's company,
    now Constable for kingdom
Oktar, new Marshal-Judicar of Tsaia (interprets Code of Gird for Tsaia)
Arianya, Marshal-General of Gird (commands entire Company of Gird)

Lyonya

Kieri Phelan, king, former mercenary commander and duke in Tsaia
Sier Halveric, Aliam Halveric's older brother, vocal member of Council
Aliam Halveric, commands Halveric Company, Kieri Phelan's mentor and friend
Estil Halveric, his wife
Garris, senior King's Squire
Arian, half-elf King's Squire
    elves
Orlith, Kieri Phelan's tutor in elven magic
Flessinathlin, the Lady of the Ladysforest, elven ruler of this elvenhome kingdom,
    Kieri's grandmother
Dameroth, Arian's father

Pargun

Torfinn, king
    Elis, his daughter
    Iolin, younger son
Einar, king's brother, traitor

Aarenis

Jeddrin, Count of Andressat
Alured the Black, former pirate, self-styled Duke of Immer, taking new name
    "Visla Vaskronin"
Fenin Kavarthin, Arcolin's banker in Valdaire

Adventurers

Arvid Semminson, Vérella Thieves' Guild
Dattur, kteknik gnome and Arvid's companion

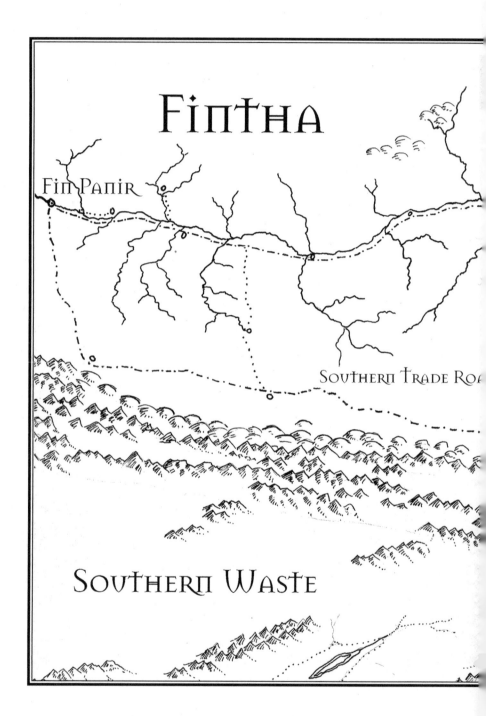

Fintha

Fin Panir

Southern Trade Ro

Southern Waste

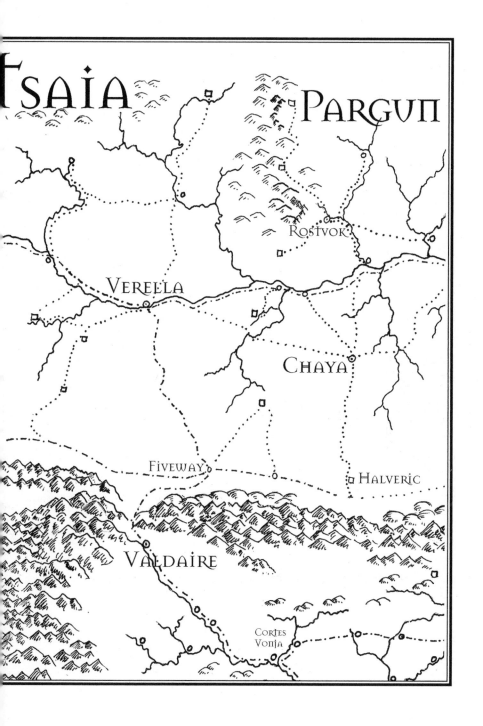

TSAIA

PARGUN

ROSTVOK

VEREELLA

CHAYA

FIVEWAY

HALVERIC

VALDAIRE

CORTES
VONJA

KINGS

OF THE

NORTH

CHAPTER ONE

Chaya, Midsummer Feast

Falkieri Artfielan Phelan, King of Lyonya, waited with barely concealed impatience for his grandmother, the elven queen of the Ladysforest, to appear for the Midsummer ritual. Under his bare feet, the moss of the King's Grove felt cool and welcoming; the fragrance of the summer night, flowers that bloomed at no other time, filled his nostrils. Yet he could not take full pleasure in the soft breeze, the cool moss, the sweet scents. Where was she?

He had spent the entire short night on the central mound near the Oathstone, expecting the Lady to appear, but she had neither granted his request to come early nor sent a clear refusal. He had hoped to use this auspicious day to ask her once again for help with his continuing effort to reconcile the two peoples, elves and humans . . . but since his coronation she had come seldom, and never for long. The whole night she had been *elsewhere,* and not even his growing taig-sense could find the direction.

He looked again at the stars overhead; the ritual must begin when the Summerstar touched the oldest blackoak's crown—and as he watched, the star slid that last short distance.

"Grandson," the Lady said. "It is time." She was there, where she had not been an instant before, and already she had begun the chant. No time now to remonstrate. He raised his arms high and sang as the sky brightened overhead. Across the Oathstone, she also sang, the two of them—so the tradition went—singing the sun over its midsummer peak. The Lady's hands drew patterns in the air, coils of silvery light, a net to capture the first rays of the sun's gold.

Kieri suspected she would withdraw into her elvenhome kingdom as soon as it was done, but as her enchantment wrapped around him, his irritation subsided. Her song, her power, held him fast. His mind soared: he knew he was in the place he belonged, performing the rituals he needed to perform. The taig responded to both of them; he felt it in his whole body, a tingling awareness of life that both nourished him and needed him. This was how it should be. But the dawn song and the Lady left him at the same time; her enchantment no longer clouded his awareness, and his resentment returned.

He knew she would not return until sundown, when they would spend another short night by the Oathstone. This time, he promised himself, she would listen to him. They were co-rulers; she should not ignore the king any more than he should ignore the Lady. She must at least explain why she had been so supportive that quarter-year ago and so ignored him now. Then he put that out of his head; he still had his own duties.

That morning he walked the bounds of Chaya, retracing the route he'd taken on his coronation day. Once more his subjects lined the streets and the city wall; now he knew many faces and names, and when a child wriggled loose from Berian, baker, and ran to him, he scooped her up.

"Jerli, where are you going?" Kieri glanced at the child's mother, who stood red-faced a few paces away.

"Give you Midsummer luck," the child said, pushing a flower behind his ear. Then she planted a wet kiss on his cheek and wriggled to get down. Kieri set her gently on her feet, and Berian snatched her up, face hardening.

"Don't scold her," Kieri said. "Kind hearts are Arianya's children." His own heart ached, thinking of his lost daughter at that age, who had run to him just as eagerly.

"If the king doesn't mind—"

"A child's good wishes? Never." He went on then, pausing at the four cardinal directions to pour a libation and break a loaf. At noon, he went to the royal ossuary to "bring the sun" to the dead with garlands of flowers. The Seneschal had a basket of fresh leaves ready; Kieri laid the leaves on eyeholes, mouths, earholes, and hung the garlands at either end of the ossuary. He felt a welcome from the bones; he sat on the stool the Seneschal placed for him between the platforms, and the Seneschal set the Suncandle before him, its fragrant smoke wreathing about him, then bowed and left Kieri alone. By custom, he would tell the bones how the year went, reassure them or trouble them as it might.

He had visited the ossuary several times since his coronation, reading over the stories incised on the bones, aware of something he could not define—clouds of feeling from this one and that, not all of them. But always the Seneschal had attended him. This was his first visit truly alone and the first when he had a report to make.

He let his mind quiet, trying to drive away that persistent resentment of the Lady's neglect, and then began, talking to the bones as if they were living men and women, his ancestors, standing around him. He told of the coronation, of the many conferences with his Council, his assessment of the Siers he had met, his concern about the lack of trade, the slow withering of the land's economy, his concern about the danger from Pargun and what seemed to him an unreasonable aversion to preparations for defense.

"And the elves and humans are still estranged," he said, into the silent near-darkness. A chill ran down his back, as if behind him someone had stepped out with drawn sword. He felt a tension in the silence: true listening, it seemed. It could not be, he told himself . . . and yet the hairs stood up on his arms. He did not glance around; he would not give in to the fear. "The Lady of the Ladysforest—"

The Suncandle flared, the flame rising to the level of his knees as he sat on the stool. Kieri felt sweat break out on his forehead. Were elves listening? So much the better, then; perhaps they would carry his message to her. He laid it all out in plain words, in a voice flat with suppressed anger. She was his grandmother and his co-ruler: she owed him the courtesy of her presence and the kingdom the courtesy of her attention and her assistance. She had changed since the coronation, and he did not know why. He was angry, he admitted to the bones, that she had neglected what he saw as her plain duty . . . and yet he was not free to act as he would if he were sole ruler. Even that day, that sacred morn of Midsummer, she had ignored his request and come to the Grove only at the final moment.

As if physical hands touched his face, he felt something—a warmth

on his right cheek, a coolness on his left. Something of his father—
the merest hint of a man's firm, warm hand on his sword-side, the
merest hint of a woman's softer, cooler hand on his heart-side. His
heart stuttered a moment, then beat on. He could not speak aloud; he
asked the question in his mind. *Are you . . . father? Sister?*

Yes.

What . . . do you want? From his father's hand—he could not
think it otherwise—came a sense of love, support, peace. He could
almost smell that dimly remembered smell, from times his father had
picked him up and held him close. From his sister's hand, something
different: affection, wistfulness, and—stronger as he listened—
anger. Then, sudden and strong: betrayal and warning.

Kieri scarcely breathed. *Betrayal? Danger? Who?*

They lie. She— But that was interrupted; his right cheek seemed to
feel more pressure.

Not now. No shadows this day.

The sensation faded, his father's faster than his sister's, leaving
the certainty that he had more to learn from them. The final
word from his father felt like *duty* . . . from his sister, like *judgment*.

"Sir King."

Kieri opened eyes he had not realized he'd closed; the Seneschal
knelt before him, picking up the Suncandle's holder, in which only a
puddle of wax remained.

"The candle has ended, Sir King."

"Thank you," Kieri said. He had no idea how long it had burned.
"I . . . I will need to talk with you after the rest of this." A wave of
the hand encompassed all the Midsummer rituals.

"I wondered," the Seneschal said. "From my post I saw the Suncandle burn higher than I have ever seen it before. When it flares,
sometimes there is a message."

"There was . . . something," Kieri said. "Something I do not understand, but must." He shook his head to clear it. "Seneschal, do the
bones ever speak to you?"

"Speak to me? You mean, do I hear voices?"

"I suppose . . . or something, some knowledge you feel the bones are giving you?"

"That, yes, Sir King. Just as you said you did, on your first visit. Is that not still happening?"

"Yes. But I do not know . . . how much is real. How much is my wish, or my . . . I was never given to fancies, that I know of."

"Nor would I think you so, Sir King. You have every aspect of a practical man, a man of experience and action. If your ancestors' bones are telling you something, then to my mind you should listen. I am at your service whenever you wish, but is it so urgent that you must ignore this feast?"

"No . . . I think not." Kieri sat down on the bench outside the ossuary to put on his boots. "I must come back again, find the time to sit awhile with them, and then—then I will need to ask you how to interpret what I think I hear."

He found the court waiting for him outside, musicians and all. He led them to feast in the shade of the trees at the edge of the Royal Ride. They ate sitting on the grass, even the stuffiest of the Siers, and watched as a parade of livestock decked with flowers and ribbons, mellow bells around their necks clonking gently, ambled past on the main street. Music eddied in and out of hearing as the breeze shifted: ballads, jigs, round dances.

"We never did any of this in the north," he said to Arian, one of his half-elven Squires. In the quarter-year since his coronation, he'd found himself attracted to her despite the disparity in their ages and his determination not to involve himself with much younger women. "I wish I'd thought of it." It did no harm to talk to her, he told himself.

"Were you even there, in Midsummer?" she asked.

"Not often. I spent the summers in Aarenis." Hot summers those had been, sweat gluing his shirt to his body, sun beating down on his helm. "When we were in a safe camp, I poured a libation on Midsummer Morn, and some of the troops would sing songs through the night." Kieri lay back on the soft grass, eyes half-closed against the gleams of sun coming through the tree's canopy overhead, and pushed those memories away; the present peace and ease were too precious to waste. After a time, the Squires talked softly among themselves. He scarcely listened, letting his mind wander to the coronation taking place in neighboring Tsaia, to his former captains Dorrin and Arcolin. He wished them well, a Midsummer prayer of abundance and health.

"But Paks said there were magelords in enchanted sleep out there," Harin said. Mention of Paks caught Kieri's attention. "If they are magelords, are any of them Verrakaien?"

Kieri opened his eyes. "What magelords? Where?"

"In Kolobia," Harin said. "When Paks was there with the Girdish, she said there were noble warriors in the stronghold the Girdish call Luap's. Didn't she tell you?"

She had, he remembered. Kieri nodded to show he understood.

"If some were Verrakaien, would they be under attainder if they were to wake?" Arian asked. She sounded fully awake herself. Kieri turned his head and glanced at her. She was plaiting the stems of pink and yellow flowers into a crown.

"Who could wake them?" Maelith asked. She fitted a wristlet of blue flowers over her hand and began work on another.

"Who would want to?" Harin asked. "Magelords were always trouble. Let them sleep, I say, until the end of time." Then he flushed as Kieri looked at him. The king, after all, had magelord blood. "The Tsaian ones, I meant."

"The Girdish are trying to find out," Kieri said without raising his head. "The Marshal-General visited me last winter—back in Tsaia—and I heard a little about it then."

"Surely whoever put them to sleep could wake them," Arian said. "And that I would like to know: how did they come to be sleeping there, and who else might be sleeping somewhere else?"

A disquieting thought. Kieri considered what little he knew of Kolobia, what Paks had told him. The magelords had taken refuge in that land, been attacked by something—perhaps the iynisin who attacked Paks—and then cast into an enchanted sleep. Why? For what purpose? And if what cast that sleep ended it, what would come out from that distant fortress? Allies or enemies?

"Maybe dragons out of the old tales are asleep somewhere, too," Maelith said.

"Dragons! They're all gone; Camwyn Dragonmaster sent them away."

"We thought magelords were all gone," Arian pointed out. "Maybe dragons are just sleeping."

"They were said to be shape-shifters as well," Sarol said, putting a pink and white wreath on his head. "We might have one in Chaya today: would we know?"

"The Lady would, surely," Arian said.

Kieri glanced around at his Squires, now all decked with flower wristlets, garlands, crowns of flowers. They looked harmless as any of the farm lads and lasses strolling down the lane but for the swords and bows laid close at their sides.

Some of them, he thought, must be barely out of Falk's Hall—certainly not more than a year or so. He felt his years of war and intrigue as a chasm separating them from him. Even Garris, leaning against a tree a few lengths away, a stone jar of summerwine in his hand, seemed young in comparison. His gaze met Arian's.

"I could make you one," Arian said, holding up a handful of flowers and grinning down at him as if she'd read his thoughts.

"Oh, just give him yours, Arian," Panin said, in a teasing tone. "Berne will plait you one to make it up."

Arian shook her head and gave Kieri a look he couldn't interpret. "No," she said, "I'll make my own." Before Kieri could move, she'd dropped her flower crown on his chest and turned away to pick more flowers.

It was not the first time he'd felt silent communications between Squires wafting past him, but he was not going to respond to it, whatever it was. If there were covert courtships or rivalries going on, better not to know. He'd learned that in the first few years he'd commanded his own company.

That Midsummer night, he and the Lady sang together again, Kieri trying to blend his taig-sense with hers. Once more she had arrived just in time, but he knew she would stay for the feast. The light of her own kingdom, the elvenhome kingdom, rose around them; the trees of the grove glowed silver-green. Other elves appeared from the trees below, circling the mound. Kieri had met many of them by now and knew their names, their families, some of their history.

After the ceremony the Lady sat enthroned on the mound, surrounded by her subjects. Kieri tried to approach, only to be stopped again and again by elves who wanted to speak with him—a courtesy he could not ignore. The Lady smiled at him from that distance but did not beckon him to her. He felt like a child—loved, perhaps, but not wanted in what was an adult conversation. For all that she was his grandmother, she seemed less cordial than the elves who spoke to him.

One who sought him out and begged him to sit with her for a time was—she had confided before—one of the youngest and formerly a friend of his own elven mother. Her crown of violets and tiny white mist-stars released a haunting fragrance. Though she looked younger than his Squires, he knew she must be older; his mother had died nearly five decades before.

"Guess my age," she said, teasing.

Kieri had been wondering but without permission could not have asked. Asking an elf's age was, for reasons he didn't understand, as rude as a slap in the face. Younger than the others . . . age of his mother . . . he tried to calculate what that might have been.

"Eighty?" he ventured.

"No, no," she said. "Your mother was older than that when she bore you. I am just over two hundred." She smiled at his confusion, and he felt like a toddler beside her, his fifty years banished by her smile. "But you are as handsome as your father, and you also are a king. And I am accounted a mere child by most elves." She twinkled at him. "Some of us younglings might even be interested in you, should you wish to have an elven queen, as your father did." The look she gave him from wide eyes the color of the violets in her hair made it clear she was one of those.

The thought of having a wife more than two centuries old chilled his loins, beautiful as she was, for he knew she saw him as the flower of a season, soon to wither and blow away and be replaced by another. He glanced toward the Lady and saw that she was watching him and the young elf with both speculation and approval. That was worse—his ancient and ageless grandmother watching him with a woman as old as his mother would have been. He murmured what pleasantries came to mind and did not touch the hand that hovered for a moment over his. The elf-maid chatted on a moment more, then shrugged slightly and withdrew. Kieri glanced again at the Lady; now her expression was remote, and she seemed to be looking past him.

Before he could reach the Lady without discourtesy to those who delayed him, she had once more withdrawn herself and the elvenhome kingdom, leaving him alone with the new dawn. His anger flared; he felt alongside it, like a thread laid alongside a rope, what had the flavor of his sister's anger and her warning. What had she known, that he needed to know?

Could she have meant the elves, all the elves? Or only the Lady?

Back in the palace, Kieri considered going directly to the ossuary, but he knew the armsmasters would expect him in the salle. For that matter, he welcomed the chance for open combat. Sure enough, both armsmasters were waiting for him with what looked like indecent glee.

"I hope you're not too sleepy, Sir King," Carlion said, tapping the blade of his wooden waster on his heart-hand.

"You do not intend to go easy on me, I take it."

"It would be a disservice," Siger said. He blew on his fingers. "Danger comes on its own terms. As the king knows."

"You are terrible men," Kieri said, grinning at them. He felt more awake already. "I shall have to do something about you." He turned to the chest of bandas, lifted the lid, then glanced back. Siger was where he had been, but Carlion—Kieri snatched a banda from the chest, whirled just in time, and parried Carlion's blade with the banda.

"I told you that wouldn't work," Siger said. He had his thumbs stuck in his belt now. "Always more awake than you think, the Fox is."

Carlion shrugged as he backed away. "I've caught a lot of 'em with that. Worth trying."

"You have no respect for your king," Kieri said.

"Not so, Sir King. I have enough respect for my king to test him. With due respect for your predecessor, I dared not test him, even as a young man. He was willing, but never strong or fast." Carlion stood beside Siger now, and tucked his waster under one arm so he could put his thumbs, too, through his belt. "I'll bide here until you're ready."

Kieri put on the banda, fetched a waster from another chest, and came back to face them.

"Pardon, Sir King, but that's not the length and weight you usually use," Carlion said.

"As you said, danger comes on its own terms. I might not have my own weapons—I might have only a branch or . . . or a jug of water or a loaf of bread."

Carlion raised his brows. "Well, then, another time I'll be sure to have them on hand so you can gain mastery with such weapons. Ready?"

Kieri nodded, and the day's practice began. A full glass later, sweaty and breathless, he felt much better despite a few fresh bruises. Physically, at least. Swordplay could not erase his worry about the estrangement between the peoples of his realm. Increasingly he sympathized with the humans. Just like his grandmother, the other elves avoided any disturbing or difficult issue by retreating to the elven-home kingdom, where even he—king of the realm—could not go without invitation, an invitation that never came. Yet whatever course of action he proposed, Amrothlin or Orlith would insist it must await the Lady's approval.

Garris wandered in, eyes bleary. "When will I ever learn that summerwine knocks me flat?" he said. Kieri chuckled; Garris shook his head. "I suppose it's your elven side that makes you impervious," Garris said. "Here's the new courier schedule."

Kieri looked at it. "You shaved another day off the time to Harway," he said. "How?"

"Another relay station. Thanks to your decision to increase the number of King's Squires and those extra horses. Though you are going to need more forage, come fall or if we have any problems to the north." Garris yawned. "Falk's Oath, I'm sleepy. Anyway, I've also set up a schedule that gives every Sier no more than a two-day courier run to Chaya. I want to know if you expect them to provision relay stations on their domains or if you want the Crown to do it."

"They should," Kieri said. "Otherwise we waste time and effort collecting our Crown due, bringing it here, and then sending it back out."

"And if the best place for a relay station is on the boundary of territories?" Garris pointed to the map.

"Both domains can share expenses. In fact, wherever it's possible, why not put it on the boundary?"

"Good." Garris made a note. Kieri felt a wave of affection for the man who had been an old friend and had become a valued assistant, excellent at his new assignment. "Now," Garris said, "while I've got you alone—have you met anyone yet? No, that's a stupid question; I know you've been introduced to one Sier's daughter after another, but—"

Marriage. Kieri scowled at Garris. Did even Garris have to bring that up? He would marry—he had said he would marry—but he would do it in his own time. With someone the right age, the right temperament, who was not ambitious or coerced. His mind drifted to the King's Squires on the schedule Garris had brought. To one particular Squire. No, he must not. They were young, and he was a king, and he must be careful not to exert any pressure. "I'll let you know first, shall I?" he said to Garris with some asperity. "You and Hanlin of Pargun are two of a kind."

"Not so," Garris said, hand to his heart.

"Nearly. She's written me several friendly notes, always mentioning Pargunese princesses." He had answered politely but without much warmth. "She says they're beautiful. I expect they're as sly as Hanlin and as difficult as their father. The Lady wants peace, but I doubt she'd be happy to get it by way of such a marriage."

"I'm not urging that," Garris said. He scowled.

"And there are more important matters than my finding a wife," Kieri said, tapping his pen on the schedule. He mentioned one he could share with Garris. "Gods grant Mikeli made it safely through his coronation."

"You think he might not?"

"Verrakaien," Kieri said. "They didn't want me king in Lyonya; they won't want Mikeli king in Tsaia."

"But they're under attainder—"

"And Dorrin warned us they can take other bodies. The prince— the king now—survived one attempt on his life. I worry about another." He blew out a long breath. "I should trust the gods, I know that. Falk's Oath, I've been faithless so long, it's hard to practice that discipline."

"About the only one you don't practice," Garris said. He poured water from the flagon for Kieri and a goblet for himself. "I understand—we need a strong ally to the west. Prealíth—"

"There's trouble in Prealíth?"

"No, not trouble there. Rumors of trouble in Aarenis. You know—or maybe not—of the river trade to their ports and the sea trade around the Eastbight from Bannerlíth to the Immerhoft ports." Garris paused; Kieri nodded. "Rumors from Immerdzan and suchlike of increased pirate activity and a pirate king building a castle right up the great river."

"That would be Alured the Black," Kieri said. "I know him too well. Started as a pirate, turned to brigandry in southern Aarenis, with some story about being the lost heir to the old duchy of Immer, which had been vacant more than a century. He was our ally for a while against Siniava. In Tsaia, we heard of unrest in Aarenis the last couple of years." He cleared his throat. "Someday I'm going to have to do something about him."

"You? You can't seriously think of returning to Aarenis—" Garris's voice rose.

"Someone must," Kieri said. "He could be worse than Siniava, and I'm the one who supported his claim to Immer—worst mistake I made. According to Paks, it's one reason the Lady thought I might not be fit to rule."

"Kieri—excuse me, Sir King, but this is madness. *This* is your realm now. That's in your past."

"I'm responsible," Kieri said. "By Falk's Oath, I cannot ignore my part in whatever he does."

"But your duty's here—"

"Yes, until I've sired my replacement," Kieri said. "I'm not planning to storm off tomorrow, after all. But in time—" Now that he had time, having learned of his half-elven heritage . . . barring accidents or illness, he could expect at least another seventy years of vigorous life and a slow aging after that. By their standards, he was now in the prime of life.

"Well, then," Garris said. "You'd best get to courting, don't you think?" He picked up the maps and schedules and left the room, his shoulders stiff with disapproval. Kieri stared after him. He had not expected that reaction . . . yet when he thought about it . . . about leaving his father's and sister's bones to go to Aarenis . . . the weight of his inheritance dragged at his earlier determination.

CHAPTER TWO

Orlith was his next visitor. Surely, Kieri thought, *he* would not bring up marriage.

"The Lady was pleased with the taig's response to you during the Midsummer ceremonies," Orlith said. "She suggested that I advance your training."

"I see," Kieri said. "And in what way?"

"She saw you talking to one of the younger elf-maids," Orlith said. "But it appeared you did not understand the maid."

"I think I did," Kieri said.

Orlith smiled, a particularly superior smile. "She liked you," he said. "She made you an offer of marriage. The Lady had permitted it; the taig approved. You did not understand—"

Kieri put up his hand. "Yes. I understood she found me attractive and might consent to marry."

"And you did not—"

"She is my mother's age—the age my mother would have been," Kieri said, trying to keep his voice level. "I cannot marry . . . someone like that."

"She is very young for an elf—"

"I understand. She told me."

"Which was a great honor and a compliment to you." Orlith folded his lips in and crossed his arms. "I tell you, you did not understand. It would fix the taig-sense in your line for generations."

"Is that why the Lady did not let me approach her?"

"The elf-maid?" Orlith's brows arched high.

"No," Kieri said, trying to control his voice. "Herself. Was the Lady keeping me away to force me to talk to the elf-maid?" If Orlith wasn't using her name, neither would he.

Orlith's mouth tightened. "I doubt the Lady 'kept you away' but merely had no need to speak to you at that time."

"I had a need to speak to her, as I have had these past tens of days, as you know. I have invited her repeatedly; I asked her to come early the first night of Midsummer—"

"She had, doubtless, more urgent matters than yours."

Kieri felt anger rise and pushed against it. "She is my co-ruler; she has responsibilities to the realm."

"Indeed." A touch of scorn and disbelief was in that. "And do you not think the Lady had the realm's welfare close to her heart when she considered your need for an heir to succeed you and thus a consort who was not—as you remarked at your coronation celebrations— a mere child and yet young enough to bear children? Is there need greater than that?"

"There might be," Kieri began, but Orlith interrupted.

"You will allow me, Sir King, to finish what I have come to say. The Lady approves this match. The elf-maid is very young, for our people, and apt for bearing children. She will commit her life to yours—"

"That is not the point," Kieri said. "I cannot marry someone the age of my mother. Or someone who will outlive me so long."

"Your father did."

"My father had need to do so," Kieri said. "And did he even know how old my mother was? He did his duty—" He realized too late that phrasing could seem an insult to both his mother and elvenkind in general. Orlith looked angry now. "And *his* mother was not an elf. It may be different with you Elders, but for us, to marry someone the age of our mothers is—"

"Even if the maid truly loves you?"

Kieri sensed withdrawal as well as anger and chose his words carefully. "I do not think she loves, or even thinks she loves, the man I am. I think she loves the idea of repeating—perhaps completing— the pattern of elf-maid marrying a human king. It is something she would do for the memory of her friend, my mother, and for closing a circle . . . but not the real desire of her heart."

Orlith's arms relaxed. "So you are not rejecting her for any flaw?"

"Flaw! No, in my eyes she is flawless. I meant her no discourtesy. You are right: I did not recognize what she said and did as an *offer* of marriage, but as permission to court her, if I wished to do so. I do not wish—not because of any flaws in her but because—" He could not tell this ancient person the exact truth; what he had said already must serve. "I will know, when I find the right woman, who it is. I felt nothing from within or from the taig."

"The taig seems not upset, true," Orlith said. He spoke more slowly than usual. "The Lady assured me it had agreed to your union with the maid if it so happened, but I sense no real regret from the taig that it did not." He paused, then shook his head. "Well. If that is so, and you have said it is, then so be it. But I warn you, the Lady is not pleased, and you may find her less understanding than I am. She is not wont to let human custom stand in the way of her plans."

Kieri opened his mouth to ask if she thought the king's will had any part in her plans but felt something sharp as a pinch in his mind that warned him not to open that topic yet. "Would she ask an oak to grow like an ash?" Kieri asked instead, hoping that metaphor would make sense to Orlith—and, through him, to the Lady. "It is the nature of humans to follow human custom as it is the nature of elves to follow elven."

"You are half-elven," Orlith said. "*You* should be able to follow either."

"I am but one person," Kieri said, "and for fifty years knew nothing of my elven heritage. Do not bend hardened wood until it breaks." He took a breath and dared more. "I am, after all, the king the Lady chose to rule with. She and I together, I thought: making decisions, taking actions. You know I have asked her, more than once, to talk with me, help me bring our people closer. Yet she does not come, and I do not believe she spent a full quarter of the year searching out a mate for me."

"You criticize the Lady?" Orlith looked furious again.

"I ask why," Kieri said. "Does she want me to fail? This realm to fail?"

"Of course not!"

"Then she should do her duty."

"You have no right to speak of her duty!"

"I am the king," Kieri said. "That gives me the right. This realm is my responsibility, and I am not going to let it fail because the Lady will not stir herself to tend it. She can spare the time for this, out of her immortality, or she can give up her claim to sovereignty."

"You dare! This land was ours; we share it with lateborn out of generosity."

"I dare because I must," Kieri said. "This land survived so long because—so the tales say, at least—elves and humans worked together. Now, as you well know, they do not—and she is not helping. Was she like this when my mother was queen? Did she help my sister when she came so young to the throne? Or did she withdraw to her elvenhome whenever my sister asked for her help?" That, after all, might explain his sister's sense of betrayal, if after losing mother and brother, her grandmother refused to have anything to do with her.

Orlith's expression was suddenly guarded. "Your sister did not ask."

"Why not, do you think?"

Orlith shrugged. "How would I know? She never spoke to me."

"Perhaps the Lady never offered," Kieri said. "I wonder if she even cares that my sister and I were her grandchildren."

"The Lady saved you," Orlith pointed out. "If she did not care, do you think she would have come?"

It made no sense. "I'm grateful for that," Kieri said. "But I don't understand why she is so . . . so changeable."

"She is the Lady," Orlith said, as if that explained and excused everything.

"And I am the king," Kieri said, "but that does not mean I can do whatever I please from moment to moment."

Orlith glared but said, "Then perhaps the king's majesty will condescend to have the lesson which I came to give. We shall go to the garden."

Kieri sighed inwardly, but he might as well comply. Though he felt—he was sure—that he was gaining taig-sense even when not around elves, he knew he needed more instruction.

In the garden, surrounded by the roses in full bloom and the other flowers, birds, insects, he tried to do as Orlith wanted, and use only his taig-sense to identify the components of the garden, but he could not keep his nose from telling him where the roses were, his ears from noticing the wasp that zipped past his ear.

Yet Orlith was pleased when he was able to sense beyond the rose-garden wall that in the kitchen garden a row of carrots had been pulled . . . there was a gap where five days before there had been a row of living plants.

"You have indeed made progress, Sir King. Now try to reach the King's Grove trees . . . do you feel them?"

"Yes," Kieri said without hesitation. "All I have to do now is reach out."

"Good. Then let us see if you can distinguish them." He handed over a polished stick. "Only one of the King's Grove trees is kin to this . . . can you tell which one?"

Kieri held the stick, admiring the gold and dark grain. "What is it?"

"Later. For now I want you to feel your way to the parent tree."

Kieri had no idea how to match the wood in his hands to his taig-sense connection to the trees . . . but the taig itself, he thought, might help. He imagined the stick as a tiny child looking for its parent . . . and as if that were true, one of the trees reached out. His hand tingled, and then he knew.

"Sunrising side of the circle," Kieri said.

"Could you put your hand on it?"

"Yes."

"Excellent! Try this one."

Dark wood, the grain barely visible. Kieri was sure it was black-wood, but he said nothing and let the taig lead him. This time it was faster; he opened his eyes and said, "Summerwards, two trees into the grove from the circle."

Orlith blinked. "Amazing. That is, indeed, the location of the tree. We will try one more—it is the traditional test—but I expect you will have no problems with it." He handed over a stick of wood with red and black grain that glittered a little in the sunlight.

"Fireoak," Kieri said. He had no need to ask the taig; it wrapped itself around and through him, and he and the tree both regarded the wood that had once been part of a particular limb on its sunsetting side with pleasure. He told Orlith; the elf nodded, smiling now.

"Well done indeed, Sir King!" Orlith stood and bowed. "It is enough for one day." Then he was gone in an instant, and Kieri realized that he had never answered why the Lady had not come, nor if she would.

Another chance gone. He wondered when Orlith would come back or if he even would.

Even as he stood up, one of his Squires appeared in the garden door.

"Pardon, Sir King—"

"Yes?"

"Master-trader Geraint Chalvers to see you—you had asked him for a quarterly report."

"Yes, of course." Master-trader Chalvers, the first merchant appointed to his Council, bowed low as Kieri came into the room. He had a cluster of wood and leather tubes under his arm.

"Sir King, I have the reports you asked for."

"Thank you, Master-trader Chalvers. Perhaps you would like some sib. I was just about to have another cup."

"Er . . . thank you, Sir King." Chalvers bowed again.

"We should go to a larger room," Kieri said, looking at the size of the rolls Chalvers had brought. "Are those maps?"

"Yes, sire. These were made for trade."

"Then we need the big table." Kieri led Chalvers to the smaller dining room.

Chalvers spread the maps out on the table. "You asked what impeded trade here. I know you've lived most of your life in Tsaia and the south—you're used to a trade network that runs at least from Fin Panir to the Immerhoft Sea. Here our largest problem is that we're at the far end of anything . . . we don't have an easy pass across the Dwarfmounts, we don't have a really good river port, and for overland transport our roads are inferior to many in Tsaia and the Guild League roads of the south."

"Have you yourself traveled to Aarenis?"

"Oh, yes, Sir King. When I was young, my father bade me follow the trail of Lyonyan goods all the way to the last buyer. I went as far east as the Immervale and as far south as Cha and Sibili, where I found them making tiles more cheaply than we could. I even came back with the secret of a blue glaze we did not have then. I was gone almost three years."

"Well, then, let's see what you're showing me." Kieri bent over the first map.

"Lyonya has many trails but only two real roads—" Chalvers pointed. "—along the foothills, where every spring the snowmelt and rain flood across the road and no one much cares to fix it. Wagons make it only as far as Halveric Steading, and some years not that far. There was a road, or so the tales run, all the way across Prealíth once, right through the Ladysforest, or what the Ladysforest is now."

Kieri nodded, thinking of his own journey the other way, from Bannerlíth to Halveric Steading: forest tracks and trails, dry leaves underfoot and more falling from the trees as day by day it had grown colder. Had he gone through the Ladysforest? He must have, and yet he had never seen an elf. A dim memory came of someone tall and shadowy, asking him questions and then walking into a silvery mist.

Chalvers was waiting for his attention, he noticed, and nodded again. "Go ahead."

"The other road is here, Sir King, along the Honnorgat. At thaw every spring, the river floods some stretches and makes it impassable for tendays at a time. That connects with an even less passable track in Prealíth but intersects one that cuts across here—" He pointed. "—from the river to Bannerlíth. Most of our traffic goes up to the river road, then into Tsaia at Harway. From Harway to Vérella, the Tsaian road is two wagons wide and passable in most weather. We do have wagon access here and here." He pointed to the southwest corner and partway up—opposite Verrakai land, Kieri thought. "But that middle way was never satisfactory with both Verrakai and Konhalt jealous of traffic. Mud holes and brigandage. We traders think the Verrakai supported both."

"So we don't get as much trade coming in or out, and it's hard for people to get their wares to a Tsaian or Finthan or southern market." Kieri looked the map over again; this one did not have all the steadings marked on it, only the few towns and the trade routes.

"Yes, my lord. T'elves don't mind; they don't depend on trade, anyway, not our kind at least. And there are Siers, you know, who are happy to live out in the woods on what they can gather and grow.

And I say nothing against that—each to his own. Only if we need an army, my lord, we need a way to feed and clothe it. I know *you* know that; I'm not meaning any disrespect."

"No offense taken," Kieri said. "You're quite right. Armies must be fed, clothed, and paid—they don't come cheap. Some changes we must make, and I agree that better roads is a good place to start. Where would you put the roads?"

"We can't do a thing about the southern trade road once it's in the Ladysforest," Chalvers said. "We'll likely never have a trade route by land to Bannerlíth. But up to the last steading before the Ladysforest, it could be improved—bridges over the runoff streams instead of fords, for instance. And the river road or that middle road, supposing the new Verrakai duke allows, could be laid out like the Guild League roads, all-weather roads for heavy traffic."

"Those cost a great deal," Kieri said, thinking of what he'd been told in Aarenis. "Where would the stone come from? And the labor?"

"That's this map, my lord," Chalvers said, unrolling another and spreading it on top of the first. Kieri stared. Chalvers had marked the resources needed for road building: where they were, what ways led to them, and his estimate of costs. "The roads alone will pay for themselves in five years—increased trade. It's true we don't have the population of Tsaia or Fintha, but perhaps we could hire rockfolk—dwarves or gnomes—to cut and move the stone." Kieri had doubts about that; he suspected the elves would not favor such a plan.

"But the real improvement—and we need the roads to make it work—is this," Chalvers went on. He put his finger back on the first map, on the Honnorgat northeast of Chaya. "The river towns have landing places and some crude wharves, but they're not adequate as trading ports. That's what we need. Water travel—down the Honnorgat to the eastern sea, to Bannerlíth at least and maybe around to Aarenis—would open new markets and be cheaper transport than overland."

"It's a long way," Kieri said, tracing the route with his finger. "Over the mountains, even going through Tsaia, is shorter."

"Yes, but Tsaians take toll of everything that passes through. Downriver, no problem. Harbor fees and cargo taxes at Bannerlíth, but I know the Pargunese and Kostandanyans trade to Aarenis without stopping there." He tapped the map again. "Look here. There's a marshy area, a double handful of little mucky streams, not good for anything: dig it out, make it a harbor off the river. What comes out to make the harbor can build up around it to support buildings." He looked up, grinning. "Our very own river port. Tsaian ports are all above the falls. They'd use our road to reach this port, and they'd pay *us* tolls. It would still be cheaper, even for them, than going overland—at least for some goods."

"You talk to the Pargunese?" Kieri asked; that had trapped his attention.

Chalvers shrugged. "Well . . . yes. There's some trade across the river—not much—but traders will talk to traders whether their rulers are friends or not. We've seen their seagoing ships heading downriver, loaded with furs and timber and whatnot. Salt fish, I expect. Woolen goods: their women are fine weavers."

Another problem Kieri hadn't anticipated. Tsaian traders, as far as he knew, had nothing to do with Pargun . . . but was that true? "So . . . you found out their routes," he said to cover his unease.

"Yes, Sir King. Right now, merchant vessels coming north have nowhere to go but Bannerlíth and one port each for Kostandan and Pargun. Pargun doesn't have a road from its port up above the falls, and they don't trade much with Tsaia anyway. Southern merchants would come to us to reach markets in Tsaia and Fintha if we had a safe port and a good road up past the falls. We might even attract the Pargunese. Better to trade than fight, eh?"

Kieri just managed not to shake his head. He had hoped for a new viewpoint when he insisted on having a merchant representative on his Council, but he had not expected such immediate results. Chalvers had the imagination his Siers seemed to lack and solid practical experience as well.

"I'm very pleased," he said. "I agree the roads must be improved. I have hopes that the new Duke Verrakai and Count Konhalt will prove able to reopen that middle road to safe travel within a year or two, but in the meantime we must see what we can do about our own roads. The river port . . . that had never occurred to me."

"It's an advantage we have over Tsaia," Chalvers said. "Theirs over us have been a few good roads and a short route to Aarenis, but they have only the one pass over the mountains. If there's war— well, I'm sure they'd go by sea if they could . . . and we would profit."

He grinned at Kieri, who could not help grinning back; the man's en-thusiasm was contagious.

"You are definitely the right man for this task," Kieri said. "Con-vincing the rest may be difficult. Though I am king, I prefer to work with my people rather than force them. Still, if we make a start with one road . . ."

Chalvers nodded. "Understood, sire. I am the newest on Council; I know that. But even a small start should begin to show its value." He bowed and withdrew. Kieri smiled after him. What a relief to deal with a sensible, practical human after Orlith! And he hadn't men-tioned marriage.

CHAPTER THREE

Vérella, Midsummer, Coronation Day

Dorrin, Duke Verrakai, sat her borrowed horse in the coronation procession, very much aware that more than Duke Marrakai's red chestnut stallion objected to her presence. The horse she understood—a spirited charger would resent her unfamiliar hand and seat. Her tact and skill should settle him quickly. But she felt the gazes of lesser peers behind her as if they were spears tickling her shoulder blades. How could she reassure them? Or would they always fear and distrust her?

Beside her, Kirgan Marrakai nodded, no hostility now in those green eyes. "You ride very well, my lord," he said, as they turned the first corner of the palace wall. Then he flushed, having revealed he hadn't expected her expertise.

"A fine horse," Dorrin said. "Kieri always preferred Marrakai-bred horses. What's his name?" She smiled and nodded at the crowd lining the street, held back by Royal Guard troops.

"Firebrand, my lord," he said. "Stable name's Cherry."

Ahead of them, the king touched spurs to his horse, and the gray curvetted; Duke Mahieran, just behind him, did the same. The red stallion jigged; Dorrin lifted her hand slightly, shifted her weight, and the stallion lowered his haunches, bent to the right, and began the half-parade. Beside her, Kirgan Marrakai did the same to the left, and the two of them formed a V behind the king and his uncle for a dozen steps before shifting to haunches out. As long as she kept him busy, Dorrin found, the red stallion steadied: supple, obedient to the lightest aid. She doubted anything similar would work with the peers.

By the time the procession had completed its tour of the city bounds and returned to the palace, the stallion had relaxed. Not so the peers, other than Kirgan Marrakai and Duke Serrostin; the others' glances were brief and ranged from anxious to hostile. The palace servants, too, as they helped the peers change from riding boots to court shoes, avoided her gaze. The same tiring maid who had giggled while adjusting Dorrin's court dress that morning now seemed terrified of her. No doubt the woman had heard that Dorrin was one of the dreaded magelords. Dorrin longed to get away, but law and custom decreed she must attend the coronation banquet.

In the anteroom of the banquet hall, she was surprised to see Duke Marrakai slouched in a chair; she'd assumed he was still in bed, under a physician's care. Dorrin, uneasily aware of the Marshal-General's displeasure and the fears of some of the other peers, stepped aside to let the others talk to him first, but he gestured to her.

"Come closer," he said. "You were Phelan's captain; I hold no grudge against you for your name."

"You are kind, my lord," Dorrin said, wondering why he said nothing about the attack in the courtyard. "But how do you feel?"

"They tell me I fell and hit my head—what a thing to happen on a coronation day, eh? But a head as hard as mine does not crack easily, whatever the physician says. I have a headache, that's all. Anyone might."

Dorrin looked at him closely, concerned. Despite his words, he looked the color of new cheese, and his gaze wavered. She leaned close. "My lord duke, with no intent to argue, I have seen soldiers take such a blow, who wore helmets. They needed to lie quiet; our physicians insisted on it. By your leave, I would have you obey the physician; you are not yet well."

"It is the coronation banquet—my last, I am sure, for Mikeli is young and will long outlive me. I do not wish to miss it." He gave her a crooked smile. "If I die now, no one will blame you. You had nothing to do with it."

So he remembered nothing of it; that in itself could be expected with a blow to the head, but as for the rest—if that were all, he should look better than he did. Dorrin looked around; the other peers, out of courtesy or nervousness, had left a little space for her and Duke Marrakai to talk, but the Marshal-General stood not far away, watching. Dorrin caught her gaze and nodded. The Marshal-General moved nearer.

"My lords," the Marshal-General said, her tone edged. "How may I serve you?"

"Tell Verrakai you do not blame her," Marrakai said. "She is worried about my health, but I am as hale as any man of my years. It was but a knock on the head from falling."

The Marshal-General looked closely at his face. This time her voice was gentler. "My lord duke, I understand her worry. Such blows are not always harmless; I believe yours did more damage than you know. Will you not retire?"

"No!" Marrakai's voice was loud enough to turn heads. More quietly he repeated what he had told Dorrin. "And I won't go off to bed like some errant boy who's displeased his tutor!"

This vehemence convinced Dorrin—and, she saw, the Marshal-General as well—that his injury was still affecting him and perhaps worsening. "Marshals have healing powers, do they not?" Dorrin said to the Marshal-General.

"So, it is said, did magelords once," the Marshal-General said, looking Dorrin in the eye. "Are you unwilling to use your powers that way?"

"Not unwilling but unskilled," Dorrin said. "Healing was the rarest of the gifts, and there was no one to teach me. All I've healed so far is a well."

"A well?"

Dorrin shook her head. "Too long a story for now. If you have the ability, Marshal-General, or know someone . . ."

Marrakai slumped in his chair, his head falling forward; his eyes had not quite closed, but when the Marshal-General called his name, he mumbled something they could not understand. Now the other peers crowded in, including Kirgan Marrakai.

"What did she do this time?" asked one of the barons; others shushed him.

"*She* did nothing," the Marshal-General said. "It is that blow to the head. Send for the physician and any Marshal in the palace. My lord Verrakai, I ask you to lend your aid, as a Falkian would."

"Certainly," Dorrin said. Every instinct told her they had little time, that something was wrong inside Marrakai's head. She had seen the same in battlefield wounds.

"Help me lift him from the chair to the floor." The other peers shuffled back as two palace servants came forward. Together with the Marshal-General and Dorrin, they lifted Marrakai—no easy task—and laid him on the floor; someone hastily handed them a folded cloak to put under his head. "Duke Verrakai, lay your hand on his shoulder—like that, yes—and one on his chest; I will hold his head. And now I ask all Girdsmen to pray with me for the healing of this peer of your realm, while I also pray and Duke Verrakai calls on Falk."

Dorrin felt hands on her own shoulders and glanced back to see Duke Mahieran and the king both standing there, as if guarding her back and joining her effort at the same time. Others, behind them, reached to form a human chain. She closed her eyes, calling on Falk and trying to feel what the Marshal-General was doing so she might aid. Power rose in her, as it had before without her bidding. She opened her eyes and looked at Marrakai's face. He had gone pale again, almost gray around the mouth. It wasn't fair—he had done nothing wrong—he had defended her; he must not die for that.

Her power moved along her arms; they first itched, then tingled, a sensation she had not felt when healing the well. She felt she could see the power moving up to his head, joining with something the Marshal-General was doing, though she could not say what that was. Something urged her to shift the power a little this way, a little that. She was unaware of time passing, of anything at all, until her power cut off suddenly and Marrakai opened his eyes and blinked. His color was healthy again, his lips pink, his eyes clear.

"What happened?" he asked in a more normal voice. "Did I faint?" He glanced from one to the other.

"Somewhat more than that, my lord," the Marshal-General said. "The blow to your head—"

"Blow to my head?" He frowned, put a hand to it. "When? How?"

Everyone started talking at once, telling what each had seen, a rising gabble of voices, until the king said, "Silence, my lords and ladies. This noise will not serve him."

Into the silence that followed, the king said, "You were attacked, my lord duke, and, when you fell, hit your head on the stones of the courtyard. You woke and were put to rest by the physician for a while but then lost consciousness again. You were healed by the Marshal-General and Duke Verrakai. You remember nothing?"

"No," Marrakai said. "Not clearly, at least, since—since the coronation ceremony. I feel well now." He moved his head on the folded cloak beneath it. "No headache—if only I could remember."

"Juris can tell you about it later," the king said with a warning look to the other peers. Kirgan Marrakai nodded to his father; the Duke shrugged and extended a hand; the Kirgan reached down, and Marrakai stood. He was steady on his feet, his gaze clear and focused. He, the Kirgan, the physician, and two Marshals both withdrew briefly.

This time the physician and the Marshals all agreed that Marrakai was as fit as he said he felt. The banquet started. Dorrin took her seat as instructed, but it seemed unreal. Too much had happened too fast. Too many people—still strangers, but now her fellow nobles—eyed her with a mixture of awe and concern. Marrakai, apparently now in perfect health, sat across from her, chatting with Duke Serrostin; Duke Mahieran sat next to Dorrin. At the head of the table, the king and his younger brother Camwyn—the boy looking uncomfortable— sat alone and at first spoke only to each other.

"It is clear, my lord," Mahieran said to her as servants produced a fish course, "that having you among the Council will ensure no dull days."

Dorrin shook her head. "I shall hope to bring no more excitement, my lord."

"I suspect you and that paladin have something in common," Mahieran said. "You cannot help what you are, and what you are is change." He chuckled. "I daresay this Coronation Day will never be forgotten, and since it turned out well in the end, the celebration's all the sweeter."

But was it the end? Dorrin kept waiting for something else to happen: a servant to leap at the king with a bolt of power or a carving knife, the taster to fall dead of poison, one of the peers to attack her.

The banquet went on smoothly, servants bringing in course after course, pouring the different wines, offering warm damp towels at intervals. Musicians played, jugglers and acrobats performed, a chorus of Girdish yeomen in their formal blue and white sang a deafening "O King Below, O Gods Above" to the accompaniment of trumpets and drum. Dorrin recognized the tune as one her troops had marched to, with very different words, some of which ran through her mind.

A stab of nostalgia smote her, but would she really be happier to be back in the field than here? She looked across and down the table draped in Tsaian white, rose, and crimson, glittering with crystal goblets, gold and silver plates, the peers in their many colors, their lace and jewels, the hovering servants in palace livery. Back there she'd had less luxury but the company of true friends. Here she might find new friends and clear her family's reputation. After all, she'd saved the king's life already, and that had to count for something.

She wondered what Paks would think. Paks, she suspected, would tell her to follow what Falk wanted, as any Knight of Falk should. Falk—when she tried to ask—said nothing. This was more Falk's world than Gird's, this magnificence and luxury, and Falk probably expected her to be comfortable with it. The next course was roast venison spiced in a way she'd never tasted. She finished the meal laughing at herself and her internal dialogues while Duke Marrakai talked horse breeding with Duke Mahieran.

"How did my horse carry you in the procession?" Marrakai asked her suddenly. "Did he give you any problems?

"None at all," Dorrin said.

"Good. I've taken care that he's ridden by others regularly, so he knows he's to behave. But he will try things, even with me."

"We had them all prancing and showing off," Duke Mahieran said. "I'm not sure if m'lord Verrakai asked for everything he did or if it was his idea."

"Both," Dorrin said. "I thought it would keep him busy, and if he offered more, I made use of it."

"What concerns me now," Duke Marrakai said, "is the security of the royal stables and stud."

Duke Mahieran nodded and turned to Dorrin. "Is it likely other grooms could have been taken over? Do you have any idea how long the transference has been going on?"

"A very long time, my lord," Dorrin said. "I looked only at the current family book, for those I thought would be alive now. When I glanced back, the same symbol was used as far as I looked. The worst of it is that some have been transferred more than once."

Duke Serrostin spoke up. "My lords, this is a matter of state; perhaps it should be deferred to Council."

"It is urgent," Mahieran said.

"Indeed. And this is a banquet hall with more ears than ours." His gaze flicked briefly to the king's table, where Prince Camwyn sat, cheeks flushed from unaccustomed wine. "Unless Duke Verrakai perceives another immediate threat, I suggest we confine our topics to those appropriate to a celebration."

Mahieran raised his glass. "And I salute your wisdom, my lord." He turned back to Dorrin. "At the Council meeting tomorrow, you'll be asked what you know."

"Council meeting?"

Marrakai leaned across the table toward them. "Of course— Verrakai's seat has been vacant since your uncle's treason, but as Duke, you're entitled to a Council seat unless the king changes his mind. You will have to spend hours—I was going to claim a headache, but you and the Marshal-General made that impossible."

Duke Serrostin, next to Marrakai, laughed. "You're incorrigible, Selis. You could let Duke Verrakai decide for herself if Council meetings are boring. Besides, complaints or no, you always show up early and are the last to leave."

"It's my duty," Marrakai said, hand over his heart. His eyes twinkled. Dorrin smiled a little uncertainly.

Serrostin smiled at her. "You'll find, Duke Verrakai, that we three are sometimes considered difficult. Once there were eight dukes in Tsaia, but after the Girdish wars only five intact dukedoms remained. The new king—the one the Girdish allowed—chose to break up the others into counties or redistribute the land to those who were left. The Code of Gird recommends dissolution whenever there's a break in inheritance—and for various crimes as well. Tsaian law doesn't require it, but the Fellowship has pushed for fewer large estates. At any rate, the Escral title died out about a hundred years after the Girdish war—that was in the northwest, bordering Fintha. Dirga, perhaps a hundred years after that—they bordered Lyonya in the southeast, from the mountains north to your own domain."

"What Counts Konhalt and Clannaeth hold now?"

"And others. There are some free towns. Brewersbridge is one, nominally in Clannaeth's rule, but it has special status. Fiveway— well, actually that's in Harbin's, I think. Counts can propose barons to the Crown Council—so there are baronies within counties—or the Crown sometimes grants them independently, when it's believed the baron will develop into someone who could manage a county."

"But very few dukes," Dorrin said.

"Yes. Well, that's natural. King at the top of the mountain, dukes next. More counts than dukes, more barons than counts, more commoners than anyone else."

"But are there only we four?"

"There's Gerstad," Marrakai said. "But he's old and never leaves home. Had no children—well, he did, but they all died in a fever. Bitter as gall, and I can't wonder at it, but he's never at court and his domain's in sad state. If it weren't for Count Rundgren—and you, Serrostin—"

Serrostin shrugged. "I do what I can," he said. "It isn't much; he won't allow it."

"So it is mostly we four," Mahieran said. "At this level, anyway. Which made it very difficult when your uncle was Duke, as we were not exactly close."

Next morning, all the nobles appeared for the Council meeting: the king named his new officers of the court, confirmed the new Marshal-Judicar officially as a royal appointment and Juris Kostvan as the new Knight-Commander of the Bells—a popular choice, Dorrin gathered, from the reaction. Then he named his Council. The others stood and applauded, then filed out, while the Council gathered around the table.

"I welcome you all," the king said, "both those who were on my Regency Council and those who are new to this gathering. As events this year have proved, threats loom over Tsaia, but together and with

Gird's aid we will prevail." He looked around the table; Dorrin saw the others smile and nod. "Now," the king said, "Duke Verrakai will report on the danger we face from Verrakaien magery."

Dorrin repeated what she had explained before about the transference of personality into unwilling victims. "And as I wrote the king, we found children—" she said.

"Their own children?" asked Oktar, the new Marshal-Judicar.

"I am not sure." Dorrin explained what she suspected about the parentage of at least some of the children who had suffered the death-sickness and "recovered."

"I do not know how you found the courage to kill them," Mahieran said softly, looking down. "I am not sure I could have, in your place."

Dorrin felt tears burning her eyes again. "My lord—I cannot say—only that the real children—the child they had been—had already died and this was a usurper. I fixed my mind on that, but it was not easy."

"I imagine not, even for a seasoned soldier like yourself." Mahieran paused, then went on. "Do you know, I think you may have more military experience than any other peer—at least until Phelan's other captain, Arcolin, comes to be confirmed at the Autumn Court."

Dorrin's heart rose. "Will he, then? I am glad to hear it. He's a fine man, Jandelir Arcolin."

"Surely you knew—"

"That he was given temporary authority, yes, but not that he would be confirmed in the grant."

"It is the king's decision, with the Council's advice—and we are now the Council." A murmur of agreement from around the table. "I favor it myself, though whether he should be made duke at once—"

"It's a big step, from captain to duke," one of the barons said, looking at Dorrin. Brenvor, she remembered after a moment. "What do you think?" His voice was challenging.

"Me?" Dorrin had not expected to be asked. "Arcolin has more years with the Company than I, and he was Kieri's senior captain all those years. He's served as his agent with all his business; he knows it thoroughly. If not a duke, what would you?"

"Count, perhaps," Brenvor said. "Even I can see the domain—and the Pargunese danger—needs a higher rank than baron to head it. But I'd like to see proof he can meet the challenge, before we grant the higher title."

Dorrin wondered what challenges Baron Brenvor had ever met, but knew she was being unfair. They had seen Arcolin only as a loyal subordinate, not in command.

"But as to the danger of those hidden Verrakaien," the king said. "Duke Verrakai, do you know any way to identify them, other than your own powers?"

"No, Sir King."

"Can you sense them from a distance without seeing them?"

"No, Sir King, I cannot."

"Then I must ask you to stay in Vérella until you have examined the entire staff and all peers." He held up his hand to still indignant murmurs. "My lords, I do not suspect any of you—I know you to have been loyal for years—but so was the groom whose body was taken over. Unless Duke Verrakai has some other way of detecting the threat, we must one by one pass examination."

"Not you, Sir King," Dorrin said. "Nor any in this room or at the coronation banquet last night. For those I am sure are not taken over."

"Are you, indeed? Then it is Gird's mercy, I say, that so much has been accomplished." The Marshal-Judicar's voice held a slight note of mockery.

"But, Sir King," Dorrin said, ignoring the Marshal-Judicar for the moment, "I do think those Verrakai in custody awaiting trial or sentenced to prison must be killed unless I can assure you they have not been taken over. Confinement does not lessen their powers, as yesterday's events prove. Any still alive could attempt a transfer—to a guard, to a servant bringing food—and might be successful. I know you do not want to kill the children—or what seem children."

"You're talking of a summary judgment on the basis of your examination? Without a trial?" the Marshal-Judicar asked. He sounded angry. "That's against the Code—everyone has a right to a trial."

"A speedy trial," Serrostin said. "We cannot risk anything long enough to allow them to change bodies. And think of the harm to the person whose body they take."

"I take your meaning." The king looked sad. "My brother's best

KINGS OF THE NORTH

friend is a Verrakai—was a page here, now in prison—and Camwyn's sure he's innocent. He keeps asking to visit him."

"He must not," Dorrin said. "If the Verrakai boy is actually no child, he might take over the prince."

"Could you tell if the boy is one of those—or guilty of anything?"

"If he is someone else, yes. But I'm not sure I could tell if he was part of the conspiracy."

Duke Marrakai stirred; the king shot a glance his way. "I know, my lord, what you said about the lad's attitude toward your son Aris."

"It's not just that," Marrakai said. "It's what the prince has told Aris since."

The king's brows raised. "Do we need to call Aris to testify?"

"If you wish. But haven't you noticed the difference yourself in the prince's demeanor and attention since he's no longer close with Egan Verrakai?"

"Yes." The king shook his head as if to clear it. "It's a bad, bad business. I cannot take chances with the realm, or with my brother's life. Duke Verrakai, you will visit the prisoners and determine if any are harboring ancients of your family. Do we all agree that such is evidence of treason and punishable by death?" Every hand smacked the table. "Then I will appoint witnesses to go with Duke Verrakai, including at least one Marshal and one judicar. But we must finish the other tasks of this meeting as well." He cleared his throat. "I have received reports from Lord Arcolin warning that Aarenis continues unsettled. Though he was hired to put down brigands, thought to be vagrants from Siniava's War, he has found instead organized bands willing to give battle and clearly supported from without, he thinks by the new Duke Alured of Immer. Duke Verrakai, you know of this Alured, do you not?"

"Our ally against Siniava," Dorrin said, nodding. "Younger than the other captains, said to be a former pirate, very ambitious. He supplied a company of woods-wise fighters, and we used his network of spies."

"Spies! In Aarenis only? Or beyond?"

"The ones we used were all in Aarenis, but now that he has a title, I expect he will have spies everywhere, including here."

"Arcolin says he is ruthless."

"Indeed. We were with him during the capture of the Immer ports, after Siniava's death—that was the price of his earlier aid. Kieri—the king—regretted he ever made that bargain when we saw how cruel Alured could be. Alured wanted to hire him—us— through the winter and another season, but Kieri refused."

"Does he pose any present threat to us?"

"Not unless he gains control of the Guild League," Dorrin said. "I'm sure he now controls river trade down the Immer to the sea, but taking over the Guild League will not be easy or quick."

"That much should be enough for anyone," Count Halar said.

"It wasn't for Siniava," Dorrin pointed out. "And if he hadn't been stopped, he might well have cast his eyes northward."

"If this Alured heard about what you found," Duke Mahieran said, "would that influence him?"

Dorrin felt a cold chill down her back; she had not thought of that. "Alured? Certainly. He would want that crown as proof of his claim that he was descended from the old royal family of Aare. Impossible, of course, but a lost crown rediscovered would, in his mind, be his family's."

"No chance it could be his?" Serrostin asked. "I mean—your family's had it, and perhaps they were related. Could this fellow be a distant relative of yours?"

"I suppose," Dorrin said. She hated the thought, but Alured's cruelty and even his slight magery fit her family's pattern. "But our family records are so unreliable, with the transfer of personalities, that I cannot possibly tell. What I do know is that he had a vast network of spies in Aarenis during Siniava's War, and it would be folly to think he had none here."

"And if he had them here," Duke Marrakai said, "he will have heard the rumors that were going around the markets."

"And are now going through the court," Dorrin said, nodding. "How many people saw me battle my father in the courtyard? How many heard of the gifts I brought the king? Whatever is widely known, he will know, and things we think confined to a few he may also discover." She turned to the king. "The regalia, Sir King, are not safe: he will seek to have them stolen for his benefit. He will hire the Thieves' Guild."

"It's in my treasury," the king said. "He couldn't possibly get to it, nor could any thief of the Guild."

"Sir King," Duke Mahieran said, "remember the assassinations. We thought we had secured the palace then."

"If he has allied with my surviving relatives," Dorrin said, "he may have powers through them."

"True. *You* had not mentioned Alured before."

"No, my lord. I thought his menace confined to Aarenis and his domain large enough to keep him busy longer."

"Have you heard from Arcolin?"

"No, my lord." She wondered at that, since Arcolin had been writing to the king, but those messages would have been carried from Valdaire to Vérella by royal courier; his to her would be by private messenger and no doubt slower.

The king nodded as if satisfied. "Is there any way we can interdict the spies' report?"

"No, my lord. If they deemed the information important—and I'm sure they would have—they will have sent it ahead already. Those rumors about the crown were circulating before your coronation."

Duke Serrostin spoke up. "It's possible that the Thieves' Guild could be convinced to cooperate with the Crown, after the scouring we gave them."

"For a price," Count Kostvan said.

"You would pay thieves not to steal?" asked the Marshal-Judicar, raising his brows.

"Isn't there a master thief the Marshal-General has invited to Fin Panir?" Serrostin asked, with a glance her way.

"Yes," the Marshal-General said, "Arvid Semminson, to tell what he knows of Paksenarrion."

"Well, it's my understanding he now stands high in the local Guild. I see no harm in asking him to report any offer he gets from this Alured."

"Indeed," the king said with a sidelong glance at the Marshal-Judicar, who had clamped his lips together as if to hold back something he might say later.

That first Council meeting lasted well into the afternoon, and Dorrin left it feeling even more that she had been caught up in a whirlwind. She knew less of Tsaia as a whole than any of the others; they talked of agriculture, industry, and trade in terms that confused her. But when the topic of defense came up, everyone looked at her.

"Duke Verrakai, I wish you to assess our readiness," the king said. "Review our resources and our training methods. If this Alured fellow tries force a few years hence, we must be ready."

Dorrin assented: he was right; she did have the expertise for this. But the looks she got from the other Council members suggested that not all of them would be eager to have her questioning the way they organized their troops.

A palace servant stopped her on her way out. "The Marshal-General would like to speak with you," he said. Dorrin followed him to the offices of the Knights of the Bells, the Girdish training order housed in the palace complex.

The Marshal-General was talking to the new Marshal-Judicar, Oktar, when Dorrin arrived. "Ah, Duke Verrakai. Have you a little time?"

"Yes, Marshal-General," Dorrin said.

"You gave us all a surprise yesterday," the Marshal-General said. "Like most, I believed all the magelords long dead or frozen in time like those in the far west. Safely distant. What I knew of your family's treason and the magicks used there, I thought due to blood magic alone. But you—" She shook her head. "Neither I nor any of the Marshals I've spoken to here have sensed evil in you. They tell me you asked for help from a local grange."

"Yes," Dorrin said. "And two Marshals came. We have not yet gone into the cellar, though, where I expect the worst."

"Now that I've heard some of your story," the Marshal-General said, "I agree the king made the right decision yesterday in sparing your life, but frankly, I find all magicks distasteful and the power you showed—and told us about—terrifying. It is one thing to face obvious evil, as I know Marshals here did in cleaning out Liart's lairs, but another to see great power and be uncertain of its source."

Oktar spoke up. "The Code of Gird, in one revision, allowed for the use of magery for specific reasons, including healing. And the Chronicles of Luap speak of a partnership between a mageborn and a Girdish peasant—"

"But that was overturned in the Edicts of Barlon—"

"I know, Marshal-General, but to my mind the discoveries made in the last few years—the scrolls that the paladin Paksenarrion brought from somewhere in the mountains and the discovery of Luap's Stronghold in Kolobia—bring those Edicts into question."

"So you would support removing all strictures on the use of magery?"

Oktar snorted. "No, Marshal-General, I would not, of course, suggest that a magelord be granted dispensation to use magery for any and all purposes, including evil."

"Good," the Marshal-General said. "Because I'm not going to take *that* proposal to my Council." She grinned at him; he chuckled. Dorrin had noticed the Marshal-General's informality at Kieri's stronghold but, after her mood the day before, did not expect the almost teasing tone. She turned to Dorrin. "If it's convenient for you, I've got the rest of the day free, and I know Marshal Tamis is at your house now."

"Certainly," Dorrin said.

When they arrived at the house, windows and front door stood open, with Eddes, one of Dorrin's escorts, sitting in the entrance hall polishing his boots. He jumped up, sock-footed as he was, and bowed. "Sorry, m'lord—didn't think you'd be back yet."

Dorrin waved a hand. "Go ahead, Eddes. Do you know where Marshal Tamis is?"

"Upstairs. I think the bedrooms."

"Thank you," Dorrin said. She would have to find someone else to watch the front door and explain to Eddes that boot-cleaning should be done out back. She led the Marshal-General and Oktar into the house. They found Marshal Tamis just coming out of the room Dorrin was sure had been her uncle's bedroom.

"If it wouldn't risk fire in other houses," he said to Dorrin without preamble, "I'd say burn this place out. Those spells are stubborn— oh! Marshal-General. I didn't know you were here."

"I came to help, if I can," the Marshal-General said. "What's the problem?"

"Blood magery, and the blood's soaked into the fabric of the house—into the wood of the floor in this instance. I think someone or something was killed here, under the bed."

The bed had been moved aside; they all looked at the old brown stain on the floor. The room seemed to darken as Dorrin stared, though the window stood open to the afternoon sunlight.

"What have you tried?" the Marshal-General asked.

"Prayer, of course, and the Relic of our grange."

Sudden nausea gripped Dorrin's belly; she gagged and grabbed for a basin on a table to one side. As the others watched, she heaved into it, too sick to be embarrassed for the moment.

"What—?" the Marshal-General said.

"It's a body," Dorrin said. "We have to get the floor up. It's— under there."

"It?"

"The body—the blood's coming up, not down." She saw their faces pale and knew her own must be bloodless as well. "And we must do it now. Quickly." She stepped to the door of the room and called out. "Bring an ax; there's one in the stable! Bring it here at once." Feet thudded in the distance as someone ran through the house.

"What do you think it is?"

"Someone was killed to hide a secret. I don't know how it was done, but the blood survives until a counterspell removes it."

"And you know the counterspell," Arianya said.

"I hope I do," Dorrin said. "Something similar guarded the vault in which I found the crown—you heard about that, did you not?"

"Yes."

"I think this is another old family secret, and it's dangerous."

Inder appeared at the head of the stairs, a towel tied around his waist, with an ax and a sharpening stone. "It's not that sharp, m'lord, but you said hurry—"

"Thank you, Inder. You should go back downstairs—do not be alarmed if you hear wood cracking, but if you see—" She paused. What might he see that would give warning for her servants' escape? "If you see an odd mist in the house, get everyone out."

"Yes, m'lord."

Dorrin took the ax into the bedroom. She heard a thin buzzing whine, as if a wasp circled her head. "You should leave the room," she said to the others. "And risk or no, set fire to the place if I'm not successful."

"I do not run from danger," the Marshal-General said. "I will witness."

"I do not know if I can protect you," Dorrin said.

"Dorrin, I don't ask *your* protection. Perhaps I can even help. Tamis, what Relic do you have?"

"It's supposed to be a piece of the Cudgel . . . of a cudgel, anyway."

"Hold it up, then."

Dorrin raised the ax; the buzzing grew louder. "Do you hear anything?" she asked, wondering if the sound were perceptible to those without magery.

"There's a fly in the room somewhere," the Marshal-General said.

"It's not a fly," Dorrin said. She brought the ax down full force on the floor. The old wood, hardened by time, rang but did not yield. The bloodstain darkened perceptibly. Again . . . again . . . and the wood cracked. Blood spurted up through the crack, the smell of it strong in the room, followed by the stench of decay. Dorrin ignored it, striking again and again, working the head of the ax into the gap and tugging pieces of board free. She had no time to think of the others, not with wave after wave of malice pounding at her. The first board yielded finally with a shriek, and then another and another. The red mist she had seen before formed in the air, but this time others were also praying, and it dissipated more quickly.

Under the floor a space the size of a small body had been framed in and covered with a blood-soaked cloth. She pulled that back and saw for a few moments a child's mummified body resting on a bed of shattered bone. Then it collapsed, the skin and flesh vanishing away like the blood-mist, leaving clean bone behind. Every prayer she knew ran through her mind; she felt her eyes burning, the hot tears on her face.

"Gird's grace," the Marshal-General said softly. She was kneeling beside Dorrin now and put out a hand to touch the small skull, stroking it. "Gird's grace on this child and—I presume—the others whose bones lie here. Poor little ones. And their families—they must have thought them run away or fallen into the river."

Dorrin blinked her tears away and wished she could erase that momentary glimpse of the body—the obvious marks of pain on those small limbs. "Marshal Tamis is right," she said. "This house should be destroyed. We burned the old keep, back in Verrakai domain, for the same reason; it was saturated in evil, centuries of it."

"I think not," the Marshal-General said. "This evil is gone—I feel it is gone."

"And I," Oktar said. "Look—the bloodstains are gone from even the broken boards."

At that moment something rustled in the cavity, and the bone fragments under the skeleton stirred. "A mouse," Marshal Tamis said.

"No mouse would—" Dorrin began, and then a battered, dusty spoon with a loop-shaped handle rose through the bone fragments to the surface.

"Holy Gird," the Marshals said together. Then the Marshal-General said, "A spoon? What does a *spoon* mean?"

"It's not a spoon," Dorrin said. Despite the horror of the whole room, she knew she had to pick it up.

Yes, the crown said in her head. *It belongs with us. With you.*

She reached out; the Marshal-General grabbed her wrist. "Be careful! It might still be—"

"It's magical but not evil," Dorrin said. "I think it will change in my hand—watch—" She plucked the spoon out—heavy silver, it felt like—and her hand and arm tingled as they had before. The spoon squirmed, re-forming into a ring, a sapphire surrounded by diamonds.

Put it on! Put it on now! The room filled with light that faded after a few moments when Dorrin made no move to slip the ring onto a finger.

"It looks like more of the regalia," Dorrin said when none of the others spoke. "I should take it to the king, to be stored with the rest."

No! Put it on!

Dorrin pulled out the lace-edged handkerchief that went with her court dress and laid the ring in the center; the cloth eased the temptation to put it on.

"It looks like the same sort of work as that necklace Paks brought," the Marshal-General said after a moment. "Oktar, did you see that when you were in Fin Panir?"

"No, only the scrolls. I had heard the necklace might be elf-made."

"The elves said no, when I asked them," the Marshal-General said.

"They were quite firm about that, but then they would not say what they thought it was. Typical, I thought. Nor did the dwarves admit to it. They did want to buy it, though, if we chose to sell. The jewels, they said, were from very far away. That was all they could tell us."

"Paks wondered if the legends had been wrong and Gird had been crowned King at some time," Dorrin said.

"No," Oktar said. "On that the records are clear. He wanted nothing to do with kings."

"We both thought—the colors being blue and white—"

"Of course," the Marshal-General said. "But our records tell that the peasants of Gird's day were not allowed to wear blue. We think blue became his color out of defiance—probably clothes taken from lords during the war."

"Blue meant something to the magelords," Dorrin said, thinking of the jewels and the embroidered cloth around the crown. "Wasn't there a cloth found in the far west? Paks mentioned it."

"Yes . . . with a star symbol on it."

"The scrolls mention a Sunlord," Oktar said. "It could be a sun symbol."

"The same design was on the cloth that wrapped the crown," Dorrin said. "Paks saw it."

"I should look at that," the Marshal-General said. "But first—what else in this house? Marshal Tamis?"

"This was the worst upstairs, after the mess in the old Duke's study. Duke Verrakai said she wasn't sure she'd gotten all the traps out, but Veksin and I dealt with the bloodstain and removed the symbols of Liart. Haven't had time to do more, with the coronation yesterday."

"The cellar," Dorrin said. "I haven't so much as touched the door yet."

"Then let us look there," the Marshal-General said. "We can at least plan for its cleansing, if we can't do it all today."

CHAPTER FOUR

"Should we call in Marshal Veksin?" Marshal Tamis asked.

"I don't think so," the Marshal-General said. "Duke Verrakai, lead the way if you will."

Dorrin led the way downstairs to the alcove near the passage out into the cobbled yard. There two iron-bound doors stood side by side.

"I think one's a simple root cellar," Dorrin said. "The other . . . not."

"Which is which?" the Marshal-General asked.

"I feel some malice from both, but much stronger here," Dorrin said, not quite touching the right-hand door.

The Marshals came nearer, and the Marshal-General nodded. "I agree."

"This is very like what we found in various lairs of Liart's priests," the Marshal-Judicar said. "And for that we wanted Marshals and knights both. I would recommend calling in another—and Duke Verrakai, are your escort sufficiently skilled in arms, or should we send for city militia or Royal troops as well?"

"They're not," Dorrin said, "though they're much better than they were a quarter-year ago." If only she'd had some of her own cohort with her. "*I* am, however."

Oktar shook his head. "My lord duke, the king would not be pleased if you died here when more good troops could prevent it. I feel evil as strong as any we rooted out back then."

Would he not? It would solve several problems for him. But she must not think so of her king, the man to whom she had sworn fealty the day before, the man whose life she had saved and who had saved her from a traitor's death.

"You think there might be a priest of Liart hiding there?"

"One, several, who knows? But I feel a great menace."

Dorrin stepped back and glanced into the kitchen, where Jaim was just emptying a bucket of water into a pot. "Jaim, do you know where Marshal Veksin's grange is?"

"Yes, m'lord."

"Run ask Marshal Veksin to come here. We're going to cleanse the cellar and need his help."

Jaim paled. "My—my lord, do I have to come back?"

"I need a message taken to the palace as well," Dorrin said. "You can go on from the grange to the palace gates and guide the troops back here." Not that they didn't know exactly where Verrakai House was. "You can stay outside the house, but I don't want you wandering around in the city. Wait a moment while I write the message."

Dorrin left the Marshals contemplating the door and ran back upstairs to find writing materials. She scribbled a quick note to the palace guard commander asking for assistance. When Jaim left, she took the opportunity to change from her court dress to her soldier's garb and met Marshal Veksin at the front door, ready to fight if necessary.

"This looks serious," he said as he came in. He, too, had prepared for a fight, bringing swords as well as stout sticks.

"Yes," Dorrin said. She led the way down the passage. "Marshal-Judicar Oktar thinks there may still be a priest of Liart alive, in the cellar."

"I brought an extra sword in case Tamis didn't have his today."

"Thanks," Marshal Tamis said, and belted it on. "Are you going to clear the house?" he asked Dorrin.

"You think it necessary?" she asked.

"Prudent, perhaps. Your servants could wait in the stableyard."

Dorrin heard the clatter of boots at the front of the house and went to meet the servants and send them toward the back. Then she collected her household. "We're about to cleanse the cellars, and that may be dangerous. For your own safety, you must do what I say.

Efla, Jaim, I want you in the stableyard, with Gani and Perin to guard you and the horses. Inder, you stand outside the front door to warn away any visitors." Not that she'd had many visitors she hadn't brought home herself. "Eddes and Jori"—her two boldest, who had made the most progress in arms, according to Selfer and Bosk—"come with me. You will be my personal guards."

The five looked more eager than afraid and jogged off to get their swords. Efla put her hands on her hips, looking remarkably like Cook back at the domain. "I have two fowl in the oven."

"You matter more than supper," Dorrin said. "Out with you now." Jaim was already out the door, as close to the outer gate as he could get. "Keep Jaim calm, Efla." That might keep her calm as well.

When they were all disposed as she wished, she nodded to the Marshals. "Do you recognize any traps on this door?" Oktar asked her.

"No. I can try the Verrakaien command words if you like."

"Do that," Oktar said. "It may save us some struggle. But stay to one side, where we have room for our blades."

Dorrin spoke the words. Nothing happened at first, then a key materialized in the lock, as if condensing from the air itself. Dorrin eyed it warily, but when it finished solidifying, it looked like an ordinary key—which it surely was not. Marshals Tamis and Veksin advanced with the Relics of their granges. "Wait," Dorrin said. "Let me try another—" She spoke again, and the key turned slowly in the lock with a metallic screech.

Tamis shrugged at the noise. "We weren't ever going to have surprise," he said.

Dorrin tried one command word after another; finally the door ground open, scraping on the stone flags of the passage. The air inside smelled stuffy and faintly sour. "Bring a lamp," she said, annoyed with herself for not having lamps ready. In moments Jori was back with two lamps, both lit.

By the lamps' light they could see a large room stretching into dimness, its level stone floor lined with chests on the left, shelves above them. Cloths draped whatever was on the shelves—by the blurred shapes, bowls, pitchers, stacks of plates. Along the right wall they saw full sacks, some plumply smooth as if they held grain or meal and others lumpy as if holding fruits or roots. In the middle of the room, a worktable with a stack of folded cloths and a hanging chain over it for lamps, though no lamp hung there.

"That's not what I expected," the Marshal-General said. "I wonder . . ."

Jori pushed past with the lamps. "I'll hang these up so you can see better," he said, and strode into the room.

Dorrin had not even time to say "Wait!" before the floor dissolved before their eyes and Jori fell with a startled cry, flailing, into the darkness below. One lamp trailed a long stream of flame as it fell; the other went out. A moment later, a thud and a scream of agony from Jori, followed by the creak and clang of some machinery.

Dorrin called on her magelight. Though feebler than Paks's, it was enough to show the steep flight of stairs leading down to the left alongside the near wall, not out into the space. "Get lamps!" she said to Eddes, and started down.

"Careful!" the Marshal-General called, but Dorrin heard others following her down the stairs.

"Block that door open above us," she called.

At the bottom of the flight Dorrin turned back along the side of the stairs; ahead was a wall, a door opening on darkness. She could not see Jori, only hear his cries, feebler now. Her own magelight, none too bright, moved with her, showing the bare stone flags of the cellar floor.

She looked through the door, her light revealing Jori sprawled awkwardly on a spiked frame; another had fallen on him, piercing him from above. A pool of blood spread from beneath him.

"Jori," Dorrin said. "Don't move."

But he turned his head a little. "My lord—please—"

Behind her, Oktar asked, "How bad?"

Dorrin shook her head. Blood trickled from Jori's mouth; his eyes were wide with fear and pain. "Can you heal him?" she asked.

"Not until we get him off those spikes," the Marshal-General said. "You?"

"The same."

"Let us go first," the Marshal-Judicar said. "These Marshals and I have seen a similar mechanism before in the Thieves' Guild lairs. Is he Girdish?"

"No. Will that make a difference?"

Oktar did not answer. He, Tamis, and Veksin stepped around the frame; Veksin bent to Jori's head and murmured something Dorrin could not hear. She closed her eyes, calling on Falk and feeling the all-too-familiar grief and guilt—how could anyone be so cruel, so determined to cause pain? And it was *her* family, her heritage . . . She could scarcely breathe for the misery and horror of it.

No. Their guilt is not your guilt. Your heritage is honor.

Tears ran down her face, but she could breathe again. When she opened her eyes, Oktar and Veksin had the upper frame lifted away from Jori. Oktar looked up at her and shook his head. She could see for herself that the spikes had dealt fatal wounds. Nor was it likely he would live long enough for a healing.

"One last pain, Jori," Oktar said, bending close to him. Dorrin could not tell if Jori heard it. "We're easing it as much as we can. Be brave now."

They lifted him off the spikes, and more blood poured out. He did not make a sound or move, as limp as if already dead, and Dorrin hoped he was.

They laid him on the floor outside, the whole front of his body soaked with blood. Dorrin knelt beside him, along with the Marshals. No breath, no pulse, no sense of life.

"His suffering's over—poor man—" the Marshal-General said.

"He was just trying to help," Dorrin said. "They—my people— were afraid to do anything on their own when I came, and I've tried to encourage them. Now this—"

Oktar put a hand on her shoulder. "My lord, you did not build this trap, and you did not tell him to rush in. He knew there was evil magery in this house. It was his folly, not yours."

"I'll send for the grange burial guild," Marshal Tamis said. He took the cloth Eddes handed him and wiped Jori's blood from his hands.

"Burial guild?" Dorrin asked. She had not heard of such a thing.

"They prepare the bodies and mount vigil until they're buried. Though he was not Girdish, he died bravely, and with your permission we will give him what honors we can; he can be buried in the grange burial ground. You have no one trained in such, do you?"

"No, I don't," Dorrin said. One more responsibility she had not thought of. "Thank you."

"I'll tell one of your people upstairs to take a message to the grange—and to the city militia. They won't make any difficulty, not with the Marshal-Judicar here."

Oktar nodded. "Their only concern will be sickness; burial must take place before midday tomorrow."

Jori's death delayed their investigation of the cellars. When the four members of the burial guild arrived, they put Jori's body on a burial board and carried it upstairs. Their grave demeanor reassured her; they handled the body as if it were precious.

"If we delay now," the Marshal-General said when they had disappeared upstairs, "whatever evil power is here will have more time to defend itself."

"You can trust the burial guild," Marshal Tamis said, touching Dorrin's arm. "They will prepare him for burial with all due respect and ceremony. Let us go on with the work."

Alert for more traps, they explored the cellars, a warren of alcoves and rooms, a maze impossible to clear quickly. They found Liart's Horned Chain on every wall: graven, painted, or an actual chain. Two small rooms had clearly been used as cells; the doors had tiny barred windows, and shackles hung from the walls. An alcove between them held an array of torturers' implements. In one of the rooms, they found signs of recent occupation: a bed with rumpled bedclothes, a pitcher with a little water in the bottom, and the end of a loaf of bread, now hard and dry. Under the bed was a red leather mask.

"A priest's lair," Oktar said, grimacing as he held the mask gingerly. "And here until a few days ago. May have fled when you moved in, my lord."

"I'm surprised he didn't attack her," the Marshal-General said.

Oktar shook his head. "That's not how they've operated in Vérella, Marshal-General. We found last winter that they'd sooner live under a respectable house, never bothering the inhabitants, who knew nothing of them. When the new Duke moved in, he'd bide his time."

"Could he be somewhere else in here?" Dorrin asked. Although they had sent upstairs several times for more lamps, the pools of lamplight scarcely lightened the shadows.

"Could be, but again, it's their habit to flee when their lairs are opened and attempt a flank attack. We never found a connection to this house and, despite the former Duke's reputation for arrogance and temper, never suspected that he was actually a Liartian until the assassinations." Oktar shook the mask he held. "That priest will be missing this. Costume's the way they terrify people. Without a mask, people can identify him." Oktar grinned at the Marshal-General. "Maybe we can trap him. He might come back for it."

Dorrin felt a cold chill down her back. "Unless it's a trap for us."

"What?"

She nodded at it. "When I was a child, one of the times I was being punished, they hung such a mask on the cell wall and told me the priest could see me through the eyes of the mask. Maybe that was a tale to frighten a child, but it seemed that it talked to me. Were I you, I'd destroy it."

"That would explain one thing that cost two lives, back in winter," Oktar said, and crumpled the mask in his fists. "Especially if it could also act as the priest's remote ears. Well, not this one. Marshal-General, shall we see?"

"Indeed."

Dorrin watched as all the Marshals prayed over the mask; it began to smoke and finally burst into flame, filling the chamber with the stench of burning leather. Dorrin felt a lessening of the pressure she associated with evil presence.

"How did he get away?" she said when they had followed every passage to its end, explored every alcove and room. "We have found no exit."

"Could he have escaped upstairs, as you came in the front?"

"Certainly," Dorrin said. "It's a large house—he might have climbed out onto the stable roof from one of the back windows, for all that."

"Or we haven't yet found the entrance to Vérella's underworld," Oktar said. "He would have more than one way out, and the underground entrances to this house are the ones we must find before we rest. Though we tried to eliminate all the Liartian priests and their followers, we knew that might not be possible. Marshal Veksin, you found several of those in that house over on Old Market Square, didn't you?"

"Yes—we'll need to tap floors and walls both. Even the interior walls. There was one instance in which the interior cellar wall was more than an armspan thick and contained a hidden staircase."

Soon the cellar resounded with the tapping of staves and dagger pommels. Dorrin went upstairs briefly. In the front room, Jori's body lay on the board, now resting between two chairs, swathed snugly in wrappings of white cloth except for his head. His eyes were closed under a blue strip of cloth; a blue pall lay over the white wrappings, and the older woman stood, staff in hand, at the foot. In the fireplace, a small pot smoked; the sharp fragrance of some herb competing with the faint stench of blood and death.

"The others are in the stableyard, cleaning up," the woman said.

"Thank you for your service," Dorrin said. "He deserves all honor."

"He died saving you?"

"He died trying to serve—he was hasty, but I had not warned him—he rushed past us and fell."

"His wounds were deep. Whatever your rituals at home, by city rule he must be buried quickly to avoid disease."

"I understand," Dorrin said. "Marshal Tamis offered to grant him a place in the grange burial ground." She paused, then asked, "May I ask your name and those of your guild?"

"I am Kosa," the woman said. "And you will find Sef, Pedar, and Gath in your yard."

"I am Dorrin Verrakai," Dorrin said. "And again, thank you."

On the way to the back of the house, she smelled the chickens in the oven and decided to let Efla back in the kitchen to finish preparing a meal. Out in the yard, the older man and younger ones from the burial guild were scrubbing at something in a bucket; laid out on a cloth on the cobbles were a few tools. Jaim squatted near the gate, looking sick; Efla stood by him. Perin had tied one of the horses in the yard and was brushing its tail.

They all looked up when she came out; Perin looked grim but went on brushing. Efla had the blank look of someone not sure what she felt. Dorrin walked over to the yeomen, who had put aside their blue tabards and rolled up sleeves and trousers. "I came to thank you," she said. "Which of you is Sef?"

"I am," the older man said, standing up. "And these are Pedar and Gath. It's their first."

The young men indeed looked like soldiers who had just seen violent death for the first time.

"Your people were upset," Sef said quietly. "I suggested they go back to work, but the boy—"

"I'll speak to him," Dorrin said. "Thank you." She walked over to the gate. "Efla, we think it's safe for you to return to the kitchen—can you do that?"

"Yes, m'lord. Jaim—"

"I'm not going in there," Jaim said. His voice shook. "There's a dead man in there! I heard him scream!"

"Jaim!" Efla said, scowling. "Be a man!"

"Go on, Efla. I'll deal with this." Efla moved away, turning her back on Jaim. Dorrin turned to him. "Now, Jaim. Sitting here scared won't help you," she said in the voice that had unfrozen many a recruit. "If you can't go inside, you must help with the horses."

With her eye on him, Jaim got up and slouched over to Perin, who handed him the brush and grinned across the yard at Dorrin. She watched a minute or two as Perin led out another horse and went to work on its hooves. When Gani came out of the stable with a cart of dirty straw and manure, she spoke to him.

"You and Perin make sure Jaim keeps his mind on his work. We'll bury Jori in the morning; I expect everyone to attend."

"Yes, m'lord. Come time, will we all go back inside tonight?"

"I'm not sure," Dorrin said. "The Marshals are at work below; I hope—I expect—the house will be safer tonight than it's been since we arrived. If you want to sleep in the stable instead, you can, but turn out clean, in uniform, for Jori's burial."

"Only, if those chickens are ruined, the Leaf Street Market closes in a glass or two."

Efla, who had loitered nearby, added, "And if we're feeding all them as is in the cellar, my lord, I'll need more."

Was nothing ever simple? Dorrin shook her head; she knew better than that. "Whose turn is it to go to market?"

"Inder's, m'lord."

"Well, then—Gani, you take Inder's place out front and send him to market." Dorrin fished coins from her belt-purse and handed them over.

"Stuffed rolls," Efla said. "And a handbasket of redroots, and some greens, any kind, but they must be crisp." She followed Gani into the house; Dorrin paused to speak to Perin about Jaim.

When Dorrin went back into the cellar, she found the Marshals clustered in one corner of the largest room.

"Do you sense anything?" Oktar asked.

Dorrin extended her hand. "It's another Verrakai lock," she said. She spoke the command words, and the invisible lock released. Slowly, the apparent stone faded into a stout wooden door heavily barred in iron. She pulled on the chain attached to a ring bolt, and the door tipped up. Under it, a ladder led into an underground passage.

"That's one," Oktar said. "We'll find at least one more."

By the time Inder came back from the market, they had found two more exits, one into the same underground passage but the other into a separate passage that appeared to lead westward.

"Do you think it goes under the street?" Dorrin said.

Oktar looked grim. "I think it leads under the palace grounds," he said. "That's how the assassins got in, I'll wager. We followed every underground passage we knew of but never found one that ended within the palace walls."

"We'll take this one," the palace guard sergeant said.

Dorrin and the Marshals went into the other one and edged forward carefully. After some time they came to five steps up and a door. They all felt something evil nearby, and the lamplight showed a pile of clothes: the red robe, gloves, and mask of a Liartian priest with the iron chain and the symbol lying on them.

The door itself, however, was untrapped, and they came out into an alley opening onto a street of shops in the cloth merchants' district. The building was a warehouse belonging to the Cloth Merchants' Guild, and inside it they found no sign of the door into the passage.

"They could hardly be unaware of a door on the side of their building," Marshal Veksin grumbled.

"It's behind that angle," Marshal Tamis said. "Whoever built the place wanted a secret entrance—the wall juts out just enough—it's not obvious. And it may have had an innocent use originally."

"Maybe, but it's going to have no use now," Veksin said. He went off to tackle the Guildmaster; she and the others returned to her house, rolling the priests' habit into a tight bundle, mask innermost.

"I'll take that away," Oktar said. "We'll deal with it elsewhere. What are you going to do about that trap?"

"Tear down the cell walls, dismantle the trap . . . Will the metal be useful for anything, or is it too saturated with evil?"

"You'll have to ask a priest of Sertig about that," Oktar said. "Or a dwarf. Depends how it's forged, they say, and if it is imbued with evil, it will take someone who knows forge magery to undo it. All the smiths now operating here were cleared back when we had that trouble."

"How should we secure these openings in the meantime?"

"We did it several ways before. If you take rubble from the cell walls, for instance—any that don't reach the ceiling can't be bearing walls—and pile it in that passage, then have a mason block the hole itself, it'll be effective. Other than that, we can mortar some rocks in there, but someone could break through in time."

"We need something for tonight," Dorrin said.

"Oh. In that case, close up the holes and—"

They heard noises coming from the third exit and Dorrin quickly drew her sword, but the dust-streaked men who came out wore palace livery, including an officer of the Royal Guard. "This passage comes out in the saddler's room in the old stables," he said. "It's illegal to build or maintain secret ways into the palace grounds. Who's in charge here?"

"I am," Dorrin said. "Duke Verrakai."

He blinked at her, apparently not recognizing the Duke he'd seen in formal court clothes in the mercenary captain's garb.

"And I," the Marshal-General said, "am Marshal-General Arianya. We just found this passage and sent your patrol back to you, suspecting where it might lead."

"How long have you been in this house?" the officer said, glaring at Dorrin.

Dorrin had to think—two days before the coronation, then that, and then today—"Less than a hand of days," she said.

"And you didn't know—"

"I was summoned here for the coronation," Dorrin said. "I had duties at the palace."

"Oh. And you had not been here before?"

"Never."

"Well, you'll have to have that passage closed up. We have secured our end; I must see this end secured."

"We have three exits to seal," Dorrin said. "A temporary seal, to start with. On Marshal-Judicar Oktar's recommendation, I'll have some of these dividing walls pulled down and piled into the passages and then stone laid into the exits."

"I suppose that will do," he said. "I'll have to talk to the Marshal—er . . . that would be you, wouldn't it?"

"Right," Oktar said. "Never mind; we're all confused by this. Duke Verrakai lost a man today in a trap in this very cellar. I'd recommend you post guards down here. The Duke doesn't have the resources right now, and the safety of your king demands it."

"Post guards in a private house? We don't usually—"

"It would be a great help," Dorrin said. She had not thought of that, had wondered how her remaining four militia could possibly guard the cellar, the front, the back . . .

"Would you want any assistance upstairs?"

"If you could post someone at the front door," Dorrin said. "My people are understandably upset at Jori's death. He and Eddes were close friends; Eddes saw how he died. But my concern is that the cellar may not be completely safe. These Marshals and I have done what we can in a half-day's time, but poor Jori's death . . ."

"How did he die?"

"He thought an illusion was real and walked off the landing up there." Dorrin pointed. "He fell into that trap."

The officer shuddered. "And you think there might be more?"

"Not that we know of. But again—not until I have had this taken apart to the outermost walls, and those walls carefully examined, can I be sure it's free of danger."

"My lord! The chickens are ready!" Efla sounded more like Cook every day.

Dorrin's stomach growled. She was suddenly ravenous. "If you can watch down here even the turn of a glass, I can offer the Marshals some supper."

"You haven't eaten? It's late."

Dorrin felt the last of her energy running out as if she were the hourglass. "We've been busy. Excuse me," she said. "I need to go back upstairs."

Despite the stuffed rolls Inder had brought and the two baked chickens, it was a somber group around the kitchen table for supper. A faint odor of death seeped through the house along with the sharp fragrance of herbs. The two local Marshals went back to their own granges. The Marshal-General and Marshal-Judicar stayed, but the talk was all of Jori: things Dorrin knew and things the others knew from the days before she became Duke.

"He had this girl," Gani said. "From the same village and all. Pretty, she was, but then one of the lord's sons saw her, and that was that."

"There was the time he lost his badge, remember?" Perin said. "You wouldn't know this, m'lord, but the old duke-that-was, he'd have the hide off a man's back for losing anything he provided, badge most of all. And Jori was sure he'd left it on the ledge in the bathhouse and someone tooken it. He even quarreled with Eddes about it."

Eddes swallowed and took up the story. "But it was Kir, really. Kir went off with them as fought the Fox—the king—that time and never come back. Anyway, he took Jori's badge and threw it to that dog—the brindle mastiff the old duke had—to get Jori in trouble. I saw it in the kennel; the kennel man, he hadn't seen it yet. Jori and me, we stole some meat and baited the dog, but it left tooth marks on the badge, and Jori was punished, just not as bad."

Jori had been, it seemed, the butt of many jokes, apparently because his girl had ended up in the Duke's son's bed. Dorrin felt sick at yet more evidence of her family's cruelty, and yet she had always known. Why hadn't she, in adulthood, told someone? Even Kieri? As a duke, perhaps he could have forced an investigation into Verrakai practices. If others had known, it could have been stopped sooner.

She had little appetite after that thought and sat waiting while the others finished.

"Is the chicken too dry, m'lord? I did it just like Cook taught me—"

"The chicken's fine, Efla." Dorrin forced herself to eat the last of it. "I'm not as hungry as I thought."

CHAPTER FIVE

After supper, all of Dorrin's people except Jaim, who refused, went to see Jori one last time. Eddes and Efla broke down, sobbing; the other three stood a few minutes and then walked out. When they had all left, the yeomen of the burial guild wrapped Jori's head until nothing could be seen but the white strips of cloth. Dorrin waited until it was done and then, as the Marshal-Judicar had quietly suggested, gave Kosa a Tsaian gold coin wrapped in a white cloth as a grange-gift.

Before she left, the Marshal-General took Dorrin aside from the others. "Do not take this amiss," she said, "but because of your family, no Marshal-General—no High Marshal, even—has visited your family's domain for a very long time. With your permission, I would accompany you eastward—meet with any Girdsmen in Verrakai lands, and perhaps—if some evil still lingers—be of assistance." Dorrin said nothing for a moment, and the Marshal-General went on. "It is not out of suspicion of you yourself, not now. But you are one alone and cannot be everywhere all the time." She smiled. "And as Paksenarrion is there, perhaps she will ride back with me to Fin Panir to see the necklace."

Dorrin shook off the heavy grief she felt for Jori's death. "Of course you can come, Marshal-General." How many, she wondered, would the Marshal-General bring along?

"I travel light," the Marshal-General said. "And since I'll be with you, I need no other escort."

Dorrin blinked in surprise, but the Marshal-General waved a farewell and went out into the night.

❧

At first light, four more yeomen in the burial guild appeared out of the fog. Dorrin had all her people up and dressed in their best; at the Marshal-General's recommendation, she wore court semi-dress. After days of clear skies, the fog felt chilly and dank. It seemed appropriate. The burial guild carried Jori's corpse, and the others followed. At the grange, Marshal Tamis waited for them, then led the way out of the city. Guards at the south gate let them through. The fog thinned, and a thin drizzle started. Tamis went down the road Dorrin had ridden so often, then turned aside to the west. Dorrin estimated they walked another ladyglass, wetter every step, until they arrived at a field set off with white stones. Two yeomen stood beside an open grave.

Dorrin had seen Marshals in Aarenis but had not paid much attention to the details of the funerals. Now, as the burial guild folded the pall and handed it to her, lifted Jori's body reverently, and eased it into the grave, she felt an unexpected comfort.

❧

Over the next few days, Dorrin talked to the peers she'd met, asking what troops they'd been assessed and how they were raising and training them. Not entirely to her surprise, she found that many peers ignored their military obligations. "I will send troops if there's a war," one said, "but I see no reason to hold men out of the fields to fight in a time of peace. Besides, the Fox always had more than enough."

The dukes did better but, with their responsibilities at court, left the raising and training of troops to their militia captains. Only a few of those had been to war, though the dukes considered them knowledgeable about handling troops in drill and field.

"Well?" the king said when she came to report her progress so far. "Are they as unprepared as I suspected?"

"It depends what you expect to face," Dorrin said. "Here's a list of those who admit they haven't drilled their troops in the past year. The escorts they brought with them are household only. This other list is those who have some kind of regular training program, though I don't know if it's actually followed."

"You don't trust the word of your fellow peers?"

"Sir King . . ." Dorrin hesitated, then went on. "I do not know the others well enough to know if they are trustworthy and diligent or not. I've been impressed by many of them. Others . . . but I could misjudge them in the atmosphere of the coronation, all the festivities . . ."

He held up his hand, and she waited. "Dorrin, you of all my peers have both long military experience and recent evidence that this realm, long at peace, may not be as safe as we always supposed. As I supposed, anyway, during my years as a prince. The Pargunese crossed the river for the first time in living memory—with collusion from here, yes—but what they did once they might do again on their own. Arcolin's reports, as you know, indicate the south is even more unsettled than immediately after Siniava's War. My ancestors came up that road. Why would not someone else follow if they perceived the north as holding riches they desired? And if he believes he is heir to the Kings of Old Aare . . ."

No. You are. The voice of the regalia tingled in her head; she felt almost faint; her vision darkened.

"Dorrin? Are you all right?"

"I am well," Dorrin said. The regalia had not spoken to her since she had laid the ring in the royal treasury—why now? She forced herself to concentrate. "I do not see that Alured would try to invade the north unless he had already subdued the south. Stealing treasure is one thing; mounting an invasion is another thing entirely. Have you had a new report from Arcolin?"

"Yes. Rumors that the Guild League will fail are all over the south, he said. Tavern gossip, market gossip: that the cities are debasing their own currency, that the Guild League cities cannot keep merchants safe on the roads. He says the cities are not—as far as he can tell—debasing their coinage, but counterfeits are imported by merchants under Alured's control. He captured one such."

"Alured was never stupid," Dorrin said. "And that makes him all the more dangerous."

"So he might decide to invade?"

"I still think he would need to conquer the south. Even if he succeeds, that will take more than a year. More likely longer."

"Read his letters," the king said. He opened his letter box and handed her scrolls covered with Arcolin's familiar script.

Dorrin read through them swiftly, more familiar with Arcolin's turns of phrase and the logic of his thought than the king could be. South of Vonja, trying to interdict brigand bands that weren't simple brigands—with a single cohort? Her lips pursed. That would be difficult; he might be taking high losses if the brigands were as numerous as he indicated. She saw none of the phrases they'd used as codes in the Duke's Company. Well, he wasn't writing to her, after all, and if he had such codes with the king, she would not know them.

"Why did he take only one cohort south?" she asked.

"That's what Phelan told him, on the basis of what the Regency Council had told him. And that's what he asked when he came with that one cohort. It meant having two in the north, in case of more trouble there."

"One's not enough. He'll need more next year."

"He'll have yours," the king said.

"Yes," Dorrin said, without enthusiasm. Her Phelani cohort had been invaluable so far; losing them would make her rule harder.

"When are they going back?" the king asked. Dorrin had the uncomfortable feeling he knew how reluctant she was to let them go.

"I'm not sure," Dorrin said. "I will need to talk to Arcolin—and to Selfer, their captain now."

"You know he's coming to Autumn Court. I expect you, too."

"Of course, Sir King."

"Now—do you have a better idea what resources we have and what we might need?"

"By the list of services owed the Crown, you should be able to raise three thousand troops from your nobles. You have no need for that many—which is convenient, since I doubt you could field more than a thousand in any reasonable time."

"A thousand . . ."

"In another two tendays, another thousand. Eventually you would have them all, but it might be a half-year before they were sufficiently trained to be of much use."

"My lords—"

"Are loyal, Sir King, but in a time of peace few prepare well for war. And consider—as a duke, I'm supposed to provide four hundred myself and have two hundred in regular training. Right now I can't. Almost all who would have been my troops were killed or wounded in my uncle's treasonous attack on Kieri Phelan last winter. I was hoping to hire two cohorts—half my requirements—from whoever took over Kieri's domain. But if Arcolin needs them, I'll have to look elsewhere. What you do have, that your present planning does not consider, is the direct contribution of trained troops from the Fellowship."

The king frowned. "But most of our troops are Girdish—aren't they?"

"That's part of the problem, Sir King. Most of this realm is Girdish, so adults are already enrolled in granges and bartons, where they train as foot soldiers using basic weapons. Your lords are supposed to train them as well, in units related to the size of their domains, but that means more time taken from whatever work their people do. It's very easy to think—especially for those who have never seen war—that their people get enough training through the Fellowship. But Girdsmen in the grange system are under command of Marshals, not their feudal lords, and they have little time to train in groups— five or six granges together—with the weapons they'd be using against well-armed foreign troops."

"What do you recommend?"

"A major change in how your defenses are organized, based on Girdish-trained troops—it will require integrating grange and feudal training, with the possibility that yeomen would be commanded in the field by their lords, not by Marshals. I'm not sure how it would work, but an agreement with the granges would give you access to many more troops—and better-trained troops—than you presently have."

"Would you have to convince every Marshal?"

"Not if I can convince the Marshal-General. She's not Tsaian, of course, and she's not sworn fealty to you, but she might work with you on this. You're Girdish, after all. Your family has long supported the Fellowship here."

D uke Marrakai stopped Dorrin on her way out of the palace that same day. He looked perfectly healthy now, as if he'd never had an injury. "I'm wondering whether you've considered taking squires," he said. "I know other peers are planning to propose their sons to you, but I exercised a little persuasion so I could be the first to ask. I have a situation, you see."

"A situation?"

"Well, perhaps you noticed that although there are girls in training to become Knights of the Bells, you never see them as anyone's squire. There's a feeling that girls of that age should be home with their families. They can train with the local grange, or even here for knighthood, but they're just not chosen as squires. They need a woman's guidance, is one thing people say. The girls don't much like it, but there you are. Now, you've commanded women in battle; you know all the things that young women get into, I daresay. And I have a daughter—"

"You'd trust your daughter to *me*?" Dorrin said, shocked into saying exactly what she thought.

His brows went up. "Is there any reason I shouldn't? You saved my life and the king's. My daughter is precious to me, of course."

"I—I'm honored," Dorrin said. "But you know a squire's tasks are both onerous and sometimes dangerous—"

"She's gone up the ranks in our local grange," Marrakai said. "She'd be yeoman-marshal if I'd agreed to it, but she has family responsibilities. She's too young to enter the Bells, and she's too old to stay home without a lot of . . . um . . . drama. A dose of reality from someone else is what she needs right now. She's not as volatile as Aris was when we sent him to Fin Panir—she's between him and Juris in age. But I will not press, if you object—"

"I had not thought of taking anyone as squire, to be honest, but also to be honest, it would be a great help to have some trustworthy assistant when Selfer goes back to Arcolin, as I'm sure he will."

"Assistants, not just one, if you'll take my advice. You have a large domain and—pardon me for mentioning it—you seem unsure, which is understandable. Do you, for instance, have a capable and trustworthy steward?"

"No," Dorrin said. "The one I had was a Liartian and attacked me. Most of my people are ignorant and still frightened; they were never allowed much autonomy. Well, except for the cook." She grinned, remembering that stalwart woman and the kitchen she ruled.

"Then let me recommend you take several of the squires you're offered. My daughter is, though I say it as her father, honest, brave, and kind. Sonder's son Beclan is the same, though perhaps a little spoiled, being the king's cousin; Sonder's going to ask you if you'll take him. I'd send you Aris as well, except the king wants him here to companion Camwyn, and it's probably best not to hand you two of my offspring at once."

"And who else?"

"I think Serrostin and Kostvan may both ask you—but I don't know how many you are willing to take. The king wants Roly Serrostin here—they're good friends, and Roly's the one who saved him and my son Juris from Haron. But Roly's younger brother Daryan is just as pleasant a lad as Roly. The Serrostins are all steady and mild-mannered. I'm not sure which of his sons Kostvan's thinking of. If you don't take one, I probably will."

"I like the sound of steady and mild-mannered," Dorrin said. "When the Duke—I mean, King Kieri—had several squires at a time, he valued those among them who were not easy to upset. But— would you be insulted if I asked to meet your daughter before I agree? She might not like me, after all."

"Small chance of that," Marrakai said. "But of course—you must meet her. Come to dinner at my town house tonight, and see what you think."

Marrakai House was on the far side of the palace complex from Dorrin's house; Marrakai had sent an escort, though she felt no need for one. The house had red and green stones worked into a decorative design around the main door. Duke Marrakai and his wife met her at the door and led her into a front room very like her own, but for having more furniture and a great patterned rug on the floor. Juris and Aris were both there, along with a tall girl whose black hair, green eyes, and bone structure all fit the family. She wore a red-and-green-striped skirt, a red leather doublet, and a wide-sleeved shirt revealing strong wrists.

"This is Gwennothlin," Lady Marrakai said. "She's been wanting to meet you."

The girl flushed a little but looked straight at Dorrin as she curtsied. "My honor, my lord Duke."

"I understand you're interested in becoming a squire," Dorrin said.

"Yes, my lord." The girl stood straight and still to answer but gave the impression of great energy barely controlled.

"Of the knightly arts, which is your favorite?" Dorrin asked.

"My lord, that would be bladework. I am . . . overfond, some would say . . . of swordplay." Her sword hand twitched, as if remembering a move.

"What other arts do you have?"

"Knightly only, or—"

"All of them. And do not fear to bore me—if your secret passion is embroidery, tell me."

Her family all laughed at that; so did the girl. "The only way to make Gwenno embroider is to tie her to a chair," her mother said. "She's passable with weaving—sashes at least—but that's all."

"Well, then, my lord," the girl said, "I ride well enough, my father says, and I can drive a pair. As you know, we are horse-breeders, and I trained my own mount. My teachers taught me reading, writing, and ciphering, enough to provision a troop or a household. I know the use of court-sword fairly well, but the battle sword I have only begun in the past year. I have done some archery."

"Tactics?" Dorrin said.

"No, my lord, not beyond what my brothers have told me. If I were admitted to the Bells for training or Fin Panir, I would learn, but—"

"It's not necessary," Dorrin said. "If you have the interest, I can teach you tactics." She liked the look of the girl—a little younger than the recruits the Company accepted, but the same kind of energy and will.

Through dinner, Aris and Gwennothlin served, Aris with more polish than his sister; Juris, the eldest son, sat at the foot of the table.

The entire family, down to children seated on pillows, ate together. Dorrin realized she had never seen a family dinner in a noble or even wealthy merchant house. Gwennothlin and Aris both wiped up the spills of younger children, straightened their pillows, cut and served their food, with the same aplomb as they served the elders, and the conversation at table included all. The youngsters finished first and left the table.

"Come, sit with us, Gwenno," Marrakai said. "Aris, when you've cleared up the children's things, come join us." He turned to Dorrin. "Many lords do not let children eat with adults, but our tradition is that once a day at least, the generations meet. It keeps us all alert."

"I never thought of that," Dorrin said. She could not imagine such a dinner as this in her childhood, nor had she thought of having the Verrakai children eat with her. She had left their care to those she thought appropriate, but what training did the nursery staff have?

For that matter, she needed a new steward at the steading and a watchman or someone to stay in the house in Vérella as well as someone—but what and who?—to help with the children. She asked.

Both Duke Marrakai and his lady were glad to help. "Of course you need a steward, and you also need a housekeeper," Lady Marrakai said. "If those children have been left in the care of nursery-maids all this time, they surely need a tutor—at least one. What staff do you have now? Are you pleased with them?"

Dorrin explained. "Some were Liartians—well, most had been threatened into saying they were, but only a few wore the horned chain. The kitchen staff—I've got a very capable head cook, and the one I brought with me is competent with the basics. Housekeeper— I'm not even sure what a housekeeper does; we never had one at Kieri's stronghold."

"Ah," Lady Marrakai said. "Then you need help, my dear—I hope you don't mind my saying that—"

"Not at all," Dorrin said.

"The proper organization of a ducal household will reassure your people as well as make your life much easier. To start with, you need experienced senior staff. Since you already have a cook, you're in luck—good head cooks are the hardest to find. How is her bread?"

"Very good," Dorrin said.

"Excellent. Now, I presume there's a garden and a fruit orchard."

"Yes," Dorrin said.

"How many gardeners?"

Dorrin was ashamed to admit that even after a quarter-year she was not sure, nor did she know anything about the training of the dairy staff, the brewing staff, or even—as Marrakai chimed in—the stable staff.

"Not to worry," Lady Marrakai said, more cheerfully than Dorrin expected. "If you have to start from the bottom, you'll know more when you're done. Gwenno, go fetch my domestic journal."

This philosophy was so alien to the Verrakai way of doing things that Dorrin felt once more how inadequate she was. But Lady Marrakai did not seem to notice. Instead, she ticked off items on her fingers.

"Steward—someone who can oversee everything—trustworthy to manage while you're gone—must be good with people and with numbers—" She paused, frowning a little. "Didn't Count Farthen mention sometime this spring that he had an under-steward who was capable of a larger job?"

"Yes," Marrakai said. "He's still in town; I'll ask him tomorrow." .

Two turns of the glass later, Dorrin was still leafing through the little book Gwenno had brought back and listening to Lady Marrakai's advice. Finally Lady Marrakai stopped short in the middle of her lecture and grinned, a grin very like Gwennothlin's. "I hope you realize I'm doing this for the fun of it—it's not that I think you're stupid or anything."

Dorrin shook her head. "No—I really know nothing about running a normal establishment. Organizing a soldier's camp or a fort is very different, barring the need for food and cleanliness. You've been very helpful." She glanced at Gwenno. "But I never gave my answer about your daughter, and she's waited with uncommon patience. Gwennothlin, if you wish to be my squire, I will be pleased to have you. There are legalities we had in the Duke's Company—"

"Of course," Duke Marrakai said. "Well, Gwenno?"

"Yes!" the girl said. "Yes, thank you, lord Duke."

"Then we can sign the papers tonight, if you will, Dorrin, and get this pesky wench out of our house—" But his look at Gwenno was tender, not dismissive.

"She cannot go tonight," Lady Marrakai said firmly. "She must pack, and I must make her shoulder knots in the Verrakai colors immediately. Two days for Verrakai-blue tunics."

"And I must find another couple of squires," Dorrin said. "There will be work enough for more, as you said."

In Marrakai's office, the Duke wrote out the legal contract specifying the duties of lord and squire, much the same as Dorrin had seen for Kieri's squires. Gwennothlin signed in a very clear hand, her expression solemn, and then Dorrin; both the Duke and his lady signed below. Dorrin wrote the copy, and all signed again.

"I thank you for trusting me with your daughter," Dorrin said. "And you, Gwenno, for trusting me with your life. I hope you will be happy—though that is not in the list of a squire's duties."

"There's no doubt in my mind about this one," Marrakai said. He gave Gwenno a hug and a kiss on each cheek. "Spread your wings, daughter."

Invitations from Dukes Mahieran and Serrostin came the next day; Dorrin met the boys and agreed. Tall Beclan had the polish of a youth who had been always at court; Daryan, two years younger, had not yet come to his growth and was a slight boy with light reddish hair. When Count Kostvan also invited her to take his second son as squire, she explained that she did not feel able to take four squires yet. He nodded, seeming resigned.

Lady Marrakai's contacts sent recommendations for a children's tutor, an estate steward, brewmasters, dyers, weavers, and housewardens to care for the Vérella house while she was away. Dorrin interviewed them all and made her choices. The housewardens—an older couple looking for a less strenuous job—moved in immediately, freeing her servants from some of the household chores. Dorrin had a final interview with the king and then her banker—a frightening glimpse of how much it cost to be a duke.

At last she could think of leaving the city; she sent word to her squires' families. They arrived at the house the following morning with horses, gear, and brand-new Verrakai livery, with the colors of their own houses at their shoulders.

"Stables down that alley," she said. "We're short-handed right now; you'll care for your own mounts. We're leaving tomorrow morning."

"Yes, my lord," came in a ragged chorus, and they disappeared into the alley. When they came back inside, she took them on a quick tour of the house.

"As I'm sure you heard, this house was seized under the Order of Attainder, so I did not bring sufficient staff with me—" That was as good an explanation as any. "The Crown has returned it, but too late to hire locals. So it's more like camping in a house than living here. Here's where you'll sleep—" Two small rooms, one with two simple beds, one with only one. "Don't settle in—as we're leaving tomorrow, you'll be helping pack up for the trip home for the rest of the day. There's a meeting at Marshal Veksin's grange tonight; you have my permission to attend."

"Yes, my lord."

"My father's sending along two pack mules," Beclan said, "with the rest of my clothes, weapons, and so on."

"And mine," Gwennothlin said. "But only *one* mule." She shot a quick glance at Dorrin, as if for approval.

"I thought girls had more baggage," Beclan said.

"I thought boys had less," Gwennothlin said.

"Are your fathers sending someone to tend the mules, or will you be doing that?" Dorrin asked, interrupting what promised to become a quarrel.

"I'll ask," Beclan said. He took a step toward the door, then paused. "That is, my lord, if I have your permission."

"How many mules altogether?" Dorrin asked, looking at Daryan this time. "And how many spare horses?"

"My father's sending a lot of clothes because he thinks I'll be growing a lot this year," Daryan said. "He said it wasn't fair to make you supply so many sizes." His pale skin flushed an unbecoming red.

"My mother wanted to send two mules," Gwennothlin said. "But I said I didn't need all that."

"Two mules each, then," Dorrin said. "There's no rank among squires of the same year. And two horses each, I'm presuming?"

They nodded.

"So one of your families needs to provide a muleteer. I will send one of you to all three families to make clear that I expect two mules, packed and ready, to be here for each of you tomorrow morning one-half glass past dawn. They can argue about who provides the muleteer." They all looked eager for this errand, but Dorrin had a plan. "Daryan, you know where everyone lives, right?"

"Yes, my lord."

"Then you go. You may ride, since we have a busy day ahead of us, and I want you back quickly."

"Yes, my lord."

"Now, Beclan, let's see how you do organizing provisions for our journey. Take inventory of the available supplies; in a glass I want a list of what you think we need to purchase today. Gwenno, with this many animals in the train, we will need supplies for them as well. See to it that all the horses are in good shape—get them shod if necessary—and check all the tack in the stable. I expect a report within a glass." That should keep them both busy while she herself dealt with the new house staff.

Dorrin had never in her life closed a house, with or without resident staff left behind. This was one more proof that she knew much less about her role as a noble of Tsaia than any of the others. The housewarden assured her that the house would be kept clean and ready for reoccupancy whenever she wished.

"If you can give us even a day's warning, we'll have the sheets off the furniture, beds made, and so on. The main thing, my lord, is keeping the vermin out and making sure any repair work gets done. I understand you'll have masons in the cellar."

"Yes, for a few days. We're blocking it off for now; there's no need for it. It wasn't being used for storage anyway."

By the end of that first day, Dorrin felt she had a good grasp of her squires' personalities. Gwenno certainly fit the Marrakai pattern: energetic, full of ideas and enthusiasm. She was quick with suggestions and obviously eager to prove herself. Beclan, more reserved and a bit haughty, was nonetheless perfectly courteous and willingly did whatever chore Dorrin asked. He seemed faintly amused by Gwenno and Daryan, though he was only a year and a half older. Daryan looked younger than he was, being below middle height with a round face that still looked boyish. He was polite and did everything asked of him but did not venture an opinion or idea.

Dorrin released them all to visit a grange if they wished, and they walked off not quite together, Beclan a stride in the lead and Daryan a half stride behind Gwenno.

The next morning, the train of animals and riders lined up to depart seemed almost a half-cohort to Dorrin. She herself, all but one of
the servants she'd arrived with, her three squires, Master Feddith
the tutor, Grekkan Havverson the new estate steward, and the
Marshal-General, plus the muleteer hired to care for the pack animals
and spare horses. Others would come later.

The few pack animals they'd come with weren't enough for the return. They now carried supplies for the journey, supplies Efla insisted were needed for the cook back home—five mules' worth, plus
a mount for Efla.

Dorrin gave a last look at the house; it seemed to have an entirely
different expression with its windows and door open, no longer grim
and forbidding. Just another city house, one that might someday be
full of light and music and friends, if she chose to make it so.

Their procession moved through the streets toward the bridge.
This early in the morning, most of the traffic was inbound, farmers
bringing produce and livestock to the thrice-weekly market. By the
time they reached the city gates, Dorrin had sent Daryan to buy a
poke of hot sweet rolls from a baker's stall, and when Beclan looked
longingly at someone carrying a basket of peaches, she nodded and
said, "Get enough for all of us." Guards at the city gates grinned as
they passed.

"Thought I saw them peaches going in just a bit ago—"

"If they were in a basket on a donkey cart led by a man with a
green ribbon on his straw hat, you did," Dorrin said. "We've a long
road to take."

"Coming back for Autumn Court, m'lord?"

"Gods willing," Dorrin said. She paid the toll for them all.

They turned onto the east river road, munching buns and fruit.
Dorrin could not but think how different this was from that frantic
winter journey to catch up with Kieri: then cold and dark, now the
summer sun, even this early, warmed their faces and gilded the
fields and orchards they passed. Mist hung in ragged streamers near
the river; the soft air smelled of fruit and flowers and hay. And
no reason to hurry: they came to Westbells only shortly before
noon. Beyond that more lush pastures, fields of ripening grain,
orchards . . .

The party divided naturally into three groups: she and the squires and the Marshal-General, her servants, and the muleteer with the extra horses and pack animals. That was pleasant enough and seemed safe this bright summer morning, but Dorrin had spent too many years in Kieri's Company to ignore possible danger.

"We'll be rotating guard positions," Dorrin said, when they had passed Westbells. "For now, I want Daryan ahead on the road; Beclan, you'll trail our group; and Gwenno, you'll be flank scout on the river side. Eddes will be flank scout on the land side."

"Surely you don't expect any trouble here, this close to Vérella— it's Mahieran land—" Beclan began.

Dorrin raised an eyebrow and noticed the Marshal-General giving him a stern look as well. "You're here to learn, Beclan," Dorrin said. "More trouble comes when you don't expect it than when you do." Not strictly true, in some of the places she'd been, but a good lesson anyway. "You'll warn us of anyone coming up behind—and that includes along the rear flanks. Daryan, you'll signal when you see any party coming along the road the other way. Stick your hand up once for every rider or the number of people in a group. Same with the flank guards. Every time we pass through a village, rotate positions. Rear guard to river-side, river to foreguard, foreguard to land-side, land-side to rear."

"How far out?" Gwenno asked. "Should I ride across the fields?" She looked eager to do so.

"We don't trample crops," Dorrin said. "Where they border the road, just ride on the verge. Stay back, about halfway along our group, where you can see any hand signals I give. We want to make it clear that we're alert, watching on all sides. If we practice that now, where it probably *is* safe enough, you'll know how to do it later, when it's not."

The squires set off into their assigned places. Eddes, now almost up to Dorrin's standard as a basic militia soldier, grinned at the squires until he saw Dorrin looking at him. At the next village, Beclan turned aside from the rear and trotted up to Gwenno. "Go on," he told her. "I've got this side now."

Dorrin turned in the saddle. Eddes had indeed dropped back to take Beclan's place, and Daryan had reined his mount to the side of the road, waiting for them to pass. Gwenno pushed her horse into a stronger trot and reached Daryan before the head of the column.

"Neatly done," Dorrin said. She waved the column on, and they started again.

That night they camped in a field near a cluster of farm buildings. Dorrin assigned one squire—Gwenno this time—and two of the militia to dig the jacks; Beclan and Daryan set up her tent and their own and took the horses to water and to graze while the rest cut out a fire ring and Efla cooked supper.

"I wondered how you'd handle them," the Marshal-General said.

"Hmm?" Dorrin stretched, arching her back.

"The squires. I suppose I shouldn't be surprised; you've handled recruits before—"

"And Kieri's squires from time to time. He assigned them to different cohorts when he had enough of them. Their fathers had sent them to us to learn military things, after all."

"What do you think of these?"

"After one day? It's too soon to make judgments." She hoped she'd know much more by the time they reached Verrakai lands.

Supper was less than successful; Efla had never cooked over a campfire before. Her attempt at bread came out scorched on the outside and gooey on the inside, the redroots burned to the bottom of the pot, and only the sausages, toasted on sticks, and the sib were really good.

"Never mind," Dorrin said, to her apologies. "Clean out the pot—we can eat the last of the city bread tonight and in the morning, and tomorrow night I'll show you some tricks about cooking outdoors."

The long summer twilight softened around them; the first stars came out as they sat around the campfire. "My lord," Beclan said, "when you're moving an army, how many guards do you put out?"

"It depends on terrain," Dorrin said, "and what trouble you expect. But here, on this road, when I had most of a cohort with me—"

"You were on this road with a cohort? I thought Duke Phelan's lands were up north."

"When I was hurrying to catch up with him on his way east," Dorrin said, "I had, as I said, most of a cohort and basic supplies. We knew there'd been trouble. From Vérella to Westbells, where we met Paksenarrion, we were riding in tight formation, moving fast enough I didn't set a rear guard, but did have assigned flank guards whose job was to watch. Beyond Westbells, Paks often rode out as foreguard. Every time we stopped to rest the horses, there were guards out on all sides."

"What about in Aarenis?" Beclan asked. "In Siniava's War, not in peacetime."

"We always had fore-guards, flank guards, and rear guards. How many depended on how many troops we were moving. A cohort on the march, not mounted, would have mounted scouts, at least a pair on each side, one on the road ahead, one on the road behind." Dorrin gestured. "If you're in open country, where the scouts can ride at a distance but see the column clearly, it's easier. In wooded country, you need people who can operate on their own and not be ambushed themselves."

"Ambushed," Gwenno said, in the tone of someone for whom it was a game.

"Yes," Dorrin said. "Take this country, for instance. It's Mahieran land and peaceful to look at, but imagine it full of enemies. From the road to the river, how many troops do you think could lie hidden as we went past? This shady block of trees we chose to camp near—how many could be concealed in it, archers or arbalestiers? No ground is completely flat; every fold could have enemies in it—and they feel the same for us." She looked at the young faces, sober now as they considered what she'd said. She nodded at the Marshal-General. "I'm going to sleep outside tonight, I think, warm as it is, but I'll take a bucket-wash in my tent first—feel free to use my tent either way, if you will. We'll each take a watch for a turn of the glass. You squires will be paired with my militia." She gave the assignments, and soon they were all asleep but the night guard.

Sometime after the turn of night, a rumble of thunder and a cool breeze woke her. Flashes of light in the distance—more thunder—Dorrin woke the camp. "Check the horses; make sure they don't stray—is the horse-line secure? Get all the gear into the tents." She herself grabbed an armful of firewood and moved it into her own tent, then checked the ropes and pegs before lying down inside.

The storm, like most summer night storms, came and went quickly; Dorrin had gone back to sleep with practiced ease, and woke in the damp dawn to see Efla poking disconsolately at the sodden fire-pit. "Here's dry wood," Dorrin said. She set it alight. "Boil water for sib and another pot for the eggs." The squires came out of their tent blinking and stretching. "Beclan, you and two of the men will fill in the jacks when we're ready to leave. Meanwhile, Gwenno and Daryan, you take the horses to water, groom them, get them tacked up. I'll ride the dark bay today." She went on giving instructions to her militia and then to Efla on making camp bread.

It took a glass longer to get this group moving than it would have a cohort, but it was, she reminded herself, their first night of real travel—inns did not count. That day she assigned Inder to ride guard with the squires, and they rotated properly all day long.

CHAPTER SIX

As the little cavalcade moved east toward Verrakai lands, Dorrin found the Marshal-General a surprisingly good travel companion. She and Dorrin traded stories of days and nights of travel: storms, difficult stream crossings, the occasional encounter with brigands. Dorrin found herself telling tales of Aarenis; the Marshal-General was one of the few women with whom she could share stories of combat and command responsibilities. The squires listened in the evenings; Dorrin kept them busy by day. They were still on their best behavior, she could tell, but personalities showed through. Beclan felt entitled to be first in everything and had an air of condescension that clearly grated on Gwenno; she showed flashes of temper, quickly subdued after a glance at the Marshal-General. Daryan, as the youngest and shortest, seemed shyer, edging away from the other two.

"You're going to have an interesting time with them," the Marshal-General said, out of their hearing. "All three of them high-born, and none of them really grange-trained."

"They're all Girdish," Dorrin said.

"Aye, but reciting the Code word-perfect isn't the same as growing up in a real grange."

"Theirs aren't real?"

The Marshal-General made an impatient gesture. "Every noble house has a grange nearby—and so it should—but nothing I do

convinces the Marshals who serve there and the yeomen who belong there that their liege is no greater in Gird's eyes than a yeoman.
So their children are tutored in the Code, and mostly go to drill with
their home grange, but they're also taught how to fight like a noble.
Which do you think they prefer? They're born into privilege, and
they like it—anyone would—but liking something doesn't mean it's
good for you."

"Mmm." Dorrin rode on a few paces. At the moment, all three
squires were out of earshot, flanking the column between her position and the rear guard. "I could see that with Beclan."

"Royal family." The Marshal-General looked as if she might spit,
but didn't. "He's not the heir, but he thinks of himself, of all the
Mahieran, as royalty. Entitled to deference. He thinks the girl should
allow him precedence. And the girl's insulted as much on family
grounds as personal ones. The Marrakaien, for all their Girdish faith,
would think themselves superior to the Mahieran if they dared."

"I don't think there's much Gwenno wouldn't dare," Dorrin said,
chuckling.

"Just so. Those two will push each other into rashness if you're
not careful. The younger boy—he's not as meek and mild as he
seems, I'll warrant." The Marshal-General took a swig from her wa-
terskin and offered it to Dorrin, who shook her head.

"If I keep them busy enough," Dorrin said, "they should settle. A
load uses up all that youthful energy."

"True." The Marshal-General twisted in the saddle, stretching.
"I'm hoping your military background will see the foolishness of letting them indulge—lean on—their privileged backgrounds."

"Oh, yes," Dorrin said. "I saw that with some of Kieri's squires,
and I have scant patience with it."

They arrived at the border of Verrakai Domain in midafternoon,
having spent two nights in Harway so Dorrin could thank the
tailor and cobbler for their work on her court clothes and order the
supplies she thought she'd need for the next few tendays. Somewhat
to her surprise, her people had made real progress on the road from

Harway while she was gone. It ran almost straight and, if not smooth, was much improved. One of Dorrin's militia met them, this time politely.

"Lord Duke, welcome home."

"I'm glad to be back, Jaren." She was, in spite of her expectations. The woods were cooler than the fields had been; they camped that night in the new way-house she'd had built—still only a rough shelter of three walls and a roof, but at least it was rain proof.

The next evening they reached the house. Now sleek cows grazed in the water meadows near the stream; in the distance, the grain looked almost harvest-ready in the slanting golden light, though she knew it would be another three tendays at least. The house, blue-gray against the light, looked friendlier without the grim keep tower looming over it.

As they neared the house, Paks's red horse lifted its muzzle from the grass and whinnied loudly. Paks appeared from the gate in the garden wall, trailed by a gaggle of children.

"Marshal-General!" she called, waving; she broke into a run, leaving the children behind.

The Marshal-General stiffened; her horse stopped abruptly. "That light!"

Dorrin said, "The sun's glow?" It seemed especially golden that evening.

"It's more than that," the Marshal-General said.

"Dorrin," Paks said, slowing to a walk. "How was it? Did the king like the crown and things?"

"It's a long story," Dorrin said. "I'll tell it all, once we've bathed and eaten. You need to meet my new squires: Gwenno, Beclan, Daryan."

She dismounted just in time to meet the swarm of children who had now caught up with Paks. "Auntie Dorrin! Auntie Dorrin!"

Dorrin looked at Paks, who shrugged. "They're your family; they needed something to call you besides 'my lord.'"

It made sense, but . . . Auntie? She supposed she was, to most of them, but she had never imagined herself as an auntie. From the looks on her squires' faces, neither had they.

"Paks said you'd come back. We worried," Alis said.

"She taught us lots, while you were gone," Jedrah said. "So did Captain Selfer. I can figure how many mules for a cohort supply train!"

"And we played outside and learned how to pick caterpillars off the cabbages—and swim—well, some of us—"

"And when Mardi and Seli got in a fight, they weren't whipped," Mila said, leaning into Dorrin's side. "I know you said it would be different, but when you left, I thought maybe it would go back— but—but we're not scared now. Paks made them share a meal, and now they're friends again. And we can play with the servants' children if we want, and they can play with us."

"And nobody's been sick all summer, m'lord," the nursery-maid said. "No fevers at all."

The children chattered all the way back inside until one of the nursery-maids, catching a nod from Dorrin, sent them all upstairs "so the adults can hear themselves."

That night, for the first time, the old house felt like home, a home she could want to live in for the rest of her life. Selfer joined them for supper, another link to her old life; he and Paks had become friends, it seemed, in the time she'd been away. After supper, the three squires joined the elders around the table, and they talked late into the night, when a thunderstorm blew up from the north.

Next morning, Dorrin showed the Marshal-General where the old keep had been.

"You did right to burn it out," the Marshal-General said. "When did you do it?"

"Spring Evener," Dorrin said. "That's when Kieri was crowned, too, so I thought of it as a coronation bonfire as well as an offering for the Evener."

"All good thoughts," the Marshal-General said. "But now I'd like to see that well Paks was telling me about."

"We could ride over today, if you want."

This time she felt no need for an escort, even though some of her relatives were still missing. She left the squires at the house, telling them to familiarize themselves with the house and environs. On the way to Kindle, Dorrin described the village to the Marshal-General. "It won't look like that in a year or two," she said. "But don't expect much improvement. They won't have had time."

"You're trying to make it better," the Marshal-General said. "I can see that and feel it. How many granges are on your domain?"

"I'm not sure," Dorrin said. "I know Darkon Edge, of course, because that's the grange Paks raised for Kieri on the way to Lyonya. The maps I have don't show grange locations at all."

"I'll see that you have a list of those on our rolls," the Marshal-General said. "If they're lapsed, would you permit them to be reestablished?"

"Of course," Dorrin said.

"There's no 'of course' about it," the Marshal-General said. "You're Falkian; you might prefer to establish fields instead of granges."

"Tsaia's king is Girdish. Some of my friends are Girdish."

"Well, then. Your people need someone good to follow. I'll send you a couple of personable, cheerful young Marshals."

They came around a clump of trees, and there before them was Kindle—but a different Kindle.

"I thought you said it looked like a wreck of war," the Marshal-General said.

"It did—" Dorrin looked around her. Where was the real Kindle? "Did Paks do this?"

"I don't know. I suppose she could have."

The ramshackle huts now looked like cottages in need of some repair, which they were getting. A wall Dorrin clearly remembered as leaning now stood upright, and two half-grown children were smearing the uneven stones with mud; another side already had whitewash up to the thatch. Roof framing had been mended, so even old grass thatch looked more like a real roof, and others were now half-thatched with reeds.

Every cottage had its kitchen garden, and despite the late start, the gardens flourished. Washing hung over fences and bushes. Faces appeared at cottage doors, around corners—women and children mostly; the children already looked plumper and distinctly cleaner.

"She's back, she's back!" a small child screeched, and ran toward them. Dorrin dismounted, recognizing the little girl who had brought her the crown of flowers. The child flung herself at Dorrin, hugging her knees. "We's water!" she said.

"Don't bother the Duke," a woman said. "Come back—"

"It's all right," Dorrin said. "She's not bothering me. Look—this is the Marshal-General of Gird, come to visit. She wanted to see your village—and you've done so much work since I left—"

"Gird's grace on this place," the Marshal-General said. The women stared. "Did you ever have a grange here?"

Frightened looks now. "No . . . lady."

"Do you know who Gird is?"

"T'old duke, he said Gird was a liar and a thief and a long time dead and good riddance." That came out all in one breath.

"He was wrong about that," Dorrin said. "Look—you know the *merin* of wells and springs, don't you?"

"'Course, m'lord, everyone knows about them."

"And Alyanya, the Lady of Peace?"

"Ye-es."

"Gird was a farmer in a village, just like you," Dorrin said. "He put flowers at the well, just like you. He blooded the spade and the plough, first time in the ground, just like you."

"Yes, but—but he's dead."

"He did a lot of good things before he died," Dorrin said, with a glance at the Marshal-General. "You should learn about them."

"Is that what you want?"

"I want you to have a good life," Dorrin said. "And I think it would be good for you to learn about Gird, at least."

"Could Gird heal our well like it was, if he wasn't dead?"

"I don't know," Dorrin said with another glance at the Marshal-General.

"'Cause you did, m'lord, and you freed us from the old duke, and now we have water and our childer an't cryin' for food. We don't know Gird."

"Tell you what," Dorrin said. "I'll have a Marshal of Gird at the big house, and maybe the Marshal will come visit you—not to poke and pry, just visit—and maybe someday you'll want a Marshal nearer than that."

"Guess I don't mind that," said a woman with a baby slung on her hip.

"Now let's see the rest of this—you've done so much work in so little time—" The villagers led them from cottage to cottage, bragging on one another. This one had found the stand of reeds, and that one had found a better lens of clay to seal between the stones, and these two men had gone all the way to a village more than a day away to learn how to use the reeds instead of grass. And would m'lord mind if someone added a room or a shed to their cottage?

"All from a well being renewed," the Marshal-General murmured.

"It saves them work, and they don't have that curse operating here," Dorrin said.

"They have hope again, because of you," the Marshal-General said. "But they need direction. You might have time to direct this one, but not all your villages. They must learn to make better decisions themselves, not because they were ordered to. Girdish Marshals and yeoman-marshals can teach them."

"They don't know Gird," Dorrin said. "And it's been less than half a year. Send me a Marshal or two by all means, but let the people see first that I welcome them."

The Marshal-General shook her head. "It goes against my training to have lords intervene between the people and Marshals of Gird."

"Particularly when they aren't Girdish themselves, I expect," Dorrin said. "And have used magery."

"That, too," the Marshal-General said. "Though here, they needed your magery." She sighed. "I cannot regret inviting Paksenarrion to join the company of paladins, but she certainly did start a cascade of events that still hurtles . . . somewhere. And I don't know where."

"You blame Paks for this?" Dorrin waved her hand at the well, the village.

"Would you say she had no part in it?" the Marshal-General said. "Was the Duke's Company the same for her being in it, even before she came to Fin Panir?"

"Mmmm . . . no. She kept Kieri from torturing Siniava, and then—when she left—it was as if by her leaving he recognized Alured's cruelty . . ."

"And then she found Luap's scrolls in that elf place, whatever it was, and brought them to us. Her capture in the far west, all that happened after . . ." The Marshal-General's voice faltered; Dorrin glanced over to see tears on her cheeks. "Her healing by a Kuakgan, her time in Lyonya as a ranger, all of that led inexorably, I see now, to her finding that Kieri Phelan was in fact the heir to Lyonya's throne. Once she named him, once Paks's sacrifice saved him from the Bloodlord—"

She spat aside. "—all your lives changed. All *our* lives changed. Tsaia and Lyonya cannot be the same. Even Fintha and the Fellowship of Gird cannot be the same. She was the rock falling from the cliff; all our lives were set in motion by that fall."

"And yet—"

"And yet she is a sheepfarmer's daughter from somewhere beyond Three Firs, and Three Firs, which I'll wager you've never seen, is nothing but a village stuck to the side of a hill by the roots of its three fir trees. We sent someone there to learn more about her. End of the peddlers' track, it is, one of a hundred such villages where the good land meets the moors. I heard all about the pig farmer's family her family wanted her to marry into—the boy was relieved; he was scared of her and is happy with the baker's daughter."

Dorrin laughed. "I cannot see her as a wife, no."

"Nor I. She asked that a sword be sent to her family if she died in Vérella. One will be, for her family deserves to know what she did, but we're trying to gather the stories of her, as we do for all paladins."

"Will you tell the bad things?"

"We must." The Marshal-General looked away. "That is why the stories of paladins are not quickly told, or lightly. I want her to come back to Fin Panir with me and share the tale of her deeds, all of them."

"The Lady of the Ladysforest, who brought her people to us in our greatest need," Dorrin said, "offered to rid her of her memories of the worst. She refused. But she does not talk about it."

"There is a thief in Vérella. Well, he says he's not a thief—"

"Paks mentioned a thief helping her after—"

"When I sent word that I wanted more of her story, he came to one of the granges and asked to speak to the Marshal. His version has been written down, but it did not prepare me for that circle on her brow."

"I will miss her when you take her away," Dorrin said, "but I know she must follow the gods' call. I do wish I had her touch with children. I have no idea how to be a proper aunt, let alone parent. I brought that tutor from Vérella, as you know, but—what now?"

"You were a child; you must remember—"

"Nothing good," Dorrin said. "I told you. I do not know how it is possible to have a childhood free of fear and evil. That's what I want for them, but if there is more . . ." She shook her head.

"I find it amusing—no, ridiculous—that I, leading a Fellowship which did its best to rid the world of nobles like you and households like this—should be asked for advice by one. And yet, before I was the Marshal-General, I managed a grange, and then a group of granges, as High Marshal. Though I never wanted children of my own, I loved the children of my grange."

Dorrin glanced at her and saw an expression she associated more with mothers than warriors. "So—do you have advice?"

"Think far ahead, Dorrin. What do you want for them when they're grown? Surround them with people who are that—the kind of adults you want them to be. Children are such mimics . . . if they see honesty and fair dealing and kindness, they will copy that."

"Paks has been here four or five tendays—"

"And you saw how they were when you arrived. Was that a big change?"

"Yes," Dorrin said, thinking back. "They were improving, I think, before that, but not this exuberant."

"Do they have chores, or do the servants do all for them? Peasants, you know, teach their children to work."

"I don't think they do," Dorrin said. "I would have to ask the nursemaids."

"Well, those above seven winters should, in my opinion. We have children in the grange do simple things—things they can see are useful. We think it's good for them, as long as they're not overworked and underfed." They rode on a little ways before the Marshal-General spoke again. "And I know you will want them taught skills of arms, but do not value those over the skills of peace, or make everything a competition."

"That I understand," Dorrin said.

"Do any of them have mage-power like yours?"

"Not that I know of," Dorrin said. "But beyond looking for those who had invaded others, I haven't looked for it."

"You must. Like any talent, it must be trained for the right reasons, in the right ways."

When they got back to the house, they found Paks and the squires at weapons practice, surrounded at a safe distance by fascinated children. Dorrin and the Marshal-General joined them, hot as it was. They had not yet crossed blades; Paks waved the others away to give them room. Dorrin stretched first, as did the Marshal-General, and then suggested they use practice blades.

They began slowly, with the usual drill, speeding up as each found the other able. They were well matched in height and reach, but Dorrin's years of battle experience soon told, and she made two quick touches with the blunted practice blade.

"Too much sitting; not enough fighting," Arianya said, breathing hard. "I should spar with you again."

"Every day, if you like," Dorrin said, feeling pleased with herself. Sweat rolled down her back, tickling under her clothes. "But perhaps in the morning or late evening. It's a bit warm."

The Marshal-General laughed; her own face was sweat-streaked. "Next time with hauks, if you have them."

"I'm sure we do, somewhere," Dorrin said. "Or sticks, if nothing else. And I'm not as practiced with them."

Two days later, the Marshal-General and Paks rode away; the children had cried when they knew Paks was going. Dorrin looked at her squires. They had been brought up in good homes; they must know what children needed. They had not become her squires to learn child rearing, but she needed their experience.

She gathered squires, tutors, and all but one nursemaid together while the children were playing on the lawn outside.

"You know already that I have no children and no experience with them. These children have had a bad start. Leaving aside what they were taught and what was done to them, their parents and elder siblings have all been taken away. Thanks to you—" She nodded at the nursemaids. "—they are better than they were. I have brought Master Feddith from Vérella—tutor to another noble family and recommended by your father, Daryan—to teach the scholarly arts. I have talked to the Marshal-General and Master Feddith at length, but one man and four nursery-maids cannot do it all themselves. Master Feddith has already suggested bringing in older children to provide a more ordinary mix of ages. You squires must understand that you are the only good models of young people these children have ever seen. They will look to you the way you yourselves looked at knights and squires when you were barely out of shortlings. They will copy you—good for good, fault for fault."

"Will you want us to . . . to care for them?" Beclan's lip did not quite curl, but distaste crept into his tone.

"Not as nursery-maids, of course," Dorrin said. "But as if they were your younger siblings, when you happen upon them, yes. These children are as impoverished as those in the villages: they have never known any other home or anyone but the family that's now gone." She paused to let that sink in. "At times, I may ask you to take one or a small group on outings, under your protection. Think—how old were you when you left the confines of your house for the first time?"

"I don't remember," Beclan said. "I can't remember not knowing both of the nearer villages . . . the house in Vérella, of course, and I was taken to the prince's birthday party for the first time when I was—maybe—four winters."

"They have been here their entire lives. None have been so far as Kindle, let alone Harway. That must change. You will be exotic to them, fascinating," Dorrin said. "So you must be good elders, as I believe you will be."

In two turns of the glass, they had worked out a preliminary daily schedule and even—Dorrin insisted—outings at least once a tenday to more distant parts of the domain.

"I'm glad you're including chores," Master Feddith said. "It's something I recommend in every house where I serve, if it's not already done."

"They've never had to do aught," the nursemaid said. "By the old duke's orders, they was born to rule, not serve." She flushed and ducked her head.

"It won't hurt them," Dorrin said. "It may take them awhile to learn, but when they see the squires serving, they will understand— we all serve, one way or another. You know them best right now; all of you and Master Feddith can decide which chores. Keep them busy enough they won't get into mischief."

Within a tenday, the children were settling into the new routine, even the youngest doing the simple chores assigned.

Master Feddith discovered that they were all astonishingly ignorant—only the eldest could read at all—and their general knowledge was less, he swore, than that of Serrostin's stablehands. Yet they were not stupid, he told Dorrin that tenday night.

"They are clever enough to learn but were never taught. They were told only a few tales of the Verrakai and their exalted place." From Feddith's expression, he didn't think much of it. "And about power and blood magery. That's all. Not even the proper terms of venery, which every lord's child I ever taught knew when I came. But they are learning now. And your squires are a good influence. Two of the eldest children have asked when they will be pages."

"Not for a while yet," Dorrin said.

"Good," Feddith said. "Make them earn it—and, if you'll take my advice, my lord, do not send any of them to other households. Let them learn here. Nor would I hurry them into weapons practice, not until you're sure all the taint of the Bloodlord is gone from them."

"Sound advice," Dorrin said. "And I will follow it. I don't want to forbid them all play, even play with toy swords, but it must be supervised. You are right; they had too much experience with cruelty and bullying before."

A few days later, she came around a corner of the house and found two of her squires red-faced and angry, and Beclan leaning on the wall looking coolly amused.

"What's this?" Dorrin asked.

"I am not a child, just because I'm younger," Daryan said.

"I never said you were," Gwenno said. "I was only trying to help—"

"I didn't need your help."

"I'm sorry!" Gwenno flung out an arm, whirling half around and glaring at Dorrin instead of Daryan. "I just thought—that's the tallest horse in the stable—"

"Stop this," Dorrin said. They fell silent. "Now, I will hear what you did, one at a time, no interruptions. Beclan, you first, if you please."

"We were to ride out and inspect the progress on the new road, as the Duke knows," Beclan said. "It was Daryan's turn to saddle the horses, and as he is . . . shorter . . . Gwenno offered to help, and Daryan took it amiss."

"You were the one—" Daryan began; Dorrin quelled him with a glance.

"Go on," Dorrin said.

"Well, I may have—I did—suggest that maybe he would need help with my horse, as he is the tallest and fidgets when being tacked up."

"And you have not trained him out of it?" Dorrin asked.

"Well . . . no . . . I'm not a horse trainer."

"And yet you have horses," Dorrin said, as mildly as she could. "I perceive you have had stable servants available your whole life to deal with the bad manners of your mounts. A wise knight makes sure his mount is reliable, Beclan. I will give you extra time to train yours."

"Me? The Marrakaien are the horse-lovers." Beclan shot a glance at Gwenno, who bit her lip but said nothing.

"Those who depend on horses must learn to manage them well," Dorrin said. "It is part of a squire's training that I will not neglect; I have seen squires die for lack of it—riding well is not enough."

"Die?" Gwenno said, before she folded her lips again.

"Yes," Dorrin said. "Unhorsed in battle, with a mount too skittish to stand, and thus easily surrounded and struck down." She looked from one to another. "Whatever else this is about—and I will ask more in a moment—you must all see that your mounts improve in training, and that starts with handling on the ground. From this day, you will each, every day, groom, tack up, and ride. You will rotate through all the horses, mine included."

"But—" Beclan began; Dorrin held up a hand.

"They are all up to your weight, Beclan, even if not as pretty as yours. You may someday have to use an enemy's horse when your own has been killed or run off. This is another essential skill."

"Yes, my lord," Beclan said. He dipped his head, but Dorrin could feel his resistance.

"You may tack up your own horse today, but tomorrow you will switch. I will write up a rotation." In all her spare time—but she foresaw considerable good out of this. "Stay and be quiet," she said to Beclan. "I will hear the others. Now, Daryan, tell me your story."

"Beclan said I might need help with his horse because it was so tall and I'm the shortest. He told Gwenno to help me. He's always telling us what to do." Beside him, Gwenno fizzed with impatience, but Dorrin ignored that; the girl needed to learn self-control. "I said I didn't need any help, and he laughed, and Gwenno said besides she was better with horses—and just because she's a Marrakai, and they think they know everything about horses. It wasn't *her* brother who saved the king's life; it was Roly. I said that, and all Juris did was sit there like a stone—"

"He was spelled!" Gwenno burst out. "He couldn't—"

"Not now, Gwenno," Dorrin said. "Go on, Daryan."

"Well, then you came. My lord."

"I see." Dorrin folded her arms and gave him a hard stare. "It was ill-done to taunt Gwenno with her brother's having been spelled by the same magery that held the Marshal-Judicar, the Knight-Commander of the Bells, and the king himself in thrall, Daryan. Your brother, I understand, was not in the room when that happened, and absence left him free. Do you think Rolyan would approve your criticism of Juris Marrakai?"

Daryan reddened even more. "Um . . . no, my lord."

"Or your using it to anger Juris's sister?"

"No, my lord."

"Courtesy to all is one of the main duties of a squire. That includes courtesy to one another. When you are grown and knighted, and especially if you come to your father's estate and rank by the deaths of your siblings—"

"No!" Daryan cried, paling.

"You will many times face slights and insults better left unanswered," Dorrin said. "I am glad to see you unambitious for that place, and like you I pray that your elder brothers and sisters live long and thrive, but even so, you are a Duke's son and must learn to master your temper." She turned to Gwenno. "And now you, Gwenno. What is your tale?"

"My lord, much the same, and I, too, let my temper master my tongue. Beclan bade me help; I am used to helping my younger sibs, and I own I have thought of Daryan—because he *is* younger, not merely because he is shorter—as I might a younger brother, not as a squire the equal of myself, which he surely is."

"Fine words," Dorrin said. "But I heard you quarreling."

"Yes, my lord, you did," she said, looking Dorrin in the eye. "I said, when he demurred and said he needed no help, that he should not fuss, that the horse was likely too tall and too difficult for him and I was glad to help. Then he said what he said about Juris—"

"Which was?"

"As he told you," Gwenno said. Her eyes shifted; Dorrin suspected it had been worse, but approved Gwenno's willingness to let it pass. "And so I grew angry and said Roly might be good enough with a map-stick but Serrostins sat their horses like sacks of redroots."

Dorrin bit her lip not to laugh. "I find you all at fault," she said. "You are bred of dukes; you inherit wealth and power. You all hope to be knights someday and do great deeds, but now you quarrel over whether someone helps tack up a horse? That is ridiculous." She let them wait in silence a long moment, then went on. "Beclan, you are the eldest, born to a royal house, and yet I find you setting up the cause of the quarrel and smirking against the wall as if it pleased you."

Beclan reddened. "My lord—"

"I did not give you leave to speak," Dorrin said, using command voice; he went still and silent. "You are the eldest, I say again, and it is to you that younger squires—and the children of this house—look for behavior to guide them. Consider the paladin Paksenarrion—is your behavior anything like hers? Do you think *she* takes pleasure in quarrels or creates them for her own amusement? You may answer."

"No, my lord," Beclan said. He looked sheepish now. "I'm sorry, my lord. I didn't—I didn't think—"

"You will think hereafter," Dorrin said. "You want, it is clear, to be seen as the wealthy son of power that you are, to be seen as knowledgeable, capable, skilled, a leader. You must become so, in truth . . . must be what you would seem. Be an example, be a true friend to your colleagues, your fellow squires."

"Yes, my lord. I will try."

"You will do more than *try*, Beclan—you will *do*, or I will send you home." She turned quickly to the others. "And the same is true of you, Daryan, and you, Gwenno. You were all reared in dukes' houses; you were taught courtesy, as I know, for I know your fathers. So there will be no *trying*—there will be courtesy, kindness, fairness among you all and to all you encounter. Is that clear?"

"Yes, my lord," they said.

"You will find me understanding of honest mistakes," Dorrin said, "but I will not tolerate squires claiming precedence they have not earned or making mischief with one another. Now: each of you go, tack up your own mount, and do the work I had assigned you today."

"Yes, my lord."

She watched them cross the yard to the stable. Would her rebuke hold them even a day? Maybe. And here came her new steward, no doubt with something else for her to solve. Well, she had accepted the king's commission; she had been confirmed as duke; she had better, as she had advised Beclan, be what she seemed.

CHAPTER SEVEN

Chaya, shortly after Midsummer Feast

E ven with the Midsummer Festival over, Kieri could not return to the ossuary immediately. He presided at the King's Court; he had more meetings with his Council. In addition, he had already planned his next assault on human-elf rivalry: a joint hunt. Both races enjoyed the sport and surely—he hoped—could forget their animosity in the pleasure of a day in the field. He had found an auspicious day, according to advice from both Siers and Orlith; he could not change that now. His grandmother did not deign to answer his invitation, nor could he compel her, but his declaration of a Royal Hunt meant all others he invited must attend. The human and elven huntsmen did not quite glare at one another when he called them into his office together—a good sign, he hoped.

The night before the hunt, he was awakened by noises outside but went back to sleep when the Squires at his door did not alert him.

"W hat was that kerfluffle in the courtyard last night?" Kieri said as the breakfast dishes were removed and the little rolled pastries brought in.

"It is the Pargunese again, Sir King," Sier Halveric said. "You would not believe—"

"What have they done this time?" Kieri asked, reaching out to the taig. No disturbance enough to signal danger to the realm . . . a few ripples here and there, travelers, but certainly not an army. Reports from traders on the river road and fisherfolk in Lyonya's few riverside towns included mention of Pargunese troops seen across the river, but nothing too ominous. Yet.

"Sent a pledge of peace," Halveric said, with the air of a man with a good tale he wants to tell. Around the table, growls of disbelief. "Indeed they have, though: she arrived last night, or rather hours before dawn this morning, on a lathered horse with only two exhausted attendants chasing after her. Their king's daughter, they said. They want a wedding."

They all looked at him; Kieri knew exactly what they were thinking. The King must marry, must get an heir. But not, Kieri thought bitterly, an enemy's daughter, no doubt a pale frightened child forced to this—the King of Pargun had a certain reputation.

"I'm not marrying a Pargunese," Kieri said. They looked at him. No one said anything, but it might as well have been scribed on their foreheads in silver and gold: the King must marry . . . someone. Perhaps marrying a traditional enemy would bring peace between the realms.

"And there is word," Sier Halveric said, "that a delegation from Kostandan is within a day's ride with the daughter of *their* king."

Kieri felt his brows rise, wrinkling an old scar. "I thought they were allies, Pargun and Kostandan."

"Against Tsaia, certainly. But in hope of influence here, perhaps rivals. We do not know whether Kostandan knew of Pargun's plan, or vice versa."

"The Pargunese knew," Kieri said. "Or their princess would have made a grand entrance, not come hurrying along the road to throw herself at the gate in the dark."

Two princesses! He felt a headache coming on. What was he supposed to do with two princesses, but bow over their hands and be polite? He had already met all those daughters of noble Lyonyan families, and one of Prince Mikeli's letters revealed that Tsaian nobles would be more than willing to have the King of Lyonya consider their daughters, too. All the women had been beautiful; no doubt these princesses were beautiful. Those he had spoken to were all intelligent, or seemed so. All courteous, as pleasant to the ear as to the eye. But beauty and fine manners were not enough. He wanted a woman whose character he could trust.

Not the daughter of a devious, cruel king, whom he had long suspected of collusion with those who had killed Tammarion and their children, a king who had sent troops into Lyonya to kill him before he could even be crowned.

Before his Council could say anything, he went on. "Sier Belvarin, I trust you will locate suitable accommodation for the visitors. It would be discourteous to house the princesses anywhere but here, and their escorts or chaperons of rank, of course, but with the delegation from Prealíth—" diplomatic, not accompanied by any more marriageable girls, he hoped "—we must be sure we don't end up with no room to move." Dzordanya, that mysterious land, had as yet sent no one.

"Sire." As he stood, they all stood.

"And don't forget, we ride to hunt this morning. With so many visitors, we must have game." He saw the looks they gave one another. Huntsmen could provide game—did, during the closed season—but could not accomplish his larger aim: reconciling humans and elves to one another. Even at informal breakfasts, and more in the formal councils, elves and humans were proving a difficult team to harness. The euphoria of finding a suitable king and crowning him had evaporated since his coronation, and years of distrust and bickering had formed habits he must, somehow, break.

B y noon, Kieri was ready to smack heads together. His hope that good sport would overcome prejudice had proven too optimistic. The two groups of nobles, elves and men, mingled only when his eye was on them, and then only formally. When the red-and-black hounds scented game, the pale hounds were called off by the elven huntsman on the grounds that it was not the proper day for scenting: this was a day for gaze hunting only. They had said nothing about that upon setting out, and from their expressions were looking for an excuse to resent any questions he might ask. He did not ask.

When the pale hounds took off shortly after that, the red-and-black

hounds lay down instead of following. Kieri whirled to see the repeated signal by their huntsman.

"Whyfor?" Humans might resent his questions, but not so lethally
as the elves.

"The pale hounds riot, my lord. My Cherry gave no tongue. I
would not have them taught bad manners."

"They saw something . . ."

"So *they* say." The look the huntsman flashed toward the elf nobles
who waited politely for the king to lead the chase was poisonous.
"No *proper* hound can both scent and gaze."

"Bide here, then, until I return," Kieri said. The huntsman opened
his mouth, but the look Kieri gave him shut it again. Kieri lifted his
reins. "Come, gentlefolk," he said in the pleasantest tone he could
manage, and Oak broke to a gallop. Behind him, the soft thunder of
hooves indicated that they'd all followed. They'd better, he thought.
He would deal with the huntsman later.

Still, after the first stag fell to his arrow and the hunt settled to
business, he felt it had not been a useless endeavor. Both packs of
hounds ended up working together; some of the men and elves exchanged near-friendly banter along with compliments on a good shot
or a handsome mount. The hunting party returned in late afternoon,
followed by the pack ponies laden with enough game for what he
was already calling—in his own mind only—"A Feast of Princesses."

What mattered more than princesses were the two packs of
hounds now trotting along side by side, the set of their ears and tails
suggesting the kind of cooperation he'd hoped for. He glanced
around. Though the bulk of the elves still rode to the left, the heart-
side, and the bulk of the men still rode to the right, the sword-side,
he saw man and elf chatting peaceably in the middle, both individu-
als and small groups. He hoped his father and sister would have approved.

Once back at the palace, he was immediately besieged by the
Pargunese princess's guardian, a sour-faced woman who declared herself Countess Settik. Complaint after complaint, starting
with the baths.

"Barbaric," she said. "*Tubs,* as if we were piles of dirty clothes! And so small. And dirty bits of weed thrown in!"

"Herbs," Kieri said. "To scent the water."

"At home," she said, "we have *proper* baths. We don't have to climb up steps and into cramped little tubs—we step down into heated pools where the water moves and is always fresh. It is an insult to guests to make them use what is nothing more than an oversized bucket. You must grant us the use of your bath. If you are ashamed to be seen as the gods made you, we can bathe at a different time, but I will not—not, I tell you—fold myself into that—that *article* again."

"I use one," Kieri said.

She sniffed. "I don't believe you. No king would."

"I do not know what your baths are like," Kieri said firmly, "but everyone here uses a tub. If you insist, you may inspect my bathing room—"

He had not believed she would be so rude, but she did insist, complaining all the way to and from it of other indignities: being lodged across the hall from the princess instead of in an adjoining room, having no separate kitchen where food could be prepared under her own eyes. Kieri declined to inflict her on his own cooks. Nor did she approve of the King's Squires Kieri had assigned to the princess Elis— all, he insisted, honorable women.

"They wear trousers," the woman said. "And they bow instead of curtsy. It is unnatural."

"It is required, when they are on duty," Kieri said. The last of his patience vanished. "You must excuse me; I have urgent business." She glared but let him go. He wondered if her husband was as difficult and suspected he was. It would take a difficult man to survive her.

Two princesses would take up the time of at least four King's Squires each, day and night: two-thirds of the women on the list of Squires. He'd have to pull some in from other tasks—riding courier, for instance. He went into Garris's office and found him scowling at the chart he'd made of King's Squires and their assignments.

"It's going to take eight King's Squires, minimum, to keep a guard on both princesses."

"I know," Kieri said. "Plus mine—you're sure you can't cut that back?"

"You may be one of the two best blades in the kingdom, Kieri, but I'm not risking your life. Not until you're married and your heir is shoulder-high."

Kieri shook his head but didn't argue. "So we're tying up half the King's Squires on palace duty . . . well, maybe the princesses won't stay long once they figure out I'm not going to marry them. Her. Either one."

"You might," Garris said. "If you did, it might seal a peace with whichever—"

"And make an enemy of the other. No. Anyway, they're just girls. Who's where?"

"Of the women? Aulin's been on duty with the Pargunese—her name is Elis—today. She says the girl's very tense and frightened of something, so she asked to stay on tonight. She'll need help tomorrow. Arian's somewhere between Riverwash and here; she left three days ago with a message to the river guard. Binir should be on the way back from Prealíth. Lieth's here, of course, and I can substitute men for the women in your rotation if that's acceptable."

"Certainly," Kieri said. "At least for a while." Once more he thought how comfortable he found the women Squires, with their easy competence. A pity they were all so young; he put that out of his mind, watching as Garris wrote out a new chart. "Do you need a clerk assistant, Garris?"

"No—not yet. When you get up to fifty Squires, then I will."

"If more princesses show up at one time, it may come to that. When you've finished, come have supper with me—somewhere far away from the Pargunese girl's dragon guardian. That woman is nothing like Hanlin at the coronation and much more like what I thought of as Pargunese."

"Thank you," Garris said. "A turn of the glass, maybe one and a half. How did the hunt go?"

"Very well. Ample game for a banquet tomorrow, and at least some of the hounds and people were mingling."

"You can't hurry things here, Kieri," Garris said. Then, with a sly wink, "Except perhaps your finding a wife and getting an heir."

Kieri rolled his eyes and made his way back to his bathing room. There, relaxing in his steaming tub of herb-scented water, he wondered about the Pargunese baths. How did they have hot pools in winter? Did they have hot springs near the palace? But hot springs usually stank—surely they didn't bathe in water that smelled like rotten eggs. Though that might explain their sour attitude.

He heaved himself up and submitted to Joriam's pitcher of rinse water, then dried himself with towels warmed by the fire. His bath was fine enough—more luxurious than he'd had for most of his life. He did not need whatever it was the Pargunese woman thought better.

Though the evening began quietly enough eating supper with Garris, after supper he had to decide where the Kostandanyan princess and her retinue should be housed, and that meant conferences with half a dozen servitors. Twice the steward brought him demands from Countess Settik and once from the count, who wanted his horse moved to a different stall and all the Pargunese mounts fed only the oats carried on the Pargunese pack horses. Kieri called in the Master of Horse.

"We just put those oats in the bins—I can scoop out the top layer, but—"

"Put some oats in a separate barrel for the beasts and tell him those were his oats," Kieri said. "Sprinkle a little salt on them, and the horses won't know the difference. Neither will he."

By then it was time to make his way upstairs and inspect the guest suite for the Kostandanyan princess—he'd decided to put her as far from the Pargunese as possible—and then he slipped out for a few minutes into the rose garden, now lushly perfumed with both the roses and night-blooming flowers. He sat on his favorite bench and breathed in the mingled scents, sweet and spicy, trying to regain the sense of peace and confidence his elven tutor insisted he needed to connect most powerfully with the taig.

In the near-dark, with the water gurgling and splashing as it ran through the garden, he relaxed slowly, touching first the garden's taig and then that to which it was connected. Outside the palace enclosure, just across the way, the trees on the margin of the King's Grove . . . and then, as his taig-sense expanded, the King's Grove itself, every tree distinct in its identity, its history . . . He sank slowly into a trance, now more familiar than the first time it happened, touching and being touched by the trees and through them other trees and all that "tree" meant—past, present, future, from the root-clutched rock below to the creatures that lived on and or visited it. He roused only when the clamor of another arrival in the palace courtyard broke through the reverie.

He took a last stroll around the paths in the garden and went up to his own rooms, not risking confrontation with another group of angry foreigners. His Squires could tell him what the Kostandanyan girl was like.

Shortly, the steward came to tell him that the Kostandanyan princess, by name Ganlin, seemed to have been injured on the way— she limped at least—and might be too fatigued to attend a banquet the next night. Kieri considered the likelihood that Count and Count-ess Settik would be angered by delay—probably, but he was not in-clined to coddle them—and reset the date.

⁂

On the night of the dinner, the two princesses and their guardians appeared at opposite ends of the passage and stopped, obvi-ously startled to see one another. The princesses, Kieri noted, looked surprised but delighted; their guardians glared.

He made the welcome speech he'd planned and then led the way into the dining room. With most of the Council gone for the summer, Kieri had invited others to fill out the table, including off-duty King's Squires. He hoped seeing the women Squires in formal garb would convince the princesses' guardians that they were well-bred, proper ladies as well as Knights of Falk and King's Squires.

Formal attire for women had never caught Kieri's interest; he had seen a lot of it since being crowned, but knew he understood little of the covert messages sent by the length and cut of a sleeve, the width and draping of a skirt, the amount and placement of lace.

On his right hand, Elis of Pargun wore pale blue, and on his left hand, Ganlin of Kostandan wore pale green. They faced each other across the wide table; somewhat to Kieri's surprise they were not eyeing each other with jealous speculation.

Countess Settik had already complained about the seating, insist-ing that Elis should sit beside Kieri at the head of the table, that no proper banquet could be given with one long table instead of a

U-shaped arrangement, the head table seating at least five. Then she had tried to insist that she sit next to Elis, "as is only decent," but he was not about to have that poisonous woman any closer to him than he must.

He found the two princesses puzzling. Elis, the taller, had silvery-blond hair and light gray eyes; she sat erect, almost stiff, in a blue gown that lent only a little color to her eyes and none to her face. She spoke little to him, in a cool, remote tone, answering his first polite questions without enthusiasm and ignoring Sier Halveric to her right. Mostly she looked down or across at Ganlin. Her hands were larger than he expected; they looked strong and capable; he saw a mark on her heart-hand that might have been a training scar. He wondered what had made it.

Ganlin, another blond, had more color—hair more yellow, blue eyes, and more color in her face. More animation in her voice and face, too: Kieri noticed her smile for the man on her other side, Sier Belvarin. She answered Kieri's questions with a smile. And yet—she looked most at Elis, as Elis looked most at her. And yet again, Ganlin's hands looked like Elis's—more the hands of a young woman trained to boys' pursuits than the soft hands of an idle princess.

Kieri glanced down the table. Countess Settik, across the table and down eight places from Elis, was obviously trying to catch her eye and signal something. The man next to her, Sier Halveric's eldest son-in-law, a man of phlegmatic temperament, already looked frayed, and Kieri was glad he hadn't asked any of the younger men to sit there. Elis avoided her guardian's gaze. Ganlin's guardian—one of her aunts, he'd been told—was chatting with Garris, the King's Squire next to her.

No, Kieri thought, nothing could make him marry a Pargunese. Yet courtesy demanded that he share his attention between the two girls. Perhaps if he got them talking more . . . "Do you know each other?" he asked. They locked gazes across the table at each other rather than at him. Both flushed a little; he had the sense that one wanted to nudge the other under the table, but it was too wide.

"Um . . . no, lord king," Ganlin said, with Elis a beat behind with her. "We've met, lord king. That's all."

So both were prepared to lie; Kieri had not lived so long not to recognize the signs of a covert agreement of some kind. "Well," he said, "perhaps you should become more acquainted. Pargun and Kostandan are, after all, neighbors."

"My guardian wouldn't—" "They don't want—" came simultaneously from both girls.

Oho. Another complication. He could imagine that the guardians would have preferred to present only their own princess to avoid competition, but since they were both there, surely it was natural for girls that age to spend time together. He struggled to find some topic that might interest them, but he had no idea how princesses were reared, what they valued. Taking a cue from their hands, he said, "Do you like horses?"

A patch of color came out on Elis's cheek. "Very much, lord king," she said quietly. "I—I like to ride. Fast."

"Then you should ride," Kieri said, relieved to have found some common interest. "We have both an indoor school and the Royal Ride—a long stretch of grass through the forest. Perhaps if Ganlin—"

"I like to ride," Ganlin said without his asking. "But—but more informally."

Kieri felt his brows rise. "Informally?"

"My—my aunt thinks it improper to ride astride."

"Does she indeed? Here, most women ride astride," Kieri said.

"Really?" Elis's voice rose; down the table, Kieri saw Countess Settik glare at her, and Elis looked down.

"My aunt says it's not proper for a princess," Ganlin said more quietly. "Certainly not while visiting . . . I used to . . ."

"We both did," Elis said under her breath. She stabbed a medallion of venison with unnecessary force.

"Then consider that you are free to use the Royal Ride," Kieri said, applying himself to his own meal. He glanced down the table to where Arian, just back from Riverwash, was listening to Count Settik of Pargun and Kaelith doing the same with Ganlin's male escort—her uncle or uncle-in-law, Kieri assumed. It would have been pleasant to have them at his end of the table; the Squires often ate with him. For a moment, he transposed the Squires and princesses, imagining them as the latter, but he put that out of mind.

Dinner progressed from course to course; Kieri tried a few more topics with the princesses but could not sustain any conversation with them, as Elis seemed both angry and frightened, and Ganlin took her cues from Elis. They were so young . . . not only in age, but in experience. Kieri found himself thinking of Paksenarrion, as he often did—not much older than these girls, the age his daughter would have been if she'd lived. His Estil would have been much more like Paks; he could not imagine either of them in a formal dress. And these girls, with their capable outdoor hands . . . were they really princesses, or . . . or what? As far as he knew, Pargun and Kostandan had no women soldiers—rude jokes had been made about that from time to time—so he would not have expected princesses to learn soldiers' skills. Yet if an enemy wanted to send in agents—even assassins—young girls pretending to be princesses might evade suspicion.

CHAPTER EIGHT

Vonja outbound, a tenday after Midsummer

I andelir Arcolin, at the head of slightly more than a half-cohort of his soldiers, had been on the move all morning, trying to catch up with a band he believed had attacked his camp a few nights before. They moved north on a trail running along the west flank of a ridge. Along the ridgetop, Arcolin knew, was a footpath, rocky and difficult. Below this trail—the widest of the three—was another, twisting around the many swampy areas at the headwaters of the little streams that fed the tributary in the valley. Beyond were fields and then the same north-south road they'd taken from Cortes Vonja.

In the humid midday heat, the woods' rich green smell competed with the sharper odors of sweaty men and mules. Sweat trickled steadily down his face, his back, his sides. Arcolin resisted the impulse to take off his helmet and let the air cool his head, but spared a thought to the men left behind in camp, including the three who'd suffered burns when fire arrows set a tent alight. The cohort was understrength now, not even counting the ones left behind in the city to help with Stammel. Thirteen dead, another eight in addition to Stammel unable to fight.

The inexorable mathematics of war would soon reduce the cohort's effectiveness to the point where he'd have to tell the Cortes Vonja Council he could do no more without reinforcements. Though his cohort had killed more of the enemy than they'd lost, the so-called brigands, unlike any ordinary brigands, had not disappeared or quit harassing them. They were being supplied from outside—that was obvious—but who had the resources of men and money? Was it really Alured the Black? Or was another adversary at work?

Arcolin's horse snorted; he yanked his attention back to the moment. Ahead of him, on the trail, he saw a pile of horse manure, fresh and glistening. His first impulse was to press forward faster; perhaps they were catching up with the fugitives. He looked around. He saw nothing, heard nothing but the creak and jingle of armor, harness, and packs from his own cohort. Too quiet, more than the simple noontime stillness. He passed back a hand signal, and his troop moved off the trail downslope, into the woods.

Silence closed around the cohort when they had moved ten paces off the trail and closed into a fighting column again. Arcolin backed his mount down the slope. He could just see Burek at the other end of the column. Arcolin's horse lifted its head, ears pricked toward the trail. A few moments later, Arcolin heard a rustle of leaves, someone moving down the slope across the trail from them. He could still see nothing. He glanced at his troop. None of them moved, waiting his signal, Devlin's eyes flicking from him back to Jenits, Jenits watching Devlin.

Louder rustling. Now, because they were so silent, he could hear a few individual footfalls, someone slipping and bumping into a tree, harsher breathing. Suddenly, far off on the left flank—what would have been ahead of them if they'd kept going—he heard a man's voice, an obvious command. Louder noises near the trail, bushes thrashing as men pushed their way into that open space, more noises now on their left front.

A well-constructed little ambush, if it had worked. Was this all of it? Suddenly his horse threw up its head and blew a rattling snort. Arcolin looked up and caught sight of someone who seemed to be walking on air parallel to a massive oak limb. His mind refused to accept it for an instant, then he knew: he'd seen sailors in Immerdzan port, feet on a rope slung below the horizontal poles—what did they call them?—resting their elbows on the . . . the yard, that was it. Guards, he'd been told, to keep thieves off the ship in harbor and fight pirates at sea. Even as this ran through his mind, he signaled Devlin, backed farther downslope . . . surely not all the trees were rigged, just those around planned ambush sites.

A shrill whistle sounded loud as a scream, and yells followed as the enemy charged toward the trail. Arcolin risked quick glances upward, aware that any one of them could end with a crossbow bolt in the eye—ropes rigged on both sides of the trail but none here . . . or here. His own troops backed down the slope in order; the brigands followed, more raggedly as they rushed to close and the slope pulled them on.

His cohort reached the lower trail, the one skirting the wet ground around tributary headwaters. Arcolin halted them, and in the seconds before the enemy reached them they had time to form the tight, protective formation—the *flexible* tight, protective formation—he wanted.

The first enemy charged out of the woods, five—six—seven—the fastest, least controlled—and tried to stop, still slipping, sliding—and then, desperate, charged into the waiting cohort and died. Behind came more—a ragged line—and hoofbeats of more than a few horses. Those on foot arrived first—fifteen—twenty—with a motley collection of shields and weapons, including two short pikes. The first rank held them off without difficulty. Devlin dispatched one of the pikemen, and Jenits took the other.

Horsemen burst out of the cover, three close together, three more behind, clearly intending to break the formation. At his signal, Arcolin's formation split, opening a lane through which the horses charged even as their riders tried to halt and turn them. One, indeed, managed this, but at the cost of slowing his mount so much that Arcolin's soldiers easily surrounded him and pulled him off.

The rest of the brigands fled back into the woods; those whose horses were mired in the swamp floundered through the muck, and a tensquad caught and killed three of them. Two more fell to the crossbows they'd captured on that first patrol.

"That's more like it," Devlin said, surveying the row of brigand bodies. "And if we were better with our crossbows, we'd have had more of them. What warned you about the bowman in the trees, Captain?"

"My horse as much as anything," Arcolin said, patting the sweaty neck of his chestnut. "And I saw how they'd been picking us off despite our scouts. They've got sailors up on the trees."

"Sailors?"

"Remember the harbors we went through? The guard sailors up on those crosspieces—the yards, they called them—standing on those ropes slung below when they weren't walking on the yards themselves? They've rigged trees beside the main trails, at least in some places, and can shoot down on us."

"That's bad," Devlin said. "We didn't see anything like that in Siniava's War."

"No. But Alured was on our side then. These will be pirate friends of his, I have no doubt. They'll be able to look right down and see our scouts—and our scouts aren't looking up. This fellow must've been four or five armspans up—that would be no height to a sailor."

"What do we do?" Burek said.

"Today? They'll expect us to pursue, and they'll try to lead us back where their aerial bowmen can attack . . . so we're not going to do that. Today we take the swamp trail back south, as if we're running away, then we'll cut back upslope, cross the main trail, and go right over the ridge."

Burek and Devlin both looked puzzled, but Jenits's face lit. Arcolin gave him a quick nod. "I don't expect we'll run into a trailing force—though we might—but we should see evidence of their tree rigging. If we can get to the main trail across the ridge before they realize what we're doing, we should be able to see how they get up and down, and estimate how far ahead they set up ambushes and the kinds of locations they pick. And then—"

"We can put our own archers up there," Burek said. "And ambush them."

"They'll need practice shooting down at that angle," Arcolin said, remembering what Cracolnya had always said about his cohort's practice on rising and falling ground. "But yes. The thing is, we know nothing about rigging ropes in trees, not even what size rope."

In the long summer afternoon, the cohort moved as Arcolin directed, encountering no brigands they could detect. Just as they crossed the main trail, Burek spotted a coil of rope tucked into the crotch of a tree. They looked up. At intervals along a nearly horizontal limb, loops of rope circled the limb, stained dark, unnoticeable to a casual glance. One end of the coil ran up the tree trunk, looking like a vine stem, to the base of a limb higher than the one that held the loops of rope.

"They climb the rope, pull it up, thread it through those loops . . . they must tie it off at the far end," Burek said.

"Now we know they have trees ready to rig along the main trail," Arcolin said. "So they can move their ambush site. We need to know how many, what kind of trees they use, how many sailors they have to climb them."

"Our siege-assault specialists could climb it," Devlin said, looking up.

"Later," Arcolin said. "For now, we don't want them to know we noticed this. We'll go on over the ridge and look there."

He wondered how many brigands were actually good at climbing trees and standing on ropes to shoot crossbows. The ones they'd just killed all wore conventional shoes or boots. He remembered the sailors aloft being barefoot, remembered asking someone about that. Boots were too slippery when they got wet, he'd been told. Bare feet callused by hard use and salt water clung to the ropes and spars.

They reached the crest of the ridge, and Arcolin looked back at the slope they were leaving, the furrow in the trees that showed where the main trail ran. He could not see the trail itself, but someone aloft in one of those trees could signal to a watcher here without being seen from below. A troop, no matter how quietly it moved, still made enough noise to cover the sound of a crossbow's string . . . and a bolt fitted with a ribbon could be seen from here.

On the far side of the ridge, they moved cautiously through woods as the light slowly waned into twilight. Scouts reported a clearing ahead with rigged trees covering the opening.

"Looks like a camp—maybe for twenty, by the size of the jacks."

"How recently were they there?"

"Hard to say, sir. Not yesterday, but within the last hand of days, most like. Fire-pit has bones in it, but there's a pile of offal still downslope. It's been dragged about by vermin but not consumed yet. They're planning to come back this way sometime; we found a barrel of meal hidden in a brush pile."

"We'll camp here tonight," Arcolin said. "They're sure to notice us, but we can't move far enough before dark to be out of their range, either. So they'll attack, but our people will be up the trees, not theirs."

"All night?" Burek asked, looking up at the trees.

"Better than theirs sneaking in and having the height on us," Arcolin said. "Short watches, since there's no way for anyone to rest up there."

That, it turned out, was an error. The first climbers sent into the trees found fishing-net hammocks tied into the crotches of each rigged tree, water jugs with lines tied to their handles.

"They could stay up in the trees for days," Burek said. "That explains how our scouts missed them."

"That and not imagining such a thing," Arcolin said. "Siniava's people never did anything like this, so none of us even considered it. And yet—I saw those ships, the last year of Siniava's War. And I knew Alured had been a pirate."

"Risky," Burek said. "But we hurt them today."

"We've hurt them before," Arcolin said. "Ordinary brigand bands would have retreated by now. There's something keeping them in this area, and they're being reinforced."

The best climbers in the cohort went up the trees and tested out the rigging. Nothing happened through the early and midnight hours of darkness, and Arcolin finally woke Burek and lay down at the foot of one of the rigged trees. So far none of his climbers had fallen.

He woke to a blow in his back, the scrape of a blade on his mail. He rolled away, yelling, grabbing for his dagger. More yells from his sentries . . . someone landed on him again, this time with a heavy cloth that missed his head but caught his arms for an instant. He stabbed through the cloth, felt the dagger go home into flesh, yanked and stabbed again—and then his people were there, the weight on him gone, and his assailant lay dead on the ground.

In the torchlight Arcolin saw a small, wiry man in short trousers and a sleeveless jerkin, barefoot—his soles horny as goats' hooves— his hair in a stiff braid. He had elaborate tattoos on both arms—sea monsters, Arcolin thought—he remembered the sailors of the south being heavily tattooed. On a thong around his neck was a medallion with a design Arcolin did not recognize. The blade he'd attacked Arcolin with, broad and curved, was much like those they had captured before.

"Was there only one?" Arcolin asked. "And how did he get past the sentries?"

"Sneaks," Devlin said, nose wrinkled. "They're good at that, if nothing else."

"Didn't see or hear another one," Jenits said. "Maybe because he's barefoot?"

"Could be," Arcolin said. "He's a sailor . . . but why would he come here alone and then attack openly? Why me, and not a sentry? Killing a sentry would open the way for others to attack. He could have avoided us easily enough."

"Something here he wants," Burek said. "And perhaps he didn't realize you were there. If he wanted to climb the tree and stumbled into you, he'd have to attack."

"Maybe," Arcolin said. "Come morning we'll see what we find."

The rest of the night passed quietly. In the morning, they found another barrel of meal and an empty cask that smelled of the wine it had once held.

"That barrel's heavy," Devlin remarked, when they'd pulled the lid off. "Let's see what we've got."

"Grain," Tam said.

"Poke it with a sword," Devlin said. "Let's just see."

Far down in the barrel Tam's sword met resistance. "We could just eat the grain," he said with a sly grin.

"Pack it up," Arcolin said, shaking his head.

In minutes, men were shifting the grain to the extra sacks. They found a heavy leather-wrapped bundle at the bottom of the barrel: a small anvil and a hammer.

"They have a farrier with them," Burek said. "We know they have horses, and most of the horses are shod. But this anvil looks small to fashion horseshoes. And there's no sign of a forge—none at all."

"They could have the forge somewhere else and keep the anvil here—though I wonder why," Arcolin said. He looked closely at the anvil; something about it tickled his memory. The street of the smiths in Cortes Vonja—the different sounds of the hammers, the anvils ringing to the blows in different smiths' halls, different sizes of anvils . . . "What would this anvil be good for?" he asked Burek. Devlin answered.

"Captain, I've seen an anvil like that in a medaller's—where they make badges and medals and things. This hole here—that would hold the anvil die—"

"Dies!" Arcolin said. "Of course! He came back for the dies."

"Sir?"

"Coins, Dev—they're striking coins. Changing the marks, at least, and maybe the composition, making counterfeits. *That's* what was worth one man sneaking back in the night, and if he came to the foot of that tree, it's because he wanted to climb it. They sent a sailor— the dies are hidden up the tree somewhere."

Those who'd spent the night in trees climbed back up and poked into every hollow, every tangle of limbs. "Found something," Forli said. "Limb broke off and they hollowed out a space." He lowered the leather sack on a line; inside were two pieces of steel. "And here's something else," he added. "Sack of money, looks like." He tossed that down.

Burek fitted the tang of the lower die into the hole on the anvil, and Arcolin set the hammer die atop it. "That much fits," he said. He looked in the sack of coins and found a mix of coins: some Guild League with different marks, some from the far south with the marks of Immerdzan and Aliuna, a few from the duchy of Fall. In the bottom of the sack was another, of thinner leather, holding pewter disks, a dozen or so plain and several bearing confusing blurred marks.

"Practice," Devlin said. "The shop I saw, a 'prentice was learning to hammer straight, and the master used disks like this for him to learn on."

Arcolin upended the hammer die and looked at the surface that would shape a coin. He could not read the design—surely it was intended for a Vonja coin, but . . .

"Let me try," Burek said. "We can use one of the practice disks. Someone get me a hammer." One of the soldiers rummaged in the tool bag they always carried and found one. Burek fitted the disk between the two dies and struck the top one a solid blow. The disk looked lopsided—it had not been exactly centered—but now Arcolin could read the mark: the Guild League symbol on one side and Vonja's own mark, PCV, on the other.

"In silver, it would be a niti," Arcolin said. "I wonder if this is the only coin they make." He pulled a niti from his belt-pouch to compare.

"Those nas and natas we found in the merchant's wagon were some of them counterfeit."

"And where did they get the dies?" Arcolin said, thinking out loud. "These are hard steel, not something an artisan can carve out."

"Mints have dies. Maybe they're stolen?"

A breeze rustled the leaves overhead, and Arcolin looked up: clouds moving in again. "Later. Pack everything up; we'll go back to our home site."

"Take the dies and anvil?"

"Of course. We need proof for the Vonja Council. Scouts, be alert for rigged trees. I think they're still north of us, but we don't want more losses, in case they sent for reinforcements."

By dusk, the cohort was back off the ridge and within a glass's march of their former campsite, where they'd left the wagons and two tensquads.

"I don't think we'll see any attacks for a few days," Arcolin said. "They'll be resupplied, no doubt, but that will take time. We must be hurting them. We'll send word back to the city. These dies could be stolen from their mint, or made elsewhere. I want to take them in myself, in case they do have a traitor who might intercept them. Perhaps if we get word about Stammel." It had been so long, he did not expect good news.

Burek nodded. "I wouldn't trust them either—not after what they tried before."

Arcolin gave the dies to their own smith, who looked them over carefully.

"This little anvil's definitely a coiner's," he said. "At the mints they'd use a water-powered hammer to strike multiples at once; this would be a merchant's set. Seen them up north, to strike Finthan coins with Tsaia's mark."

"I thought both passed easily in the northern realms," Burek said. "Doesn't the north have a sort of Guild League?"

"No," Arcolin said. "Finthan and Tsaian coins are commonly accepted at mint value—at least in Vérella and Fin Panir—but everything else must be changed—at a cost—and some are regulated."

Burek looked puzzled. "But doesn't that impede trade? I mean, if the money changers take their snip, and the realms—"

"Yes, but not so much that most people mind it. We use letters of credit, as you saw. And the periodic bankers' caravans—heavily guarded—often carry gold bullion and lump silver, so it can be fresh-minted in Tsaia. There's no tax on letters of credit and much less on unminted metals."

"What about the others, like Pargun and Lyonya and so on?"

"Pargun doesn't trade in Tsaia."

"But they trade on the coast," Burek said, scowling. "I've seen Pargunese coins—not many, to be sure, but some."

"I suppose . . ." Arcolin had not ever considered where the Pargunese traded. Down here? They must go by sea, down the river. "I suppose they trade in Bannerlith, on the northern coast, north of the Eastbight—perhaps they themselves have come to the southern coast."

"Even Andressat uses Guild League standards for coinage. It would be simpler if everyone did."

"True," Arcolin said. "But the money changers would hate it. They'd lose half their trade."

"I suppose," Burek said. He had picked up the dead sailor's medallion and now turned it over and over, examining the designs on both sides. "I wonder what this means."

"I never saw it before," Arcolin said. "It's not the device Alured picked when he claimed the duchy of Immer. He went with one from the Cortes Immer ruins." He poked through the pile of coins, setting them in stacks according to size, metal, design. "Some of these wouldn't fit the dies at all. If you stamped this one width of the die—" He held up a small silver. "—it would be obviously thinner than standard. There must be more dies."

"Unless they want them to be noticed," Burek said.

"Not this obvious, I don't think. If the idea is to show that the city mints are adulterating their coins, they'd want them to look nearly the same."

That evening, Arcolin wrote out a report for the Council, and Burek added notations to the map they were making. Next day, by daylight, he set Burek to making a fair copy of the map to send back to the city with his report. In midafternoon, a farm boy came to the camp to report that his father had seen "fancy men" moving along the woods' edge.

"Fancy?" Devlin asked. He was questioning the boy; Arcolin listened from inside the tent where he worked.

"Hats w' feathers," the boy said. "And they leader has shiny things—around he neck and he arms."

"How far away was your father, that he could see all that?"

"Oh, he hid in a log," the boy said, scratching one bare leg with the dirty toes of the other. "He's lookin' for berries, this time summer, an' he heard 'em, and into a log he went, same's I would, on account it's t'other village's berry patch."

"And?"

"And they come right by 'im, walkin' proud, he says, but some limpin' and blood on they clothes. And pickin' every berry they saw."

"How many?"

The boy stared at his hands, scowling, moving his fingers up and down, and finally said, "Two hands maybe."

"They'll be no trouble to us for a while," Burek said. "But to the farmers . . ."

"It's late to move today; we'll move tomorrow," Arcolin said. "I'm not going to risk our people on the trail at night. The woods are more open up that way—we should be able to pick up a trail."

CHAPTER NINE

Cortes Vonja

Once a tenday the grange drilled outside the city, in the water meadows. As soon as the Marshal allowed, Stammel went along, his hand on Suli's shoulder. He wore his own uniform again, though it was loose, and a banda over it. The Marshal insisted on a straw hat over his helmet; he was sure it looked ridiculous, but the Marshal wanted to protect his eyes.

"I'm blind," Stammel said. "Why worry about them?"

"Because an infection in them could kill you," the Marshal said. "And if there is any chance your sight might come back, staring into the sun you can't see will finish it."

So now he followed Suli and the others, stumbling only a little now and then. She was good at noticing what might trip him and murmuring warnings. "Rut here. Big root ahead, high step."

This was drill as he knew it, but with slightly different commands. The yeomen knew them and started off at a strong walk; Stammel, next to Suli, felt out of place this close. At least he hadn't tired on the walk out of the city, and when the Marshal called a rest, he wasn't out of breath like some of those he heard huffing and puffing.

"Unarmed next," the Marshal said. "Pair up. Stammel, you're with Groj."

Stammel grinned. He'd won the argument, then; he hadn't been sure until this moment. Unarmed fighting, once in grip of the other, wasn't about sight but about feel . . . and he was sure his feel would come back. Groj might throw him, but he would be fighting again. Suli guided him some twenty paces.

"I'm Groj," a voice said in front of him. "I'm one of the smiths. Marshal says I'm not to kill you."

"I'd prefer not," Stammel said.

"I'm a head taller," Groj said. "He said I should tell you that."

"I could tell from your voice," Stammel said. He could feel his body's adjustments, the same as always. For a taller man, this shift. Around him he heard other pairs moving into position.

"But I won't let you win," Groj said. "I told 'm I wouldn't, and he said that was all right."

"I won't let you win, either," Stammel said. Just as he wondered whether pairs signaled each other some way or the Marshal started it, he heard the command.

All the pent-up emotion of the past tendays exploded as he charged. He heard the rasp of Groj's boots on the grass as the man tried to swing aside, but he was faster, and his arms, reaching wide, caught the man's belt. Pivot, yank—Groj's big hand touched his shoulder, but he already had the leverage, and Groj went down. He rolled up quickly, caught Stammel's arm, and then they were in grip, hands and elbows and knees, struggling for mastery.

Groj was bigger and very strong, but Stammel had more speed and many more years of experience; he fought silently, exulting in the expertise he had not lost to blindness, feeling and hearing Groj's surprise, the grunts of effort, the gasps as Stammel found yet another way to pin the bigger man. If demons could not defeat him, no big hamfisted smith—

"Hold!" came the command. Groj fell back, gasping; Stammel pushed himself away a little, only somewhat winded.

Footsteps on the grass. "Well," Marshal Harak said. "What do you think now, Groj?"

"You're right, Marshal. He'd have half-killed anyone else. I'm blown."

"Sergeant, I expected you'd explode some way, so I gave you Groj. I didn't think you could hurt him, but you've left marks on him will take tendays to vanish."

He hadn't realized that. He'd been so happy . . . "I'm sorry," he said.

"No need," the Marshal said. "You've been entirely too controlled since your ordeal; it had to come out sometime."

Arcolin's Camp

The messenger from Cortes Vonja carried two letters for Arcolin, one with the seal of Gird on the flap and the other addressed in Arñe's writing, sealed in the same wax as the other but without a seal. Arcolin felt his heart sink. Good news would have been Stammel riding into camp with the others.

He slid his dagger blade under the flap of the Marshal's letter first. *Your sergeant lives,* the Marshal had written.

> *But he is blind, and like to remain so. Despite this, he has been drilling with my yeomen, greatly to their improvement, I may say. The first time he attempted unarmed fighting, with the biggest in my grange, he threw him down. Though he is not yet recovered to his full strength, I judge his health improved enough to leave the grange, and so does he. The Council, at the urging of all three Marshals and the Captain of Tir whom you met, and also a Captain of Falk you did not meet, awarded him a small pension, enough to survive on if he chooses to stay. I understand he will have a pension from your Company as well. He knows of the pension but has said nothing to me. He wants to know your will in this and considers himself still under your orders.*

Arñe's letter was less formal:

> *Captain,*
>
> *Sergeant Stammel is well and strengthening daily, but he is blind. We have all done what we can; Suli has a blind uncle and so guides him the most. We have been calling her Stammel's eyes. I know—*

That part was scratched out. Arñe added,

*He wants to come back, but he won't ask. He would do any work
you gave him.*

What work could he give a blind man when they might be in
combat at any time? Yes, he had hired a half-blind captain, but the
man still had one eye. Stammel . . . Arcolin squeezed his eyes
against the thought of telling Stammel he must leave the Company.
At least he must take Stammel back north, back to the stronghold, to
safety. He called Burek into his tent and showed him the letters.

"Blind!" Burek said. "I thought he would live or die, and if he
lived, recover."

"It is . . . hard to imagine," Arcolin said. "Hard for us all; you
knew him only a short while, but for many of us . . ."

"You will pension him, surely."

"I will think," Arcolin said. "Go find Devlin and send him to me."
Devlin, who had been Stammel's corporal for so long before the dis-
ruptions of Siniava's War had promoted him.

"You have word," Devlin said as he came into the tent.

"He's alive, but blind," Arcolin said. Devlin looked stunned, the
way he himself felt. "He can walk; he can even drill, after a fashion.
He threw a yeoman in an unarmed fighting drill. The Marshal pressured the Council to give him a small pension, if he wants to stay
there, and will find him a room in someone's house."

"No," Devlin said. "No, that can't be."

"I'm sorry," Arcolin said. "But it's true."

"That's not what I meant, sir. I understand: he's blind. But he
can't—he will die—if he's penned up in some spare room, alone,
without us. Sir, you have to bring him here. He can walk; he can
march with us. If he can drill, he'll get stronger. He knows so
much—he can teach me, and Arñe and Jenits and the rest."

"But if we're in combat—he can't fight—"

"He can at least be with us," Devlin said. "I know that's what he'd
want—he probably won't ask you—but it's what he wants. What he
needs. And we need him. If he'd lost a leg or something, if he
couldn't keep up—but you say he can—"

"The Marshal says he's well enough to move out of the grange,
but—ours is a hard life for men with sight."

"And the life he knows," Devlin said.

"The Duke—" Arcolin began; Devlin interrupted him.

"It's not Phelan's Company anymore, sir, but yours. Maybe you think Kieri Phelan would have sent him back north, but you can do what you want."

He wanted Stammel back, but he wanted the Stammel who no longer existed, the Stammel who had not lost his sight because Arcolin had agreed to a civilian's request. But he wanted Stammel back here to talk to, to steady the troops.

"They'll need horses," he said. "Let me think—Stammel should have my ambler; he's steady and a smooth ride. He won't have ridden in a while. Arñe or Doggal can ride the fast one I left up there. And four more. We don't have four spares, unless we don't move and send the wagon teams . . . or switch out mules . . ."

"I'll take care of that, sir," Devlin said. "Thank you, sir!"

Arcolin wrote out the orders for Arñe. He wanted to go himself, but the cohort could not afford to lose another senior person; the courier could take the orders back. He wrote a letter of thanks to Marshal Harak and one each for the Captains of Tir and Falk.

Only a few days later, a small party of horse travelers proved to be the missing six, all wearing absurd floppy straw hats over their helmets. Arcolin thought Stammel looked perfectly normal at first and wondered if he had regained his sight, but then he saw Suli, riding beside him, touch his arm and take the rein of the horse.

Arcolin strode forward, but Stammel had dismounted by the time Arcolin reached the group, and Arñe greeted him. "No problems on the road, Captain."

"Glad to have you all back with us," Arcolin said. "You'll want to see Sergeant Devlin; we've made some temporary assignments. He will explain." Arñe told Tam and Doggal to put the horses up, then, at his nod, headed for Devlin, who was near the fire-pit. The other two, at another nod, headed for their companions. This close, Arcolin could see that Stammel's eyes did not focus on him, but wandered, as if searching for the light, their once-clear brown clouded. It was eerie; he tried not to shudder. At least the whites were no longer red. Stammel stood upright, rigid as if at inspection, his face unreadable.

"Stammel—" Arcolin said; he felt his throat close, took the two steps forward, and gripped Stammel by the shoulders. The bones were closer to the skin than they had been. "I thought—I was afraid we'd lose you, man."

"Thank you for letting me come back, sir," Stammel said. He sighed. "But you have lost me, one way. A blind sergeant—not much use in a fight. I'll try to be useful at something, until—until we go north. I can still scrub pots and chop redroots."

"Stop that," Arcolin said. "I didn't order you back here to scrub pots. We need you, your expertise. You're the senior sergeant, just as if you'd broken a leg and were riding in a wagon. From what Marshal Harak told me, you were already starting to train his yeomen."

Stammel's face relaxed. "Just wanted to give you a chance—"

"What, to waste the best sergeant I ever had? I may not be Kieri's equal, but I'm not stupid. Let's start this over. Welcome back, Sergeant Stammel."

"Glad to be back, Captain," Stammel said.

"Devlin already has some ideas for you," Arcolin said. "But I wanted to brief you on the situation. It's gotten complicated."

"Complicated?"

"It's not just brigands we're fighting. I don't know if someone—Alured, for instance—is trying to infiltrate a whole army into southern Vonja or something else . . ."

"That money the merchant we captured had. I heard in the city it was counterfeit." That sounded like the old Stammel.

"You heard?"

"People see a man being led around by a young woman, they think neither of them can hear. Or think. Suli's my eyes now, sir, but I'm the ears. I don't think I hear better, but not seeing . . . I pay more attention. Anyway, she'd take me out on walks in the city. We stopped in a tavern . . . and I heard men talking. Merchants, I think, because one was talking wool prices, and then their voices got lower and it was about coins. That some of the Guild League cities are minting false coinage, cheating their own people."

"I wish I'd thought to look at those money bags," Arcolin said. "All I saw was silver and copper coins; when he said it was his own, I thought I'd let the Council figure it out."

"Well, they have. 'Course, what I heard could be just rumor, but I heard other things that fit in. Those coins were supposed to have been minted here, in Vonja—had the Vonja die marks. But the Vonja Council swore they weren't, by some secret mark no one's supposed to know. The odd thing is, most of 'em were the right weight and passed the float test, whatever that is. Only some of the silvers were too heavy. Why would anyone make counterfeits with too much silver?"

"I'm not sure," Arcolin said. "Burek told that last season, most of Golden Company contracted there and the bankers turned back a lot of their contract payment as counterfeit. Those were Sorellin natas . . . or they bore Sorellin's mint marks. Burek said it almost caused riots."

"Did M'dierra tell you about it, sir?"

"No. She did mention some counterfeiting—so did the banker— but she didn't tell me specifically about her experience."

"Burek still doing well?"

"Very well. And I found out what Andressat has against him. He may be a bastard grandson of the old man, and he chose not to take the job the count offered him. That would be enough with Andressat; he'd think it ingratitude. His foster father is a horse master at the count's stud."

Talking to Stammel the way he always had eased the strangeness; Stammel sat the same way, held his hands the same way, had the same expressions on his face. Arcolin tried not to look at his eyes.

"The thing is," Arcolin went on, "there are more brigands—or whatever they are—in the woods around here than can possibly be supported without regular resupply. You know that village we camped near at first?" Stammel nodded. "They came down on that village, destroyed a couple of the cottages, killed some of the villagers and took the rest—left a trail a blind—sorry—anyone could follow across the grain. We stayed there the night after I left Cortes Vonja. No attack. We went as far as the deserted village beyond the one where we found the merchant."

Stammel scowled. "Is that the one just south of a stretch of woods?"

"Yes. I remembered it when I rode out into what had been fields; we passed that way coming up from Sibili, last year of Siniava's War. The cottages are all collapsed now, but someone's tending the well. Flowers, and that."

"And the merchant came that way . . ." Stammel said.

"Yes. There's a ford in the woods, well out of sight or hearing of either village if they were both occupied. In the old days, it had stones laid down—they've been moved, to make a hole—wagons can't get through without risking an axle unless you unload and load them. And there's a footpath—a wide one, with bootmarks—along the stream to the east."

"So the merchant could deliver the food and money there. Why did he have it still when we found him?"

"I think the brigands gave him the money," Arcolin said. "It's backward, I know, brigands giving money to merchants instead of robbing them, but if you wanted to put counterfeit money in circulation, who better than a merchant going to trade? As for the food, I think that's farther from their camp, wherever it is."

"I suppose," Stammel said. "But it only makes the merchant richer, doesn't it? I mean, if it weren't discovered? And if it is, he's dead and they don't have a supply line." He shook his head. "I don't see the gain for them—or whoever hired them."

"If the coins aren't discovered, then with more silver or gold—or what's taken for gold—I suppose that would spread somehow . . . but I can't figure out if prices would go down or up."

"Up," Stammel said. "They always go up."

Arcolin laughed. "Seems so, indeed. But scarcity always makes them go up more, and sometimes they go down in a good harvest year."

"One of the conversations I heard," Stammel said, "one man said if the Guild League cities started adulterating their coinage, there was no use to have a Guild League at all. He said . . . he said there was only one reliable mint in all the south. The others laughed at him and called him a fool."

"Did he say where that was?" Arcolin said.

"No, sir. I think he showed them a coin—I heard one fall to their table. But I couldn't see—and Suli was away just then, for a few moments, and didn't see."

"Sounds like a spy," Arcolin said. "And very much as if someone doesn't want the Guild League itself to prosper. I can think of only one lord down here who might have ambitions that high. Most of them are still recovering from Siniava's War. But that only adds to my concerns. We're only one cohort."

"We'll be all right, sir," Stammel said. "Where are we, exactly? Other than two and a half days' ride from Cortes Vonja?"

"Sitting athwart one of their main trails," Arcolin said. "We move every two days—they've become better at attacking our camps, but we've had only minor casualties. Here—I'm going to take your hand and put it on this map—I've put out sticks and things to show how the land is here."

Stammel grimaced but put out his hands; Arcolin took one and guided it to the map. "These stones are the last village we passed. Only six huts; three more in ruins. About half the fields they used to farm are overgrown; they run pigs in the woods and let cattle have the overgrown fields. I'm trying to find as many of the trails as I can, and thus figure out where their camp is."

"You don't think they're moving about like we are?"

"No . . . largely because the villages differ so in how they react when asked about them. If they were always on the move, I'd expect the villages to have about the same contact with them, but that's clearly not so." Arcolin swallowed. He had to talk to Stammel about the effect of his blindness on the cohort, but he dreaded it. He tried to keep his voice light. "I wanted to ask you about Suli—she's your usual guide, isn't she?"

"I'm used to Suli now, sir. I know it's strange, having a woman as my guide—all the things we've said—but there's nothing—"

"I didn't think that." He was sure of Stammel, less sure of a young girl whose good heart might lead her too far.

"It's her experience, you see. Her uncle went blind. She understands just how much help I need. She doesn't try to smother me, and she doesn't leave me lost." Stammel swallowed. "It's not fair to her, o' course. She signed on to be a soldier, not a blind man's guide. She says she doesn't mind, but—"

"We'll let the two of you train others," Arcolin said. "This may not be the last time we have someone blinded. Most of our people know how to tie up a bleeding arm or leg now; they might as well learn this. Then she can rotate back into her regular duties."

"Makes sense," Stammel said. "Whatever the cohort needs, sir, you know I'll go along."

"Your needs count, too. You've already brought me valuable information. But now, I've kept you long enough. Suli can take you to find Devlin; you and Dev decide who to start training as Suli's assistant."

Arcolin stood under the tent flap, watching Suli and Stammel walk across to the tent where Devlin waited, talking to Arñe. Except for his hand on Suli's shoulder, Stammel seemed the same as ever: his carriage upright, his steps firm and even. With a guide, he would be able to march with them; he would not need a horse or a seat in a wagon. His mind was as clear as ever . . . he would gain weight and muscle, Arcolin knew, with time. Stammel alive, sane, healthy—should he be grateful for that and consider sight a small price to pay? He closed his eyes, shutting out the sunlight, the familiar faces of his cohort, trying to imagine it, but he could not. Sight was not a small price, no matter what else was left.

By evening everyone had greeted Stammel, and the mood of the whole cohort seemed better. Devlin, in particular, had lost his worried expression; Arcolin had seen the two of them, Stammel's hand on Devlin's shoulder, doing a circuit of the camp.

"I did not think it would make so much difference, having him back," Burek said.

"You hadn't had time to know him," Arcolin said. "Those here who hadn't fought with him before trained with him in the north. He's everyone's favorite uncle or older brother."

"M'dierra has a sergeant like that—the recruits are first terrified, then adoring."

"Minicor?" Arcolin asked. When Burek nodded, he said "I met him years ago; you're right; he is very like Stammel. The troops could stand to lose me better than Stammel."

Burek looked horrified. "But sir—if you—then I—"

"Not ready for it yet?"

"Not if it means you—something happens—"

Arcolin shrugged. "These things do happen, you know. I believe you'll do well if it does, but in the meantime, I do wear my helmet."

Burek laughed. Arcolin's adventure without his helmet had indeed spread through the cohort.

"So, now that things are more as they were—not that they will be, if he doesn't regain his sight—let me tell you what I learned from Stammel and the others who returned today." He gave Burek a précis of the information they'd brought. "So—together with what we've discussed before, do you see anything else, any pattern I've missed?"

"No," Burek said. "I could wish they'd gone into the markets and noticed prices, especially the horse market, because that's what I know most. If there's bad money about—or more money than there should be—the price of horses goes up. Shoeing, too. I wonder if any of them noticed that."

"They were staying in a grange in Smiths' Street. Surely some of the yeomen were smiths. But then, the Girdish are set against false weights and measures, and in Fintha they control prices. I don't know if Marshal Harak would approve if they raised their prices, unless the cost of iron and coal went up."

"When we go back to the city, I can go to the horse market and talk to the smiths," Burek said.

"In the meantime," Arcolin said, "let's make sure the camp isn't so happy to have Stammel back they get careless with the watch."

But Stammel himself took care of that; they heard his voice from across the camp, the familiar bellow. "And while you lot are sitting here like spinsters gossiping, who's keeping watch? Less talk and more work!"

A startled silence, then camp noises resumed, this time with a different timbre.

Over the next few days, Arcolin grew used to seeing Stammel with a hand on someone's shoulder, his head cocked a little sideways. Neat in appearance as always, attentive, alert, quick to silence idle chatter, ready to respond to any orders Arcolin or Burek gave. They moved every few days, marking the trails they found on the map; Stammel marched as fast as the others, needing extra help only on the rougher ground. Everyone called Suli "Eyes" now, but many of the troops had a nickname; he thought nothing of it.

Arcolin suspected—but knew better than to ask—that Suli, Devlin, and others gave him special help. That didn't matter. They had Stammel; Stammel had them. If some chores were quietly diverted from him, and others came to him because sight was not required, it was only common sense. A familiar voice, a familiar presence.

They were attacked again one night, an attack as carefully planned as the other, and this time killed only five; two of their own were wounded. Arcolin heard Devlin, voice harsh with effort, tell Stammel to get back, get down. He felt a stab of grief, but there was no time—they fought off the attack, and when he came back, Stammel was busy, talking to one of the wounded as he held the man's shoulders down and Master Simmitt stitched the wound. He made no complaint.

But just before dawn, as Arcolin made the rounds, he found Stammel standing with one of the sentries. "I was wondering," Stammel said. "About archery."

"Archery?"

"I know I can't use a sword without eyes. But I think I could shoot."

Arcolin felt his brows rising. "But you need eyes even more—the targets are farther away."

"I need someone to tell me where. I was thinking about Paks, and that trip she and the others made from Dwarfwatch. Canna was shot by someone who never saw her, Paks said. Someone just shooting blindly into a thicket. Now, if we were attacked, and I had someone to tell me where to aim—"

"Sergeant—" Arcolin shook his head, glad for once Stammel could not see. "I never heard of a blind archer," he said finally.

"There's a legend," Stammel said. "And I've seen inns with that name—always thought it was a joke about the ale, to be honest. But still— if I could try with a crossbow . . ."

Arcolin looked at him. "You've spanned one already, haven't you?"

Stammel nodded. "And the thing is, Captain, you know we usually have Cracolnya's cohort. We need archers. If I can—they'll never expect it. It's like you said; they're spying on us. They know I'm blind; they think I'm helpless." His hands clenched and opened, clenched and opened. "If I can hit a target, then anyone could—we could train our own—maybe a half-file?"

It was impossible; it could not work, but sparring in unarmed combat was not enough for a man like Stammel. He had to feel he could fight. Arcolin understood that very well. And Stammel was right—they did need more archers. They had the captured crossbows . . .

"If we were in the stronghold, I'd say yes," Arcolin said. "You'd have the space there; we'd have armsmasters to teach you. But here? We're on campaign."

"Just let me try for one day, sir. If I make no progress by the end of it, I'll say no more."

"All right." What, after all, could it hurt? They weren't moving that day, anyway. He could let Stammel try to get over the notion— though what would replace it he could not guess.

Stammel took a typically Stammel approach to the practice. "How many of you think you can outshoot a blind man?" he asked a glass later. Silence. "Come on, don't be shy. I'm betting someone a jug of ale, when we get back to Valdaire, that I can outshoot you. Maybe not today, but another day. To make it fair, you can start practicing with me." A chuckle, somewhat nervous.

Stammel held up one of their five crossbows. "This is a crossbow. It's nice and short and thus good for use in the woods. Some of you have never used a crossbow, because Siger, being from Lyonya originally, likes longbows." He pointed out the parts of the crossbow, naming them. "Simple to use—aim, pull this, then re-span and you're set. Even if you don't hit anyone, they won't like the sound of death from the air." Meanwhile, targets were set up, not far away at all.

They were using blunt quarrels, but Arcolin still worried that someone would lose an eye.

Stammel's crossbow had a twig bound to the stock so it stuck out one side—to identify it, Arcolin assumed, but why? Then Stammel picked it up and brought the stock up . . . and the twig touched his neck just when the arms of the prod were level.

"Ready!" he called. Downrange, Suli and Devlin stood one to either side of the target, an arm's length away. Both said, "Here." Stammel aimed, Arcolin could see, between the voices. He pulled the trigger. The bolt skimmed over the top of the target.

"Two fingers above the target," Devlin called.

Stammel had re-spanned the bow and lifted it. Again it was level. "Ready," he said. The other two called, and again he shot. The bolt bounced off the middle of the target. He spanned the bow again and this time shot without waiting for the others to call. The bolt hit the middle again.

Silence. Arcolin could not believe what he had just seen.

"Well?" Stammel said finally.

"I think some people will be regretting that bet," Arcolin said. "Gird's arm, man, I didn't think anyone could do that. How—?"

"I'm not sure," Stammel said. "When I found I could walk and then make my way around the grange, I remembered that even on dark nights I had good balance. I always knew where my arms and legs were, when I was upright and when I wasn't. Siger used to say that crossbows were the lazy man's bow—you remember he said a blind man with one hand could shoot a crossbow. Then it was a jest, but I thought . . . if I could figure out a way to hold it level without someone having to show me each shot . . . and then there were the redroots."

"Redroots?"

"I was slicing redroots a few days ago, and Dev made some awful joke. I threw a redroot at him—just joking, you know—and it hit him square, he said. I threw at his voice. Turned out I could throw to any of them, though I couldn't catch. I could throw to someone I knew was between two voices, who said nothing. Well, if I could aim a redroot, why not a crossbow?"

"What about range—what will you do there?"

"Practice. The sound's different enough—I know how far away you are, Captain. I need practice to understand how much over the sound to aim for different distances, but—I can help, sir, in a fight, and not be helpless."

"Yes, but—none of our people will be out there to give you a direction and range. You could hit one of them by mistake."

"Not if I shoot beyond all their voices, at distant enemy voices. I know I'm not likely to hit anyone, but I can certainly scare them."

Arcolin still had doubts, but this was Stammel, after all.

By the end of that day's practice, Stammel was hitting the target four times out of five at a distance twice as far as at first. The others, using crossbows without the twigs to signal when the prod was level, did worse. Stammel was grinning when he came back, one hand lightly on Bald Seli's shoulder and his crossbow hanging from the other.

Over the next days, Devlin helped Stammel pick those who were learning fastest, and they were assigned to more practice sessions. The armorer devised a better way to attach Stammel's levelers: iron rods with the ends beaten into smooth flanges set into the stock. As they all improved, Stammel managed to maintain a slight lead on them; Arcolin realized that would not continue forever, but they were all proficient enough to be useful in a fight, and two or three of the best were close enough to Stammel's level to make a contest fair.

The days shortened perceptibly, though the southern heat lingered; Arcolin thought of the coronation that had happened tens of days ago in Tsaia and wondered what it had been like. He could not imagine Dorrin as a duke, really. Or the young prince as a king, for that matter; and he must attend Autumn Court. He began counting how many days it would be, how soon he would have to leave the south to make it there in time.

CHAPTER TEN

River Road, Tsaia

Marshal-General Arianya rode steadily westward, glancing aside now and then at her most unexpected paladin. If, indeed, Paks was in any way *her* paladin despite being on the list in Fin Panir.

Paks at Kieri Phelan's northern stronghold had been surprise enough—alive and well, with the powers a paladin should have—after the way in which she had left Fin Panir. That had been miracle upon miracle, Arianya thought, though complicated by the actions of a Kuakgan.

But now—though it was hard to see the paladin in the blithe young woman who rode along so easily, plum juice running down her chin—now Paks was more than that. Arianya had never heard of such a thing as that silver circle on her brow. The stories she'd already been told, including that meeting with the thief who claimed to have brought her out of Liart's lair, went beyond imagining.

"Want a plum, Marshal-General?" Paks asked, holding out a handful. She'd bought the plums from a farmer that morning, just after they left Thornhedge Grange, and clearly intended to share them out before lunch.

"Thank you," Arianya said, taking one and biting into it. "I hope the king will let us see Dorrin's gift again when we pass through Vérella. I'd like to make a sketch of the designs."

"If the necklace *is* part of that set," Paks said. "I wonder if it's magical as well."

"I was worried about that," Arianya said. "Magelord jewels . . . possibly royal . . . that's not something we should have in our treasury."

"Why not?"

Gird wouldn't like it was the obvious answer. Arianya paused. "It's a danger to those who don't know how to control its power," she said instead. "I'm not sure Dorrin could. Though anyone who could mend a well the way she did . . . that's power, all right. Remember the old story about the magelord who sent a whole river into a well and flooded a fort that way?"

"That's when Gird's friend Cob was hurt, wasn't it?" Paks asked. "It's in the histories we had to read. Those scrolls I brought—do they tell the same story?"

"Yes, in more detail. But the point is, magelords could control water, or some of them could. And Dorrin can."

"She thinks it's because of Falk," Paks said. "She prayed."

"She may wear Falk's ruby, but she's not just a Falkian knight," Arianya said. "When she killed the man—her father, she said, wearing another man's body—that wasn't a prayer to Falk. That was magery."

"It could be both," Paks said. She bit into another plum and spat out the stone into her hand, then tossed it to the base of a hedge to the river side of the road. "Alyanya's blessing," she said.

Arianya glanced back, half expecting the stone to sprout then and there and bear flowers and fruit by the end of summer. No, that was silly. "I don't see how it could be both," she said. "Gird wouldn't— surely Falk wouldn't—"

"But she's his knight," Paks said, as if that made everything clear. "And I know he talks to her."

She sounded so certain. Arianya remembered feeling that certain and being wrong, terribly wrong. But she was not a paladin. "I wanted to ask you about that place where you found the scrolls—was it like Luap's Stronghold in Kolobia?"

"No—at least—not exactly," Paks said. "It was more elvish. Macenion—the part elf I was with—said elves had built it."

"I never heard of elves going under stone," Arianya said. "Even in Kolobia, there was no sign elves lived under stone."

"Iynisin—"

"Yes, of course, iynisin—but they're evil. Elves are—are the Elders, guardians of the green world."

"They can be wrong," Paks said. "Just like us. The Lady thought Kieri Phelan was unfit to rule."

"You think they were wrong to build the elfane taig?"

Paks shrugged. "I don't know."

Neither did Arianya, but as Marshal-General she had a duty to the Fellowship; she must know right and wrong beyond the limits of the Code of Gird, to govern wisely. A chill ran down her back.

"Tell me everything you remember about that place and about the Lady," she said.

When they reached Vérella, Arianya pointed out the Verrakai city house to Paks as they rode past. Though the street door was closed and the ground-floor windows shuttered, upstairs the blue-and-white-striped curtains waved gently in the breeze. A new staff had been fitted beside the front entrance, now bearing a small pennant with a small blue V on gray.

"Her house wards must have done that," Arianya said. "She had no standard out at Midsummer." They rode on to the palace gates— opened at once for the Marshal-General of Gird and a paladin. Arianya asked audience with the king, and within the turn of a glass had explained her request.

"If the necklace is royal regalia," the king said, "how did part of it end up in a brigand's lair so far away from the rest?" He led the way to the treasury, where the Verrakaien gifts were set apart from the rest. He opened the chest, then lifted out the items one by one, setting them on a table.

Arianya stared at the crown, the goblet, the contents of the box. "I can't imagine any of the Verrakaien selling part of the set, but it certainly looks similar in design."

"It could have been stolen," Paks said.

"What bothers me," Arianya said, "is the way the pieces seem . . .

alive in some way. I saw that ring Duke Verrakai found under the floor. And you and she both say these things were controlled, somehow, by blood magery—that can't be good. I wonder how dangerous it will be to bring the necklace and the others together."

"Did the ring make the whole stronger?" Paks asked.

"Duke Verrakai didn't say anything about that," Arianya said. "She didn't think it was evil in itself. Then again, she's a magelord." Arianya shook her head. "It's annoying. All my life I've considered magelords inherently wicked—any with magery, at least—but I can't see Dorrin that way."

"I must know," the king said. "One way or the other, I must know if it is part of the same set. If it is . . . would you sell it?"

"To you? Why would you want it? It's not your regalia; you already have a crown."

"I don't know," the king said. "I just feel that if it is part of the same set, they should be together. They're not really mine, but for now I'm their guardian."

"You say that as if they were alive," Paks said. "As if they had a will."

"You said you saw the crown rise in the air," Arianya said. "So did the king." She turned to the king. "And if they are not yours, then whose are they, and what will happen if you keep them?" Arianya did not want to imagine the king—or queen—who might come to claim them.

"I don't know," the king said. "I would be more comfortable, to tell the truth, if they were not here. What do you think now, Marshal-General? Is that necklace part of the set?"

Arianya nodded. "If it's not, it's made by the same hand as made these—and both rockfolk and elves claim they did not, whoever that may have been. And there's only one way to tell. They must be brought together. I don't suppose you'd lend them to me to take to Fin Panir."

He hesitated. "If it were me alone . . . but, Marshal-General, if it is known that the Marshal-General is bringing a magelord crown to Fin Panir, how will that sit with the Fellowship?"

Arianya thought for a moment. "Not well," she said. "But the cloth that wraps the crown is definitely the same design as what we found in Kolobia, and we know there was a priest of Esea, which is what they called the High Lord. The High Lord's Hall in Fin Panir is the only surviving holy place built for Esea Sunlord. Perhaps these were made for such worship, and would be at peace in those precincts."

"I had not thought it might be made for a god," the king said. "Would these things be worn by a priest, then?"

"Possibly. Who knows what their priests wore?"

"I will think on it," the king said. "To some of my nobles, the obvious value of these things is taken as surety for the behavior of Dorrin Duke Verrakai. To dispose of them—even to you and the Fellowship of Gird—may cause comment for me, as well as what Girdish opinion might be of you."

Arianya felt a prickle of irritation. "We cannot live our lives by others' opinion, Sir King."

"No, but neither can we utterly ignore them if we wish to rule our people well. You could consider bringing the necklace here, you know."

"So I could," Arianya said. "In fact, that was my first intent, to see if it matched. But seeing again that embroidered cloth, so like an altar-cloth, it occurred to me that we might learn more—and more safely—if the pieces were brought together in a place of worship."

"I will consider," the king said. "Understand, Marshal-General, it is not my greed that wants those things in my treasury. Duke Verrakai bade them rest here. I am not certain how they will react if moved."

"You did not mention that at first."

"I did not think of it until we were here, faced with them, and I recalled how they seemed to obey her."

"I do wish," Arianya said, "that she was not quite so full of virtues. Centuries of Girdish predecessors tell me she should die, and yet—"

"She's not evil," Paks said.

Arianya eyed her. "I haven't said she was. It would be easier on me if she were, that's all."

"We could test them," Paks said. "What if we tried to move them to another room in the palace?"

"What good would that do?" Arianya asked.

"If they're obeying her command to stay here . . . maybe we can't."

Arianya sighed. That abundant energy, that flow of ideas, could be exhausting. The other paladins weren't like that—well, not all. Camwynya, she reminded herself, was much the same.

"We could try," the king said.

The king signed out the box, explaining that they wanted to test something. He lifted it from the chest. "It's heavier," he said. He took a step, then another. "And heavier yet."

"Let Paks try," Arianya suggested. "It was her idea; maybe it will trust a paladin."

The king handed the box to Paks, and she took another step. "No," she said. "It grows heavier with each step. Let me see." She turned back toward the chest; her arms bobbed up a little. "It's lighter now—almost weightless. And it's tugging me toward the chest." She turned back to the door; her arms sagged. "It doesn't want to go anywhere. I think we have no choice but to leave it here." Once more facing the chest, she nodded. "It's very clear—into the chest or nowhere."

"Well," Arianya said. "That settles it for the present. I am still concerned, Sir King, that if it is obeying someone else, it may not be safe to house in your treasury."

"It has caused no trouble so far," the king said. He grinned at her, suddenly looking more his age than kingly. "It is a welcome guest, but I will not claim ownership."

"It wants in the chest," Paks said. "May I put it back?"

"Certainly," the king said.

Paks carried the box to the chest; it seemed light in her hands as a feather. She laid it in the box; light flared for a moment and then subsided.

"That's new," the king said.

When Paks replaced the other items and closed the chest, the lid—plain wood as it was—seemed to grow into the rest of the chest, so it looked all one piece.

"And that," the king said, eyes wide.

Arianya felt a pressure in her head and then a voice she did not know. *We are not your enemy.* "Are you not?" she said aloud; the king looked at her oddly. "It spoke to me," she told him. "I would let it alone."

"I intend to," the king said. "And if it speaks to me, I will be prudent—" His face changed expression. Then he relaxed and shook his head. "Well, it told me I was not its enemy and it would abide here until its sovereign came to take it away."

"But is its sovereign your enemy?" Arianya asked. "Witting or unwitting?"

NO! came the voice in her head, and by the king's expression, it said the same to him.

"It is lonely and wants to go home," Paks said.

"It spoke to you, too?"

"Not spoke—more like sang. It is from far away and grieving, homesick. I don't understand it all, but I believe it is right to protect it, and then . . . then something will happen."

"Something always happens," Arianya said. "Perhaps it will happen in the time of the next Marshal-General and not on my watch. At least you need not worry about thieves."

Halfway from Vérella to Fin Panir, Paks suddenly reined in her horse. "I must go," she said.

"What—you have a call?"

"Yes. Somewhere south . . ." The red horse jigged, sidling off the road and bobbing his head.

"Do you know what?"

"I never know what," Paks said with a grin. "But I must go—I'm sorry, Marshal-General, but there's no time."

And with that she was gone, the red horse kicking up clods from a field as he surged into a gallop.

"Well," Arianya said to her horse. "*You* are not going anywhere that fast, so don't get ideas." The rest of the journey to Fin Panir, she put her mind firmly onto her many tasks, including finding the right young Marshals for Duke Verrakai's domain. And the necklace . . . should she send it to Vérella? If it joined the rest of the regalia—and would the box open for that?—it would be safe from thieves, but she felt certain no thieves would breach the treasury in her own hall.

CHAPTER ELEVEΠ

Cortes Andres, Aarenis

Jeddrin, Count of Andressat and the South Marches, sat in the cool of his loggia on the east side of his residence, overlooking the walls of Cortes Andres. He had a fine view of the pastures where his horses grazed, steep vineyards, and the walls of a village clinging to the slope, its white walls gleaming in the late afternoon sun. Though the day had been hot, on this side of the house he had a little breeze, and the damp cloths his servants had hung chilled the air just enough to make it pleasant.

He had been up at dawn, as always, for a Count of Andressat (as he said daily to his sons and grandsons) must be diligent if he was to do the best for his people. He had duties, not merely privileges; it was in the performance of such duties that a true nobleman distinguished himself from pretenders, those who thought wealth alone or power could make gold from lead by painting it yellow. Ruling—ruling well—could never be easy, and was less easy now, though he had hoped—believed—that with Siniava gone, it would be easier.

He had claimed the South Marches, the cities of Cha and Sibili that Siniava had ruled so badly, and at first this security on his southern border gave them all confidence. His son-in-law Narits governed Cha; his son Ferran governed Sibili. That should have given Andressat direct access to the Immerhoft trade, but he had recurring problems with Confaer, the only port he'd captured, and pirates controlled the island that lay in the harbor's throat like a stone. Andressat wine and

Andressat wool piled up in the warehouses of Confaer, easy prey for thieving gangs—pirates ashore allied with pirates afloat. None of the allies of Siniava's War had the resources or will to help him clean out the other port cities or the island towns.

Other problems had arisen, as well. Duke Phelan had allied with Alured the Black in Siniava's War to gain unhindered passage through the southern forests and so outmaneuver Siniava's army and pin them at last. Alured now claimed the title of Duke of Immer and moreover claimed it was his by birthright, not merely conquest.

That led everyone the Count knew to ask him, for he was known as a genealogist, possessor of the most complete archives of Aarenisian families and their relationships, whether Alured's claim could possibly be true. Jeddrin was sure it was not, for Alured had none of the qualities of nobility.

The man had been a pirate from nobody knew where, had made a reputation at sea, then—for no reason anyone knew—had come ashore and begun gathering a force in the great southern forest that lay between the Immer valley and the Chaloquay drainage. Phelan had befriended him and used him in Siniava's War, but Phelan was— had been—he had *thought* Phelan was—merely a northern duke, whose title reflected nothing of blood or bone.

And now Phelan was shown to have had royal blood after all, royal and elven, and he had treated the man as a mere mercenary captain. Well, that was done and he could not undo it, but he did not want to make any mistakes about this new Duke of Immer.

Now, having brought up another stack of documents from the family archives, he spread them on the table and began looking them over.

He ran his eye down the pages of a bound book—very old, the leather binding flaking away; he preferred scrolls—recording the yields of wheat and the produce of vineyards in a time before his father's father's father's father. Rainfall records, damaging storms: the same kinds of records he himself kept. Nothing in that one about families, politics, or even trade. He put it aside for a stack of flat sheets tied with a ribbon faded gray from its original color; it had left marks on the outer pages. He turned them one by one.

One page had genealogy . . . he recognized his great-great-great-great-grandfather's name at the bottom in spidery writing. Up the page . . . he began jotting the names down; this was older than the Family Roll in which he'd listed his sons.

The sheet beneath, the ink much faded, bore the inscription "To the right honorable, the faithful, the most noble Va-Jeddrinal—This being the copy you asked for, the which I most humbly present for your pleasure, of the oldest known record in the north, of the Fall of Aare and the King's Quest, as recorded by Mikeli himself in the fifth year of exile in the north."

Jeddrin stared. No one had a copy of the Fall of Aare, though the story was known. The lords of Aare suffered a defeat of some kind and came north across the sea . . . could this treasure have lain so long in his archives unrecognized? Apparently so.

In another hand, the work began, "I, Mikeli, heir of the kings of Aare, sing the lament of Aare's fall, the Sandlord's ruin, the towers that shattered and the waters that vanished, as a lament but also a warning to those who follow, that they may escape the ruin that still roams the world below."

That was plain enough. Ibbirun, the Sandlord, god of chaos, had sent waves of sand to swallow the cities of Aare. Jeddrin felt his skin prickle with awe and dread. He read on and on, as the light faded and servants brought lamps and food and drink. He ate nothing, absorbed in the story he thought he knew, but had known wrong, from the start. Though the language was archaic, he had studied old texts before, and few of the words puzzled him.

When he finished at last, in the dark, silent hours, and lifted his gaze to the sky, the stars before morning hung before him, challenging. The men of Old Aare, the men he had thought of with respect— his ancestors, those who had survived the Fall and the hard journey north, the sea and its storms, to land on the shores of this land and conquer it, who had even—in attenuated blood, as he thought— gone over the pass of Valdaire to conquer the north—those men, those magelords, had not been, but for Mikeli and perhaps a few others, the nobles of Aare.

They had been servants, crafters, merchants, and—Mikeli made it clear—thieves and whores as well, the scum of the city, lifted on a tide of disaster and tossed away, while the nobles—nearly all of them—died.

"For of the princes of Aare, and the princesses, the lords and ladies, all those of high degree, now so few are left that to populate one palace with those of pure blood is scarcely possible . . ."

The nobility of Aarenis, Jeddrin read, had been created out of what was left: "As I was sent ahead, to be saved against my will while all around me knew their doom, so I must do what I can to redeem my guilt, and theirs, and make this story plain . . . and for Aare to continue in men's hearts, I must create from nothing a semblance of its greatness." Mikeli then explained how he had chosen this one and that to be duke or count or baron and how he had striven to ensure that literacy survived, and arts and crafts.

For a long bitter time Jeddrin stood looking out at the night, hands clenched on the railing of his loggia. So the despised mercenary captain proved a true king, the born son of a king and an elf-queen, while he—who had been so sure of his lineage—traced back, as the tale made clear, to a stonemason and a count's bastard daughter. Kieri Phelan was royal, and he himself as common as dirt, all his pride of blood based on lies, on the accumulated wealth of a fellow—a great-father those many generations back—who was strong and honest— the qualities for which he was chosen—and whose wife, chosen for him by the prince, could read and write. Mikeli in his wisdom—if that is what it was—had assigned masons to the stony lands and wood-crafters to the forests.

"If the gods favor us, perhaps the gift of magery will survive, but if it does not, so many being drawn from crafters will ensure that none go naked or roofless."

Jeddrin thought of his own domain, where indeed skill at masonry and abundant rock meant none of his folk lived roofless, and the sheep provided ample wool for spinning and weaving. Yet in Siniava's War he had seen vagrants enough, barely clothed in rags, starving, sleeping in heaps under bushes. That had not been Mikeli's intent; he had wanted to create a land where hunger and rags and misery did not exist.

A wish-tale . . . but a better wish-tale than Siniava's, or Alured's, who wanted only to rule.

His eyes burned; his back ached. Far to the east, the first dull red of false dawn showed below the stars. He was too old to read the night through and then work all day. He shuffled the papers together, retied the ribbons carefully, and carried the stack indoors, to put safely on a table, away from any morning breeze that might scatter the pages. A few watch lamps burned to show the way. A sleepy servant woke at the sound of his step, jumping up.

"Never mind," Jeddrin said; he could not scold servants anymore, he but a stonemason's get. "I read too late; I will sleep late as well. Tell the cook, if you will."

In his bedroom, the curtains had been pulled back, as he preferred on summer nights; he drew them, put the documents on his table, and then undressed and washed himself before sliding between cool sheets. His mind produced scenes from Mikeli's account, a city filling with sand and refugees struggling to get away, carrying their tools or a few days' food . . . not the nobles riding away on horseback he had imagined before.

When he woke and dealt with the day's work and then once more delved into the archives, he found more. Some were but fragments: "A man came to the shores of the lake and being thirsty, he drank, and in with the water he swallowed a seed, as it seemed, a seed small and eager to be swallowed, and therein began the ruin of the towers and the land." Others, also attributed to Mikeli, were longer, parts of a journal describing years of struggle to make a new Aare in a land unlike the old.

"The keys are gone," Mikeli wrote in one entry.

It took days to figure out what the "keys" were and what had happened, or what Mikeli thought had happened. Days in which a message from Alured, Duke of Immer, arrived, along with a squad of stern-faced soldiers and a man who claimed to be a scribe, demanding access to Andressat's archives, from which he hoped to prove Alured's right to the kingship.

"I will gladly show you the archives," Jeddrin said, "but we do not allow anyone to remove materials or to shuffle them about. I received the duke's earlier request and have been searching."

"But you are a busy man, Count Andressat," said the squad's

commander, who named himself Captain Nerits. "The Duke is pleased to lend you a scholar to assist in the search."

"I have archivists of my own," Jeddrin said. "It is not our custom to let strangers poke and pry."

"It is not the Duke's custom to have his vassals disobedient," the captain said. He did not draw a weapon—Andressat had his own guards in the room—but the threat was clear.

"Duke Alured's domain lies in the Immer valley," Jeddrin said. "Mine was never part of it."

"I would not be too sure," the captain said. "And all the more reason for the duke's scholar to study in your archives, as it would be in your interest to conceal evidence to the contrary. Nor should you miscall him Duke Alured now; he has chosen a new name to fit his new status, an ancestor's name from records he found in Cortes Immer. He is Duke Visla Vaskronin: remember that. As the duke means to rule, it would also be in your interest to show your submission now."

Cortes Immer was far from Cortes Andres: leagues and leagues lay between, forest and vale. Cortes Andres had never been breached, not even by Siniava, and in the aftermath of that war, Alured, Vaskronin, or whatever he chose to call himself could not have raised a large enough army to invade Andressat.

"Surely your duke has enough to do without bothering a poor stony land far from his own," Jeddrin said. "I mean no discourtesy, but I will not see my hospitality abused, either. If your duke's claim is proved true, I will accept his authority, but until then *I* rule Andressat, and none other. I will escort your scholar to the archives, to see for himself why it takes so long to read and check every scroll and book."

"We will escort him—"

"You will not. You will remain here," Jeddrin said, with all the command voice he could muster. The captain shrugged; Andressat told his own guards to find them quarters in the citadel's outer ring. The scholar followed as he himself led the way into the inner citadel and then into the palace and finally, the main library.

The room was long, almost the full depth of the building, lit by tall narrow windows with shelves between. "This is one of the archives," Jeddrin said, watching the scholar's face.

"It is . . . impressive," the man said. He did look like a scholar, stoop-shouldered, his fingers ink-stained.

"It does not contain what the Duke of Immer seeks," Jeddrin said. "This room has been searched and cataloged. My own archivists—" He gestured to the end of the room, where a man sat working at a desk and a woman reached to a high shelf with a long pole.

"What is that?" the scholar asked, pointing at her.

"It is for retrieving scrolls or scroll cases from the top shelves," Jeddrin said. "My father invented it. He is the one who began the re-organization after a series of wet years brought a spring up—yes, even up here on this height—in the middle of the old archives. Things had to be moved in haste, dried, stacked anywhere room could be found, and the same weather that brought the spring gave his archivist lung-fever. Some records were lost and could not be restored, he told me—I was not yet born—and others damaged. It was some years before he could find someone qualified to begin copying the damaged materials, and as I'm sure you know, some once attacked by the black stain continue to decay—it was a race against the stain, not entirely won."

"But why were the archives on the floor in the first place?" the scholar asked.

"According to my father, his father and his wife's father both increased the collection—already large—buying up any antiquarian documents they could find. They were enthusiasts, and they vied in finding old and rare scrolls, books, loose sheets. My father's father had not expected to inherit, and so had more leisure than I. But let's see how you do with this one—" Jeddrin pulled out a scroll he knew had been written but seven generations back.

The scholar peered at it. "It's old."

"Yes. I'm wondering if you can read it."

"I think—let me see—it is a record of . . . of goat breeding?"

"Yes. With notes of weather, diseases, and so forth."

"I don't recognize some of the words—" The scholar pointed. Jeddrin said, "Rain."

"Really? It's not the same—"

"No. Our word for rain drops the second sound, and the breath-sound has narrowed."

"You've studied this?"

"My father insisted. I was to be his scholar, you see; my elder brother was to inherit—much the same situation as with my father's father. My elder brother slipped and fell on a vine stake and died of it; neither of us had married yet."

"So you can read all these?" The scholar waved at the shelves.

"Of course," Jeddrin said. "And older, besides. But now I'll take you to the store-pile, as we call it, things still unsorted. Apparently all my ancestors collected writings; it may not be fully cataloged even in my lifetime."

"I could help," the scholar said.

"I think not," Jeddrin said. "If you cannot read it, how could you catalog it?"

The store-pile filled a series of connecting rooms, divided by function. The farthest held unsorted materials, heaps and piles on floors and shelves. In the next, baskets and bins held roughly sorted items, those tainted by blackstain or blue carefully segregated from the rest, in closed containers. The two outermost rooms had tables where scribes copied out the most damaged materials.

"I employ five archivists and scribes at present," Jeddrin said to the scholar, whose jaw had dropped. "In my father's day, only one of these rooms had been cleared for copyists. Now two."

"I am sure the Duke of Immer would hire even more, if you would trust—"

"No," Jeddrin said, without heat. "Every family has records it does not share, and I am not handing over unsorted materials, that my family guarded for generations, without knowing what is in every one."

"How much work do you do here?"

"I? I have little time for it, though I try to spend an hour a day reading, to retain my skills. I am presently reading a series of letters between my great-great-grandfather and someone in Pliuni, discussing the breeding of goats and whether our goats here were brought from Old Aare or tamed from wild goats in the Westmounts."

"But if you aren't looking yourself, how do you know what the Duke seeks has not been found already?"

Jeddrin gave him a look that made the man step back. "Does your

Duke, then, cook his own food? And will he himself read every item in the archives, should I send them?"

"N-no. He will hire scholars—"

"Even as I have done. He is a ruler; I am a ruler. I made it clear to my scholars what they were to seek, and they report to me. It might be found today, or tomorrow, or by Midwinter, or three winters after I am dead . . . or it might not exist at all. I wrote the Duke that if I found proof of his legitimate succession by blood from the nobles of Aare"—the words hurt as he said them, considering what he now knew about his own family—"I would tell him and publicly acknowledge it. And I will. In *my* family, we keep our word." That, too, sliced his spirit, for the documents Alured sought were hidden away in the secret chamber off his bedroom, until he could decide what to do, the proof of his own lack of noble blood. "It would be helpful," he want on, "if the Duke knew more of his parentage."

CHAPTER TWELVE

Gray Fox Inn, Fin Panir, Fintha

Arvid Semminson, now effectively master of the Thieves' Guild in Vérella, finished his dull but satisfying lunch and picked his teeth while watching the staff of the Gray Fox common room at their work. He had not been in Fintha for several hands of years; the Girdish realm had outlawed the Thieves' Guild. He would not be here now, but for the Marshal-General's invitation; the Girdish wanted to know everything he remembered about their paladin Paksenarrion. The Marshal-General's seal on her invitation to him brought instant respect from the innkeeper, and he'd been given a table in the quietest corner of the big common room all to himself.

A heavily-bearded dwarf in typical clothing—yellow doublet over a checked shirt, green trousers, a blue hat with a red feather—and a beardless one in a green shirt over blue trousers came in. Arvid looked at the older dwarf as a servant led the two to a table near him. No clan ring on the dwarf's heart-thumb. A chain around his neck—not gold—which might hold a Guild symbol, like his own, tucked well into that shirt. Arvid looked away, listened to a serving maid stumble through a polite greeting in dwarvish and the dwarf's stilted but understandable Common in reply. The beardless one said nothing; the bearded one ordered for both.

Most people would have thought the beardless one a youngster, a mere boy, and the bearded one his father or other relative. Arvid knew better. He waved to the skinnier serving maid the next time she came by and ordered a pastry and herbal drink to round off his meal. She brought it on the same tray as the dwarves' food: Arvid shifted a little to face more away from that table and pretended to be absorbed in watching the more buxom serving maid flirt with a tableful of merchants across the room.

A dwarf thief and a *kteknik* gnome—and not a dwarf from Vérella, because he knew every dwarf thief in the Vérella chapter of the Thieves' Guild—would not be here in Fin Panir for anything less than business. Drawn by rumor or on assignment? Arvid considered what he knew of Fin Panir from both previous visits and Thieves' Guild intelligence. Only one prize seemed worth the risk: that necklace—the one the Marshal-General thought might be part of a set of royal regalia.

After a few minutes, the sounds of eating behind him—dwarves were notoriously noisy eaters—slowed and the two began to talk. Arvid missed the first, as the merchants finally stood to leave, scraping chairs on the floor and paying loud, slightly drunken compliments to the serving maid, the landlord, and the room at large. He watched the maid sashay to the bar, grinning over her shoulder before she dropped her tip into the box.

At last he could hear the two behind him. They spoke low, in the language of rockbrothers.

"I tell you, *we* did not make it." That was the gnome, Arvid was sure by the timbre of his voice.

"Nor we." The dwarf cleared his throat and lowered his voice. "But the elves say—"

"The elves care nothing for truth." The gnome, though wearing blue and green instead of sober gray, had not lost the gnomish accent. "Perhaps they made it, perhaps not. The question is, what should be done?"

The buxom serving maid came by with a full pitcher of summerwine and Arvid's herbal drink; she set it on the table, and he winked at her. Behind him, he heard the pitcher being set on the table, a resonant thunk. The girl went back to the bar; Arvid sipped his drink.

"We take it," the dwarf said. Arvid smiled to himself. What had promised to be a boring, hot midsummer journey now offered a delightful complication, perhaps even adventure. "And I still want to know where the stones came from," the dwarf went on. "Not from our mines, but where? Where are such mines, with such stones? Do we have brethren there, and if so, why do we not know it?"

"Take it where?" the gnome asked. "To whom? To whom does it belong now? That paladin?" Arvid could almost see the lift of the shoulder a gnome would give to the dwarf's other questions.

"It matters not whose it was," the dwarf said. "But the stones—"

"Not from your mountains, not from our hills; beyond that does not matter."

Arvid risked a casual glance all around the common room, including the table where the rockfolk talked; they were ignoring him, leaning across the table to talk to each other.

"Nor the Westmounts," the dwarf said, counting out the ranges on his thick fingers. "Nor the red rocks of far Kolobia, nor the gray rocks within sight of there."

"So far it does not matter," the gnome said again, impatient now. "But there is something . . . the rock sings trouble."

"Indeed it does," the dwarf agreed. "But it might also sing profit. Trouble and profit go oft together."

"You are greedy," the gnome said.

"I am not," the dwarf said. "But if gold falls into my hand, I will not let it slide through my fingers."

"If it is not your gold—"

"All the better." The dwarf grinned. "Is it not obvious that the Girdish do not need that necklace? It came to them by thievery, after all—contaminating their paladin-candidate that a thief gave it to her. We serve her reputation by taking it away, that reminder of her impurity."

"We cannot keep it!" the gnome said. "It is not ours; we neither made it nor bought it!"

Arvid had heard enough. Checking the hang of his sword, he rose and without hurry moved to their table. "Excuse me." He put his hand flat on the table between them. The dwarf should recognize the small tattoo on his thumb web. "Arvid Semminson, of Tsaia. It would be impolite to conceal from rockbrethren my fluent command of their speech, and perhaps by so doing discover that of their plans they would prefer not to have revealed." He smiled, showing very human teeth; rockfolk noticed such things. They would smell the metal of his sword and dagger and the hidden blades he wore here and there about his person as well. Good steel. Excellent steel. They would know the ore from which it had been forged.

"You are that thief who brought her out alive," the gnome said, recovering first.

"I am no thief," Arvid said, without heat and still in their tongue. "It is true I am in the Thieves' Guild, and of some consequence there—"

"It is said you saved her life."

"No. The gods saved her life; I but saw her carried to safety."

"You killed the accuser."

"That I did, but killing is not thievery."

"Of breath it is," murmured the gnome, but the dwarf shook his head.

"To kill one bent on murder is not murder," he said. He smiled up at Arvid. "Would you drink with us?"

"I would sit with you, but not drink; I have had what I can hold, and still do what needs doing this night."

Arvid felt the tension rise; the two nodded, however, and he pulled the chair from his own table to theirs. "You heard us speak of a necklace," the gnome said. "You have knowledge of it?"

"Little," Arvid said. "That lair was full of things, large and small, valuable and worthless. I found it; I gave it to her."

"Her. The paladin?"

"Yes; she was but a mercenary then."

"Why? Were you besotted?"

"It was a whim," Arvid said. He leaned back in his chair. "Clear to see she'd been born poor, and a mercenary doesn't make much. Yet she came with treasure, and no word from her mouth to explain it. Not the treasure that comes from looting burning citadels in the south. The money changer in Brewersbridge wouldn't talk, and I had my task there anyway, no time to put hot wires to his fingers. But from one of his servants, who liked mulled wine, I heard enough to know the treasure was old and varied, from deep in some cave, mayhap. Yet she was such a simple girl, happy with a full belly of the plainest food, comfortable with woodsmen and smiths and the like more than with the worthies of the town. Made friends with the innkeeper's daughter. I thought I'd see what a pretty necklace given as a gift would do for her. Would she change?"

"Where exactly did you find it?" the gnome asked.

"The thing that ruled there had it," Arvid said. "When it died, and everyone else was keening over the dead yeoman-marshal, I explored the private chambers. The thing was dead; the hoard was surely stolen goods, but we had been granted the right to the value of what we brought out, less a tax to the town. I confess—" Arvid chuckled at this. "—I did not declare the necklace, nor have it valued; I don't know if Paks did. She had an almost gnomish attachment to law." He winked at the gnome. "Stronger than yours."

"I am—" The gnome stopped, confused.

"You are a *kteknik,*" Arvid said blandly. "I have met your like before. Do not worry; I feel no need to share this knowledge with others of my kind."

"We know where Paksenarrion's treasure came from," the dwarf said. "Would you ask that?"

"I know already," Arvid said, "and do not need to ask. It is no great secret, though the location of the elfane taig is not certainly known to my informants."

"It is to me," the dwarf said. "But we do not go there." He paused, as the serving maid reappeared with a platter and picked up their used dishes. Another appeared with bowls of custard.

"Have the Sinyi moved back in, do you know?" Arvid asked, when she had left and the two rockbrothers had begun to eat.

"Oh, yes," said the gnome, his voice now bitter. "They say they are cleansing the hall and we will all be invited when it is done—the Elder Folk, that is. They denied my prince's request to send a delegation to search for any kapristi bodies, and said they would bring them to us if they found any." He spat a small bone onto the floor.

"Ungracious," Arvid murmured. "You were involved, were you not, in its construction?"

"In small ways only," the gnome said. He glanced at the dwarf.

"We assayed the stone," the dwarf said. "Declared it suitable; it was a . . ." He paused, then went on. "An agreement was reached between dwarf and elf, for the stone-right—"

"It was not a fair exchange," the gnome muttered.

"It was not *your* stone," the dwarf said. "It was ours—the king's to give, if he chose, but he chose to trade."

"Stone belongs to *us*," the gnome said. "As Sertig wrought, so it should be: the rockfolk to the bones of the earth, the singers to the trees above."

"Are you saying the king had no right—?"

"I am saying no prince would have so abused Sertig's gift," the gnome said. "And for a female to rule—"

Arvid cleared his throat; the rockfolk looked at him, eyes narrowed. "Rockbrothers, I am not of your kind, though I speak your language, and would not choose to hear that which might displease you later to know had been heard. Pray warn me away, or abate your quarrel."

"Courteous," allowed the gnome.

"Fine words," growled the dwarf.

"So we were discussing a necklace," Arvid went on, "of which I know but little, save that in my hands it seemed a thing of rare beauty, such stones as only rockfolk bring from the ground." Silence, but for munching and swallowing. "And yet I heard you say it was not of your making."

"It was not," said the gnome. He wiped his mouth after a long swallow of ale. "Neither dwarf nor gnome, to our knowledge, brought forth the stones or wrought them into that necklace. Nor was it elf-made."

"Surely," Arvid said, "it was not made by men."

"It did not make itself," the dwarf said. "And who else might have made it, if not dwarf, gnome, or elf? Humankind it must be, but not from here."

"From across the sea?" Arvid asked, tenting his fingers.

The two rockfolk looked at each other and back at Arvid. They said nothing.

"Old Aare, perhaps?" Arvid said, smiling from one to the other.

"I am thinking you know little and ask much," the gnome said. "Your answers to our questions told us nothing."

"I do not ask," Arvid said. "I but think aloud. If not from here, or Aarenis, or across the eastern sea, or far Kolobia, or the Westmounts, then it must be from somewhere else, and the only somewhere else I can think of is Old Aare."

"Cursed land," said the gnome, pinching his lips after.

"We don't go there," the dwarf said. "The rock is nedross."

"Mmm. So you," Arvid said, looking at the dwarf, "would simply take the thing, if you knew where it was, and—and then what?"

"It's valuable," the dwarf said.

"Yes, but its value varies. Where would you sell it, if you could?"

"Why should one tell you?" the gnome asked. "What value would you return for this information?"

Arvid shrugged. "Perhaps it would not be worth your while to know what I know." He was aware of sharpened attention. "It is not the first time I have been in Fin Panir, though it is the first time I have been invited into the Marshal-General's own library." The quality of their silence changed again. He smiled at them. "But come, rock-brethren, finish your meal. You have traveled far today, I'll warrant, and the day was over-hot for those used to the shelter of stone."

The dwarf found his voice first. "You—a thief—are invited to the Marshal-General—"

"To the library. To meet with scribes, I understand. The Marshal-General, as I am sure you're aware, is away." He knew, but perhaps they did not, that she would be back on the morrow.

"You know where the necklace is?" asked the gnome.

"Does that information have value to you?" asked Arvid.

A stir at the doorway; Arvid did not glance that way, but watched the gnome and the dwarf, who did.

"Aye, he's here," he heard from the landlord a few moments later.

Arvid smiled at the two who still had food before them. "I expect it's my guide; I will be sleeping tonight in the Girdish headquarters. I shall hope not to see you before sunrise." Then he turned and raised a hand to acknowledge the bearded Marshal edging his way between tables. "I'm quite ready, Marshal, if you won't join me for a mug."

"Thank you, no," the man said. "Marshal Perin, that's my name. Evening, rockbrothers." He spoke in Common, not their tongue, and the two merely nodded. He turned back to Arvid. "You've a horse needs stabling, I understand?"

"Yes, if you've room. I've paid a night's bait for him here, but since I'm moving, I'd prefer to take him along."

"No problem. Settled?"

"Oh, yes. My pack's just here—" Arvid plucked it from the shelf that ran along the wall, and handed the landlord the wooden tag on a thong that proved it his.

By the time they reached the complex of buildings where the former king's palace had once been, Arvid had told Marshal Perin about the dwarf, the apparent dwarf who was really a gnome.

"Really? He's not wearing gray, and he's with a dwarf; I didn't know they did that."

"He's a *kteknik*," Arvid said. "A spy. It's his punishment for something he did in his own tribe—Aldonfulk, he said."

Marshal Perin scowled. "They punish their people by making them spies?"

"For some crimes, yes. Service to the prince, it's called. He can't wear his tribe's uniform—"

"They're all just gray, aren't they?"

Arvid sighed to himself. "Not quite, Marshal. They're all gray or black, but each princedom has a uniform—it may be the lay of the collar, the buttons, the cuffs—and it is death for a gnome to wear the uniform of another tribe, to which he is not entitled. He cannot wear his own again until his prince decides the information he brings back balances whatever it was he did. The usual thing is for a *kteknik* to work with a dwarf, because in colored clothes he can pass for a young dwarf."

"How many of the beardless dwarves we see are ktet-ketick-whatevers?"

"Most to all," Arvid said. "Didn't you know that?"

"No, I did not," Marshal Perin said. "*We* did not."

"It's true," Arvid said. "Young dwarves do not go out into the world until they have beards, and they grow beards early. Only very rarely will you see a true dwarf lad out with his father, and never in a large city. They're very protective, dwarves."

A groom came to take Arvid's horse. He followed into the stable to see where it was stalled.

"You will be sleeping in the School dormitories," Marshal Perin said. "You will have your own room, of course. But please do not mingle with the students. They are apt to fall on any guest or traveler and ask questions when they should be studying."

"School?" Arvid said.

"We're the training facility for the Knights of Gird, also paladins—

though they're housed separately—and we also have a junior school where Girdish . . . I suppose I must say nobles, mostly from Tsaia . . . send boys for whom they cannot find acceptable fosterage. Wealthier Finthans, as well. Most end up as Knights of Gird or Knights of the Bells."

"Only boys?"

"For the younger ones, yes. For knights' training and paladin candidates, we have both—as you must know, because of Paksenarrion." Marshal Perin paused in the great forecourt. "Would you like to see the High Lord's Hall?"

A little chill ran down Arvid's back. "Perhaps another time," he said. "It is late—"

The Marshal's mouth quirked. "Not that late. Admittedly, the windows are more beautiful in the morning, with sunlight coming in the round one, but . . . I'm sorry to be blunt, but you must know that we know who you are. We honor you for saving our paladin, but . . . a thief—"

"I'm not a thief," Arvid said. "Not all in the Thieves' Guild are thieves."

Marshal Perin smiled and nodded. "I understand. But still, you consort with thieves. Fortunate for Paksenarrion that you do, for then you were able to help her."

Arvid shivered again. The memory of that time would not release him; he still saw her wounds heal, heard the gasps of the crowd, smelled the rank fear, felt the buffeting of those fleeing the scene. He had come prepared to ensure honorable burial for her . . . and she was not dead. The other one, he had killed quickly, efficiently, with the poisoned daggers he always carried.

Then Paksenarrion had wakened . . . alive, not crippled, and in behavior the same as she had been a few years before, when he had enjoyed playing the sophisticate with the naive soldier-girl. And said . . . that Gird might want to save the Thieves' Guild. Ridiculous. He had not told *that* to the Marshal who first interviewed him about Paks. He wasn't sure he'd ever tell anyone.

"I was glad to help her," he said.

When they entered the School courtyard, cloaked in the blue shadows of summer dusk, Arvid glanced around, automatically noting ways in and out. Windows, drainpipes, gates . . . it would be easy, should he need to. His skin tightened. His room, one of five kept for guests on the ground floor, was small but clean and furnished with sufficient to his needs: bed, chair, table.

"The rockbrothers will try to steal the necklace tonight or tomorrow night," he said suddenly.

Marshal Perin stared. "Necklace?"

"The one I gave Paks in Brewersbridge. They know it's here— well, everyone with wit in Tsaia knows that."

"But surely—"

"Guard it well this night, Marshal, wherever it is. Such a thing might redeem the *kteknik*'s place with his prince, or a dwarf's with his king."

"They said this?"

"They were talking of the necklace when I joined them, and said it plain out. I speak their language, you see."

"If they are caught, they will know you betrayed them," Marshal Perin said. "Dwarves, at least, do not take kindly to betrayal."

"I gave warning," Arvid said. "I told them I hoped not to see them before sunrise—and they know who I am. I do not know if it will stop them. This is a pleasant room for guesting in, but it is more likely to deter such thieves if they see me with drawn blade here and there about the place. Let them think a thief—as you think, and they also—was set as guard."

"You . . . want me—us—to show you where the treasury is, and trust *you* to ward it?"

Arvid shrugged. "It is up to you, of course. I quite understand your reluctance and would not suggest, in any event, that I be the only guard. Merely that I am the one most likely to spot gaps in your protection large enough for one small gnome to wriggle through."

"You have no desire for the thing yourself?" The Marshal's gaze was keen; Arvid met it squarely, having no fear that his face would reveal anything of his thoughts.

"I had none, when I left Vérella," he said. "I am not a poor man; what I need, I have. And yet I admit that as I came closer to Fin Panir, I felt . . . something. From what I have heard—and you may have as well—the crown and other regalia have some ancient magery to them, and draw or repel persons without their will. If this necklace does belong with the rest—if it is part of that—perhaps it seeks to join the others, or they seek to call it."

"Magery!" The Marshal's face tightened to a grimace of disgust. "Do you mean the old—the magelords' magery?"

"Yes," Arvid said. He had opened his pack in full sight of the Marshal, unrolling his spare clothes and laying them neatly on the shelf, along with his own cup, plate, bowl, and eating utensils. He shook the pack, demonstrating its spurious emptiness, and hung it on a peg. "Surely you heard about the coronation—that the new Duke Verrakai killed a Verrakaien who had taken disguise as a groom, and thus saved the king's life. So he pardoned her for her use of magery in doing so."

"We heard that, but did not credit it," Marshal Perin said. "The Marshal-General was there; she would not countenance such a breach of the Code of Gird. Killing by magery is an offense for which the only sentence is death."

"The king rules in Tsaia. And you can hardly blame the Tsaians for thinking a live king, new-crowned, is worth the exchange. His younger brother is but a child, and not like to become the man the king is, so I hear."

Marshal Perin shook his head. "It is wrong, and nothing can make it right. That's what Gird's war was about: clear right and wrong, no excuses."

This was exactly why the Girdish had always seemed so naive and even stupid to Arvid: their insistence that everything was simple at root. Their paladins used what amounted to magery, but no doubt they'd say it was the gods' favor. How did they know the magelords had not had some god's favor? But this night he had a reason to convince this Marshal that he should be allowed to guard the treasure. What approach would work?

"It would be wrong to let it be stolen," Arvid murmured.

The Marshal turned sharply. "You seriously think the necklace is in danger—you do not trust that we have secure locks?"

"I trust that in a center of Girdish learning, surrounded by those who follow the Code of Gird, you have little experience with really skilled thieves or—since you forbid magery—with the way enchanted objects can sway minds. I know that two determined rockfolk—and rockfolk will know things about this place you do not—expect to make away with it."

The Marshal shook his head. "Impossible. The buildings here are on bedrock."

"*Rock*folk," Arvid murmured.

Silence. Then, "Oh," said the Marshal. "You mean they could—"

"Tunnel through it? Certainly."

"But how would they know where to tunnel?"

"It is said that the rockfolk can perceive the jewels they desire through a league of solid rock—that is how they find them. I do not know if that is entirely true, or what sense they use, but we had a dwarf in the Guild at one time who proved uncannily accurate in a test of that ability. We drilled a hole to the center of each of three blocks of stone, and put a single jewel in one, then asked him to name the stone holding the jewel. He did so. The safest place for your treasure, Marshal Perin, is aboveground, in a room large enough for multiple guards, all of them known to you."

"Which excludes you," Marshal Perin said, "since you are not known to me."

"If the others are your fellow Girdsmen, they will not let me steal."

"I will ask," Marshal Perin said. "But I do not know if they will follow your advice or wishes. Will you wait here or come with me?"

"I will wait," Arvid said, for that, he thought, would ease the Marshal's mind a bit. "Leave the door open, if you will, for the breeze." The first cool breath of air had come through the window into the stuffy little room. Marshal Perin nodded and left. Arvid took his pack off the peg and removed from it those items he might need in the night, then hung it again. He checked his blades, one by one, and when satisfied lay down on the narrow bed and waited. It was not long before someone paused at the door and looked in: a bright-eyed youngster in the gray tunic and trousers of a student.

"Are you a visitor?" the boy asked, then flushed as if he'd realized it was a stupid question.

"Yes," Arvid said. "But I'm not supposed to talk to students."

"Why not?" Now the boy leaned on the door frame. "Have you done something bad?"

Arvid made a show of thinking about that. "Not lately," he said finally. "Have you?"

"Not really bad. I did say a bad word when I hit myself with a hauk—see, here's the bruise—" He pushed up his sleeve to show a bruise on his upper arm. "—and I didn't think Marshal Gerrit would know it was a bad word because it's dwarvfish—my brother taught it to me—but he did."

"What was it?" Arvid asked.

"*Char-chardnik*," the boy said. "All the words ending in *-nik* are dwarvfish, Olin said."

Arvid struggled with laughter and choked it back. "Sorry, Olin's wrong. Do you even know what *chardnik* means?"

"Horse droppings?"

"Er . . . no. It's not a dwarvish word; lots of words that aren't dwarvish end in *-nik*, and it means something your father would whip you for saying."

"But—but *what*?" From the boy's gleeful expression, Arvid knew he was imagining what he'd say to his older brother.

"Something vile," Arvid said. "And aren't you supposed to be studying something?"

"Writing pages of 'I will not use foul language' over and over, but I brib—got Tamis to do it for me."

A boy with talents. Arvid smiled at him. "I would not have either of us in trouble for this conversation—the Marshal who bade me not interfere with your studies might come back any time."

"Do you have to stay here?" the boy asked, with a glance up and down the corridor.

"I said I would," Arvid said. "And I expect Marshal Perin to return."

"From?"

"Over there," Arvid said, gesturing out the window.

"Then I can see him and he will not see me if I'm not right in the doorway." The boy came into the room without waiting for an invitation and flattened himself against the wall, where he could see out the window. "I'm Baris, by the way, Baris Arnufson."

"And I am Arvid Semminson," Arvid said, sitting up on the bed.

The boy went pale. "Oh—oh, you're the one—in the—the—you know. And you saved *her*! We heard about you!"

Arvid kept his jaw from dropping by main force. He had not expected that a boy in Fin Panir would recognize his full name, and if the whole school did, no wonder Marshal Perin told him not to chat with the students. "Um . . . if you mean Paks—"

"Of course! Paksenarrion, the greatest paladin ever! My brother was here when she was; he saw her. He *talked* to her."

"You might want to lower your voice," Arvid said. "You can be heard even if you aren't seen."

The boy spoke more softly but with the same intensity. "She was just a student when she came—just going for knight's training, he said. He had a room on the same corridor . . . There was this other boy, who almost challenged her when he thought she was just a peasant girl, but she wasn't, she'd been a soldier. In the south. With Duke Phelan, only now he's king of Lyonya and she's why, that's what they said."

"True," Arvid said. Nothing was going to stop the whole recital, everything this boy knew about Paks, he could tell. "Don't forget to watch out the window."

"I won't. And then—" He rattled off the tale as told by students in the training college; Arvid corrected nothing. "And why are you here?" the boy asked when he'd done.

"To tell the Archivist what I know about Paksenarrion, for your records," Arvid said. "At the Marshal-General's request."

"Tell me," the boy said. "Please, please . . ."

"I cannot, at least not until I have told the Archivist, so the tale will not have details worn off by retelling."

The boy scowled. "Well . . . a promise to the Marshal-General. I suppose you mustn't, then, but after . . . afterward, please come and tell me . . . us . . ."

"If the Marshal-General permits. See here, Baris, I am not your tutor; I have no right to interfere."

"But you're in the—" The boy's voice dropped even lower, to a murmur. "—Thieves' Guild." Louder, again. "Why do you care about the rules?"

"We have rules, even in the Guild," Arvid said. "Just different ones." He caught the faint sound of a door closing across the courtyard. "You had better go now, Baris, and if you wish to know what that word means from my lips, I trust you will not chatter about meeting me, more than a glance in the room and being sent away."

"Oh, I wouldn't," the boy said, moving to the doorway. "This is too good a secret."

Arvid lay back on the bed and closed his eyes, listening to the boot-heels and voices in the paved yard outside—Marshal Perin and another Marshal had met and paused to talk—and wondering if any boy that age could keep a secret even one turn of the glass. He had, he recalled, but he had been brought up to it. Still, it was comforting to know that Girdish boys were normal: mischievous and wily. He might find something other than stuffy sanctimoniousness here.

He opened his eyes when Marshal Perin knocked on the door frame.

"You must come to the High Lord's Hall and swear before witnesses you have no intent to steal the necklace and that you believe it is in danger," he said. "And I warn you, you are not likely to fool us or the gods in the Hall."

"And then?"

"And then the senior Marshals' council will do as you say, to safeguard it," Marshal Perin said.

CHAPTER THIRTEEN

The necklace lay, glittering in lamplight, on a folded cloth in the middle of the table. Arvid did not come near it. It would have looked good on Paksenarrion; he wished she'd put it on. Around the table four Marshals of Gird stood guard, and Knights of Gird guarded the door, inside and out. Arvid had suggested bringing in the rockfolk who were presently guests of the Fellowship, envoys from their respective kingdoms, but the Girdsmen did not agree. He looked at their arrangements and nodded.

"What you must understand," he said to those suspicious faces, "is that your fine stone walls are as water to them. They command stone the way you command your own flesh. Stay alert—change guard often, to others you trust, at the first hint of sleepiness—it can be a glamour."

He himself would not be in the room with the necklace, but in the treasury chamber where it had been kept, now bare but for the sapphire and two gold coins he placed in the center on a stool as a lure. He lit the lamps—he would need them, though the rockfolk wouldn't—and settled himself in a corner to wait. A carafe of water, a bowl with a hunk of bread for the hollow feeling one got midway between the turn of night and dawn, should he need it. Outside, in the corridor, Knights of Gird stood guard, lest the dwarf and gnome get past him.

Arvid eased his legs from time to time, wiggled his shoulders, waved his arms, but did not walk about. Without a glass to watch the

fall of time, he had only his own instinct to tell him when the turn of
night came. He expected the incursion—if it came—to be shortly
after that.

When it came, it was, by his reckoning, a turn of the glass after the
turn of night. He felt increasing pressure in his head, a desire to close
his eyes, lie down, sleep. He ignored that. Refusing the invitation to
sleep was a basic skill all in the Thieves' Guild learned early.

Though he listened for the chink of pick on stone, he did not expect to hear it. With pick and shovel, even rockfolk could not have
delved from the inn to Gird's Hall so quickly: they would use rock-
magic, he was sure. The Guild dwarf had told him of it, but could not
or would not describe what it was like. "The rock parts," was all he
would say.

A faint vibration came through his boot soles. Arvid took the
bread from the bowl and poured in water. It stilled, then the surface
shivered again, showing concentric rings. A faint groan, and the rings
steepened.

No sound from the knights outside the door: they might have
fallen asleep naturally or yielded to the rockfolks' enchantment.
Arvid slid a little buckler onto his left hand, checked once more that
he could reach all his small blades, then drew sword and dagger. The
groan again, then a noise like a board breaking, and a gap opened in
the stone an armspan from the jewel he had placed. Two heads rose
through it, one bearded, one not, one with bright eyes scanning the
room, the other's eyes closed, skin sickly pale.

"Rockbrethren," Arvid said in their tongue. "Did I not say I had
so hoped not to see you this night? It would be better to depart now,
and not return."

"Sertig's curse on you!" the dwarf said. He glanced at the single
sapphire and two gold coins. "You took it yourself and now you
would mock us?"

"I never touched it since I gave it to Paksenarrion," Arvid said. "It
is neither mine nor yours. Give up this quest, for your own health,
before you kill your *kteknik*."

"He is not dead, merely drunk," the dwarf said with a shrug. He
had risen, finger by finger, from the crack.

"Gnomes do not drink themselves sick by their own will," Arvid
said.

"You knew we were coming," the dwarf said. "Why did you not stand here and run us through before we could move?"

"I saw no benefit in it," Arvid said. "So it was not my intent to kill you, although—if you sling that ax you're trying to raise without my noticing—I may be forced to action."

The dwarf's shoulders drooped. "What would you have us do?"

"Go back as you came and heal the rock you wounded," Arvid said. In their language, that sounded more powerful than in Common. "It is your charge as rockbrethren, is it not, to care for the rock as the elves care for the taig?"

"A human lectures a dwarf on his duty!" The dwarf laughed harshly, but sweat had broken out on his forehead, glittering in the lamplight. His eyes shifted about. "Besides—rock once broken like this will never be dross."

"It was ill done, then, to injure healthy rock, and for the sake of so little. Sertig's curse will not fall on *me*."

The dwarf seemed almost to shrink, but then he burst out of the crack, letting the gnome fall back into the crevice. "You at least must die, having seen our rock-magic." He had his ax in hand now and a blade longer than Arvid's dagger in the other hand.

"This is foolish," Arvid said, moving out of reach. "You and the *kteknik* could escape. Why attack me?"

"Vengeance," the dwarf said. "You betrayed us; you ruined our plan; you are my enemy and the enemy of all rockfolk, for what you have seen." He waved the ax in a complex design and spoke words Arvid did not know. In an instant, with a shriek and showers of grit, stone flowed across what had been the doorway. Even if the knights outside awoke, they could not help him now.

A moment's panic almost cost him his life, as the dwarf charged. Arvid shifted aside just in time, taking a slice from the dwarf's knife on the outside of his left arm. His body took over, years of training producing parries and attacks, over and over, as the dwarf, rock-strong and angry, came at him without pause. *Simyits! Help!* But here in Gird's Hall, the trickster god, the two-faced, had no power, if indeed he ever had. Arvid wondered, in the fourth time around the margin of the room, using the wall to help ward him from the ax blows, if he dared call on Gird.

That thought struck him as funny, and in that moment of utter relaxation, he managed a kick at the dwarf's elbow, and the ax flew clear. With his next thrust, he buried his blade in the angle of jaw and throat. The dwarf staggered; Arvid shoved and twisted; the tip of his sword was stuck in the back of that hard, thick skull. The dwarf grabbed at the blade one-handed and thrust at Arvid with the other, but could not reach him. Finally—too slowly—the dwarf slumped to his knees and fell over. Arvid waited . . . the dwarf was, at last, obviously dead.

So he hadn't needed Gird after all? A man's laugh—whose?—rang in his head, and someone—who?—asked how he planned to escape. The lamps were guttering now; the air already smelled close and stale. He could die here—suffocate here—and be entombed forever. Even if other rockfolk came, they would not give his corpse any honor, not with a dead dwarf in the same chamber. No one would ever know—

Panic returned. No one would ever know what he had planned to tell the Archivist about Paksenarrion.

Well, then, the voice suggested, *best use the wits the gods gave you and find a way out.*

Panic receded; the pain in his arm returned; blood dripped off his fingers. Arvid tore off his bloody sleeve and used it to bind the wound, an awkward task one-handed, but it was not the first time he had tended himself. He would clean it properly later, if he made it out of here alive. He had a grisly time removing his sword from the dwarf's body, then cleaned it on his cloak before sheathing it again.

He went to look at the crack in the floor. There, an arm's length down in the shifting shadows, the gnome lay huddled, filling the space. Even as Arvid watched, the gnome's eyes opened; he could see the gleam. Beyond the gnome was a passage that might lead to the outside, if the rockfolk had not closed it behind them.

He reached in, grasped the gnome's shoulders, and hauled him up into the room, then laid him gently on the floor, facing away from the dwarf's corpse. He bore no visible weapons; Arvid forbore to search him closely. The gnome lay still, gazing up as if confused.

"You were ill-used, rockbrother," Arvid said in their language. "Your companion drugged your ale and then reft the rock-magic from you. You will want water, I daresay, and perhaps some bread. May I fetch it for you?"

"Why—help me? What trade?"

"You are injured; we will talk trade when you recover," Arvid said. He turned aside, slipped the knives from their pockets in his cloak, and laid the cloak over the now-shivering gnome, then fetched the bowl of water and the bread. "May I lift your head?"

"What price?" the gnome said again.

Arvid sighed. "Rockbrother, I know not if you are fully aware yet, and I know that among your people a valid contract may not be made between one who is aware and one who is not. I honor your desire to set the terms and be sure they are just, but you must recover first—"

"You named me *kteknik*."

"So I did, and so you are. But I do not treat you differently for all that. I am not your prince; I have no cause to punish you. If you permit, I will lift your head so you can drink; I think water and bread will help rid your mind of the drug, and then we can bargain."

"I am thirsty," the gnome said. "I will pay what you require for water."

"I require only your permission," Arvid said. Indeed he felt pity for the gnome, who was probably *kteknik* for something he himself would not consider a crime, and who had been abused by one he trusted. He lifted the gnome's round head, noticing as he did that it felt rock-hard for all the thick hair on it, and held the bowl to his lips. The gnome sipped, sipped again, and then brought his own hands up to hold the bowl. Arvid slid an arm under his shoulders to lift him a little more. "There is bread," he said, indicating it.

With a bowl of water and some bread, the gnome became more alert, looking around. Arvid stayed between his gaze and the dwarf's body. The gnome stared at the sapphire.

"That?" he asked. "*That* is what he aimed for, one single jewel and a bit of gold?"

"Indeed," Arvid said. "And he blamed me for that, and would have killed me, had I not killed him first."

"Fool," the gnome said. He looked down at himself. "Was it you or he who took my blade?"

"I took nothing," Arvid said. "He had an ax and a long knife or short sword—I know not how you call something that length."

The gnome turned, still sitting; Arvid moved aside and let him see the dwarf's body, the blade lying beside it and the ax some distance away. The gnome looked back at Arvid. "You were wounded," he said. "By my blade, I judge. The ax would have severed your arm."

"Wielded by someone else," Arvid said. "I bear you no ill-will for that."

"Under our law, wounds dealt by my blade are my responsibility," the gnome said. "Only in part, if someone else dealt it, but it was still my blade, and I did not prevent its use." He looked at the water carafe, and Arvid poured more into the bowl. The gnome drank, then spoke again. "You may think it strange, that I do not ask now what you expect from me. You have shed blood from my blade and, I deem, in my service—for that dwarf would have killed me. My life is yours, until the debt is paid, and my debt to the prince as well. It is the Law."

Arvid stared. "Rockbrother—what is this? It was not your fault: he put something in your food or ale and took your blade. He used your power as well as his."

"It is the Law," the gnome said again. Though still shaky and gray about the mouth, he got up to his hands and knees and kissed Arvid's boot. "I will serve you in any way that does not break the Law, and I must interpret that law leniently, toward human laxity. Accept my service; say the words that seal the contract."

But you are kteknik hovered on Arvid's lips; he did not let the words pass. "I accept your service," Arvid said instead. "But I ask only that you guide me from this place, which the dwarf sealed with his rock-magic—I deem you too ill as yet to use yours again this night." He waved to the wall that had once had a door in it.

The gnome peered at the wall. "It is true, my lord, that I cannot open that rock this night. It will be days before I can use my powers again, for you said truly that the dwarf, may he rot in the light, drained me near to death. You are my savior; it is my delight to do your will."

"Can you tell if it will take long for those outside to break through, should they choose? There is a passage, where men wait—they might hear me pounding—"

The gnome shook his head. "It will not be done, my lord. That is no skin of rock across a door: that is solid stone, encasing door and—" he winced, hands to his head. "He brought rock upon them in a trice; they were made one with it. Wicked, wicked—"

Arvid felt cold through. He had not imagined such a thing. The deaths of those knights . . . he should have insisted they stay farther back—

The gnome, was watching him, obviously fearful. Weak as he was, he must have realized Arvid could slay him easily.

Arvid forced his voice to calm. "Can we then use the passage through the rock that you came in?"

"Indeed, though it will be uncomfortable for you, being made for us. It is wide enough, but low."

"More than one has told me it would do my soul good to bend," Arvid said. He caught up the gnome's blade; his own blood had thickened on it, and it took scrubbing with the remaining water and the dwarf's cloak to clean it well. "Take this," Arvid said to the gnome, and handed it over. He looked around the room and shrugged. "We might as well take the sapphire and gold as well; those above will not find it."

With the carafe and bowl, the sapphire and gold, they descended into the crack, Arvid finding it awkward. Below, the opening the rock-folk had made was rough, wide enough for a man Arvid's size but so low he found it easier to crawl than crouch. For a time, a little light came from the lit room behind and above, then at a turn all went black. He was acutely aware that if the gnome lied—if he had any power—he could bring rock down on Arvid and still himself escape.

But the gnome stayed close ahead, quietly warning Arvid of every twist and turn, every steep slope. Down they went, and down, this way and that. Arvid knew the city sloped down above them; Gird's Hall and the High Lord's Hall were on a hill. A stench came to his nose.

"Defilement," the gnome said from the darkness ahead. "The mageborn cleft the stone to carry away their filth, long ago in your time; they dirtied clean stone, being too lazy to carry it away to the fields. The dwarf opened too close to it—"

"Sewers," Arvid said, in Common. "Our name for such tunnels. If this is at all like other mageborn work I've seen, there will be a place to walk alongside. Is there an opening?"

"It is poison!" the gnome said.

"Not if we do not drink of it. Or have open—alas, I do have an open wound, and you are wiser than I."

Past the stench, farther and farther. His knees hurt; his shoulders complained; his hands felt raw. He could feel warm blood trickling from the bandage he'd tied on his arm; he could scarcely bear weight on that hand. He tried walking in a crouch, one hand up to ward his head from the stone above, but that hurt as much after a short time. He was more and more tired of this, and afraid of being trapped. He forebore to ask the gnome how much farther, for fear of hearing an answer that would wrench a complaint from him.

Then he smelled freshness in the air and saw dim light ahead . . . and then more light, defining the surface on which he crawled, the gnome's shadow on it clearer and clearer. Was it daylight already? It could be. He stayed on hands and knees until at last the rock above him receded. The gnome waited, hand out to help him rise, and he needed that help.

Morning sunlight blazed on the open land around him—not the city or its walls. They had come out the side of a hill that rose above them to the north and cut off the view to the west as well; to the east he saw a patchwork of fields and woods below.

"Where are we?" he asked. When he glanced at his injured arm, blood soaked the bandage he'd applied, glistening in the light.

"A half-day's walk from Fin Panir," the gnome said, "over the land, that is. It is shorter, under the ground, but you, my lord—you are sore wounded. I know where clean water is, and herbs for your wound."

"I must go back," Arvid said. "I must tell them—"

"Not now," the gnome said. "Stone comforts me," he said in response to Arvid's look of surprise. "We were under stone for hours; though it could not restore my strength completely, it removed the taint of the drug he used."

Arvid felt the bright sun fading, the light going gray, and the next he knew he was lying on half his own cloak, with the other half pulled up to form a shade. Footsteps neared, a slight crunch on the pebbles, and then the gnome handed him a bowl. "Drink, my lord. It is good water."

"Thank you," Arvid said.

"And now I will clean your wound. Close your eyes; I must move the shade."

Instead, Arvid turned his head and watched as the gnome took down the shade and laid that half of the cloak flat. On that he set the carafe, a pile of herbs whose clean sharp smell tickled Arvid's nose, and one of Arvid's small knives, gleaming in the sun.

The wound, revealed, oozed blood and looked already swollen. The gnome, gently enough, bathed it with water and what had been, Arvid realized, his own handkerchief, the lace-edged one he used to prove solvency from time to time.

"It's not that bad," Arvid said, though he never liked seeing his own flesh torn.

"A clean slash," the gnome agreed. "But needing to be purified, and I have no numbweed or even ale."

"Be at ease," Arvid said. "I have felt worse."

The gnome, he decided, could have taught the healers he'd used before a thing or two about wound cleaning; he had to use every technique he knew not to cry out before the gnome had the wound packed with herbs and rebandaged. But when it was done, he could feel a change in his arm—pain, but a cleaner pain. The rag of his sleeve, blood-soaked, the gnome had rolled up and tossed away, washing his hands after.

"And now you must chew these leaves," the gnome said. "They do not ease pain at all, but they will strengthen your blood."

Arvid chewed them—a bitter, sour taste but not disgusting—and after that was able to sit up, back against a rock. "Thank you," he said. "If it is acceptable, I consider your debt discharged."

"No," the gnome said. "It cannot be. It does not balance. Without my aid, if indeed the dwarf had killed me, you would have gone down the passage anyway, would you not?"

"Well . . . yes."

"And I perceive you to be a man of strength and determination; you would have made it to the opening. Your wound was serious, but not immediately fatal; you could possibly have found aid at a farm, and would have found water. So by my honor I am still in your debt."

The implications of the night's events came into Arvid's mind: what had happened, and what the Girdsmen would think of what had happened. Their knights entombed in rock that now blocked the passage . . . his absence . . . and, if they did manage to break through, a dead dwarf, a missing gnome and master thief, and no jewel or gold. They would be after him, as furious as hornets whose nest had been kicked. And he afoot, without his purse . . . and no Thieves' Guild hostel nearer than Tsaia. Only one thing might work.

"I must go back," Arvid said. "I cannot think you would wish to return."

The gnome shrugged. "In reality, I did nothing against their law: I was overpowered, and by human law that makes innocence, does it not?"

"Ye-es," Arvid said. "But will they believe it? I fear I have damaged your reputation, for I told them you and the dwarf were talking thievery—that's why I was there, alone."

The gnome shrugged. "But you erred. Do you not remember I expressed shock at the dwarf's plan? Or was that before you came?"

"I heard that—I had forgotten. My pardon."

"We can stand surety for each other's tale," the gnome said. "Your wound also speaks for you, and if you speak for me—"

"Then we had best start," Arvid said. The herbs had cleared his head and steadied him; he would have preferred an excellent lunch, a bath, and a long nap, but he had seen hard times often before. He was able to stand, and the gnome pointed northward.

"From the top of this hill, you can see the city," he said. "But there is a sheep trail easier to follow."

"I am glad," Arvid said. Standing, in the full force of the midday sun, without his hat, he felt unsteady at first. He hung his cloak from his head, for that small protection, and smiled down at the gnome. "Let us be off, then."

"Is it not a problem for you humans to leave your blood behind?" the gnome asked, pointing to the blood-soaked rag of his sleeve.

"There are no blood-mages in Fintha," Arvid said. "Girdish don't allow them."

The gnome gave a curious rasping sound. "*Human* blood-mages are not the only ones who work magic with blood."

"Then what?" Arvid asked.

"Bury it deep or take it along and do so later. I have no strength to do it without tools."

"I have pockets in my cloak," Arvid said. He stuffed the stiffened thing into one of them, and they headed for the city along the sheep trail on the side of the hill.

Heat beat up from the rock outcrops on the hill, intensified the smell of sheep droppings and wool. Arvid told himself it was only the heat that made him unsteady enough to stumble now and then. A hot breeze came up from the land below, smelling of hay and flowers. To the east, clouds gathered slowly into clumps, then more swiftly into towers, dark at the base. It would rain—might already be raining—there, but here on the uplands the sun reigned.

Around the shoulder of the hill, Arvid caught a glimpse of the city wall in the distance. It seemed near and far at once, as if he had doubled vision showing the real distance and his sense of how fast he could travel. He glanced at the gnome. "Do you think we can make it by sundown?"

"I do not know all the country," the gnome said, "but I do know there is no chasm or steep between here and there." He squinted. "If that is a gate—if there is a gate on this side—we should find a road soon."

In another three hundred paces they could see a road. Here and there a tree hung over it; Arvid longed for that shade. Once on the road, Arvid fixed his mind on staying upright and moving as steadily as he could; the gnome, at his side, said nothing until they came to a well, four trees, and a bench set ready for travelers.

"Water. We stop."

Arvid leaned on the well coping, feeling the cool damp air ease his face. The gnome was already up on the coping, working the windlass. "I should—" Arvid began.

"My lord, sit on the bench. I will fetch water. I have still the carafe."

Arvid staggered to the bench; it felt a half-season cooler in the shade there. He let the cloak fall back from his head. The gnome brought the bucket back to the well coping, filled the carafe, and brought it to Arvid. After a bowlful of water, he felt a little better. The gnome drank, and then Arvid again. Now Arvid was aware of hunger, but no worse than he'd known other times. He wet his face and looked around. Under one of the trees, a few hardy summer flowers bloomed: blue sage, star-eye, tinset. He plucked one spray of tinset and laid it on the well coping; the gnome added the silvery-gray leaf of blue sage.

They had scarcely started again when a party on horseback, all in Gird's blue and white, rode up behind them and surrounded them.

"Ho, travelers—did you see aught of a man in black and—" The speaker paused. "You! You are that thief! And this must be—"

"I am not a thief," Arvid said. "I am Arvid Semminson, come to Fin Panir at the request of the Marshal-General, and this is my companion, who will share his name if he wishes."

"Liar!" The man, red-faced now, spurred his horse closer to Arvid. "You killed Girdish knights; you stole—"

"I killed a dwarf," Arvid said. "I killed no knights, nor did this gnome. I stole nothing."

"It is gone, and your horse and pack; you must have done it!"

"It" must mean the necklace. His horse, his pack? Had there been other thieves, and he had not noticed? In the meantime . . . "Do you see a horse and pack?" Arvid said. "If they are gone, someone stole them—it was not I, for if I had taken my own horse, I would be riding, not afoot."

"It threw you and ran off, and no wonder," the man said.

Arvid sighed. Girdsmen had heads like stone; facts shattered on their preconceptions. "I am not so ill a rider," he said instead. "I left my horse in the care of your stable, and my pack hanging from a peg in a guest room. If they are gone, then they were taken by someone else."

"Are you, a thief, accusing Girdsmen of thievery?"

"I accuse no one; I merely state the facts. If it is gone, someone else took it because I did not."

"Where were you last night and this day, then?" the man asked.

"Last night I was in the treasure chamber of Gird's Hall," Arvid said. "With the knowledge of your Marshals' council, I had baited that chamber with a sapphire and two pieces of gold. While I was there, as I had expected, the dwarf I warned Marshal Perin about made an entrance through the rock itself. He had overpowered this gnome, and stolen power from the gnome to make an entrance. The dwarf was angry and grew stone across the door I had used; the only way out was through the passage he had created. I killed him, taking this wound—" He held up his arm. "I found the gnome still alive, and he led me through the passage to the outside."

"You trusted him?"

"I had no choice," Arvid said. "I needed his help to get out of that place—I cannot burrow through stone."

"He is rockfolk; he could—"

"His power was spent; I told you. The dwarf stole it."

The man leaned forward, resting a forearm on his horse's neck. "Let me tell you another tale, Arvid Semminson, that I think runs truer than yours. You and these rockfolk planned the whole thing. You let them into the treasure chamber, after they burrowed along; together you killed the knights in the corridor, you taking that wound you show so proudly. Then you and the gnome came out the secret passage; the dwarf meanwhile sealed the passage with rock, bespelled those who watched the necklace, and made off with it and your horse and pack, and—since he failed to meet you at the appointed place—you came trailing back, feigning innocence, hoping to escape the just punishment you deserve."

The man sat up, drew his sword, and all around the circle of horsemen came the rasp of swords being drawn. "Liar," the man said. "Thief. You deserve death, and death you shall have, and we the reward for bringing back your corpse. Dead or alive, the High Marshal told us when we rode out. Dead it shall be."

Arvid did not move. "I have not yet told all I know about the paladin Paksenarrion," he said. "It is for that I was invited here. Do you think the Marshal-General will be pleased to know you silenced one she herself asked to speak?"

"You—!"

"I can be killed, if so she judges, after I have spoken of Paksenarrion. But I cannot speak, if you kill me now." He shrugged. "It is, of course, your decision."

"He is right, Pir," one of the others said. "And the Marshal-General should arrive today; it will do no harm to wait. We won't let him escape again."

Arvid considered pointing out that he hadn't "escaped" in the first place, and had been coming back on his own, but in view of the drawn swords held his peace.

"Very well," the first man said, with bad grace. "Then get a march on, you, and don't dawdle."

"Considering that I've had no sleep, no food since yesterday, and have a wound, and my companion is not at full strength either, you may have to accept a slower pace than you, riding, would find reasonable," Arvid said.

"A day's fast never hurt anyone," the man said, wheeling his horse discourteously close to Arvid.

"Pir—" one of the others said.

"I'll go tell them we found him," the man said, and spurred to a gallop. The others looked down at Arvid with less hostility.

"You could ride pillion," one of them said.

"I don't ride," said the gnome.

"It would be quicker," Arvid said to him, "but if you cannot ride, then I, too, will walk. My thanks," he said to the rider who had offered. He took a few steps forward, but standing in the heat had affected his balance, and he nearly fell, his vision darkening.

"My lord!" The gnome was at his side, a hard-muscled shoulder under his arm, helping him. "You cannot go on."

Arvid shook his head. "I can. It's just the standing—"

"No," said one of the Girdish. "It's not right." He dismounted and eased the reins over his mount's ears. "I will help you mount, and I will lead my horse."

"Torin, are you sure?"

"I am sure that it is not courteous to force a wounded man to walk such a distance in the heat, without food or water. And we must go at a foot-pace anyway, for the gnome's sake."

"Pir won't like it."

"Pir can—" The man swallowed whatever he might have said and offered Arvid his hands to mount. Arvid would have ignored that, but when he tried to raise his wounded arm to the saddle-bow, he could not. Mounted, he looked down at the gnome.

"I'm sorry—"

"It is nothing, my lord. I am quite able to walk."

CHAPTER FOURTEEN

A rvid draped his cloak over his head again. In such wise they made their way to the city faster than Arvid could have walked it, and neared the gate by late afternoon. He would have dismounted when they came to the gate, but his guide would have none of it.

"You do not need to exhaust yourself up the steep to the Hall."

They found the forecourt in some confusion. The Marshal-General had just arrived, having been overtaken by a search party sent out on the river road to catch the fugitives; it had returned with her. Others, sent north and west, had not yet returned. As well, two students had gone missing. Clusters of Marshals, knights, and staff were huddled here and there, all talking against one another.

In this chaos, the arrival of another seven riders caused no notice at first but to bring grooms running out to take the horses. Arvid slid off, wrenching his arm in the process; the gnome moved up close to him.

"There they are!" Pir, spotting them across the court and pointing, had a voice that affected Arvid like a squealing saw. "We found this one at least!"

Faces turned toward Arvid, including the Marshal-General. She came toward him, the others shifting out of her way, and looked him up and down.

"Arvid—you look the worse for wear."

"Yes, Marshal-General."

"You don't look like a man who successfully killed four Girdish knights and made off with a stolen necklace, a horse, and a pack."

"No, Marshal-General."

She glanced at the gnome and to Arvid's astonishment said, "Greetings, rockbrother. Was it you who bound up this man's wound?" in the gnome's own language.

"Yes, Marshal-General," the gnome said, eyes alight.

"And you were with him in this . . . situation?"

"Yes, Marshal-General."

"An accomplice, I'll warrant," Pir said. "I'll tell you what I think—"

"Later," the Marshal-General said. "I will see Arvid, whom I invited and who is my guest, cared for first."

"But—"

She turned her shoulder to him and spoke to the man leading the horse Arvid had ridden. "It was well done, Torin, to offer him a mount. I suppose the rockbrother refused?"

"Yes, Marshal-General."

"Arvid, come with me, you and your friend. You will sleep in the main Hall tonight." Arvid was not sure he could walk that far, but one of the Marshals offered him an arm, and he made it inside the cool entrance chamber of the Hall without disgracing himself. "You both need a chance to bathe and change," the Marshal-General said. She spoke to a young man in gray. "We need a suit of clothes for this rockbrother and also for this man."

They moved down a passage past a long room filled with tables and benches and turned left into one furnished with two beds and opening into a small chamber with a tub and spigot and a stool. A window in the bedchamber opened onto a walled garden.

"You will wish to stay together, I imagine," the Marshal-General said. "You will be more comfortable here than in the School barracks, and anyway, there's a disturbance over there right now." She turned to the gnome and again spoke in that language. "Rockbrother, I honor your skill in wound care and do not doubt you have applied the best herbs you could find, but Arvid is a man, and I would ask that you permit one of our healers to see him. I am sure it will not lessen whatever ceremony of exchange you had with him."

"He was wounded by my blade in another's hand, and he saved me," the gnome said. "The debt is mine; my life is his; do what you will."

The Marshal-General glanced at Arvid; he opened his mouth to explain, but his vision darkened and he was hardly aware when he slumped, other than to think, *Oh, no.* He came to himself again in one of the beds. Snoring from the other bed proved to be his gnome companion, sound asleep. A dim lamp burned in the bath chamber. Outside, it was dark, as he could see between the slats of the shutters, now opened for a nonexistent breeze.

Beyond the closed door, he could hear footsteps and voices, but not what they said. Some passed . . . more silence . . . then immediately outside the door he heard voices again.

"I'll just look," one said. The door opened. The Marshal-General, in a simple blue shirt, sleeves rolled up, over gray trousers.

"I'm awake," Arvid said. "But he's not."

"I'll be brief. Do you remember waking once before?"

"No." He hated the thought of that.

"You roused enough, after you were cleaned up, to drink a little soup. Your wound has been healed, though we can do nothing for the blood loss. If that bloody mess in your cloak pocket—and *dear* Arvid, I do not wish to think what purpose you find for all those pockets—is all your own blood, our healers think that is quite enough to explain what happened."

Arvid squeezed his eyes shut a moment. So now the Marshal-General and doubtless all the other Marshals knew some of his secrets . . . and the cloak was the easiest of his tools to use, most times.

"I travel a lot," he said, his voice coming out in a croak. He had never felt more like a rain-sodden rooster, tail feathers limp and dragging.

"Indeed you do. I will not worry you tonight, but if you are awake, the healers say more food would be a good idea."

"And then?" Was this a last meal?

"And then a night's sleep, and in the morning we shall talk."

His stomach grumbled, and she wrinkled her nose at the sound. "I'll have a bowl of beef broth and all-heal sent in, and some bread. And more water."

"The door—"

"Is guarded. You have nothing to fear, Arvid."

He wasn't so sure, but as the gnome snored on, and a woman with a broad friendly face brought him the food, he ate and—snoring or no—slept. He woke to children's voices in the garden outside; it was broad day already, and they had been sent, he gathered, to pick herbs for the kitchen.

The gnome's bed was empty, but he could hear splashing from the bathing room. He lay, feeling less soreness in his shoulders and hands than he'd expected, even if his arm was healed . . . he looked, and the bandage was gone, but a clean white scar, thin as a string, outlined the slash.

Well. He sat up; his head spun for a moment. A cream-colored shirt embroidered with stars and flowers around the neckline and a pair of gray trousers were folded on the table. He glared at them. *He* wore black. He did not wear Girdish clothes, except he had no others, and he was not going to walk around bare-skinned. He put on the clothes—they smelled of sun and herbs and were pleasantly soft-rough on his skin—and tried standing. Yes, he could stand, but he felt weaker than he'd hoped.

The gnome came out of the bathing chamber, dressed now in a sleeveless brown jerkin and green trousers, both too wide for him and held on with a leather belt. "They had only dwarf things," he said to Arvid. "It is not discourtesy. Our clothes will be clean and dry later today, they said."

"Do you have others at the inn where we met?" Arvid asked.

"I do," the gnome said. "But I am not sure—the dwarf may have hidden them, or perhaps he did not even pay the score. And he could have taken my money—"

"We have two gold pieces," Arvid said. "Those were mine, from my own purse." At least . . . he'd had them the day before. But there they were, on top of his folded cloak. His sword belt and sword, too, and all his other blades, neatly laid out. Either the Marshal-General wasn't planning to kill him, or she hoped he'd give an excuse. He thought about that as he went in the bathing chamber, splashed water on his face and hands, and made use of the jacks-hole, here set in a raised platform and provided with an elaborately carved seat. Surely that wasn't Gird's idea . . . but he remembered this had been a palace before Gird's time.

He was pulling on his boots over thick gray socks when a tap came at the door. It was, again, the Marshal-General.

"You look better," she said. Her gaze flicked to the table. "Feel free to arm yourself if you wish. I was quite impressed, by the way."

"If you were going to kill me, you had your chance," Arvid said. The embroidered shirt soured his mood. Flowers!

"You're my guest," the Marshal-General said. "I don't kill guests. You need breakfast, you and your companion."

She led them to a small empty dining room off the vast kitchen, with a table just large enough for six, and then fetched breakfast herself. "For you, Arvid, meat to make up the blood you lost. For you, rockbrother, what I believe your folk prefer: fruit and seeds. If that is not to your taste, please tell me." The gnome chose berries over stone fruits, and crunched away at the various seeds and nuts. Arvid ate steadily: the slice of ham, the eggs, the bread. When they had done, the Marshal-General carried the crockery out and came back.

"Rockbrother," she said first, "I need to speak with Arvid awhile, him alone. Will you walk about the garden, or accept a guide around the Hall?"

The gnome looked at Arvid. Arvid shrugged. "Do what you will, rockbrother, while the Marshal-General and I have speech. I will be with you again later."

"I would see your High Lord's Hall," the gnome said, to Arvid's surprise. "I understand this is to you what our Giver of Law is to us."

"That pleases me," the Marshal-General said. "I will send for a guide, one who speaks some of your language, to answer any questions you may have."

The gnome bowed; soon a young woman in a Marshal's tabard appeared and greeted him in his language. "Rockbrother, you would see the High Lord's Hall? May I be your guide?" And off they went together. The Marshal-General sat down across from Arvid.

"Well, now," she said.

"Marshal-General," Arvid said. He had not expected to feel anything in particular face-to-face with her—he who had been face-to-face with others in power—but her steady gaze quickened his pulse.

"You are not a stupid man, Arvid Semminson," she said. "I do not believe you stole the necklace, nor did you entomb those Girdish knights. You would not commit such obvious crimes."

"Thank you for your good opinion," Arvid said, past a tight throat.

"So I will hear your story, in your own words, taking as long as you will, and as completely as you remember." Her mouth twitched in the tiniest of smiles. "I imagine you understand me."

"You have no scribe here to record—"

"No. If I decide a record is necessary, I can write it myself."

"I begin with the showing of the regalia, then," Arvid said. Without naming names, he explained how word of the regalia had passed to and through the Thieves' Guild.

"Do you know the first date the crown was heard of?" the Marshal-General said.

"Before the coronation? No, only that there was rumor the new Duke Verrakai had a secret crown and would have another try at the prince, then or after he became king. As soon as word passed that Dorrin Verrakai would be the new duke, I would say. Certainly the rumors built in the last few tendays before the coronation itself."

"I was surprised to find you had left Vérella when I came through."

"My pardon, Marshal-General, if that was discourteous. I had not visited Fintha for years and thought I might familiarize myself with the land and the city."

"A tactical talent, then," the Marshal-General said. "I do not blame you; it merely surprised me. And my Marshals, as well, to find the Thieves' Guild so quiet with you gone."

Arvid looked at his nails. "Well," he said. "You have skilled staff . . . and so, in my way, do I."

"So you arrived here and stayed a night at the Gray Fox . . . but did not await my arrival to present yourself the next afternoon at the Hall. May I ask why?"

"I had your safe passage to show, Marshal-General, and thought again that I would prefer to scout the territory ahead of you. I would not beg more than one night's extra lodging—"

"You knew I would come yesterday? How?"

"A messenger from the grange where you stayed the night before stopped for a mug of ale at the Fox and told the landlord you would be back at Hall the next day. Then, when I arrived here, your people told me the same. But the other reason I came was to warn the Hall of the intended theft of the necklace by a dwarf—a dwarf who was with that gnome. You do know, Marshal-General, that he's *kteknik*?"

"Of course," she said. "Go on."

"The dwarf was intent on the theft; the gnome was not, but I thought might be persuaded to it after I left. So I warned your people, and suggested the ruse of putting a single sapphire and some gold in the room where the necklace had lain, and a separate guard on it upstairs somewhere, as far from rock as possible. I said I would remain in the chamber alone, with guards outside, and explained I expected the rockfolk to come through the rock." He paused for a swallow of water. "As they did. But the dwarf had drugged the gnome and then used his rock-magic to rend the rock silently and swiftly. The gnome was unconscious and nearly dead when the dwarf broke through."

"Why didn't you call for help?" the Marshal-General asked.

"I was a fool," Arvid said. "I am not stupid, but a man of wit may outsmart himself, and I did so. Seeing the gnome senseless, and knowing my skill and experience, I thought to disarm the dwarf myself—kill him if I must—and then—" He shook his head. "I knew the guards were spelled—"

"What? You didn't mention that."

"I forgot. Before they broke through, they sent the rock-cold . . . the spell that makes men tired and cold, their eyes heavy as if pebbles lay on them. I have faced its like before; I stayed awake, but suspected the others slept." He shook his head again. "And for that, and for my pride in swordplay, I caused their deaths, for the dwarf caused the rock to spread across the door. I thought then it was only a single stone's thickness, but the gnome told me later—but let me tell it in order."

"Go ahead," she said again.

Arvid told of the fight, of tending the gnome and the long difficult crawl through the passage, of the gnome's claim that since his blade in the dwarf's hand had wounded Arvid, the gnome owed him a great debt.

"I told him that leading me out and tending my wound cleared the debt, but he said no," Arvid said.

"How did the troop find you? There on the hillside?"

"No. I knew I must come back to the city, so we walked—I don't entirely remember until we found a road. It was on the road your people found us. The—Marshal? Knight?—named Pir would have killed me there and then."

"Would he, indeed? That would have been discourteous and unwise." Now she looked dangerous, her face hardening in anger.

"I told him you wanted to hear more of Paksenarrion, and I could be killed just as easily after I talked to you." Arvid drank more water. "I could tell you his idea of what happened—"

"No, I will hear it from him," she said.

Arvid went on with his story, ending with, "I may have a few things out of order there, for truly, with the night and day's exertions and the wound and the heat of the sun, I was not as alert as I prefer to be."

"Um."

"You said students were missing?"

"Two. Did you speak to anyone but Marshal Perin in the School? Any of the students?"

"One boy stuck his head in. I told him I wasn't supposed to talk to students, and he came all the way in."

"Let me guess. That was Baris Arnufson."

"Do you know everyone's name?"

"Don't you know the name of everyone in the Thieves' Guild in Tsaia?"

"A fair question. Yes, that was the boy's name. A right piece of mischief, I thought, but not a bad boy at heart."

"He's gone."

"I didn't take him for a thief," Arvid said. Would that boy have stolen his horse? His pack? "A conniver, yes; he told me he'd persuaded another boy to do a task for him."

"He's not the only one gone. I don't know if they're together, if one followed the other, if it's unrelated . . ."

"You want my help."

"I wanted your information about Paksenarrion, and hers about the necklace, as you know, but having come home to this, I need most to know if those boys are alone in this or if someone else was involved."

"I don't see Baris as the thief," Arvid said. "This theft has a more adult feel, of someone with experience. And it's someone here, Marshal-General, inside Gird's cordon of righteousness: someone who knew that the necklace was no longer in the cellar, and someone who knew how to maze the guards watching it."

"I was afraid of that," the Marshal-General said.

"The boys—or one boy—may have been gulled into helping, especially if in awe of high-ranking men. Baris is less likely for that role. Or one or both may have seen something inconvenient to the thief and been . . . silenced."

The Marshal-General paled. "You mean—killed?"

"It's certainly possible. That, or locked away somewhere long enough for the thief to escape. But you will have searched everywhere, I'm sure."

"Not everywhere . . . Just where we thought boys might hide to escape a class or a chore. And then, with the horse gone, and your pack . . ."

"Yes. I suggest you send someone down to the marketplace and see if my horse is for sale or if a horse of that description sold yesterday. Dark bay, looks black from a distance, touch of white on the off rear pastern. Well-built, no brands or other marks. If he's there, he knows my call—better the whistle that was in my pack, but that's conveniently gone. My pack would be easy to lose down any cistern."

"If you believe it is someone from here, I cannot send anyone," the Marshal-General said. "If you're well enough, let's go."

"Now? In these?" Arvid glanced down at his flower-embroidered front.

"They will not recognize you," she pointed out, but she was laughing at him; he could see it in her eyes. "We will let your *kteknik* gnome know where you've gone, and then see if your horse was sold, while others look for the missing boys."

In those clothes Arvid felt as conspicuous as a cow in a kitchen, despite seeing at least half the population dressed similarly. A disguise, yes, but he preferred concealment by shadow, in the night, not this.

The first of the horse-dealers specialized in teams; Arvid left the Marshal-General chatting with the man and strolled through the barn . . . no, his horse was not concealed in a back corner or in the yard where an old swaybacked roan dozed in one corner. The second, nearer the east gate, had more saddle horses, including a dark bay with three stockings and a thin stripe, drinking from a stone trough alongside two chestnuts and a gray. "There he is," Arvid said.

"You said white only on the off hind."

"So I did. That's not natural white—it's whitewash." Arvid pursed his lips and whistled. The horse jerked up its head and looked around.

"Well, that looks—" The horse dipped its head again. "—like a horse that alerts to whistles," the Marshal-General said. "So how do you propose to prove it's yours?"

"Soap and water," Arvid said. "It's an amateurish job. I can tell that from here."

The horse-dealer protested. "It can't be stolen. That Marshal told me—a Marshal from up there." The man pointed his thumb up the hill. "He said it was his, and he wanted something quieter, not so flashy."

"Did he say why he bought it in the first place?"

"No . . . t'horse was jerking on the lead. I thought maybe he was heavy-handed." The horse-dealer watched Arvid scrubbing at the white on the near fore. "I swear, Marshal-General, I didn't know . . . he was a Marshal; I never even thought about it—"

"There we go." Arvid spoke up. Patchy black showed through the white now. "See that?"

"Yes." The horse-dealer grimaced. "And I paid . . ." His voice faltered as Arvid looked at him. "Two gold crescents."

"I'll wager he didn't haggle," Arvid said.

"No, but I thought . . . he's a Marshal, see."

"Did you record the purchase?" the Marshal-General said.

"Yes, Marshal-General, just like the Code says."

A full glass later, Arvid's horse was back in a stall at the Gird's Hall stables and the gnome was back at his side; he had finally told

Arvid his name, Datturatkvin. "But for humans, Dattur alone is enough," he said.

Arvid nodded. "Thank you, Dattur, for the gift of your name." He turned to the Marshal-General. "Are there other stables here, or just this one?"

"The knights have their own, and so do the paladins and paladin-candidates," the Marshal-General said. "Why?"

"Would someone instantly notice an extra saddle and bridle, do you think?"

"Not with all the concern focused here," she said. "I'll go with you."

Dattur found Arvid's saddle stuffed into a grain bin in the knights' stable; Arvid recognized his bridle in a tangle of those awaiting mending in the tack repair area. "Someone is clever," Arvid said. "He—or she—had limited time to suggest I was guilty . . . to dispose of my horse, tack, pack in only a few turns of the glass, without being noticed. I wonder, how many non-knights come into this stable? Would the stable help know if someone did?"

"In daylight, certainly. At night, there's a watch going the rounds, but no specific guard."

From her tone, this might change. Arvid nodded. "So anyone who knew the watch schedule could come in here, dispose of the tack . . . What about the guest stables?"

"The same. But do you have any idea where the boys might be, if they weren't killed?"

"No. I don't know this city. You've tried cisterns, I suppose, and granaries . . . any place big enough to hold boys and secure enough they couldn't get out?"

"Not yet. Not all of them." She looked pale; Arvid realized she must feel responsible for the boys' safety.

"If I were the thief," Arvid said, "I'd be busy enough disposing of that horse and my tack—that must've been done while the horse-dealer was still up, willing to make a deal. Then finding a hiding place for the necklace. I don't think I'd waste time putting the boys anywhere difficult . . . just enough to keep them out of the way while I escaped. It would take a hard man to kill two boys who happened to see him, which is what I suspect happened."

"Would you?" she asked.

"No," Arvid said. "I might knock them on the head enough that they'd be silent. Put them in a pantry or something." He thought a moment longer. "Say the boys were in the School, as they ought to have been, and heard something—saw something—maybe my things being taken from my room. They're discovered—maybe they didn't think to conceal themselves. It's not easy to silence two boys and then carry them any distance. I'll wager they're still in the School barracks."

"Nobody's reported anything."

"Let me look."

As they came into the forecourt, Arvid called over two boys carrying a barrel slung from a pole. "When you don't want to be found, where do you go?"

They glanced at each other, then at the Marshal-General.

"It's important," she said. "We think Baris and Tamis are hurt."

"Well . . . there's the back cellar. We're not supposed to go there, but Baris found a trap-door."

"Show me."

There they found the two boys, bound and gagged, both with bruises suggesting they'd fought hard and unsuccessfully and been knocked unconscious. Tears had left streaky tracks down their dusty, bruised faces.

Baris, as soon as the gag was out, said, "It was a Marshal—a Marshal of Gird—I couldn't believe—"

The other boy, smaller, said nothing; he seemed scarcely aware.

"Get him to the infirmary," the Marshal-General said. She turned to Baris. Arvid had cut his hands free, and the boy was rubbing his wrists. "So, Baris, can you walk? Or shall we carry you upstairs for a good meal?"

"I—I can walk," he said. He staggered with his first step, but his gait steadied. He accepted help on the stairs, but beyond the bruises and paleness, he seemed unharmed.

The Training Master insisted on his cleaning up before a meal, but soon enough he was seated in the Training Master's office with a tray in front of him and the Marshal-General and Arvid seated on either side. While he attacked his food, the adults talked of other things.

As the color came back into the boy's face and his eating slowed, the Marshal-General said, "Baris, can you tell us now what happened? You said a Marshal of Gird—do you know which one?"

"No, Marshal-General. It was my fault, anyway—"

"What was?"

"Tamis being involved. You know the older boys are in the upper bunks—he had the lower one. I woke up—I needed the pot—and as I was climbing down, I heard something—and I slipped and kicked Tam, by accident. He woke up. Then he heard it too."

The rest of Baris's story included seeing a grown man in a Marshal's tabard in Arvid's guest-room, stuffing Arvid's clothes into his pack. The boys had watched; Baris had to keep shushing Tamis, who wanted to ask questions, but they'd been caught when the man came into the corridor. Before they could do anything, the man had knocked Tamis senseless; Baris, shocked to stillness for a moment, found himself gagged with a glove before he could cry out. He tried to struggle, but the man overpowered him with a few blows. A hand at his throat, and the next thing he knew, he was bound and gagged in the cellar, with Tamis beside him.

"Did you see anything distinctive about him?"

"No . . . well, he had something glittery around his neck."

"Glittery?"

"I just saw it for a second, when he had my throat—a bit of it, anyway, where his shirt was open."

"The necklace," the Marshal-General said.

"I'm sure," Arvid said. To Baris, he said, "You are lucky to have been found."

"It was not luck," Baris said. "It was Gird. I prayed, and I'm sure Tamis did, too. I knew someone would find us. How's Tam?"

"In the infirmary," Arvid said. "Luck came almost too late for him."

"Gird came soon enough," Baris said.

Arvid sighed. Apparently fear had driven the boy back into his narrow faith. He made another attempt to inject some realism into the discussion. "Gird punished you for trying to stop a thief?"

"No . . . it was a test . . ."

The Marshal-General gave Arvid a warning glance. "Baris, do you remember anything more about the man. Young, old, bearded, clean-shaven, dark hair or light?"

"There wasn't much light. He was about as tall as you, Marshal-General, and his hair was . . . not black, and not really light. Brown, I guess. He had a short beard, like a lot of Marshals. Hair to here—" Baris touched his shoulder.

"Would he look like a Marshal out of that tabard, Baris?" Arvid asked. "Would you recognize him in ordinary garb, say, if he cut his hair?" The boy merely looked confused.

CHAPTER FIFTEEN

Once back in her office, Arianya summoned the Archivist to see what more had been learned from Luap's scrolls while she was away.

"Quite a bit, Marshal-General, but the most important things may be these: that cloth we found was an altar cloth for the High Lord's Hall made by a mageborn woman named Dorhaniya. That's in both Luap's writings and the records here. Gird himself gave permission for her to show it to a mageborn Sunlord priest named Aranha, and it was dedicated at the altar."

"In Gird's time?" Arianya asked. "I thought the rituals of Esea Sunlord were forbidden, as being tainted by blood magic."

"It's clear, Marshal-General, that our records of the period deviate from Luap's and from the writings of his followers as we found them in Kolobia. Another thing—not all the scrolls Paks brought us are Luap's. Some are even older than that, relating to events in Aarenis so distant in time, our only referents for the names and places are legendary. The language, too, is difficult."

"But the altar-cloth," Arianya said. "You're sure it was made for the High Lord's Hall and there was an actual priest of Esea Sunlord present?"

"According to Luap and the archives, Marshal-General."

"I need to see it again," Arianya said. "I believe I have seen a duplicate in Tsaia." She described the cloth that wrapped a crown now hidden from view, a crown from magelord times. "And," she said, "a magelord lives now, magery unlocked, to whom that crown answers."

"Answers?"

Arianya nodded. "I must talk to the Council about all this, but ask you to hold it close until I convene a Council meeting—but you scholars must know what to look for. That regalia is surely royal, from kings of old, and it speaks to Duke Dorrin Verrakai. Paksenarrion— whom I met again, and more must be told of that—helped unlock Dorrin Verrakai's mage-powers and was there when the regalia first showed power. Dorrin Verrakai gave it to Tsaia's king, as a coronation gift, and it lies presently in the king's treasury, but only Dorrin Verrakai can move it. The crown is wrapped in a cloth that, to my memory and Paks's, is the same design and style of embroidery as the cloth found in Kolobia. Moreover, that necklace Paks brought us— the sapphires and diamonds—is much the same design as the other regalia. Paks thinks it's part of the set." Arianya sighed. "I need all these threads untangled and the pattern laid clear, to know how best to proceed. Two years ago, I thought I understood all—now I know nothing, or so it seems."

"Here's the cloth, Marshal-General," said one of the scholars, who had gone to fetch it. She unfolded its wrappings and laid it out.

"It's the same," Arianya said, leaning over it. The scholar hovered, as if to be sure Arianya didn't touch those tiny stitches. "I shouldn't be surprised, I suppose. An altar-cloth would be made to an older design . . . at least, I'm assuming the regalia are from before Luap's time."

"We haven't started on the priest's journal," another scholar said.

"Another question," Arianya said. "Have you found anything from Luap's Stronghold to indicate that elves ever lived there?"

"Elves? No. Their holy symbol is carved there, and Luap said one appeared, along with a dwarf and a gnome, but no sign of their living understone. Why?"

"We never asked Paksenarrion, when she was a student here, about what she saw in the banast taig that became the elfane taig. And more—we never asked any of the elves visiting here, though some were of the Ladysforest."

One of the scholars looked startled. "That's true—we didn't."

"Glamour," Arianya said, slapping her thigh. "They cozened us with a glamour, not to ask. Those patterns—in Kolobia and the High Lord's Hall and that cave Gird found—they must be elven."

"Or dwarven?"

"No. The rockfolk need no patterns to move in stone. We do. Elves do." Arianya shook her head. "I don't understand. But I will. And we must still record everything Arvid Semminson can remember about his encounters with Paksenarrion . . . any detail might be important, not just as a record of her deeds."

CHAPTER SIXTEEN

Vonja outbounds

The cohort had just moved to a camp south and east of their first area, where the ruins of another village and its overgrown fields gave them a defensible position along an old east-west market road, now barely more than a track. Arcolin planned to stay there a hand of days to map the trails found in this section of forest before heading back to Cortes Vonja; sixty days past Midsummer was the end of their contract. He had the camp fortified as if for a longer stay: a ditch, staked in the bottom, a dirt parapet topped with brambles pushed down over upright stakes. On the fourth day, he called for a contest.

"If we just counted hits from the first day of practice, the sergeant would win by a double-fist—but to be fair to the rest of you, the bet will be decided in one contest. Fifty shots, twenty at two distances, ten at the nearest. A point for the nearest, two for the middle, three for the farthest." He looked at Stammel, who seemed not at all daunted. Well—Stammel never minded being bested by someone who was actually better. "Some of you didn't take the original bet, but you've all had the practice, so I'm telling you—for a jug of ale in Valdaire, you're all in it. If Stammel wins, I hope he can drink that much . . ." Laughter. No one complained that Stammel's guides—the two who gave him the direction and distance by calling from near the target—gave him unfair advantage.

All of them placed all ten shots in the near target, as he'd expected. In the middle distance, Stammel and two others—Coben and Suli—placed all twenty; the rest missed one to three each. In the long, no one hit with all twenty shots; Stammel and Coben both got nineteen, Suli eighteen.

Before Arcolin could decide what to do about the tie, scouts called a warning. Out of the tree line on two sides, the enemy appeared—in daylight as they had not before—a troop of horse and another of infantry. Fifty—sixty—his cohort was already falling back behind their defenses. The soldiers who had, a moment before, been laughing and cheering on their favorites were now already armed and positioning themselves. Another ten horse appeared, on another side. Arcolin had no time to wonder why the warning came so late or where such a small army had come from—he was back inside their barricade, glancing to see where Burek was—where he should be, taking command of the south side of the camp—when he saw Stammel still standing outside, crossbow raised.

"Stammel!" he yelled. Stammel didn't answer or move. Arcolin's heart lurched. Who had left him there? Who would—well, he had, thinking Stammel would follow his usual guide. "Stammel," he yelled again. "Back! This way!" Beside him now, Suli started to climb the parapet. He grabbed her arm. "No—not you, Eyes."

"I have to—"

One of the enemy yelled, then others. Stammel turned a little and released the bolt; immediately he bent, spanned the bow, placed another bolt, and again stood poised, waiting. Arcolin stared as the first bolt struck; a man went down. Another yell; another shot; another man went down. The enemy advance slowed. In the golden afternoon light, the bandage on Stammel's eyes showed clearly, its ends fluttering in the breeze.

One of the horsemen yelled, spurring his horse forward. Stammel turned and shot. This time the bolt pierced the horse's chest; it stumbled, went down; the rider fell and lay still. The other horsemen reined in.

Then Stammel's voice: "I am the Blind Archer!"

The hair stood up on Arcolin's body. "Holy Gird and Falk!" he muttered. Beside him, around him, others were muttering, too.

"You are one; we are many!" one of the horsemen yelled.

"I am the Blind Archer," Stammel said again, releasing that bolt. The man who had yelled fell from his horse.

At the rear of the enemy, Arcolin could see a few men back away—not turning to run, but easing back from the others. One in the front rank leveled a crossbow at Stammel; Arcolin yelled—but the bolt missed Stammel by an arm's length, and his return bolt dropped the man.

"Archers," Stammel said, this time in his usual voice. "Volley fire."

Suli pulled away from Arcolin's grip and with the other archers stepped up on the parapet and on Arcolin's count fired, some at the horsemen and some at the infantry. A few in each group went down. Return fire was ragged and ineffective, as Stammel—standing calmly alone and re-spanning his bow quickly between shots—hit one after another. Each time he called loudly, "I am the Blind Archer." Arcolin called for volley after volley; the small group of horse on the far side, charging in as a distraction, could not get through the ditch and up the parapet. The less able at archery, those not formally in the archery group, had grabbed spare crossbows and picked off almost half the ten horsemen on that side as they tried to dismount and charge the barrier.

The enemy wavered, foot and horse both, and finally some charged forward while others turned away. The cohort sallied to meet those still coming, surrounding Stammel where he stood with a fixed smile on his face.

"Are they gone?"

"No. But they will be." Those charging forward had not yet noticed that their formations were half the size they had been; a mere thirty crashed into almost three times that many Phelani, and in half a glass they were all dead.

"Stammel, what was that?" Arcolin asked, watching the others strip the brigands—or whoever they were—of weapons. More curved blades, some straight, crossbows, half a dozen Vonjan pikes with the Cortes Vonja mark stamped on the blade.

"Burek told me more of the legend, Captain," Stammel said. Now that it was over, he wiped the sweat off his forehead. "You know that tavern in Fossnir, the Blind Archer?"

"Yes—"

"There's another tavern named that, in Cortes Vonja, and one in Cortes Cilwan. All named for a story old as Torre's Necklace. A man blinded by a usurper, for loyalty to the old king. He comes back, a beggar everyone thinks, and because he's blind and harmless, the usurper has no fear of him—but he kills him, an arrow to the throat."

"I didn't know that," Arcolin said.

"Nor I, Captain. But down here, many do, Burek said."

"Did *he* tell you to stand out there?"

"Of course not," Stammel said. "I just thought—what if I can scare some of them, and anyway . . ." He flushed a little. "Something came over me," he said. "I felt—I felt it was right."

"Well, it worked," Arcolin said. "But the next time you don't follow orders, Sergeant, I'm docking your pay." He put a hand on Stammel's shoulder and shook it. Under his hand, Stammel's shoulder felt like oak: all that muscle regained, all that strength. "Dammit, man," he said, fighting back tears. "I don't want to lose you now."

"I'm not lost, Captain," Stammel said. "Not while I'm with the cohort."

They moved on the next morning. Though they had killed more than half the attacking force, Arcolin was sure now the brigands outnumbered the cohort, and he was three days from easy communication with Cortes Vonja. The Blind Archer legend wouldn't deter them all, or any for long.

Back on the west side of the forest belt, Arcolin considered how best to finish the season's work. The maps he and Burek had made showed multiple trails in the forest and the tracks of old farm and village lanes where wagons might go. The Vonjans, if they had the will, could use those with their own militia, especially in the fall when the leaves fell, to locate and defeat the brigands. They had more forces at their command. He suspected they would not, but in their various skirmishes they'd killed over a hundred; even with regular supply, that must have cut back the brigand strength considerably.

The villages along their original route south were now fully involved in harvest; Arcolin spread his force out to ensure that market traffic moved safely. He paid city market price for fresh fruits and vegetables, to the delight of local farmers.

CHAPTER SEVENTEEN

Chaya

The two northern princesses and their guardians seemed to take up more space and time than any other six people. Kieri had to fit in visits of courtesy with them and their guardians around his other duties. Count and Countess Settik were particularly scornful of his lessons with Orlith, which had resumed without further discussion of the Lady. The Squires assigned to the princesses reported that both had been extremely guarded at first.

"We think neither is here willingly," Arian said. Along with Aulin, Lieth, and Binir, she had been assigned to Elis. Kaelith, one of those caring for Ganlin, nodded. "Aulin says Elis seemed glad to wear trousers but was afraid her guardians would see her. She has the right calluses for sword training—we all agree on that—and she walked in the garden like someone used to walking in trousers and not skirts. But she had no blade at all, not even a lady's dagger to cut her own food. Binir got her talking about horses—she knows a lot, and said she always wanted to breed Pargunese Blacks, but then blushed and took it back."

"They don't like our baths," Kaelith said, wrinkling her nose. "They say they have bigger ones at home, with hot water that comes from a pipe. They call ours barbaric. Ganlin says it's hard to climb in and out—but she's got that sore hip. There's certainly more between the two of them, Elis and Ganlin, than they've yet told us.

Ganlin wanted me to carry a message secretly to Elis, so I gave it to Aulin—and then Arian gave Suriya one from Elis to Ganlin."

"How does Ganlin feel about her guardians?" Kieri asked.

"She doesn't like them," Kaelith said. "But I don't think it's more than being made to do something she doesn't want to."

"Elis is frightened of hers," Arian said. "I'm not sure why. I also sense a deep anger in her, but she's so young—they both are, really—that it could be any little slight."

Kieri almost chuckled—it seemed an odd thing for Arian to say—she could scarcely be that much older than Elis—but instead he said, "Perhaps we should offer them something they're sure to like—if they're sword-trained, a chance to work out in the salle?"

Kaelith shook her head. "I don't think her guardian would allow it; we've all heard her scold Ganlin and remind her to be ladylike and demure. 'None of your wild ways,' she says."

"The same with Elis," Arian said. "Her guardians stick close as ticks to a hound, and everything we've offered—suggestions to go for a ride or a walk in the forest—even to walk in the gardens alone—they refuse for her. Her eyes light up sometimes, but it's no use."

Kieri considered. It was well past Midsummer now; the princesses had settled in as if they meant to stay until he married them, which he was not going to do. Their guardians had become increasingly insistent—when would he decide?

"I must see them alone," he said. "Despite their guardians. I must know more about them before I can refuse them without insult—I do not want to hurt the girls, however much I am willing to risk angering their families."

"Refusing them won't hurt their feelings," Kaelith said. "Neither one has shown that kind of interest in you, Sir King. But what about their guardians? They are so protective—or that's what they call it."

"A walk in the rose garden in the afternoon," Kieri said. "With you Squires for chaperons. It is an insult to me if they think that dishonorable. As Elis's guardians are more likely to be difficult, we will ask her first. Arian, please convey to Elis my earnest wish that she spend a short time walking with me in the rose garden this afternoon. Who's with her now?"

"Binir, Sir King."

"Do you have night duty tonight?"

"No, Sir King."

"Then you also attend us, and we will see if I can learn more from her. Tomorrow, Kaelith, I will walk with Ganlin."

At the appointed hour, Kieri waited in the rose garden, now a fragrant glowing haven of color. Elis appeared with Arian and Binir. Her expression was, as always, guarded and cool; she curtsied gracefully. "Sir King, I am honored that you wished to see me."

"I am honored that you wish to be my queen," Kieri said, and noted the instant withdrawal and stiffening. She was no more eager for a marriage than he was. "Let us walk."

She moved with him down the path between the roses and other flowers, silent and pale.

"My mother planted this garden," he said. "She loved roses above all flowers, I am told. Does your mother?"

"She did," Elis said, in a choked voice. "She had some in a pot. She . . . died. My father threw them away."

Kieri felt a jolt of sympathy. "My mother died, too," he said. "But luckily, my father also loved roses and chose to remember her by preserving her garden." He did not know if that was true, but it seemed reasonable.

"My father says they are weak southern flowers, not worth the trouble."

"They do not seem weak to me," Kieri said. "But I never grew them in the north."

Her hands, clasped at her waist, relaxed a little. "If—if I were to—to marry—would I have to stay here?"

"Stay here?"

"Inside the walls." Her voice rose a little. She stopped and resumed very quietly. "If—would it ever be possible to—to walk abroad. Even—ride?"

"Your guardians are concerned for your safety," Kieri began, but Elis made an impatient gesture.

"At home," she murmured, "I rode . . . in trousers like those the Squires wear. But—but then—"

"Come this way," Kieri said, and led her farther along the path, where an artfully designed waterfall gave an excuse to face away from the palace windows and the falling water would cover their voices. "Now," he said, when he was sure they would not be overheard or their faces seen. "Watch the water and listen to me. You are unhappy: the women attending you have seen that. They tell me you have the hands and walk of someone who is used to weapons, and that you and Ganlin are passing secret messages. No—do not turn around and do not jerk like a frightened horse at its lead."

She was instantly still, but tense. "I—I cannot talk about that."

"I think you are here against your will, and that you and Ganlin were planning something your families did not approve. You're both related to that woman who came here for my coronation—Hanlin, her name was, a sister of the queen?"

"A sister of the current queen and Ganlin's aunt," Elis said. "The king married again after my mother's death." She took a breath and hurried on. "If they find out I told—Sir King, you are right. I did not want to come. Or marry. They drugged me that night at dinner. I was to leave the next day for my own place—my very own—my father promised—and then—"

"Breathe slower," Kieri said. "So you were drugged and brought here . . . and did you then try to escape? Is that why you arrived in the middle of the night?"

She nodded. "I thought I could outride my guardians—escape completely or arrive long before them, and beg you for mercy."

"For mercy?"

"For—for meaning—" She gulped then and Kieri realized she was about to cry.

"Pinch your nose," he said.

"Wh-hat?"

"Pinch your nose. Hard. And think of something funny. You must not be seen crying. It leaves your eyes red, and they will ask questions."

Startled, she complied, and in a moment was calmer.

"Soldier's trick," Kieri said, grinning. "For a sneeze, for a sob." He sobered again. "Elis, I will not marry anyone who does not want to marry me. It was wrong of them—I suppose it must have been your father—to drug you and send you unwilling to me. But before I can find a way to help you, I must know more. Why you? Are you the only girl?"

"No," Elis said. She let go her nose for a moment and looked almost cross-eyed down it. "I have sisters who would have been willing, but I am the eldest. And I am, my stepmother and father both say, an embarrassment."

"Embarrassment?" How could this pretty child be an embarrassment?

"I am . . . not ladylike enough. I like riding—in trousers—and working in the stable, and I made my brothers teach me swordplay. When I was younger I wanted to be a soldier, but I knew that could not be, so then I wanted to be a horse-breeder." She said that fiercely.

Kieri looked at her in astonishment. She had color in her cheeks now, and her pale eyes sparkled. She reminded him of all the eager young recruits he'd had, male and female alike.

"Or I could be one of your Squires," she said, looking up at his face. "I would work hard, I promise."

"And what would your father say, if you were a King's Squire and not a queen?"

She turned white again in an instant.

"I'm sorry," Kieri said quickly. "I did not mean to frighten you."

"It is not you." She pinched her nose hard; the tears that were in her eyes did not brim over. "I can't tell—"

Years of experience with frightened young people came to Kieri's aid. "Yes, you *can* tell me. Do it now."

"He wants me to kill you," she blurted out.

"Who? Your father?"

She nodded. "They told me—on the boat—if—when—we married—she would give me a knife with poison to stab you—and then—if I killed you and got away, my father would give me the land he promised."

So his thought of possible assassination hadn't been nonsense, after all.

"I don't want to kill you," she said in a small voice.

"I'm glad of that," Kieri said. "What do you want?"

"I want to kill—" She stopped herself, then went on. "No, but I do want—the life I always wanted. Oh, please, Sir King, let me stay here! I'll do anything—cut my hair, work in the stables—" She went down on her knees; Kieri pulled her back up.

"Don't do that. Your guardians."

Tears welled up in her eyes, but she pinched her nose again. She was younger than the flowers in the garden, he thought. And yet— something in her held more than mere naive youthfulness, mere rebellion. She had been kidnapped and taken where she did not want to go, but she had refused to do evil. That he could respect.

"Tell me of Ganlin," he said. "How do you know her?"

"We visit Kostandan every year or so," she said. "My stepmother and Hanlin and I. We became friends—we both love riding and being outside and hate embroidery and tatting and women's gossip. We swore eternal friendship—we made a blood-bond and traded locks of hair. She knew I was going to have my own farm—my father had said so—and she was going to run away and join me. We were never going to marry."

Kieri clamped his lips against a smile that would have insulted her. How likely was it, after all, that two princesses would really set up a horse farm and spend their days mucking stalls and cleaning hooves?

"And if one of you fell in love and *wanted* to marry?"

Elis looked at him. "With the men I knew in Pargun? Never. And Ganlin feels the same, I know."

Kieri had his doubts. Elis had never given anyone a flirtatious look, but even at that first banquet, Kieri had noticed Ganlin watching one after another of the young men in the room. One of Ganlin's attendant Squires reported that Ganlin had asked repeatedly after Berne. Elis had better find another partner. With that thought, he had an idea.

"Elis, it's possible I can help you, but you will need to be discreet. It cannot be done in a day—"

"You will let me be a Squire? You will send my guardians away?"

"Do you know the Knights of Falk?" he asked.

She frowned. "No . . ."

"The Falkians train both men and women of noble birth to be knights; some then become soldiers—one of my captains was a Knight of Falk, and I trained there myself. My Squires are all Knights. You would have the best training in all kinds of weapons, in management of military units."

She was glowing again, thinking of it. "Is it possible? Please!"

"If I spoke to your guardians, what would they say?"

"They would refuse," Elis said, "and then punish me for having let you know I wanted it."

"Then we must plot in secret. And that means, Elis, you must be like a soldier in enemy territory, pretending to be what you are not, and hiding the glee that even now covers your face. Think how miserable you are—think of being married not to me, but to an old drunk at home—never to ride again, never to be free. Sulk. Frown. I will need time to organize this."

"You must rescue Ganlin, too," Elis said. "I know she'll want to come—"

"I will talk to Ganlin tomorrow," Kieri said. "In the meantime, tell your guardians you tried to charm me, but I was cool. Can you do that?"

"Yes!" she said with far too much enthusiasm. He gave her a quelling look, and she reverted to the sulky Elis he had seen before.

They walked back across the garden, chatting only of flowers and inconsequentials. Her guardians waited at the garden door, glowering because the two King's Squires would not let them out.

"We had a pleasant walk," Kieri said. "Princess, thank you for your time." He bowed; she curtsied, eyes downcast.

CHAPTER EIGHTEEN

The next day, Kieri escorted Ganlin around the rose garden at the same hour. "Did Elis pass you word about our talk yesterday?" he asked. He already knew, from the Squires, that notes had gone back and forth.

"She said not to be afraid of you," Ganlin said. She gave him a glance under long lashes. "She said there was hope."

"I know what her hopes are," Kieri said. "But not yours. You are friends of old, I understand."

Ganlin flushed. "We are. She is what I wish I were."

"You are very like," Kieri said.

"She is stronger and braver," Ganlin said.

"You were limping the night you arrived," Kieri said. "Were you injured on the way?"

"No, Sir King. I fell from a horse years ago—they said I might not walk again, but now it's only when I'm tired that I limp. And I love to ride, like Elis."

"That sounds like bravery to me . . . to ride again after a bad fall."

"Outside is always better," Ganlin said. "Well—except when it rains."

"You were going to go to her when she had her horse farm?"

Ganlin hesitated, then nodded. "I would try, at least. She was going to be in the north of Pargun, next to the grasslands, but in the forest so there would be wood for the barns and house. But to get there from home—alone—I said I would, somehow, but—but I wasn't ever sure."

"It would be a difficult journey," Kieri agreed. "Tell me, Ganlin, if I told your guardians I did not want to marry you, what would happen to you?"

She scowled. "They would take me home. No one there suits me, or wants me, really. I have a horse—a real horse, a big gray—and I can ride. But Elis said if she's sent home they'll lock her up, and without her I don't know what I'd do. Where could I go?"

"Would you want to stay here if you did become my queen?"

"Here in the palace or here in Lyonya? I do not want to be mured inside walls forever, even with a garden as lovely as this." She waved an arm at the roses. "I want to ride, to walk in the woods—"

"To practice swordcraft?"

"That, too. I liked it, learning—but it's—I don't think I could be a soldier, the way Elis wanted to be. It's not just my hip and leg—it's the thought of killing people."

Kieri nodded. "And yet, Ganlin . . . not all who train as knights become soldiers."

"No?"

"No, not here in Lyonya. I told Elis, and I tell you, that if you wish to learn knightly skills and manners, as would suit men and women of high birth, I know where you can get such training: in Falk's Hall."

"Men *and* women?"

"Yes. I was sent there, as Lord Halveric's squire; one of my captains was a Knight of Falk, who is now a duke in Tsaia. And the King's Squires are Knights of Falk as well."

"Do—do women who become Knights ever . . . ever marry?"

"As they choose," Kieri said. "One of the peers of this realm, a widow with children and grandchildren, is a Knight of Falk."

"I would like that," Ganlin said. Unlike Elis, her color did not come and go as readily; Kieri suspected that the pain of her injury had taught her a control Elis had yet to learn. "If you send Elis there, can you send me?" Then she frowned. "But how? Our guardians will not allow it, I'm sure."

"I'm thinking," Kieri said. "And I will ask the Knight-Commander's advice. In the meantime, you and Elis must both be discreet. Don't pass too many notes." Ganlin flushed and started to speak, but he held up a finger. "If your guardians suspect you have a great secret, it will become much harder. Be a little difficult; act as if you were serious rivals for me. I would rather not start a war with either of your fathers." They walked awhile longer, to equal the time he had spent with Elis, and then he took her back to the garden door. Her guardians were not scowling but chatting pleasantly with the Squires.

Later, alone with that day's assigned Squires, Kieri laid out the plan he'd thought of. "If the Knight-Commander agrees, it is an honorable place for them that does not insult their rank. They will be happier—at best, at home, they would become troublemakers in their realms. This way, they have a chance to become what they want—whatever that is—"

"Do you think they'll stay together?" Aulin asked.

"No," Kieri said. "I think Ganlin saw Elis as a way to escape the role laid out for her, but she is not like her in anything but a desire for freedom. But at Falk's Hall Elis will find others like herself, and so will Ganlin. And the mistress of the barracks is wise enough to recognize and deal with any problems."

"She did with me," Suriya said with a grin. "How many of us, I wonder, think girls who want to ride and hunt and fight must be sisli? Did you have that problem in your Company, Sir King?"

"A little," Kieri said. "But again—we knew what to look for, and I'd seen how Falk's Hall handled it. Also, in some parts of Tsaia and in eastern Fintha, there's more general knowledge. They don't think boys with harps are all gemsul or girls with swords are all sisli. And I'm not even sure Elis is sisli—she's mostly angry and frustrated, I'd say."

"I'd say she is," Arian said.

"And I," Suriya said. "May she know the joy I've known."

"I hope so," Kieri said. "I wish joy to both of them, but getting them where they need to be, without any excess drama, will take thought and planning. They cannot travel without an escort, even with the Knight-Commander."

The Knight-Commander, when Kieri summoned him to discuss the possibility, pursed his lips and shook his head at first. "We've never had a Pargunese or Kostandanyan—that could be trouble."

"Or a first step to peace," Kieri said. "There's at least one Par-gunese who doesn't want to kill me." He meant it as a joke, but the Knight-Commander didn't laugh.

"I must meet them," the Knight-Commander said. "I have come on business—at luncheon, perhaps?"

"We will have their guardians too," Kieri said. "The Pargunese—tongues like razors, the both of them. I'll seat you near the others."

He had no way to warn the princesses and could only hope they retained their composure. In the event, Countess Settik's usual string of complaints covered the young women's first reactions—that moment of glee, quickly suppressed, when Kieri introduced the Knight-Commander of Falk. After that, they both managed to look demure, leaving conversation to their elders. The Knight-Commander directed a few questions to each; Countess Settik answered for Elis, but Ganlin was able to say, sweetly enough, that she had heard of the Knights of Falk only since arriving at this court. No chance of the Knight-Commander having a private interview with either after the meal, because Ganlin's uncle cornered him to ask questions about the Falkian doctrine.

Later, alone in Kieri's office, the Knight-Commander finally agreed. "I'll take them both," he said. "But they'll have to meet the same standards as the others. I understand you think this may create a friendly bond between the realms—I'm not at all sure of that, but no young person deserves to be around that Countess Settik, or co-erced into evil. Ganlin—you're right, she's a different case, but you're sure she doesn't want to marry?"

"*Me*," Kieri said. "She doesn't want to marry *me* and be a queen, and she knows I don't want to marry her. I think she may marry, if she finds the right lad, and Falk grant it's someone her family will approve of."

"So she doesn't want to do what she was sent for, and she thinks she has no future at home. She's not the first we've taken in that way. But again—if she doesn't measure up—"

"I understand," Kieri said. "But it's a chance for them both."

"I'll tell the barracks mistress. When will you send them?"

"When I've contrived a way to convince their guardians to let them go. They're princesses; it must be done legally and with the ap-proval of their guardians."

"I'm glad you understand that. I was half afraid you'd give them horses and let them gallop off on their own."

Kieri snorted. "I've matured, Knight-Commander. No wild exploits: they will arrive with you and an escort of King's Squires, and their guardians will have only good tales to tell of their treatment on return."

"I'm glad you're using King's Squires. I wasn't looking forward to having Countess Settik as my guest at the Hall. How long do you think all this will take? I do have duties back at the Hall, you know."

"Very soon, I hope," Kieri said.

A few days later, both princesses quarreled with Kieri in front of their guardians and then with their guardians: they were tired of the confinement—Kieri was too old—their guardians were cruel—it was too hot—the bathing facilities were barbaric—the food turned their stomachs. They yelled, they threw dishes at the Squires, they ripped their clothes. Their guardians yelled back; Elis's slapped her face; Ganlin's locked the door on her. Elis's tantrum had been carefully timed to occur two glasses earlier than Ganlin's, so that Kieri would not be interrupted as he talked to Elis's guardians. He explained, coolly, that he did not think he and Elis were well-suited; although she was beautiful and accomplished, she did not like him.

"You could master her," Lord Settik said. "You are a strong man; she is only a woman."

"She is a child," Kieri said. "Even if I turned her over my knee, she would still be a child. No."

"You are saying you cannot master a child?" Lord Settik said with a sneer that made Kieri want to remove his head and kick it down the hall.

"Marriage is not only about mastery," he said. "The girl does not want to marry—that is enough for me. But I have a solution that may work for all of us."

"What is that?" Settik said, sticking out his jaw.

"You surely know her type," Kieri said. "She loves the outdoors, riding, even swordplay." Settik said nothing. "Such women," Kieri said, "sometimes find later that they want to marry, and they make good wives. My first wife was such. Here in Lyonya we have the finest of all training schools for nobly born warriors, Falk's Hall. You met the Knight-Commander."

"He runs the School?"

"Yes," Kieri said. "And he heads the order of Knights, as well. She would be among men and women of high rank—entry to Falk's Hall is restricted. I will sponsor her there—pay for her training, even. She will learn superior skills and courtly manners—which you must admit she needs—and who knows what might come of it?"

Settik stroked his beard. "Well . . ."

"If I send her back, that could seem to be an insult, which I do not intend."

"I do not think our king would approve," Settik said.

"What if you presented it as something that happened before you knew about it?" Kieri asked. "She refused to return—I arranged this because I did not want to force her to return."

"And is that not what you are doing?"

"In a way, but I am not doing it without getting your permission," Kieri said. "From what she screamed at us all just now, she doesn't want to go home, she doesn't want to stay here, she wants to run free. We both know girls from palaces cannot run free, not really."

"Mmmm . . ." Settik seemed to be thinking about it; he nodded slightly.

"But this is something that might satisfy her and yet do her no harm. Even help her."

"It might work," Settik said. He glanced at his wife. "It might indeed . . ."

"Suppose," Kieri said, "you have a nice night's sleep. Perhaps even oversleep in the morning."

"You have good ale," Settik said. He licked his lips. "It has been a hard day. Juncis?" His wife nodded. "We will leave the wildcat to herself tonight and enjoy ourselves."

Kieri took that for acquiescence. His interview with Ganlin's guardians went even more smoothly. Her aunt and uncle were tired of her whims, they said. If she was not to marry Kieri, then something must be done with her; she had no future in Kostandan, where she was considered both difficult and a cripple.

By dawn, the two princesses were out of the house and on their way to Falk's Hall, escorted by King's Squires and the Knight-Commander himself.

"I hope you know what you're doing," the Knight-Commander said before he left.

"I also, but I could not think of anything else," Kieri said.

The next day, the princesses' escorts started for their respective homes, apparently satisfied and bearing with them parting gifts and letters to the princesses' parents explaining why Kieri had chosen Falk's Hall.

"And that," Kieri said to the Squires who met him in the salle for practice the following morning, "is that. We all hope. At least it's quieter and not so crowded. We will all take the day off and have a picnic lunch in the Royal Ride—I'm sure you've had as much of princesses and the palace as anyone could stand."

Watching them, listening to them, he thought again how companionable they were. They handled their horses, their weapons, the setting up of even such a brief camp as a picnic, with such easy competence. He tried to imagine Elis or Ganlin doing so well, and could not, at least not until they'd become knights. He felt at home with them, as he had not felt with any other women but soldiers before. But nearly all were too young for him, and one of the two old enough—or almost old enough—was sisli. The other had shown no more interest in him than he felt for her.

He sat quietly, watching and listening, and after a time Arian came over. "Sir King? Do I disturb you? I wanted to talk to you about Pargun."

His pulse sped; he ignored it. "What is it?"

"You recall that before the princesses came, I had been up near the river, carrying messages to Talgan."

"Yes."

"I've been keeping up with the dispatches coming in—I know you have as well—and I'm concerned about those troops."

"So am I," Kieri said. "I may ask Aliam to send me another cohort."

"I can't understand why they'd send their princess to you and then prepare an attack."

Kieri had not told any of the Squires about Elis being instructed to kill him. "They wanted me dead," he said, and went on to tell Arian everything Elis had told him. He pitched his voice so all could hear if they wished. Arian's face expressed the horror he had felt. Then it softened.

"A hard trial for such a young girl," she said. "No wonder she was so difficult to understand."

CHAPTER NINETEEN

ow that the princesses were gone, the Siers in Chaya began making comments about marriage again. Was he looking? Could he use some advice? Kieri wondered when they thought he had time to look; every day had some crisis he must deal with, and that on top of his regular work. He understood their concern, but it had not even been a half-year yet.

"The thing is, my lord," old Joriam said, soaping his king's back, "you may be young, as half-elves go, and you may be strong as oak and lithe as willow, but if some rock drops on your head, you're dead. Or a fever: even kings get fevers. It's your duty, same as wearing a crown or visiting your father's bones."

"I know that," Kieri said, feeling smothered by the constant attention to his single state.

"She doesn't have to be royal, my lord. Or even noble. Just . . . you know . . ." He left it there, and poured the clean water over Kieri's soapy body. "Fertile," was what he meant.

Kieri tried looking at all the women around him with marriage in mind, but he hated thinking of them that way, as breeding animals. They were people, people he had come to know and care for. And they were, mostly, too old to have children or too young for a man his age. He wanted companionship; he wanted someone he could talk to.

That thought sent him to the ossuary, one hot afternoon. This time he lit no candle, just sat and listened . . . to nothing . . . for a long time. Then once again he felt presences gathering around him. One conveyed the combination of wistfulness and stubborn anger that he now associated with his sister.

I'm here, he thought.

Once again: *Betrayal. Danger.* He sat quietly, trying to open his mind as he did to the taig. *They lie.* She had conveyed that before, but who lied? *She trusted.* Who trusted? A fuzzy image of a face leaning down, a sense of warmth and safety. Kieri finally realized this was an adult's face as a very small child might see it . . . a face he almost knew . . . did know, as he noticed the elven bone structure, subtly different from human.

Our mother trusted? Trusted whom?

This time the image was clear as if incised in crystal: the Lady. Their grandmother. A wave of distrust and anger came with it. Kieri tried to think it through: their mother had trusted their grandmother, and his sister thought their grandmother had . . . had what? Neglected her in some way? Betrayed that trust? But how? The obvious was behaving as she had with him, staying away, not helping in some way.

You trusted. All wistfulness with that, a palpable stroke along his left cheek. *You left. You never came again.* Followed by a burst of anger.

The hair stood up on Kieri's body; he could feel it prickling in his clothes. Betrayal . . . could she mean his mother's *death*? His *captivity*? Nausea roiled his gut; he stood up, gulping, struggling not to pollute the ossuary, and staggered into the anteroom.

"Sir King!" The Seneschal stared at him. "What's wrong—what can I—?"

Kieri could not speak; he lurched up the stairs barefoot with the Seneschal behind him, still talking. His Squires, at the entrance, turned to him; he saw the shock on their faces. It didn't matter. It could not be true, she must be mistaken, it could not be—he made it to a corner of the courtyard, leaned over, and spewed, choking, tears suddenly burning his eyes and overflowing.

Moments later someone handed him a cloth; he wiped his mouth. Another cloth, this one wet; he wiped his face and tried to stand, but his stomach betrayed him, and he had to bend and gag, bile burning his mouth. Hands steadied him; he began to know where he was, that the Squires were screening him from view, that they had brought water, towels, his cloak, that his feet burned from the hot pave stones.

Finally, aching as if he had a fever, he was able to stand, clean his face again, turn away from the mess on the stones.

"Come, sit here," the Seneschal said. He had brought a chair and set it in the shade of a wall. Kieri leaned on a Squire's arm without noticing whose it was, made his way to the chair, and sat. The Seneschal washed and dried his feet, put on his socks, helped him into his boots. His breathing steadied. He accepted the mug of cold water someone brought, sipped. It stayed down.

"I'm . . . sorry," Kieri said.

"Sir King . . . Something happened—the bones." The Seneschal's wise gaze held his.

"I . . . believe I misunderstood," Kieri said. "It must be that I misunderstood." Out here, under the bright sky, what he had been shown and events he had surmised from it were impossible to imagine, let alone believe real. His sister had been a tiny child, barely walking, when their mother died; how could she know what their mother thought—whom their mother trusted—who had betrayed their mother and him, if indeed it was not a random attack by brigands? Whatever his sister believed, he could not—he would not—believe that his grandmother had connived at his mother's death. "And," he said, trying to straighten more in the chair, "I may have a touch of summer fever. I drank from a spring yesterday—" A spring the taig had assured him was safe, but tainted water could cause summer fever.

"Sir King," the Seneschal said. "Bones do not lie."

Kieri looked up at that old, wise face. "Bones can be mistaken," he said.

"Yes," the Seneschal agreed. "But if it comes to the living tongue or the bones: bones do not lie, and tongues do. Whatever you learned from bones will have truth in it. I pray you, come again to the ossuary and listen."

"Not today," Kieri said. He felt cold sweat break out at the thought.

"No, my lord, not today. But such reactions—if it is not summer fever—suggest the bones have urgent messages."

He went back to his rooms, feeling hot and cold by turns. Summer fever. It must be summer fever, with the ache, with the nausea, with the loss of appetite—he refused supper and went early to bed, waving off the palace physician. Despite the open windows, not a breath of air stirred; sound carried from the courtyard below, the stables, the streets of Chaya. A child cried out suddenly; he flinched, squeezing his eyes shut and then forcing them open to see . . . nothing but the vague outline of the window.

Toward morning, thunder rumbled in the distance, then nearer. A chill damp gust of air blew in, and then the storm broke overhead. He fell asleep then, waking sticky-eyed, with a foul taste in his mouth, much later than usual. Rain fell steadily outside. He lay, listening to it, and turning over in his mind what he had experienced. Hints. Suggestions. His own mind had made a connection out of his own experience, something his sister could not know. He had created his own nightmare out of such fragile materials.

By breakfast, when his appetite returned, he had himself firmly in hand. It made no sense that his grandmother had betrayed his mother and him . . . if she had, why would she have accepted his coronation? Tried to find him an elven bride? A vast gulf yawned between her not coming when he asked for her and deliberate malice, an attempt to kill. Perhaps she and his mother had been, like many mothers and daughters he'd known in his life, annoyed with each other—perhaps they had even quarreled—but that didn't mean anything worse. A young child, his sister, could misunderstand—

He welcomed the interruptions to his musings—messages brought in by couriers, appointments, meetings—but he hoped Orlith would not come until he felt calmer.

"Sir King, there's a message from Tsaia—" Arian, with a letter from King Mikeli in Tsaia. He took the letter from her and tried to focus on King Mikeli's concerns about the theft of the mysterious necklace from Fin Panir. Some, Mikeli reported, were saying that Dorrin Verrakai had arranged the theft.

"Ridiculous!" Kieri said aloud.

"Sir King?"

"This—" Kieri read her the letter. "Dorrin gave the regalia to the king; why would she steal the necklace?"

"That fellow you told us about in Aarenis might have sent thieves," Arian said.

"Yes—that's what Mikeli suspects," Kieri said. "Alured's dangerous. Though why he thinks the necklace alone will do him any good . . ."

"Perhaps he thinks he can use it to call the rest of it to him?"

Kieri shook his head. "I don't think it works that way. The crown or the ring should be the most powerful, assuming that the items are innately magical. They might be drawing the necklace to themselves— in which case it should show up in Vérella."

Night after night Kieri's sleep was troubled, though he could not remember specific dreams, only an undefined menace. He would have to do something, he realized, about the bones and their hints. He wasn't ready for another trip to the ossuary, and didn't want to ask the elves. Instead, he began asking who in the palace had known his sister or even his parents.

He started with Joriam, who was polishing the big brass ewers in his bathing room. The old man's eyes lit up.

"Yes, my lord, I do remember. Your mother now, my lord, she was a beauty, she was. Fresh as a snowdrop, but strong, the way elves are. She didn't ride just the air and water horses, but any color—she liked to match with your father when they rode out together. The two of them, on matched horses . . . it brought tears to the eyes."

"Did the Lady come to visit often then?"

"No . . . I wouldn't say that. At your birth, yes: said the elven needed some elven magic and upset the midwives no end. *Out with you all*, she said, and there was words spoken, I heard from one of the maids. And at Midsummer, of course, and usually Midwinter, bringing snow sprites."

Kieri had never heard of snow sprites.

"All sparkly they are, in the dark. Elf-light I suppose. Swore it did not break the rule against fire . . . well, they aren't warm at all. They dance."

"Did they ever quarrel?"

Joriam's face changed; he looked wary. "I wouldn't like to say, my lord. I was young then, you know, and the queen was our queen, and the Lady was the Lady. And mothers and daughters, you may know, are not always in accord."

"Joriam, I need to know . . . what did you see or hear?"

Joriam put down the rag and box of polish he had been using. "My lord . . . your mother had spirit, and she may have said more than she meant—"

"But she said . . ."

"I overheard—I shouldn't have, but I was in here, cleaning the brass same as I am now. They knew it, but their voices rose anyway. She said your father was king, and the Lady must deal with him herself. She was not going to be—" Joriam blushed but went on. "—not going to be ruling him . . . between the sheets. And then the Lady said your mother would regret it."

"And?"

"And then the Lady came to the door of the bathing room and told me to be gone and keep quiet. Forget what you heard, she said. I did not look at either of them as I came through the bedchamber; I could feel their magery beating at me."

"Yet you did not forget."

"No . . . my lord, I did not. For your mother said remember, and she was *my* queen."

Kieri forced himself not to pace back and forth. Joriam looked anxious enough. "Joriam, I know you're no gossiper, but this is a matter of importance to me and to the realm both. I have no parents left to guide me; when the gods send dreams or visions, I must find a way to interpret them."

Joriam ducked his head. "My lord, you came from the bone-room in a state—"

"Yes. I learned things, but not enough. Not everything a king needs to know."

"And you want me to tell you more."

"Yes."

"She was so beautiful," Joriam said. "They both were, mother and daughter, but when they were angry, it was like a fire. Not often. The Lady . . . I think she did not understand how your mother could love your father. We all saw that. She had not married him from a duty to pass on the taig-sense; she truly loved him, and he loved her. She never put on airs with him, as the elves do so often. Never treated him as lesser. The Lady said, 'You're losing your nature,' and your mother said, 'I am what I am.'"

"Did she get along with other elves? My mother, I mean?"

"Some. Not all. There was some, you know, just like now, thought themselves too great to associate with humans at all. Your mother argued with them; they couldn't nay-say her because she was the Lady's own daughter, but they did say she was young and would learn better. Her brother, he was older—"

"Amrothlin?"

"I don't know all those names, my lord. Only that another time, she said to the Lady, 'You must tell my brother to treat the king with more respect.'"

Kieri shook his head.

"My lord?"

"No—I was scolding myself, Joriam, for not having asked you before about my parents and other matters. Only you have been such a quiet presence, and so many other matters claimed my attention . . ."

"If there's more you need to know, you should talk to Tekko as well . . . you know, the old huntsman. And Erda, she was one of your mother's maids. Dressed her hair and all."

"Sir King?" Sarol, King's Squire, spoke from the door.

"Yes?"

"There's a courier come from Captain Talgan. I thought you'd want to know."

"Joriam, thank you—and I will want to talk more with you later. And the others. It's time I knew more about my family. But I must go now." He followed Sarol downstairs, his mind leaping ahead to the Pargunese situation. He wished he could get reports from Cracolnya, who would surely have posted troops on the Tsaian-Pargunese border. Though Mikeli had agreed to send any information he had on Pargunese troop movements, so far that had produced nothing useful.

Talgan's report included observations by forest rangers as well as his own troops: everything he had been able to glean about Pargunese activities both on the river and in Pargun itself.

Something is happening in Pargun, but I do not yet know what. Lyonyan fisherfolk say the Pargunese who used to chat with them freely are now close-mouthed; they don't feel welcome across the river at all. Trade is down in Riverwash, where some Pargunese ships used to bring in goods from downriver. We have no reliable

spies in Pargun; I've asked in Harway, but the Tsaians also seem
to have no one. Several forest rangers made it across, as I told you
was planned, and came back with reports of troops on the move.
But none of the rangers speak Pargunese.

"Do we have anyone who speaks Pargunese?" Kieri asked Sarol.
"I can't," Sarol said. "I don't know if any of the Squires can . . .
we've never thought we needed it."

"We do now," Kieri said. He knew Pargunese, but he could not
spend days creeping around across the river to find out what they
were up to. "I'll write Talgan . . . surely some of the people who live
along the river speak some Pargunese."

Once again he felt torn between multiple demands. He needed to
know what Pargun was up to—but he also needed to know about the
elves. If he had to mount a defense against Pargun—if they invaded—
he needed to know if the elves would help defend the taig or if they'd
hide in the elvenhome and leave all the work to the humans. What
did they really intend? What might explain the Lady's behavior?

Over the next days, he found scraps of time to talk to the other
older servants, retired and still active. Tekko the huntsman spoke of
his mother's prowess on horseback, with weapons. "Bold, not afraid
of anything," he said. "They told us she was ages older than your father, but she rode like a young girl. Armsmaster then—he died years
back—told us she was fastest he'd seen with a blade. She never
missed a shot with her bow. But your father, Sir King, was as good—
the two of them, with just one huntsman to manage the hounds,
could bring meat enough for a banquet. Fine pair, they were."

Was that why she'd gone alone with him on that journey? he asked.

Tekko sucked his teeth. "Dunno, Sir King. There was talk. Some
said she refused an escort of Squires, expecting to travel with elves—
but we didn't see them here. Your father, now, he was angry with
himself he didn't insist on Squires or Royal Archers. There was a
Queen's Squire said more, but she was killed in a riding accident not
long after."

"Riding accident?"

"Aye. Horse started bucking, there in the palace courtyard, finally
went over backward. Broke her neck and its, both." Tekko paused,
then went on. "Odd, that was. You know the Squires' mounts, all

well-trained. But everyone was still mourning the queen's death; this seemed just another sorrow."

A convenient accident, Kieri thought, but too long ago to leave useful clues lying about. He listened to the rest of Tekko's tales, including that of the hound pup he'd long forgotten about, until someone interrupted them. After a few more conversations, he realized that some treachery had indeed taken place, but he was not at all sure whose. A lifetime of dealing with courts and councils had taught him how easy it was to foment quarrels, misdirect attention, cast blame on the wrong person.

Finally he called the Seneschal to his office one morning. "What I most need to know now," he said, "is the limit of the bones' knowledge. I have talked to others who knew my parents, and they remember things that seem to corroborate what the bones hinted. But can bones know more than the people who bore them?"

"No one knows for sure," the Seneschal said. "I have not known them to convey anything beyond the lifetime of the flesh."

"What I say now must stay between us for the time," Kieri said.

"Of course, sire."

"My sister's bones hinted at treachery, treachery somehow related to our mother's death—and that means treachery related to my captivity as well. I think my sister believed the Lady complicit in this."

"The Lady!" The Seneschal's eyes widened.

"And the thought of it made me sick," Kieri said; even now his stomach cramped as he spoke of it. "I have talked, as I said, to others who were here at that time. I am not so sure who it was—but I am increasingly sure that treachery was involved. There was, at the least, tension between the Lady and my—our—mother. Someone else could have exploited that. Human or elf, but elf, I fear, is more likely."

"Not a random attack by brigands?"

"No," Kieri said. "By several accounts, she expected an elven escort on the journey—refused a human retinue—and as a full elf should have been able to enter the elvenhome with me if danger threatened. As well, she was skilled with weapons—she would not have been easy to take down. Yet she had no elven escort—they did not arrive when expected, and she chose to leave without them. A Squire who mentioned treachery at the time was soon thrown from her horse and killed. So treachery seems likely—but my sister's suspicion of our grandmother could be based on as little as a minor argument she overheard."

"Your sister lived to adulthood," the Seneschal said. "She could have heard more than you, firsthand, from those who knew your mother and the Lady."

"My father's bones have indicated no such suspicion," Kieri said. "Would he not have known more?"

"Not . . . necessarily." The Seneschal frowned. "Knowledge can pass from mother to daughter, or father to son, through bone and blood. Your sister might have some awareness of what your mother knew, from before your sister's birth."

"How is that possible?"

"I don't know." The Seneschal spread his hands. "In the old days, the old humans believed such was possible. That was one reason for raising the bones and honoring them. They had true wisdom that their descendants might share, at least in part. Certain knowledge and certain skills passed mother to daughter and father to son. Parrions, they called those."

Kieri thought of something else. "Did you ever hear rumor that the Lady was unhappy at her daughter's wedding a human? At the need to reintroduce taig-sense into the royal family?"

"No . . . though elves have always acted as if it were a greater honor to the king your father than to your mother. But I thought that natural." The Seneschal paused, then went on. "Sir King, will you ask the Lady of these things?"

"If she will talk to me," Kieri said. Bitterness flooded him again. "She can always hide there, in the elvenhome . . . and she has been doing just that."

"It must be settled," the Seneschal said. "It must be settled for the good of the realm . . . that is what the bones want, I am sure."

"I will speak to Orlith," Kieri said. "Or any elf I can find."

But when he looked, he found none. Not Orlith, not Amrothlin his own uncle, none of them. His half-elven Squires, when he asked, said they thought all the elves were having a meeting in the elvenhome.

CHAPTER TWENTY

Vonja, in Aarenis

Three days before the contract was over, Arcolin camped outside the walls of Cortes Vonja and went into the city to deal with the Cortes Vonja Council. As he expected, they were not pleased that he hadn't eliminated the threat, but after some hours, during which he showed the maps, the daily journal of activities, and the number of enemy killed, they agreed that he had done as well as a small force could. He turned in the money taken from the fallen brigands and the counterfeiting dies they'd found, as well as the ten Cortes Vonja pikes. They stared at those last as if they were vipers, not needing to be told what it meant that their weapons had shown up in enemy hands.

"We could hire you until the Fall Evener," one councilman said.

"No," Arcolin said. "I must attend Autumn Court in Tsaia; my king commands it. And I have scarce time to travel there as it is."

"How long will you be here, then?"

"Only long enough to let the men spend a little money and complete the business I have with those who helped my sergeant."

With coinage the banker considered legitimate, Arcolin paid the troops enough to let them go—one tensquad at a time—into the city for a few hours, while he visited Marshal Harak and the others.

"I'd like to see him again," Harak said. "I'm sure Tir's Captain would, too."

"I'll tell him," Arcolin said.

"What's this about the Blind Archer?"

"You've heard of that?"

"It was all over the market last week: the Blind Archer has returned. I thought at once of Stammel, but surely—"

"He can shoot a crossbow," Arcolin said. "And when we were attacked, he stood there in the open and called out that he was the Blind Archer—I'd never heard that story—and shot the first man that yelled at him. And then others. Eventually about half of the attackers fled. Don't ask me how—it must have been the gods."

"Hmm." Harak turned and pulled a ragged scroll from the stuffed pigeonholes in his office. "It's in here: Cornlyn's Instructive Stories. Sometimes it's told of Falk, but in this . . ." He unrolled the scroll, frowning. "Here. Balester of Gaona—not on any map we have—being blinded and exiled by the malice of Tagrin for having failed to kill the princeling and heir of the former and rightful king as ordered but instead placing him in safe fosterage, learned archery by the grace of the Master Archer and returned to kill the said Tagrin of hated memory, to the glory of the Lord of Justice and as proof that no infirmity need make a man—or woman—incapable of serving the right." He rolled the scroll again. "A southern tale; I doubt Gird ever heard it, but I've used it in homilies. So did my predecessor. And so now Stammel thinks he's the Blind Archer?"

"He's blind, and he's an archer—he's too sensible, I think, to believe more than it's a tale with a use—and a good use he made of it."

At the Field of Falk, the Captain greeted him warmly. "I have the Halveric sword cleansed, blessed, and ready for travel," he said. "I took the liberty of having our Field leatherworker make it a scabbard—it may not be the Halveric scabbard, but it is good quality and will not dishonor the blade." Arcolin thanked him, took the sword in its scabbard, and went to find the Captain of Tir.

He found the gruff-voiced Captain bare to the waist and trading buffets from a stick with two soldiers. "So, how is our blind hero?" the Captain asked. "I hear tales of the Blind Archer returning to end corruption and evil."

"Not that," Arcolin said, and explained.

"A brave man," the Captain said. "An honor to Tir, that one. Send him to me; I would give him a blessing before he leaves. And Tir's thanks to you, for not wasting his courage, for letting him return to the life he knows."

Back at camp, Stammel was on the point of leaving with Suli for guide and another eight. Arcolin told him he should visit Marshal Harak and the Captain of Tir, and Stammel nodded. "I meant to," he said.

The night before they left Cortes Vonja, Arcolin offered Stammel a choice.

"I must go north, to Autumn Court in Vérella," he said. "I will be granted the North Marches permanently then, and from there I must go north again, to the Duke's—to my stronghold. Burek is well able to command the cohort on the road and in winter quarters. It is up to you whether you come with me or stay in Valdaire. You would be of use either way. If you choose to stay south, I'll take Devlin."

Stammel thought for a long moment. "The cohort needs a sighted sergeant," he said. "Burek, too. He's good, but he'll need someone who knows all the local tricks."

"Well, then. We ride tomorrow, you and I, at speed."

One of the horses went lame between Foss and Fossnir; they had made good time before that, and Arcolin decided they would stay at an inn that night since they had arrived far too late to ride on. On a whim, he thought of the Blind Archer, which proved to be, in the way of inns in Foss Council towns, a clean whitewashed place with good stables.

They came into the common room to eat; it was moderately busy, mostly with obvious merchants. Arcolin chose one of the smaller tables to one side of the main entrance, where he could see both the door and out the window to the busy street. They ordered, and while they were waiting for their food someone behind him—a man he had barely noticed—asked for paper and ink in a querulous voice. A voice he knew—but the other conversations in the room grew louder; he could not hear the man's voice anymore.

Stammel leaned forward. "It's Andressat," he said softly.

"What?" Arcolin did not turn around. "How could it be?" But Stammel was right. It could be Andressat's voice.

Stammel shrugged. "I don't know, but it must be."

They ate when their food came; Arcolin wanted to turn and look, but did not. What he could remember of the man from his first casual glance around the room had not matched his memory of the Count of Andressat.

Later, in their room, a knock came on the door. Arcolin opened to find one of the servant girls, who curtsied and handed him a tightly folded paper. He opened it.

You do not know me, but I recognize you and your uniform. I have urgent word for your Duke. I travel incognito. I would speak with you. Jeddrin, Count of Andressat.

"It's Andressat," Arcolin said. "He wants to talk to me; he's traveling under a false name. And being Andressat, he names no place or time, nor does he give his alias; I'm supposed to find it myself."

He went back downstairs. Andressat had wedged himself into a back corner seat, hat pulled low. In the room full of merchants and travelers, all chatting amiably about something, he might as well have been dipped in whitewash. Arcolin went over and without lowering his voice said, "There you are! I forgot to tell you earlier, the price of that cloth in Cortes Vonja was only two natas a roll lower, and the transport—well, you know. So can we make agreement on the price now?"

A few heads had turned casually at the greeting, but an almost completed agreement for the purchase of a few rolls of cloth wasn't as interesting as their own conversations.

Andressat, hunched over a bowl of fish soup, glared at Arcolin, then gestured. Arcolin sat down. "You didn't say when or where," Arcolin murmured. "Or what name you were using, or what occupation you claimed. But cloth merchant is safe enough, and I would have the authority to bargain for cloth for uniforms. Wool, winterweight."

"I—" Andressat cleared his throat. "It is nothing. I have chosen this out of necessity, and I must carry it through. I need your help."

"I cannot delay my journey," Arcolin said. "I am summoned to Autumn Court in Tsaia. But if I can help without delay, I will do so."

"Phelan is now king of Lyonya, I hear," Andressat said.

"Yes," Arcolin said.

"The legitimate son of a former king, it is said."

"Yes, indeed," Arcolin said. "Half-elven—none of us knew that, including him."

"I must see him," Andressat said. "I found—" He leaned closer. "I found things in the archives—in Cortes Andres—he must see and know. You must ask him to come and see for himself."

"I am not likely to see him," Arcolin said. "I doubt he will come to Autumn Court in Tsaia, and from there I must go north, to take formal possession of the land that was his, and is now mine."

Andressat sat back, scowling. "You cannot go to Lyonya first? It is not far, is it? I thought all the northern lands were just the other side of the pass at Valdaire."

"The Eight Kingdoms are larger than all Aarenis," Arcolin said. "I have maps with me—would you like to see?"

"I—yes. I suppose if you cannot—but you are a hire-sword, can I not hire you?"

The Count, Arcolin realized, was frightened, being out of his own place. No one had ever heard of Andressat traveling—and so ignorant of lands he did not know that he thought a side journey from Tsaia to Lyonya would be a matter of hours or a day or two. "I'm sorry, my lord," Arcolin said as gently as he could. "I am bound to my liege, you must understand, and when he bids me come on a day, then I must come."

"I see that," the Count said. "But—but it is most inconvenient." He looked around the room, flinching a little as someone banged a jug on a table in a demand for more ale.

"What name do you travel under?" Arcolin asked. "It will seem more natural if we call each other by name. I'm Jandelir Arcolin; a merchant would call me Captain."

"I am naming myself Manis Turgold," Andressat said.

Arcolin pushed back his chair and stood. "Well, Master Turgold," he said, "come up to my room when you've finished your meal, and we'll settle it then. Third floor, end of the passage, left side."

"Certainly, Captain," Andressat said. "Less than a glass."

Up in Arcolin's room, Andressat was the same proud, prickly man Arcolin had met before, though he seemed far more provincial than Arcolin had suspected. When Andressat looked at the maps Arcolin showed him, he seemed astonished at the size of the land north of the mountains.

"And the duke—the king—is over here? How many days' travel? And I must visit the Tsaian court as well, I suppose."

Arcolin shook his head. "No, my lord, at this time I do not advise it. They've had trouble this year and are wary of strangers. Take the southern trade road—go with a caravan, if you can, as far as the Lyonyan border, then ask directions to Aliam Halveric's from there. You know him, and he will give you the best route north to Chaya."

"You have been there?"

"To Aliam's? Yes, but never to Chaya. You are welcome to ride with us—with me and my sergeant—to Valdaire and over the mountains; when the road turns north, it forks; the east fork is what you want. In Valdaire I can find out which merchants are headed east to Bannerlith; you can travel with them safely enough, and then, as I said, turn aside once in Lyonya to find Aliam. Send a courier ahead to Kieri—to the king. You do have some of your people with you, don't you?"

"I do," Andressat said. He glanced aside at Stammel. "Send your man to the stable to find Daslin and bring him here."

Arcolin shook his head. "My pardon, my lord, but I have reason to keep him close. An inn servant can go." He rang the handbell on the table.

The next day, Andressat and his servants rode with Arcolin and Stammel on the road to Valdaire. A three-day march, it was but a two-day ride with a change of horses. By then, Arcolin was sure that Andressat's sergeant could find the way to Lyonya; the man had traveled to Valdaire before and even over the mountains once on the count's business.

"South trade road, yes, sir. I never took it, but you say it's well-marked. But how do I find Lord Halveric's place?"

"Ask one of the Lyonyan rangers. I can see it in my head, but I can't think how to tell you." Arcolin wrote a note to Aliam and another the man could show to anyone in authority in Lyonya, explaining that the king knew the Count of Andressat and this was his courier. "Go ahead of him, so they know he's on the way and can prepare a welcome."

When they reached Valdaire, the winter quarters compound was empty and clean; the gate guard seemed to be expecting them and made no difficulty about unlocking the gates. Arcolin invited Andressat and his men to stay with them, but the count looked at the bare, swept rooms, the plain furniture, and asked where to find a good inn.

"White Dragon, foot of the hill." Arcolin pointed. "I'm going there shortly, if you want a guide, but I'm putting these horses up first." Andressat shook his head and rode off down the hill.

The next morning, Arcolin visited his banker. Kavarthin seemed glad to see him, but then—Arcolin told himself—bankers usually were glad to see those who arrived with money or letters of credit. Arcolin handed over Kostin's letter and explained the extent of what his cohort would be bringing in to sell.

"And I have news for you," Kavarthin said. "When my son looked into your factor's books, he found the man had been less than perfectly honest, as we suspected. Did you get the letters I sent?" Arcolin nodded. "Good—mail from the east has been dilatory this year, and I was not sure. Well, then. Your factor was cheating you, both years Phelan did not come south. My son has recovered from him a large sum, rather than drag him before the court, where the fees would cost you most of it."

Arcolin suspected that the son's fee for this service would be almost as large, but it saved him having to appear in court. "Thank you," he said. "And your son—is he here?"

"Not today, no. I sent him on business—but I will give him your thanks. I assume you will need a letter of credit to take north."

"Yes," Arcolin said. "I must attend Autumn Court, and I need court clothes." He grinned at Kavarthin. "They tell me I cannot become formally Lord of the North Marches without a fancy robe edged in fur and a ruffled shirt."

Kavarthin smiled back. "Well, Captain—my lord Captain, I suppose that will be next season—you may find you enjoy such clothes. I'm certain you will enjoy your new rank. Most men do." He glanced at the sleeves of his traditional banker's black gown, where four narrow rows of velvet decorated the black cloth.

Arcolin had not noticed them before and was moved to ask. "If it is not impertinent—and forgive my ignorance—what does that signify?"

Kavarthin smiled. "That I am of the first degree in the guild. And this—" He pointed to the ring on his finger. "—this says I am Guildmaster here in Valdaire. All members of the Moneychangers' Guild answer to me." His smile broadened. "At a certain profit to me, of course."

Arcolin remembered the merchant stripped of his Guild membership in Cortes Vonja. "What happens to those you dismiss?"

Kavarthin shrugged. "It matters nothing to me. Of all the trades, my lord Captain, the trade of money itself must be most closely observed. It is too easy to cheat, too easy to shave a coin or pass false coinage, too easy to take as one's own the money entrusted to us by others. We must be diligent, we must be honest, and we must be unfailingly harsh with those who lie to or steal from those who trust them. Else no one will trust any of us, and when that trust fails, we are all back to trading a cow for two pigs or a shirt for a loaf of bread. Commerce would cease; cities would fall; it would be worse chaos than Siniava's War. And so I, and the other city Guildmasters, keep watch over our guild members."

And who kept watch over the Guildmasters? Arcolin did not like to ask, but Kavarthin was already answering.

"You will wonder who watches over us—we also are men, and all are tempted at some time or other. At any time, members of my guild, or certain other guilds, may demand to go through our accounts, and even count what is in our vaults. If I were not honest, this would keep me so, for the penalty for a Guildmaster's dishonesty is unpleasant in the extreme." He paused, his nose wrinkling. "Public torture and death. It is that serious."

Arcolin spent the rest of the day preparing for the cohort's arrival and buying the few supplies he and Stammel would need on their ride to Vérella.

CHAPTER TWENTY-ONE

Arcolin and Stammel rode away from Valdaire several days before the cohort was due to arrive. They made an early start and by midday were well above the city. The air was already crisper, and a cool breeze slid down the mountains toward them.

They switched to their spare mounts and rode on. That night they avoided the clutter of wagons and animals, the noise and smells of the one caravansary, and camped higher on the mountain slope, the pass itself looming above them. It was chilly but quiet, peaceful. When the horses had been grained and hobbled, Arcolin unrolled their blankets on a soft stretch of ground, and they ate supper looking back down the Vale of Valdaire.

"I can see it in my mind," Stammel said. He had been quiet all afternoon. "We're up above the road, around the bend from the noise . . . and that way is Valdaire . . . it's getting dark; we'll see— I'd see the lights soon, even from here."

"D' you remember the first time you saw it, Stammel?" Arcolin asked.

"Oh, yes." Stammel smiled. "Just a lad I was then, a recruit who thought he knew more than he did. I'd seen Vérella and thought I knew all about cities. Mountains, too, I thought I knew. And then we came over the pass, and the Vale of Valdaire opened out below, all the way to the sea, it seemed, and a southern breeze came up with smells I'd never imagined. I've seen it on their faces every year since, the northern recruits."

"I saw it first from the west," Arcolin said. "You know I came from the Westmounts. Very different view, walking in from Czardas. Lived there a year, off and on . . . but I never really knew it until I'd gone north and come back, over the pass."

"I suppose . . . now . . . there's no chance my sight will come back, is there, sir?" Stammel's voice held no complaint, only resignation. He lay stretched out on the ground, hands behind his head.

"I don't know," Arcolin said. "There's always a chance of healing."

"If the gods choose," Stammel said. "The Captain of Tir—I saw him in Cortes Vonja." Arcolin waited. "He said Tir must be pleased with me, but he said, too, that I should face the reality: I was blind, and would always be blind."

"Tir doesn't heal eyes?" Arcolin asked.

"No, sir. Or, the Captain said, maybe if a Blademaster—closest thing Tirians have to paladins—but not the same, really." Stammel turned on his side. "Captain, if I don't—if I'm not ever going to see again—I can't really be your senior sergeant. You need someone who can see what the troops are doing, in a battle. See if the merchant's giving good weight, spot trouble in the street."

"Like scare off forty or fifty enemies by standing there shooting them one by one without looking at them?"

"That—was different. I don't know what that was."

"*You*, Stammel. That was you and your years of experience. Think if our troops could use crossbows at night—shoot accurately at sounds."

"It's still not the same." Stammel sat up and faced Arcolin directly. With the angle of light, Arcolin could see the cloudiness deep in his eyes, not the same as the film old men got. "And the Captain said I should tell you I want to quit, but—but I don't want to. But I should. For the Company."

"It's not your Company," Arcolin said. "It's mine now." Even as he said it, he knew that was wrong. It *was* Stammel's Company—not his to command, but his in the same way it was Arcolin's, by right of all those years. He couldn't unsay it, so he went on. "And I think you are good for it, blind or not. There are things you can't do—well, there are things I can't do, and one of them is hit a target with a cross-bow with both eyes open, let alone blind. I can't stop you from quitting—you've long since earned the right to retire, and a pension with it—but I don't want you to retire. I think the Captain of Tir was wrong. You've had a hard time; you will have a hard time, but you are and always will be a soldier and of value here. Besides, there are other sources of healing. A Girdish paladin—"

"You're Girdish, Captain."

"Yes—so?"

"So maybe it's different with Girdish, but I—I don't think I should change allegiance, just for the hope of seeing again." Despite the words, longing colored his voice.

"I can't think of a better reason, if you wanted to," Arcolin said. "There's nothing dishonorable about wanting your sight back." Stammel said nothing more that evening.

The rest of the trip went smoothly enough—always less rain at this time of year—and they reached Valdaire with several days to spare before the Autumn Evener.

As they rode up to the gates, one of the guards said, "There he is! Sir, a message for you."

"For me?" Arcolin scowled.

"Yes, sir. Duke Verrakai asked if you would care to stay at Ver-rakai House. Said there's a message from the king."

Which king? Possibly Kieri, he thought. He had not heard from Kieri since writing to him about Stammel's blindness.

"Where is it?" Arcolin asked. The guard gave directions and waved them on.

The streets seemed normally busy, the people in them not as tense as they had been before. When they came to Verrakai House, Arcolin realized he had seen it before but never noticed it, though it faced the palace walls, across a wide street. Plain, unremarkable, and always—now he thought of it—shuttered tightly. Now the upper-floor shutters stood open, though the day was cool. Blue-striped curtains hung at either side. As the horses came to a stop, the door opened. A man in Verrakai livery looked up at them.

"Yes?"

"Captain Arcolin to see Dorrin—the Duke," Arcolin said.

The man smiled. "She was hoping you'd be here yesterday, sir.

Just let me get someone to take the horses—" He turned and yelled something into the house. Arcolin dismounted and held the reins of Stammel's horse while he, too, dismounted. Soon they heard footsteps coming, hard heels on a tile or stone floor. First was a young man in Verrakai blue with the rose and white colors of Mahieran at his shoulder, clearly a squire.

"I'm Beclan Mahieran," he said. "M'lord's on the way but bade me make you welcome. I'll take your horses." He took the reins from Arcolin just as Dorrin appeared behind him.

Dorrin in blue and gray instead of maroon and white was still Dorrin, that familiar sharp-boned face, dark hair pulled back. "Arcolin! Falk's Oath, I've missed you!" They clasped arms, and then she looked at Stammel. "Stammel—what happened?" A sharp glance at Arcolin.

"A tale best told in private," Arcolin said.

When they were inside, sitting at ease in one of the ground-floor rooms, with refreshments spread on a low table, Dorrin said, "I see you're blind, Sergeant—and yet I see no scars." She had handed him a mug of sib.

Stammel answered as frankly as always. "I don't understand it all, my lord. It started with that fellow Korryn—" He and Arcolin together told of the merchant's capture, Stammel's realization that one of the caravan guards was the man branded at the stronghold years before, the attack on those in the prison office, Stammel's collapse.

"They tell me a demon invaded," Stammel said, "but it didn't—I don't think that's what a demon would feel like. It was just fire and a voice."

"Tell me everything," Dorrin said. Her expression was grim.

"Dorrin?" Arcolin had not expected that tone from her.

"Jandelir, I have learned things about my family I do not want to remember, but I must. This Korryn—I never met him either, but from what Stephi and Sejek said, he might have been a bush-relative of mine. Tall, dark—"

"Ugly," Stammel said. "Not like you."

"That's kind, Sergeant Stammel, but hardly to the point. You say—both of you—that he boasted of having lent himself or given himself to someone better or more powerful."

"Yes."

"Some members of my family were able to transfer themselves—their minds, their souls—from one body to another. Typically, they weakened the victim—I think by slow poison—and then with another poison induced a fever. To those watching, it seemed a crisis, much like comes with lung-fever, and when the victim was near death, they could invade. I don't know how, exactly. I only know it happened. The magery in our family is not merely inherited, Jandelir—it is continued, generation after generation, by those who put themselves in their children's bodies. And others, as well. If Korryn *were* a Verrakai bastard—if he accepted, for some reason, a Verrakai invader—then what you faced was a fully trained adult magelord. Though I have not seen this before, he might have been powerful enough to attempt a transfer to Stammel, even as he died—living in Stammel, hoping to drive Stammel out."

"He had a fever," Arcolin said. "It started at once—when his eyes turned red. But I thought that was from the choking."

"It could have been. I don't know. Sergeant—" She turned to him. "You saved more than yourself when you fought that invader off. If you had been defeated, you would not have died—your body, at least—and you would have been a secret weapon. Against Arcolin, against Tsaia, and certainly against me. Look at me."

Stammel faced Dorrin; she peered into his face, hers intent. "What are you looking for?" Arcolin asked.

"Any sign that some part of that being lurks inside. If it is there, and strong enough, Stammel could not tell us."

"You mean—I could still be invaded?"

"Possibly," Dorrin said. "Sergeant, I've known you for what, fifteen, sixteen years? I've seen you work with recruits, seen you train, seen you in battle. And there is something . . . different. Do you feel anything?"

"I'm blind," Stammel said.

"And yet . . . you're not blind the way other men are. I've seen blind soldiers—former soldiers—before. Leaving aside your ability to use a crossbow, there's a difference. Your eyes are neither fixed nor wandering the way most blind men's eyes are."

"They wandered more at first," Arcolin said.

"I want to try something," Dorrin said. "Here—" She pulled the ducal chain over her head. "Put out your hand. Hold this."

"What will it do to him?" Arcolin asked.

"Possibly nothing. Possibly—" She stopped, mouth open. Arcolin felt his skin crawl. Stammel had gone rigid; his hand trembled; his fingers twitched toward and then away from the jewel on his palm. Sweat burst from his forehead, ran down his face.

"Not—again—you—bastard!" Stammel said. "Take it, Captain—take it away!"

Arcolin snatched the jewel from his hand and gave it to Dorrin, but Stammel's taut expression did not ease.

"It's—he's—" His body jerked; he tumbled from the chair to the floor.

Dorrin came alight; Arcolin recoiled into his chair, nearly overturning it. Her radiance filled the room, golden as afternoon sunlight, and she had drawn her sword before he could say a word.

"Get OUT!" she said. Oddly, her voice was calm. "Verrakai karakkin tsam! Tsam!"

Stammel, red-faced and sweating, crouched on the floor, his eyes and mouth tight-shut, muscles straining. Dorrin put the sword to his throat, lifted his chin. "Verrakai!! Tsam! Forzam!"

Another light bloomed, this one crackling and spitting like witch-fire, a greener yellow than hers.

"No, you will *not*," she said. "I have the full magery; you are a shadow. Begone." And then more of the words Arcolin did not know.

A throat-tearing shriek from Stammel, and out his mouth came a gobbet of dark blood and a spurt of the green-yellow light. Then the light failed, and he collapsed on the floor. Dorrin's light slowly faded; Arcolin scrambled forward. "Dammit, Dorrin, what did you do? It's *Stammel*, not some monster."

"It's Stammel *now*," Dorrin said. She knelt beside him, laid her hand on Stammel's forehead. "It's gone. He's safe now. Falk's blade, he was strong, to have survived the attack at all."

"He's damn near dead now." Stammel breathed, but in rapid grunts; Arcolin glared at her. "If he'd died . . ."

"Jandelir, there was no time. It knew me; it knew where it was; it knew how to access the patterns of power in this house. If you had seen what I have—children inhabited by ancient mages, men tortured beyond endurance to provide the blood power—bones—this is better for him, I swear to you. He is safe; it is gone forever."

Stammel's breathing eased. Arcolin sat back. Dorrin looked tired and worn, much like the comrade he had known so many years and yet not like. "You are different, too," he said.

"Yes. As I wrote, the Knight-Commander released the magery that had long been bound, and there was . . . more than any of us antici-pated. Yet I am the same, in the eyes of those renegades of my family we have not yet captured: I refuse the blood magery. I am true to Falk. And a loyal vassal of King Mikeli, as I hope you will be."

Arcolin had forgotten, for the time, about the coming ceremony. He took a long breath, watching Stammel's breathing, his color. He looked now like someone who might wake soon. "I have to find a tai-lor," he said. "Someone who knows about court dress."

"Ah, that," Dorrin said. She grinned. "Kieri sent you a present— or rather, he had it sent for you. His court robes. He had his ducal robe with him, of course, but the others were stored in the north, and shipped down here for you. The king's messenger will tell you which to bring. It will not take much to make his other court clothes fit you: you're much of a height, and not that different in build. And you said you had something for me to take to him?"

That jogged his memory. "Cal Halveric's sword," he said. "We re-covered it, found it with other blades being transported illegally. I had it blessed by a Captain of Falk. The scabbard was lost; the Cap-tain had a new one made, to make it easier to carry."

Stammel opened his eyes. "Where am I this time? And when?"

"It has not even been a half-glass," Arcolin said. "You're with me, and you're in Dorrin Verrakai's house in Vérella."

"I need to get up," Stammel said. Arcolin stood and took his hand. "I thought it was the burning again."

"It almost was," Dorrin said. "But my relatives, even the worst, are obedient to one they believe has the right to rule them. Unfortu-nately, that's not the king, but for now—they obey me." She turned to Stammel. "Sergeant, I expect you'll be tired and need extra sleep. You've endured a great ordeal, and such things leave no one un-touched. Let me have someone guide you to the bathing rooms so you can clean up and then rest."

Stammel did indeed look worn out, Arcolin thought. "I can guide him."

"Certainly," Dorrin said. "Follow me, then." She led the way through the house. "This place was full of traps when I first came; it's safer now, but I'm still using the scullery for a bathing room. I had water put on to heat this afternoon, anticipating your arrival." As they passed through the kitchen, she said, "Jaim, go find their packs in the stable and bring them in, then run to the grange and ask Marshal Tamis to come. Efla, we'll need a supper for the sergeant."

"A Marshal?" Arcolin said.

Beclan came in the back door before Dorrin could answer; he had their packs and quickly took down a bath basin from the wall rack.

"Warm water," Dorrin said to Beclan, then turned to Arcolin. "A precaution merely," she said. "This house was steeped in Verrakai evil for generations; the Marshals and I have cleansed it, but in Stammel's present condition, if there is any lingering evil, it might try to invade again. I want the Marshal's advice; it might be better for him to stay at the grange."

"I'd rather stay here," Stammel said. "With the captain and you."

"I understand," Dorrin said. "And if the Marshal thinks it's safe, you'll be welcome. At least, you will bathe and eat here, and I will have a room prepared."

By the time Stammel and Arcolin had bathed and dressed in clean uniforms, Marshal Tamis had arrived. Dorrin told the story with additions from Stammel and Arcolin. Tamis nodded at the end.

"I think he will be safe here, my lord Duke, though I would not put him in a room alone. Let one of your servants or squires stay with him, if you and the captain need to be elsewhere. As for his sight, I cannot answer whether anything can be done. If the Marshal-General were in Vérella, we could ask her, but she's gone back to Fin Panir."

"It's early," Dorrin said, "but I think you should rest, Stammel, if you can."

"I agree," Tamis said. "He's the only one who's survived an invasion, isn't he?"

"One small boy," Dorrin said. "I was able to intervene before the transfer was complete. But holding down, controlling an invader for so long . . ."

Stammel yawned. "Sorry, my lord, Marshal."

"Let's get you to bed, then. I need to talk to Jandelir, Stammel, but I'll have someone in the room with you, if you need anything."

Arcolin watched as Stammel lay down, falling into what looked like normal sleep within a few breaths.

"Extraordinary," Marshal Tamis said. He turned to Arcolin. "And congratulations to you—I understand you're to be confirmed as lord of the north to replace Kieri Phelan."

"Yes," Arcolin said.

"I hope you'll visit my grange—with your sergeant—while you're still in the city. Both of you have stories to tell that would do my yeomen good to hear. Not before the ceremony, of course, but after."

"We'll come," Arcolin said. "But I don't know when—"

"Any time—give me a day's warning if you can." With a bow to Dorrin, he left.

"Come upstairs, Jandelir," Dorrin said. "The old duke's study's safe enough now." She led the way, and he followed up the broad stairs into a large room furnished with a few simple chairs and a plain table half-covered with neat stacks of scrolls and books. It didn't look the way he'd imagined an old family's study. "It was more impressive when I first saw it," Dorrin said. "But everything was full of traps. Here—have a seat. These chairs may be plain, but they're safe."

Arcolin stared at her. A thousand questions raced through his mind, along with a rush of fear; even when she seemed the old Dorrin, she wasn't. He cleared his throat and said the first ordinary thing that came to mind.

"I don't know anything about court ceremony. All I had to do was take and receive messages."

"You're still ahead of where I was," Dorrin said, chuckling. She had taken a chair across the table from him. "Remember how I avoided any contact with the court, lest I meet my relatives?" Arcolin nodded. "Then I had to come to the coronation and be confirmed there, as a duke no less. I knew nothing: the protocol, the people, the dress."

"I'm sure you did well," Arcolin said, still struggling with his mixture of relief in Stammel's recovery and fear of her power.

"Like a puppet," Dorrin said. "I wore what they told me, went where they told me, said what the others said. Falk's honor—it was terrifying at first, but then I realized more than half of them were scared of me. A Verrakai. Born magelord, using magery—they had to know that, just as I'd had the prince's permission to use it. And then the aftermath—" She explained about the attack she had foiled and the king's pardon. It did not make Arcolin any more comfortable. "It's better now," she said, "You've noticed my senior squire; he's the king's cousin. The king's pressured them to accept me, but most are still so formal. I've missed you, Jandelir. The way we could talk, back north or in camp. I have no one like that now."

"I've missed you and Cracolnya both—and at least I've still got Cracolnya. It's not good, your being so alone. Will you marry?"

"Marry! Falk's Oath, no! Why would I? I'm too old to bear a child, and don't want to anyway. Ganarrion—distant cousin, cleared of treason and now back with the Royal Guard—will be my heir. I don't want more complications, but I'd like someone—someone I can trust absolutely, who was never under Verrakai control—just to talk with. My people are improving, but they were ruled by blood magic for years. I have Selfer and my squires, but . . ."

"And I wanted to talk to you about that," Arcolin said. "Selfer and that cohort. It's rightly mine now, you know."

She stared. "I hadn't thought of that. You're right; if you've got the Company, then that cohort is yours. I've been paying—could I just hire them?"

Arcolin shook his head. "I need more force in the south, Dorrin. The way things are down there, one cohort is too weak, and gives me too little flexibility. There's plenty of work, but for larger units. Trying to find and replace a whole cohort this winter? No. I need them back . . . unless it's critical for you."

"No—though I trust them more than my own militia, my militia's improved by having their example. I'll miss . . . it's my last connection to my whole life, Arcolin."

"If a veteran wants to stay with you, I won't argue," Arcolin said. "Except Selfer—I can't afford to lose a captain."

"He wants to get back to the Company," Dorrin said. "He asked for leave to spend Midwinter Feast up north. You have lost Siger already, though. Once we got to Chaya, he told Kieri he wanted to stay. He came from Lyonya originally."

"I knew that but hadn't thought of it in years. I'll miss him," Arcolin said. "He was with Kieri before I was. But there's still Hofrin.

And Stammel's success with crossbows suggests to me that we could expand the archery units into the regular infantry."

"Well, back to your court appearance," Dorrin said. "Let's see how well Kieri's things fit you, while I explain the ritual."

"Do I have to bow to you because you're a duke?"

"No. But you do have to defer. And you do have to understand the argument that's ended with you being made a count instead of a duke."

"A count? I thought I'd start as baron."

"The North Marches are too big and too important to be a baron's grant. In fact, by size and position, it should be a dukedom, as it was. But because you're still an unknown quantity to most of these people, and the population's small, they're unwilling to go that far. Count's the middle choice. That means you won't have to take the sleeves off Kieri's count's robe. Be glad it's the Autumn Court, not Midsummer—I nearly suffocated in a ducal robe."

"But—ribbons at the knee?"

"Kieri did it. You can too."

The thought of Kieri Phelan in court dress with short breeches, ribbons at his knees, and those ridiculous court shoes . . . Arcolin wished he'd seen it.

His own appearance in court went more smoothly than he'd feared. As a "count-nominate," not yet confirmed in rank, he waited behind the others, as the nobles—herded like errant sheep by the Master of Ceremonies—were urged into the right order in the procession. Dukes in front, then counts, then barons, the more senior titles in front of the more recent. He would be the lowest-ranking count, after his investiture.

Bells rang; trumpets blared; ahead of him the line edged forward. Another count-nominate—for the established county of Konhalt, whose count had been attainted as a Verrakai supporter—and two barons-nominate, both heirs of men who had died in the past year, waited with Arcolin. Behind each, a servant carried the court robe, carefully folded, and another held the staff with the nominate's pennant showing the mark and colors.

When the nobles were all in place, ranged on either side of the hall, the nominates were led in by the Lord Herald in order of seniority. Duke Mahieran presented count-nominate Konhalt to the king and Council; when he had made his oath of fealty to the king, the king put on him the chain of office, kissed his forehead. When he stood again, the servant helped him into his robe, and Mahieran led him to his place in the row of counts, who moved aside for him.

Arcolin came next. Dorrin, as his sponsor, proclaimed him to the king and led him forward. He knelt, made his vows, received the chain of office and the kiss, and then felt the weight of the court robe on his shoulders. As he was the lowest-ranking count, only barons had to shift position to give him room.

The barons-nominate went through their investitures without incident, and when the king declared the ceremony over, they all moved on to the reception rooms. Arcolin had expected to find himself isolated among the other counts, but the dukes he'd met while carrying messages from Kieri all came to congratulate him.

"We need someone strong in the North Marches," Duke Marrakai said. "Someone who knows the territory, who has troops already there. Of course we all have sons who might like a grant of their own, but you're far more qualified than any of *my* brood." From the emphasis, it was clear Marrakai thought his own brood more qualified than anyone else's.

Arcolin felt out of place at first, but by the end of the day, being addressed as "my lord Count" and chatting with other counts and dukes as if he were, in truth, a noble of Tsaia, felt normal. He sensed no real hostility. For all the opportunity the North Marches offered, the dangers of its position next to Pargun, the history of orc attacks and invasions, meant that second thoughts had cooled the interest of many of the lords and their sons.

He could not help but notice another factor: barons, counts, and even dukes introducing their families to him, particularly those families including daughters of marriageable age and sons who might benefit from a few years as someone else's squire. He was careful to give no immediate encouragement, but thinking ahead—Kieri had had squires, and they had been helpful. Dorrin had squires now, all dukes' children. He would need squires. A wife, though . . . he was not ready to consider that. Though the girls, in their best court dress, were certainly lovely, he could not imagine any of them being content in the north while he was away in the south every year. As well, he did not yet grasp the undercurrents within the court; a hasty alliance could be disastrous for him and for his land.

His land. He thought that now without hesitation, automatically. His land, his people, his Company . . . his king, in that palace. He wondered when Kieri had felt it normal for the first time . . . Kieri had been younger and perhaps had imagined it before, as he himself had not. And how was Kieri coming to grips with a change every bit as great as his own? Had Kieri chosen a wife?

In the next few days, Arcolin dealt with the necessary business: the banker, the judicar, a courier to ride south and tell Burek what had happened and where he was going, another to ride north at least as far as the Duke's—no, *his*—south border and let his people know he was on the way. He and Stammel paid their visit to Tamis's grange; it was packed full that evening, and Stammel's story brought gasps and tears to many.

Finally, Arcolin and Stammel rode north, carrying with them the royal warrants of Arcolin's title. At Burningmeed, his subjects gathered to hear the proclamation of his title in the grange; they cheered him loudly. Vestin paraded the southern cohort for his inspection. The veterans stared at Stammel, but said nothing, and cheered Arcolin after the inspection.

The next day the two rode on into lowering clouds, a miserable cold drizzle sifting through the trees. Sodden leaves quieted the horses' hooves, and the bare fields of farmsteads, with cattle huddled together but still steadily grazing, suggested endurance more than abundance. Arcolin looked at each, noting the soundness of the buildings, the condition of fences, the apparent management of fields and orchards, the condition of the road itself. Here and there it was clear the cohort had done roadwork; and in some places he could see where work needed to be done. He let himself imagine how it could be in two hands of years . . . four . . . as he continued the work Kieri had begun. Sound roads, passable in all seasons. Sturdy houses, ample barns filled with grain and fodder, fat cattle, heavy-fleeced sheep, trees loaded with fruit or nuts . . . his horse stumbled a little and jolted him back to the present.

"Sir?" Stammel asked. He had heard the horse stumble, no doubt. He was sitting his horse upright as always and had no doubt felt the downward slope Arcolin had missed by daydreaming.

"I was thinking," Arcolin said, "when I should have been watching the road. We should reach Duke's East later today."

As he came in sight of Duke's East, he reined in. A sharp wind blew from the north through trees bare but for a few stubborn leaves. They had ridden through heavier cold rain earlier, but those clouds were behind them now. Ahead was the hard blue of a winter sky.

"We're close, aren't we?" Stammel asked.

"Yes. Looking down at Duke's East—I can see Kolya's orchard—leafless now—her cottage—the bridge over the stream—" He glanced over at Stammel, who looked gray and pinched. "Are you all right?"

"I can see it in my mind," Stammel said. "But what I see is not what other men see." He cleared his throat. "Does it look different, now that it's yours?"

"I was thinking how familiar it was," Arcolin said. "A comfort to come back and see this shape of land, those trees, the village . . . but yes, in a way it does look different." It had been Kieri's worry, and now it was his.

"It will always look the same to me, if . . . sorry, sir. Let's get on."

They rode down the slope. Kolya's cottage had a plume of smoke out the chimney, and several people gleaning late apples in her orchard turned to look at the riders. Waving, they ran toward the lane; Arcolin reined in.

Kolya was first to speak. "Sir, we heard you were the new duke—is it true?"

"Not duke," Arcolin said. "Count only, at this time."

"Did you see—" She stopped abruptly, staring at Stammel. He sat his horse with the same composure he had shown from the beginning. Someone else started to speak; Kolya's gesture was emphatic and hushed them all.

"We need to get out to the stronghold," Arcolin said. "I'll want to meet with the Councils of both Duke's East and Duke's West tomorrow; you need to see the new warrants, and we'll talk then. If you could let Mayor Fontaine know, and send a messenger to Duke's

West. Right now—we're still damp from the past few days and could use a hot fire and dry clothes."

"Yes, sir. Of course." Her eyes never left Stammel's face; his expression never changed. "Welcome home, both of you."

Stammel nodded at that, then legged his horse into a quick walk. Arcolin caught up with him and led the way over the bridge, through the village—waving at those who waved, but not slowing.

He heard the trumpet's call borne on the north wind when they were in sight of the stronghold; he could just see the sun glinting from helmets. He was home . . . his home now. He looked around at the wide, windswept fields, the distant line of scrubby trees, the hills to the north and west. He would ride in, and someone would take his horse, and when he walked into the inner court . . . it was all his now. For one last instant, panic swept over him—he could not do it all, he could never be as good a lord as Kieri had been. Then it blew away on the crisp winter wind, on the memory of that summer's campaign, when he had done what he thought right. He was Count of the North Marches. It was enough. *He* was enough.

CHAPTER TWENTY-TWO

Lyonya, near Halveric Steading

Many days on the road had confirmed Jeddrin Count Andressat's opinion that he did not like travel. He took no pleasure in novelty of place or person, and he was all too aware of duties he was not performing while he was gone. A ruler should stay at home, with his own people.

His thoughts ran on familiar lines. Foreigners were ill-bred; travel obliged one to mingle with such people, even traveling with one's own servants and guards. He had never, in his entire life, been over the mountains to the north, a place of barbarians and those who gave themselves ridiculous titles. Only a few in the north held titles for which he had any regard; he knew their lineage as he knew his own. The new king of Tsaia—well enough, the best they could do, all things considered. But Fintha, with no nobility—ridiculous. Three of the Eight Kingdoms—Pargun and Kostandan and Dzordanya— had kings, but of no lineage that meant anything. He found no trace of ancient blood in them, no indication that their authority came from Old Aare.

He could respect, he had told himself, an honest merchant, if such existed, or a mercenary captain like Aliam Halveric or Jandelir Arcolin. Such men had expertise, and if they did not presume to consider themselves equals of their betters, he gave them the respect they deserved. That was the duty and responsibility of a noble, after all: to recognize worth and reward it.

But necessity demanded that he travel, and travel incognito at that. He must seek aid from someone he had misjudged as—to be honest—he had misjudged himself. He had bowed and scraped like any commoner—which, he reminded himself yet again, he was. He had slept in ordinary inns—hideous places in which he'd been forced to show coin before every mug of ale, let alone a bed for the night. Even in Valdaire, where, had he used his own name, the bowing and scraping would have gone the other way.

He huddled in his cloak as another autumn rain blew down from the mountains, roaring in the trees overhead. A horrible country, worse even than the pass over the mountains. Too many trees, blocking the view in every direction, closing him in. Mud and not rock under his horse's hooves, storms in the air that could not be seen until they were upon him. Only a few villages and fields—unfamiliar crops in the fields, unfamiliar fruit trees instead of the neat terraces of vines and oilberries on his own land. Green everywhere, too much green.

If not for the vision of his own land and its fields and vineyards, his own people toiling there, the smell of the herbs strong under the sun, the clatter of goats' hooves on the rocks . . . if not to save them, who had done no wrong and deserved no harm . . . he would not have stirred from Andressat, from those golden hills, those rocky bastions, summer's heat that dried the creeks, winter rain that filled them. He ached in every bone and cursed the day he'd first heard the name of Duke Kieri Phelan.

Aliam Halveric listened to the rain drumming on the stable roof, breathed in the fragrance of horses, good hay, oiled leather, and a hint of ripening fruit from the trees trained along the inner court wall, and wondered when it was he'd become an old man. Estil insisted he wasn't old, and she didn't seem old—barring the silver strands in her dark hair—but he *felt* old, joints aching, responsibilities almost too heavy to bear. His grandchildren sprouted day by day, it seemed, rising up around him like saplings around an old storm-blasted tree.

And now he had to deal with the Count of Andressat, whose

envoy had announced the count's intention to visit on his way to Chaya to see the king. The king. Kieri. Once his servant, his squire, dear to him as a son or brother. His rival, at times, but always that bond of friendship. And now king, but king so much later than he should have been, because of Aliam. That still hurt, hurt enough that he sagged onto a chest, leaning on the wall and staring out at the water streaming on the courtyard stones. Kieri had forgiven him; he knew Kieri bore no grudge. But he could not forgive himself. He had known, and he had done nothing. Oh, he'd had reason enough to do nothing, but no reasons seemed enough now, when Aliam laid out for the thousandth time the consequences of old decisions.

He shivered, as a chill breeze blew damply into the barn, and rubbed hands no longer as callused and hard as the summer before, the summer he had still trained daily with his soldiers. He could not sit here all day. He had work to do; Andressat would be here today or tomorrow.

Across the courtyard, where rain now fell more gently, a girl peeked from the main keep door and then, apron flung over her head, dashed to the stables. "Grandfather! Grandmother wants you!" Aliam sighed and pushed himself up. He remembered the birth of this child's mother, and now the child of that child ran light-footed to his side, throwing her wet arms around him, grinning up with Estil's grin. Pain stabbed him. He was old, too old, and what would he leave this child?

In the main hall, tables had been laid. Estil smiled at his expression. "You said he was proud, Aliam. And he's been traveling incognito; his pride will be rubbed raw. We shall guest him as he feels he deserves, and he will reach Kieri in a better mood."

Aliam had to smile. "You always thought a little humility was good for proud men."

"I did. I do. But he's old, you said. And he's a guest."

"I'm old," Aliam said. The weight fell back on his spirit again; he could feel himself sagging.

Estil looked at him, a long considering look. "Do you miss the summer campaigns? Does it seem dull here?"

"No, it's not that." The years when he had taken his soldiers south each spring, the raw excitement of campaigning mixed with the drudgery of it, seemed long ago, little bright images from a different person's memory. "It's not dull here," he went on, forcing a smile. "Not with the children and their mischief; not with you . . ."

"It's not like you to brood, Aliam. You were never a brooder, but you are not happy now."

"I'm old."

"You're no older than I am," she said. "You've been . . . strange . . . ever since last winter, when the . . . the paladin came." When the Lady of the Ladysforest had come, but they could not speak those words, for the Lady had locked their tongues on that.

"It's my fault," Aliam said. Tears stung his eyes. "If I had—"

"You couldn't know," Estil said, a hand on his arm. "You couldn't be sure. You had reasons . . ."

"Reasons!" Aliam said. The bitterness in his voice shocked him, and two of the servants passing through the hall turned to look at him and then hurried on. "Tammarion died because of me," he said more softly. "I'm the one who tutored Kieri in the courtesy of warriors and taught him how women fighters should be respected; it's not just the sword, but . . . if not for me he would surely have drawn it sometime or other. Their children would be alive, she would be alive, he would be whole."

"He is whole," Estil said. "You are the one who's not." Then her hand flew to her mouth, as if to take the words back, and her face paled.

Aliam looked at her. "I know. I know I'm not. I can't live with it, Estil, what I've done and not done. I'm sorry. I'm sorry for all of it, and that it can't be changed, and that I . . . can't go on."

"Aliam—"

He shook his head and moved past her. Up the stairs, each one harder to climb than the next, and into his study, where a bowl still held a sprig of undying apple blossom, a gift of the Lady. The scent should have refreshed him, but now . . . now it was another wound. He sat down heavily.

Estil could manage without him; she'd done it summer after summer, all those years. The steading was more hers than his; she had managed it for him with all the skill and grace a man could ask for. His sons were all alive, barring Seliam—more tears came when he thought of Seliam, killed in Aarenis. Cal had heirs of the body; his eldest son was as old now as Aliam had been when he hired his first soldier. Kieri certainly didn't need him; he would be only a constant reminder of what could have been, if Aliam had had the courage to say what he knew. He could trust Kieri to treat his family well, in matters of inheritance; that was all he could ask for.

All he had to do was make it through the Count of Andressat's visit, play the host as he'd done for so many others, and then . . . his imagination failed. Old men died so many ways. Their eyesight dimmed; they tripped down stairs and stumbled off walls. Their hearing dimmed; they did not hear stampeding herds, shouted warnings of danger. They fell off horses and broke their necks; they fell into rivers and drowned. He had to be sure it was not seen as anyone's fault; he wanted no more guilt carried by his family than they already bore.

On that resolution, he stood, feeling a little stronger now, breathed in the scent of apple blossom, and went out to find Estil striding along the hall looking angry. "There you are—"

"Is he come?" Aliam said. "I just remembered, he has a fondness for cakes sprinkled with that southern spice, the yellow one. I can't think of the name—"

"Figan," Estil said, diverted by a cookery problem. "We have some, yes. Cooked in or sprinkled on after, do you know?"

"I don't," Aliam said. "At his own house, he gave us such cakes. The flavor was more on the top, but baked in or added after, I can't say." He pushed away the memory of that day, when the count had made it so obvious how little he respected Kieri and he himself had done nothing about it.

"Mercan just came; the rain's stopped, and the count's just a few hours' ride away. I have just time if I start now . . . but Aliam, please—please don't—"

The smile came easier now, and must have looked natural, for Estil seemed to relax even as he spoke. "I'll get over it," he said. "Maybe you're right, and I am missing summers in Aarenis—all that heat, sweating and stinking in my armor—" He tried for a mocking tone and she chuckled. But he thought . . . all those ways to die. Old men slowed down; old men were easier to kill. Maybe he should go south again.

"I love you," she said. "And now I must get to the kitchen. Just check the guest chambers, will you? I've tried to make them as southern as I could, with things you brought back, but I don't know . . ." Her voice trailed away as she set off back downstairs.

Aliam looked into the guest chambers she'd set aside for Andressat, with hangings in Andressat's colors, piles of pillows re-covered in blue and gold, southern carpets spread on the floors. The rooms smelled of fresh herbs and a hint of rose essence. But out the windows, instead of Andressat's open plains and rocky slopes under the burning blue of the southern sky in summer, he saw the rich green of northern grass, summer pasture ending in a wall of forest, a forest so different from those in the south. He himself had found the south exotic, exciting, but he still loved this best; he still loved the cool deep shade under trees the size of houses, the creatures that lived in those woods. He suspected Andressat would find the north oppressive, that he had traveled unwillingly and thus with no intention of enjoying what he found. He would be stiff and difficult, as he had always been.

Estil Halveric and one of her daughters-in-law mixed the dough for sweetcakes in a flurry of activity that did nothing to ease Estil's mind about Aliam. Less than a year ago he had been the same vigorous, joyful companion she'd known for so many years. Balder, grayer, a little more stooped, perhaps, but by no means old, nor had he thought himself old. Just as she could outwork most of her daughters and her sons' wives, Aliam could outwork his sons and his daughters' husbands.

But lately . . . not just lately, but since that visit, and more since Kieri's coronation, Aliam had changed. He had less energy, spent more time resting by the fireside or sitting under a tree. She'd worried that he was sick, but he showed no signs of illness, just a strange lassitude. She'd thought perhaps he missed campaigning, missed the yearly trip to the south. For years he'd gone south every summer with his company to fight, and then, with no explanation, he'd stayed north the summer before, and this one.

She'd had no idea he blamed himself so harshly, so unfairly, for the deaths of Kieri's wife and children, for the delay in Kieri's restoration. And yet, day by day he did less, ate less, grew more and more remote . . .

It wouldn't do. It wouldn't do at all. Estil pinched off bits of dough, shaped them with practiced hands, sprinkled them with figan, and set them to bake, still thinking hard. It had started with that paladin, or with the Lady, and it had been about Kieri. One of them, surely, would help her. People could grieve to death; she knew that, but it was not going to happen to Aliam. Not while she lived.

The cakes were just out of the oven when she heard the sentry's warning call. "I must go," she said.

"Your apron! Your head scarf!" her daughter-in-law said. Estil looked and saw that more than her apron had smudges and streaks of flour from baking.

She dashed for the stairs; Aliam was on his way down. "I have to change," she said. "I'll be quick."

᠅

The rain had finally stopped, and late-afternoon light pierced the forest canopy. Somewhere ahead, more light suggested an opening. The Count of Andressat booted his tired horse onward. Probably some peasant's hut, or another miserable village, though if he were lucky . . .

Beyond the trees, a swath of green, vivid in the golden light, and a sizable stone keep, not a village . . . the count looked at it appraisingly. More than a bowshot from the forest wall, neat fences divided grazing land from plow. Cattle in this enclosure, horses in that. An orchard of what must be fruit trees. The keep itself looked nothing like his . . . but it was stone-built, to its credit, and the roofs were slate, not straw thatch.

A horn call rang out; he had been seen. Not recognized, of course; they would not know who he was until he announced himself. A small troop of men on horseback rode out the gates, keeping a disciplined order he approved. A pennant flew from a pole one of them carried—Halveric's colors.

As they neared, he saw that the man in the lead was Halveric himself. "My lord Count!" Halveric said. "Be welcome here!"

"You expected me today?" Jeddrin's brows rose. He had not seen anyone all day, or heard any horn signals.

"Your envoy gave us warning days ago, and one of my outguards sent word more than a glass since."

Andressat relaxed. A properly managed estate, then, and secure enough that he need not fear, as he had feared every day after leaving home, attack by brigands or other enemies.

"You will be tired from your journey," Halveric went on. "And I see the rain caught you this afternoon."

"It has rained every day since I came over the mountains," Andressat said. "It's a wonder the whole land isn't a sea." He looked more closely at Halveric. The man seemed much older than a few years would account for; he sat his horse stiffly, as if in pain. What had happened? Halveric was younger than he himself . . . he had always seemed so vigorous. "Your country house looks very comfortable."

An odd expression crossed Halveric's face. "Thank you," he said. "Come on in; Estil's ready to welcome you."

Estil. A brother? Surely not his wife . . . but in a few minutes he saw an outrageously tall woman, dark hair streaked silver, poised at the entrance to the hall. Halveric called her over, even as a servant held the count's horse. Northerners. Even Halveric, who had seemed so urbane and civilized in Andressat.

The count smoothed his mustaches and bowed over the lady's hand. "The honor is mine," he said. She had powdered her hand with something like flour; he wondered why.

After a hot bath and shave and haircut from Halveric's barber, Jeddrin Count of Andressat felt much better. Everyone here knew his name, though he didn't know all of them, and Halveric had welcomed him with appropriate ceremony. His assigned suite was large, graciously furnished, items from the south laid out to lend familiarity. Even, when he came out from his bath, a basket of warm spiced cakes—dusted with his favorite figan—waiting on the table in his bedchamber. True, out the window were northern fields and that forbidding forest, but his host had done his best.

And his host's wife. He had no way to address women who bore no title and yet were not servants . . . he could not just use her name, no matter that Halveric had suggested it. Traveling as he had been, he'd not met any lords' wives; the townswomen he'd seen had looked, to his eye, like ordinary people, just dressed differently.

Estil Halveric was taller than her husband, straight-backed where he was stooped, with an easy smile that yet had no hint of flirtatiousness. She looked strong, as if she instead of her husband could captain a troop. She moved briskly, yet with grace . . . he was used to women of position moving more slowly, languidly, yet perhaps that was the difference in climate.

He had already seen the hall where they would dine, the tables set in the same pattern they might have been at home, had it been a formal banquet. Halveric had asked if he preferred a quiet meal alone, but his curiosity was aroused. How would a northern lordling set out a banquet? How would they come in? Halveric had eaten with him, but only informally.

At the high table, he and Halveric and Halveric's wife and the two eldest sons and their wives . . . down the side tables, the other sons and daughters and spouses.

"It is the growing season," Halveric said. "We do not travel much then—and I was not sure you wished many to know of your errand, so I did not try to gather a large party. It was in no disrespect of your honor, my lord Count."

Andressat relaxed. No insult intended; a family meal merely. That was comfortable, and for a family meal, nicely laid out. Solid, good-quality dishes, southern ware, painted with flowers and birds, heavy silver, fine blown goblets and flagons, all laid on sun-bleached linen cloths. Herbs and flowers strewn the length of the tables. And the fare . . . he could hardly believe the northern lands produced such bounty. Platters of sliced meats, small birds spitted between unfamiliar vegetables on thin rods, roast fowl, fish, tureens of soup, bowls of vegetables, baskets of bread in three colors, small dishes of oilberries . . . all served at once, instead of discrete courses. Southern wines, white and red. Halveric had explained that as a courtesy to a guest who had traveled all day.

"What fish are these?" he asked Halveric. He had expected salted fish, if any, so far from the sea, but these were fresh.

"Our own," Halveric said. "Netted from the stream this morning. We call them speck-sides." He smiled. "I remembered your fondness for river-fish. Ours are smaller, but I thought you might like them."

"They're delicious." Andressat accepted another serving. "And those meats?" He pointed with his little finger, politely.

"Beef, mutton, roast pork. The birds are ground-chucks and of course chickens."

"And you raise all this here, yourself?"

"Estil does," Halveric said, gesturing to his wife. Andressat had to turn, and meet that broad smile.

"Aliam's been gone so much," she said. "He's left it to me, you see."

He didn't see, not completely. "I did not see any goats," he said. "Do you not have goats here?"

"Not here," she said. "Steadings closer to the mountains do. They are not happy in thicker forest."

He understood that. At home, goats throve on hillsides too steep or barren for cattle. "But you have sheep."

"Only in fenced pastures," she said. "They are too hard to find, if they get loose in the forest. We keep enough sheep for wool, and eat some mutton, but we depend more on cattle for meat, though we also hunt."

It had been long in Andressat since hunting could provide reliable food for table. "What game?" he said, turning to Halveric.

"Deer, mostly," Halveric said. "Wild boar, on occasion. And then birds . . . the ground-chuck, rather like your quail in the south, and a bird we call the toris, like your hill-pheasant, only much larger. Toris are rare; I don't hunt them anymore. They're quite beautiful."

Andressat tasted a little of each dish—all quite good. The wines were good, too; he recognized his own product, and remembered that Halveric had always bought directly from his factor. That was a nice compliment.

He watched the demeanor of those at the lower tables, pleasantly surprised to see more civilized behavior than he expected, completely unlike the common rooms of inns where he'd stayed on his journey. True, men and women sat together, but there was no unseemliness, and they all seemed courteous.

He had eaten as much as he wanted; he glanced along the high table to see how the others were doing, and Halveric immediately turned to him. "If you would care for a stroll and then dessert in private—"

"Yes, thank you."

Halveric rose; the others all rose with him, and Andressat followed Halveric out into the courtyard and into a garden enclosure he had not noticed with a suitable facility at one end.

"I will understand," Halveric said, "if you do not wish to tell me why you travel so far in such haste and incognito, but if I can be of assistance . . ."

Andressat looked up and around. No one in hearing, but the danger lay not only in humans, he knew. "It is a matter of grave import—"

"Of course," Halveric said. "You would not travel so far without great need."

"I find it amazing that you would leave so pleasant a home each year to risk danger in the south," Andressat said, waving a hand at the espaliered fruit trees. "You are a man of breeding, of family—if you had stayed here—"

"I would not have this land," Halveric said. "Lyonya is not like the south. You do know about the duality of sovereignty?"

"Of course," Andressat said. "But not how it forced you into the south."

"I wasn't forced, exactly," Halveric said. He sighed. Once more Andressat noticed how old he looked, his broad shoulders stooped. "By agreement with our elders, not only the elves but also the other elder races, human holdings in Lyonya may not increase. This is all of Halveric Holding, or Halveric Gift, as the elves prefer to call it. It would have gone to my elder brother, had he not preferred a life at court. But in dividing the heritance, he gave up the land to gain the wealth allowing him to live in Chaya. I could not support this—" He gestured broadly. "—by trading farm goods. And as a young man, I knew I had military ability. That skill was salable, once I had a reputation over the mountains."

"Will you return?"

"Me? No . . . I'm too old." Halveric sighed heavily. "My sons, maybe. Cal might. We have to do something; my people deserve it and they aren't all suited to this life."

Andressat looked around again. No visible eyes or ears; this little walled space should be secure. He hoped. "I am going to ask your king for aid," he said. "You remember that Alured the Black—"

"Yes," Halveric said, with a look of distaste.

"Now he styles himself Visla Vaskronin, Duke of Immer, and the new Duke of Fall confirms him—"

"Vaskronin? Where did he get that?"

"He claims from an ancestor." Andressat paused, trying to order his thoughts. "My archives are, I believe, the oldest and most complete in Aarenis. Those of Fall and Immer once contained records as old, but war and mischance befell them. Fall asked me, when first Alured-Vaskronin claimed Immer, for copies of my archives, to see if they agreed with Alured's claims. In the search for any that might be of use, I found . . . I found things I had not known." He glanced sideways. Halveric was leaning to look at something on the limb of one of the espaliered pears.

"I'm listening," Halveric said. He reached out and pinched something from the limb. "I listen better when my hands are busy."

"Well, then . . . I should have known everything in there, but I didn't. And the oldest were written long enough ago that the writing and the words are both difficult. It is no proper excuse, but my life has been busy; I never looked back more than a few hundred years until recently."

Halveric nodded, his gaze now fixed on a row of herbs. He rolled a fragrant leaf in his fingers.

"The earliest—" Andressat swallowed. He still found it hard to frame the words to describe what he'd read, the horror he'd felt, the urgency of his concern. "—the earliest are from Old Aare itself. I had no idea we had anything that old. There's a little glass pitcher supposedly from Old Aare, and a small tapestry hanging that was in my mother's room, but I always thought that was a fabrication. Nothing could last so long."

"Jeddrin," Halveric said, looking him in the eye. "Just tell me."

Andressat stiffened. But Halveric was right; he had been dancing around the core of it. "I found scrolls from Old Aare, describing what happened there, why people left—fled—to Aarenis and, more than that, across the Eastern Sea. Evil came to Aarenis before them; more came with them, and lingered even to this present day. The elder peoples left Aarenis, as that evil invaded and took over their own powers. I do not know how—whoever wrote that scroll does not know how—only that some weakness, some division, among them made it possible."

"Lingers even now?" Halveric said, facing him once more, his face furrowed. "Are you sure?"

Andressat spread his hands. "How else explain that once rid of Siniava, we have one who is, I swear to you, just as evil. How explain the constant warfare, the constant draining of our resources?"

"Evil gods are everywhere," Halveric said, making the avert sign with his heart-hand.

"Everywhere, but not with the same power everywhere," Andressat said. "As water flows downhill and gathers in hollows, so evil finds ways and places where it can gather and then . . . then flow out, to poison the world. By supporting Alured, you and your king opened such a conduit, I believe, and I see no one who can save Aarenis—not just my land of Andressat, but all of Aarenis—but he."

Halveric scowled. "You want *Kieri* to come back to Aarenis? And do what? He's our king now; he can't just leave."

"I don't know what he can do, but he must at least know what is wrong," Andressat said. "If he cannot come himself—and I understand he has responsibilities here—he can send his former Company, perhaps."

"Over whom he has no command, now," Halveric said. "And I will tell you this, as well. Kieri knew he had erred in Aarenis, in the end. He regretted that he had not recognized Alured's nature, but he could not think of any way to restrain Alured that would not make things worse—lead to more protracted war, more damage for people who had done no wrong."

"And is that why he did not return the following year?"

"No, not entirely. The Royal Council in Tsaia were most unhappy with him for taking his reserves south, and forbade him travel the next season. The Duke of Verrakai—you may not know the Verrakais, I suppose."

Andressat shrugged.

"One of the most powerful families in Tsaia—or they were. Very—" Halveric paused, looked slightly embarrassed. "—very proud of their purity of blood," he said finally. "Magelords from before Gird's time, they claimed. They had long hated Kieri for rising to the rank of nobility, thinking him but a bastard, and also because one of his captains was their close relative. Dorrin, whom you met, was Dorrin Verrakai until her family disowned her for becoming a Knight of Falk."

"Magelords . . . that's part of the problem I must bring to your king." Andressat was surprised that Halveric would still call his king by the familiar name.

"My point is," Halveric went on, "that Verrakai hated Kieri, and even after the paladin proved Kieri's birthright, and the Council granted him royal protection and an escort to Lyonya, Verrakai raised a force against him. Imported Pargunese troops as well."

"Are they not enemies of Tsaia?" Andressat asked.

"Quite so," Halveric said. "And then the Verrakai attacked the royal family, and were put under attainder, all but Dorrin Verrakai— Kieri's former captain—who is now the new Duke."

And so, Andressat realized, the new king would have much to occupy him besides trouble he probably thought he had left behind in the south. It would be hard to convince him—and yet, he must try. He glanced aside at Halveric. The man was staring at the path this time. He had hoped to win Halveric to his own view of the urgency before tackling the king—Halveric had been the king's friend so long—but the tired, beaten old man Halveric had become would be no strong ally. He would simply have to convince the king himself.

The next morning, he walked out with his host and saw more evidence that Halveric was not what he had been. His servants, his soldiers, even his family, eyed him with concern as Halveric led him from house to gardens to barns to fields. Everything was in order, well-organized and well-kept, but Andressat felt something missing. Halveric talked of plans made, but now abandoned . . . of people who left and none replacing them, as they had in the past, attracted by a living, growing holding.

Yet fields were tended, animals healthy, fences in repair, buildings mended and clean. Andressat sensed no loss of energy in the others; Halveric's tall wife bustled about the place as if twenty years younger, keeping the household staff at work. His own room, when he returned to it before lunch, had been freshened. Only Halveric himself seemed faded, weakened by something . . . and yet essential characteristics lingered.

"I will travel tomorrow," Andressat said at last. "My mount has recovered."

"We will provide an escort," Halveric said. "And supplies, of course. There are few settlements between here and Chaya; this is a quiet corner of Lyonya."

"You need not," Andressat began, but Halveric's wife, entering at that moment, spoke out.

"Of course we must. You are our guest, and moreover a stranger from afar; even if you were not an old friend of Aliam's, you must have the best we can offer and safe passage. If your courier has reached court, the king will probably have sent King's Squires to lead you in."

That seemed incredible. He was only a count; kings did not send escorts for mere counts. Not unless they wanted to imprison them . . . he shivered, remembering Alured's threats.

"Are you all right?" Aliam's wife asked.

"I'm fine," Andressat said. She said nothing more, for which he was glad, soon leaving the room to do whatever women's work she did. Aliam excused himself shortly after.

After dinner, when he returned to his room, twilight still lay on the fields. Andressat stood by the window, watching a line of cattle move across a pasture, heads nodding in rhythm; behind them a young person—boy or girl, he could not distinguish—swung a stick and whistled tunelessly.

A tap at the door caught his attention; he turned, expecting Aliam, but instead his wife stood there, hands folded over something hidden in her skirts.

"I have a favor to ask," she said. "I apologize, as it is a favor with a sting to it."

"Madam?" He could think of nothing else to say.

"You are going to see the king. You have a message for him; I have one as well . . . one that Aliam does not know about." She looked at him, her face dim in the dying light. When he said nothing, she went on. "I can't go," Aliam's wife said. "But you can carry this to the king." She held up a folded sheet, wax-sealed.

Andressat blinked. Women of his family did not approach male guests and ask them to carry secret messages. It was . . . unseemly, except that Estil Halveric was clearly not attempting an assignation. She was a woman of power; he could feel that even as he thought how odd it was.

"Kieri's his closest friend," the woman went on. "Close as a brother. He needs to know that something's wrong with Aliam—"

"But what can he do?" Andressat said. Immediately he realized how that must sound: he intended to ask the king to intervene in Aarenis, and she was merely asking the king to help a friend. And she was right; something was wrong with Aliam Halveric. Still, Andressat felt uneasy, alone with his host's wife, despite the open door, the voices of others in the passage. And yet it was unthinkable that what he was thinking could ever be, with this woman, in this household. She was not like the women of the south, was the best way he could define it. His own wife would never have done such a thing, but his own wife never wore a servant's apron, never made bread with her own hands, never—as he had seen this woman do earlier that day—taught a grandchild to milk a cow by milking it herself.

"You are a man of honor," she said now. "Aliam has told me that, and I can see it for myself. You will not like this favor, and I sympathize. But I swear to you, the message is sent for help, not harm. I cannot ask any of your escort, Aliam's sworn men, to take it; they have a specific loyalty to him that you do not, and I do not think a guest's loyalty would prevent it. But it is your decision, of course."

"You have no other way?" Andressat asked.

"Not that I can think of," she said. "If I could go myself—but I am afraid to leave him." Her voice dropped. "He talks of dying," she said, almost a whisper. She laid the paper on the table beside the door, turned, and left.

His decision. Andressat looked at the table, once more surprised at Halveric's wife. She had left him every option. He could open the message . . . he could show it to Aliam . . . he could leave it there, for her to find and dispose of . . . he walked to the table, picked it up, tapped it lightly against his other hand, and tucked it away in the inside pocket of his tunic. Whatever else she might be, and however different from the women he knew . . . he knew she loved and respected her husband, and wished him no harm.

CHAPTER TWENTY-THREE

Chaya

The King's Squires escorting the Count of Andressat led the way into the palace court. Andressat's courier had reached them in plenty of time; Kieri was at the head of the steps when Andressat dismounted. He knew Andressat well enough to recognize that the Count was uncomfortable.

"My lord Count," Kieri said coming down the steps. "You are welcome here—I never expected to see you north of the Dwarfmounts. We are honored."

"Sir King," Andressat said, bowing low. "I would not trouble you if it were not a matter of grave import."

"Then come inside," Kieri said, "for it looks to rain again within a short time." He noticed Andressat's eyes widen at the carpets and tapestries—Andressat had prided himself on the textiles his estate produced. If Kieri had wanted revenge for all the slights Andressat had heaped on him, this would be ample, but in fact he wanted Andressat to enjoy the visit. The old man had a shrewd understanding of southern politics, and a dry wit Kieri had enjoyed whenever Andressat let it show. "Urgent as your news is," Kieri said, "you will want to bathe and rest before sharing it, I'm sure—"

Andressat shook his head. "I have two things first, and then I will be glad of a brief rest. I do not, alas, have the endurance of the young."

"Very well," Kieri said, and led him into his smaller office. "Have a seat."

Andressat sat down, then reached into his tunic, pulling out a folded sheet of paper. "It is a delicate matter," he said. "I received this from Aliam Halveric's lady—she asked me to carry it to you without his knowledge, which ordinarily I would not do. But Lord Halveric is not well—even as a visitor I could see that something is wrong there, and I do not know what." He handed the paper to Kieri.

"Aliam not well?" Kieri said. "He was fine in the spring—" But a memory of Aliam's letter came to him, and he frowned as he broke the seal. "And the other?" he said, beginning to read.

"I met your Captain Arcolin in Aarenis, in Fossnir, traveling with his sergeant, the blind one—"

"Blind!" Kieri said. He looked at Andressat. "He has no blind sergeant—who?"

"Stammel, the man's name was. Some injury this past summer. The man seems well but for that; he rode without a leading rein; we traveled together from Fossnir to Valdaire. But I was supposed to tell Lord Halveric, and I forgot—I was shocked at his appearance, to tell the truth—that your captain had found his son's sword in Aarenis, and will send it to you—he thought you should give it to Lord Halveric."

Kieri stared at the paper he held without seeing the words written there, thinking of Stammel blinded—when? How? Had Arcolin written to tell him and the letter not come? Then, with an effort, he focused on the words Estil had written.

Kieri, I write you as a friend—as one of Aliam's dearest friends— for I fear for his life. Something is wrong, I know not what nor how to act, but since Paksenarrion left us last winter, when she went to find you, he has sunk bit by bit into a strange torpor. Your coronation brought him out of it briefly, but as soon as we were home, it began again. He is older, but so am I. He takes no joy in life, Kieri. Please—I do not know what you can do, but as you love him, please come. See for yourself. I believe he will be dead by Midwinter if you do not. Estil.

Kieri looked at Andressat, who was watching him closely. "Does Aliam seem in bad health to you?"

"Much older than two years account for," Andressat said. "Exhausted, I would say, and full of some sorrow too great to bear. If he were one of my family, I would say he has the death-wish on him, but I do not know why."

Kieri felt a nudge, a sense of urgency even stronger than Estil's letter. He raised his voice. "Berne!" The Squire outside the door opened it and came in. "Berne, make ready to ride to Halveric Steading as soon as possible. They have need of me. We will need extra horses."

"At once, Sir King."

Kieri turned back to Andressat. "My lord, I'm sorry, but I must beg you to tell me the rest of your concerns as quickly as you may. Aliam is my oldest and dearest friend, and if you and Estil are right, I have scarce time to reach him before some crisis."

"Sir King, it is the archives—" Andressat repeated what he had told Aliam Halveric. Kieri listened, trying to be attentive, but with half his mind on Aliam and the sense of urgency he felt. Still, he felt the hairs rising on his arms.

"My lord Count—I suspect I may know what some of those things are. Did your archives mention the Verrakai?"

"Yes—and also some great evils—" Andressat stared at him, as if expecting Kieri to produce a miracle: answer and solution in one utterance.

Kieri gathered his thoughts. What Andressat said had importance both north and south, but Aliam needed him immediately; he felt torn. "My lord, you are welcome to stay here, and rest as long as you need—until I return from the Halverics, if you choose—but you must, before you return south, visit the new Duke Verrakai, my former captain, Dorrin. She found relics her family kept hidden for hundreds of years; I believe they may bear on your problem. I will send word to her that you are coming—"

"I do not know her," Andressat protested.

"She was my captain; you met her. She is trustworthy, and now stands high in the court of Tsaia." After nearly being killed, but Andressat didn't need to know that. "I understand that you have had a hard journey and must rest. But Dorrin Verrakai must have this news, and Tsaia's king as well. I will supply an escort; you will not be traveling alone. Before that, however, rest here awhile, as long as you like."

"I—I suppose I must," Andressat said. "If you must leave—I was hoping . . ." His voice trailed away, then he spoke again. "You—my pardon, Sir King—but you seem oddly younger."

"They tell me it's my elven heritage," Kieri said. "Once I touched the sword—" He nodded to where it hung on its rack. "—its power released that heritage, and as half-elven I am not considered old at all."

A knock at the door; Arian put her head in. "Sir King—if you wish to leave tonight, we will be ready immediately after dinner—or within a half-glass if necessary."

"But it's raining now," Andressat said, glancing at the window, where a dreary autumn rain fell steadily.

"I would ride through worse to help Aliam," Kieri said. "He saved me, long ago. Will you take dinner with me, or would you rather rest first?"

"I'll eat with you," Andressat said.

"Dinner in a quarter-glass, my lord," Arian said, and shut the door.

"Time enough to wash up," Kieri said. In the passage, he signed to Gavin, the youngest Squire. "This is Count Andressat, who will be staying here as long as he finds convenient, and then going to Tsaia, to Duke Verrakai. See that he has everything he needs. When he is ready, arrange an escort of honor to Verrakai's estate. If he wishes to stay until I return, he is welcome to do that, too."

Gavin guided Andressat toward one of the guest rooms; Kieri ran up stairs to his own apartments, where he found Garris just strapping together a pack of his clothes. His riding clothes and all-weather cloak were laid out on the bed.

"I should come, too," Garris said. "Whatever's wrong at Halveric's—"

"No," Kieri said. "I need you here, at the center of my courier service. You'll have to organize Andressat's travel to Tsaia for me. There's no one I trust more, Garris."

"How bad is it?"

"I don't know yet, but I know I must leave now, not tomorrow. If you don't get regular reports from the river patrols, send a courier to demand them. Something's going on there. I'd feel better if the king had replied to my letter about Elis."

"Kieri—tell Aliam I love him too."

"I will, Garris. Gods grant I'm there in time."

He changed to riding clothes and went down to dinner. Andressat waited there, eyeing the dishes arriving on the table. "What is that?"

"An apple sweet the cook here makes; I don't know what she calls it. My lord Count, pardon me, but I need to eat quickly." Kieri nodded to the servants, and they withdrew. He stacked slices of meat on a thick wedge of bread and bit into it. Andressat put slices on his own plate and investigated the pots of sauces, smiling when he found the one with southern peppers.

Andressat was still eating when Kieri excused himself. He rode away in the wet night, raindrops sparkling in the torchlight. He knew Andressat would consider his abrupt departure discourteous, and wished he had not needed to ruffle the old man's composure, but he had no choice, not if he was to arrive before Aliam died. The taig itself now urged him on, hinting at some danger beyond even Aliam's death.

From Chaya to Halveric's steading could be a long road or a short one, depending in part on the weather, forest rangers, the elves, and the forest taig itself. Kieri tried to infuse the taig with his own sense of urgency, and a way seemed to open, almost straight and wide enough for several to ride abreast. Still, it was days of riding, in the shifting autumn weather—that wet night was followed by a dry morning, with a cold wind blowing up behind them. The forest darkened their way even as some leaves blew before the wind. A day—another day—even with extra mounts they had to stop to rest the horses, and Kieri slept in snatches, but for the one night they spent at a farmstead deep in the forest, where the startled housewife insisted that the king must have their best bed.

Then they were coming out of the woods into the lower fields of Halveric Steading, and the familiar house and outbuildings were there before him. The same as always—but not. He could not define the difference. Kieri let his standard-bearer ride ahead of him, the royal standard snapping like a whip in a brisk wind.

Estil and Aliam both met him at the gate; Estil's eyes thanked him silently, but Aliam scarcely smiled. He looked as Andressat had described: old, tired, sick, a man ready and willing to die. Kieri hugged them both, then said, "Invite your king indoors, man—we're cold and hungry!"

Aliam winced; Estil said, "Come in! There's sib still hot, and I'll heat spiced cider."

Kieri led the way; he knew every stone of that courtyard. He shed his cloak in the main passage and hung it on one of the hooks out of sheer habit. He could see, from the alert glances his Squires gave, that they, too, felt some menace here. Arian started to speak to him, but he shook his head; he had to speak to Aliam first.

"You don't understand," Aliam said. They had drunk sib and eaten a quick meal, then he'd led Kieri to the little walled garden—an odd choice, Kieri thought, in that weather. Aliam sat hunched on the bench, as if he feared a blow. "If I had only said something . . . all those years, all the pain . . . Tammarion and the children would not have died if I'd said something. They'd have been safe, here—"

"I'd never have met Tammarion then," Kieri said. "Never had children."

"But they were killed—"

"Would you wish Cal unborn because he was captured and suffered Siniava's torments?"

"Cal is still alive. Your wife and children are dead, and it's my fault."

"It is not. Aliam, listen to me. Without you, I would be dead, dead of starvation or, if I survived in body, dead in soul from what my captor did to me." Aliam stirred a little. Kieri felt a rush of warmth, as if the taig touched him. "You saved my life," he went on. "You saved my sanity. You were my father, my elder brother. From you and Estil I learned what goodness is, how good people behave. From you I learned how good men govern others, how they lead others, how even in war honor and wisdom have a place. From you came the ideas that first let us—you and me and Aesil M'dierra—form a code of honor for mercenaries in Aarenis. If, years from now, my people think I was a good king, it will be because of *you*, because of your kindness and your example."

"But still—" Aliam was sobbing now, tears running down into his beard. Kieri's eyes burned, but this was no time for tears. Either he was a king, with a king's powers, or he was a title only, hollow.

He reached out and pulled Aliam into a hug, as Aliam had once hugged the terrified boy he himself had been. The taig's power he'd felt before surged up in him from the earth below; he could feel it reaching outward to Aliam, warming them both. "But still, Aliam Halveric, I tell you *as your king* that you did me no harm. You did me only good. As your king, Aliam, I tell you that you are my oldest friend, my dearest friend, and nothing you have ever done or would do will change that. And as your king, I command you—lay down this guilt you feel. Walk away from it. I believe it was put in your heart by some evil being." He pushed Aliam just far enough away to see his face, to see the startled look, the relief that showed in Aliam's eyes, as whatever pain held him was lessened . . . faded . . . and blew away like smoke on the wind.

"I feel—"

"Better, I hope," Kieri said. "A visit from your king is supposed to have that effect, they tell me."

"What did you do?" More life, more alertness came back into Aliam's face, as if he were waking up from a long illness.

"I have been taking instruction in the arts of kingship," Kieri said, as lightly as he could. He was still gripping Aliam's shoulders; he could feel in his fingers some change in the man, something that felt like the difference between a diseased, dying tree and a healthy one. Had he really done that? Or was it just his words? "My elven relatives," he went on, "tell me that here in Lyonya a king's main task is restoring harmony and health, not resting his royal rump on a throne being flattered."

Aliam made a sound between a sob and a laugh, then drew a long, shaky breath. "Well . . . Sir King . . . whatever you did, and however you did it, I feel . . . better. I still think—no, all right, I won't say it. I feel better. Almost . . . almost younger, though at my age that is not a possibility."

"Why not?" Kieri asked. "I feel younger, too."

"But you're half-elf and I am not."

"Aliam, this is no time to start an argument."

Another shaky breath. "You're right, Sir King—"

"And didn't I tell you to call me Kieri, at least when we're alone? And do you see a horde of courtiers standing around ready to be jealous?"

"Er . . . no . . . Kieri. But it's so . . . I don't know what—"

"Something . . . I know there's something but not what. You would not have felt that much misery all on your own."

"You remember I said—in Chaya—"

"Yes, and I remember what I said and that you were—or you acted—reassured. Were you trying to fool me then, Aliam?"

"No. I think I *was* reassured then, there in Chaya with you. I wouldn't try to fool you anyway; you were always able to see through me, at least as you began to grow into your ability. That was one of the things that made managing you difficult when you were a squire. And made you a comfortable friend, once we were grown."

"So something happened . . . something or someone changed your heart, your mind . . . when did it start, can you think?"

Aliam shook his head. "Before you came—last winter. Maybe it was just the long winter closing in . . . not enough to do . . . brooding indoors . . . and then after your coronation, when we came back here . . . I thought it was the summer heat . . ."

"Nothing to make you think one of the evil gods might have laid a curse on you?"

"Not since Paks left to find you."

"What?"

"The night before she left. The . . . um . . . Lady had been here." Aliam looked startled suddenly. "I haven't—we couldn't say it—but I suppose I can to you, as you're her grandson . . ."

Kieri waited as patiently as he could.

"The Lady came to talk to Paks; the elves did not at first think you were fit to be king, as you know. Paks insisted; the Lady agreed that at least you should have the chance to prove yourself. Then the Lady locked our tongues about her visit; only Estil and I remember it, and we cannot speak of it."

The elves had opposed his kingship? For a moment Kieri's mind veered to that, but then he pulled his attention back to the immediate problem.

"What exactly happened the night before Paks left?"

"Achrya came. The Webspinner. To attack Paks, but she spun

webs throughout the house. Paks routed her; we cleared the webs, and then Paks left. We've seen nought but ordinary little spiders since, and no harm in them."

"Maybe," Kieri said. "But I suspect she used some other bane to cloud your mind." He looked around at the garden walls, his gaze caught by movement, a flake of stone perhaps, breaking off and falling to the ground behind the peach trained on the wall. "Come with me," he said, drawing Aliam closer once more and laying an arm across his shoulders.

Outside the walled garden, his Squires waited.

"Sir King," Arian said. "By your leave, I must speak." He nodded, then stepped away from Aliam. She spoke quietly. "My lord, there is a daskdraudigs . . ." Kieri raised his eyebrows. "A rock serpent," Arian explained. "Evil invading rock—it comes alive. We must get them out at once, and call rangers. I have only one daskin arrow, and none of the other Squires have any; it is not enough."

He remembered now: Paks had mentioned a daskdraudigs, but he'd been more interested in her healing than what had come before. "Aliam," Kieri said, as casually as he could. "Would one of your people know where the nearest forest rangers might be?"

"They have a camp at a spring about a half-day's walk sunward," Aliam said. "The children love to ride out there to escape their chores; we know they're safe, if they overnight with the rangers."

"Send one of your people, then, and ask them to come here quickly."

"A problem?" Aliam asked, looking worried.

"Yes." Kieri tried to keep his voice light.

Across the courtyard, a girl perhaps shoulder-high led a bay horse from the stable; she wore riding gear and had a long green feather in her cap. "Estilla!" Aliam called.

"Granfer?"

"What do you ride for?"

She turned red. "Um . . . sir . . . to . . . exercise Bayberry . . ."

"Exercise him to the ranger camp, then, and ask them to come here. The king wishes to speak to them."

A smile broke out on her face. "Yes, Granfer! At once!" She mounted and reined the horse toward the gate.

"Quickly, Estilla!" Aliam called.

No answer but the horse leaping into a gallop, and the beat of its hooves on the turf outside, rapidly diminishing.

"We call her little Estil," Aliam said, as if that weren't obvious. "She's actually named for her mother's mother, as is proper, but she's exactly like Estil at the same age. Even her mother's mother calls her Estilla."

Cal Halveric came out of the stable. "Father? Is there trouble?"

Kieri spoke before Aliam could. "I feel something wrong with the taig, Cal. I want the rangers' help in understanding what it is."

"Should I call alarm?" Aliam asked.

Kieri extended his taig-sense. There—the garden wall. The house? He could not be sure. But the garden wall and . . . the back wall of the stable.

"Do not say the name loudly, Sir King," Arian said quietly. She was watching the garden wall. "It must not know we know."

"Quietly, then," Kieri said to Aliam and Cal. "Do not go into the stable yourself, Cal, but have your grooms bring the horses out—to—to show me their paces in the field, especially any in the south aisle stalls."

"We haven't been able to keep horses in there since late winter," Aliam said. "They fret, but we couldn't find anything wrong. What about the house?"

"Move everyone from the garden side, just in case."

"*Outside,*" Arian murmured. "A picnic?"

"It's a clear day," Kieri said. "Let's make a party in the meadow, watching the horses. Tell Estil." Into Aliam's ear he murmured, "Daskdraudigs." Aliam startled, then nodded.

Aliam went back inside; Kieri watched the garden wall. Were the seams between the stones moving? He couldn't tell, for the cover of vines and the branches of trees espaliered there. He remembered Paks had said only daskin arrows could kill one. Arian stood near him, saying nothing; Kieri had bade the other Squires help bring out the picnic.

People streamed from the house. One of Aliam's daughters-in-law shepherded a string of giggling children, all carrying bundles, out the gate. Grooms led horses from the stable, held them back while another gaggle of children scampered past with pillows on their heads.

Would the daskdraudigs know alarm had been given? Would it

wait to strike? And how did it do what it did? Kieri stood still, trying to feel the extent of the danger without alerting it, as more people, more animals, passed behind him and out of the main courtyard to what he hoped was safety. Aliam's older grandsons and some of his soldiers lugged the big camp tents and their poles . . . Estil herself, bow slung on her back, had one end of a pole on which two steaming kettles hung; another daughter-in-law held the other end. Back and forth, back and forth. Kieri watched another flake or two fall off the wall, sparkling in the slanting light, until the garden enclosure had lost the sun for the day.

Thundering hooves caught his attention; he did not look away, but heard one of his Squires greet the newcomers. In moments, two rangers were beside him. "Sir King?" one said.

"Arian says it's a daskdraudigs," Kieri said softly. "I think it's taken the south stable wall and most of the wall around the kitchen garden. Bless your speed in coming."

"We knew you were here," one ranger said. "We came to see and met Aliam's granddaughter on the way. We sent her on to our camp, to fetch the others. A daskdraudigs? They almost never invade set stone."

"It is, though," the other said. "And something drew it, some lure." He unslung his bow and looked through his quiver.

"Sir King, you must withdraw," Arian said. "You have no weapon to deal with a daskdraudigs, and I have but the one daskin arrow."

Kieri obeyed, joining Aliam and his family across the field from the compound. "It's definitely a daskdraudigs," he said then. "And they think it was lured here."

"Something Achrya left?" Estil asked.

"No doubt," Aliam said. "Thank all the gods you came to visit, Kieri."

"Indeed," Kieri said, watching across the field. The rangers reappeared, one on the roof of the house and one on the forecourt's wall. He saw them draw their bows, the streaking flight of arrows. Then the monster moved. The ranger on the house roof staggered and fell as the south wall of the house heaved up and sideways, breaking roof-beams like twigs and sending slates down in a rattling cascade.

Estil and the other women gathered the children into a knot, closing them in and comforting those who began to cry. Aliam's soldiers looked to him, but he held them back. "Can't fight that with swords," he said. "They know what they're doing, the rangers. But be ready to move back if we need to."

The monster's other end, the south stable wall, rose and came down on the rest of the stable with an impact that shook the ground where Kieri stood, then rose again and crashed into the front wall, barely missing the ranger standing on it; the shock of the impact knocked him off the wall, and he landed on the ground just outside. The ranger on the roof rolled down the slope of a sound portion into a chimney, scrambled up, and shot again and again, immobilizing that end of the monster. The other ranger, slower to rise, barely missed being hit by falling stones as the other end struck the front wall again, but his arrows flew true, and soon that end as well was immobilized.

Was the danger over? Kieri held up his hand to still the excited clamor of voices around him. It still felt . . . wrong. Whatever had drawn the daskdraudigs was still there.

The two rangers, arrows ready, clearly thought the same thing, though the monster was motionless now. Paks had said rockserpents died, became once more inert stone, safe. Was there another one? Or some other menace?

He looked at the forest behind them. The forest taig held nothing of evil; it was alert, wary, but not hostile. Whatever evil he felt was centered there, in the ruins of Aliam's house. That made sense, with Achrya's visit, if the Webmistress set the lure that brought the daskdraudigs. But why did he feel evil still near if the daskdraudigs had died?

Aliam's people set up a camp and had food cooking before full dark. Halveric troops laid out a perimeter, set sentries. The two rangers near the house came one by one for supper but then went back near the walls to keep watch on the daskdraudigs, they said.

Shortly before dark, four more rangers arrived with Estilla.

"She rides like a ranger," one said. Estilla grinned, but it was clear she was exhausted; her mother took her away for food and sleep. Kieri hoped it would be sleep. These rangers had brought many more daskin arrows from their camp and shared them out with the two who'd arrived earlier. Kieri gave them no orders, as they seemed to know what to do, and he finally lay down in his tent with the King's Squires outside.

He woke before dawn, in the death-hour, his skin drawn up into prickles. His sword's jewel pulsed with light in a way he'd never seen; he drew it and had just reached the tent's door when sentries raised the alarm, and a blast of dark malice slammed into his mind.

Not the daskdraudigs with its slow leaching of joy and will to live but something greater. Kieri called on the taig, waking it as he'd been taught this past season, and saw—as if he had the night-vision of a full elf—the field itself heaving, rippling like a shaken rug. Nothing more was visible, but the malice bore down on him, on them all. Children were awake now, the youngest screaming in terror, the older asking questions—adults trying to soothe them, voices shaky with fear.

Kieri struggled with his own battle-trained response, the anger that had carried him through so many times of fear. He'd been taught that anger wounded the taig, drove it away. *If you rouse the taig, you must do it with joy and love,* Orlith had said. Now he pushed anger aside and spoke to the taig of the love he had for Aliam and Estil and all they cared for.

Out of the ground, from the trees behind their camp, a silvery light rose. Where it rose, the field lay still. Kieri felt the hairs rise on his arms, his scalp, his whole body. Around him, frightened cries softened into silence. He wanted to know what that light was, but he knew he must hold the taig, strengthen it, pour his love for the land and its people into it, and let the taig itself be what it was meant to be, an unfrayed fabric of life.

Nearby, someone began a chant his elven tutor had taught him, both prayer and song to the taig. He joined in, only just aware that he was singing louder, and in the elven tongue, as the light strengthened. Across the field fire blossomed in the ruins of the stables, followed by a hideous noise as something exploded and stones rose in the air, falling just short of the silver light.

Another voice, and another, joined his. The light strengthened again, now almost day-bright, as a wave of music flowed over him from behind. All around now were elves, a crowd of them centering on the Lady. The light spread outward from her, from them, quieting the heaving field, pushing back the malice. Kieri felt the malice retreat, though a final whirlwind of stones and dust and sticks beat at the light's protection . . . and then it was gone.

"Sir King," the Lady said, turning to him. "Once more you bring alarms—"

He took a step toward her, thinking to make proper courtesy, but the next he knew, he was flat on the ground with his head in her lap. Inside a tent. A tent? His thoughts wandered; he could not seem to think.

"You spent yourself," the Lady said. Her expression was tender, her voice soft and musical. "I should not be surprised, grandson, for your parents were the same. But did not Orlith warn you about yielding so much to the taig?"

"What's happened?" Kieri asked. He tried to move, but his body didn't respond. "Aliam—Estil—the children—?"

"Are very well," she said, laying a hand on his forehead. "Rest. You are young in the mastery of your magery; you do not yet know how to measure what's needed, and you gave much. It is no more than the exhaustion that comes after great labor. The taig will restore you; let it do its work."

He realized then that he was not merely flat on the ground, but unclothed as well, skin to grass under a cloak. Instead of cold autumn soil, he felt warmth, the warmth of a summer sun almost, the taig's gift to him. "What did I do wrong?"

She laughed. "Not wrong, grandson. Just overmuch. You waked the taig; you gave it direction; you gave it your king's power. All that was very well done, and Aliam tells me without one curse uttered. But you let the taig take more than it needed."

"I knew I wasn't supposed to be angry," he said. The warmth beneath made him drowsy, but he was determined to stay awake. He needed to ask her something, if he could only remember. Her hand on his brow pushed the question back below his awareness.

"Especially here, where it's been nurtured so long," she said. "I wonder, though, that Estil Halveric did not sense the daskdraudigs and the lure."

"Estil has taig-sense?"

"Oh, yes. She has both old human and a little elven blood, and in her line the awareness, and the care, of the taig is uncommonly strong. She should have known something was wrong."

"You were there last winter, she said. Did you find anything wrong with her taig-sense then?"

"No . . ." The Lady's eyes widened. "Singer of songs! *I* did that!"

"What?" Heat pulsed from the ground; Kieri felt fully awake, aware that a glamour she had laid on him was fading. He sat up, pulled the cloak around him, and turned to face her.

"When I was there," she said. "I touched them all so my visit would not be spoken of, lest some evil discover your identity before the paladin reached you." Kieri felt a touch of her glamour like a silk veil across his mind. What was she hiding? "Only to Aliam and Estil I left the memory, but I barred their speech . . . and that must have interfered with Estil Halveric's taig-sense. Because of me that vile monster came and tore down their house, and Gitres Unmaker—"

"Gitres? I thought it was Achrya."

"She may have laid the lure to punish the Halverics for aiding you, but it was Gitres you held off this night, Sir King, and proved beyond any doubt your right to kingship. Not that I have doubted you since I first met you." She turned away. "I must apologize to Aliam and Estil, if you will excuse me."

CHAPTER TWENTY-FOUR

"Of course," Kieri said, still astonished. Light remained—her light? His light? Now he recognized his own tent, his own neatly folded clothes nearby. Before getting up, he laid both hands flat on the ground. "Thank you," he said to the taig, and without realizing he was going to, bent down and kissed the turf.

His clothes felt warm when he put them on. When he came out, dawn painted the eastern sky rose and gold. Off to his right, a fire crackled and steam rose from pots set on and near it. He smelled sib, bacon, porridge. To the left, a group of elves looked at the ruins of Halveric Steading; one noticed him, said something to the others, and they all bowed, then went back to staring. The Lady, Aliam, and Estil were talking quietly as they, too, watched a thin trickle of black smoke rising from the stable wreckage.

Kieri could think of nothing to say at first; he put an arm around Aliam's shoulders and stood in silence. "I seem to have made a mess of your house," he said finally.

Aliam prodded him in the ribs, as of old. "You seem to have saved our lives, you mean. Don't try to play humble, my liege." And into Kieri's ear: "I can't call you Kieri with *her* around; she'd skin me and eat me."

"I don't eat humans," his grandmother said austerely, without looking at either of them. "No elf would touch man-meat. Call him Kieri if you wish; I do."

Aliam stiffened; Estil chuckled.

"I could eat whatever's for breakfast," Kieri said. Moment by moment he felt his mind clearing. "Unless we have need of haste to do something."

"We have need of sunlight, and that is coming soon," the Lady said. She smiled. "You, grandson, have need of breakfast. Others have eaten already."

"You?" Kieri asked Aliam.

"Indeed." He patted his stomach. "My daughters say I will grow fat if I eat so much." He looked ten years younger, this morning. Kieri glanced at Estil.

"There is enough work to do, rebuilding," Estil said. "I will not worry about your appetite unless you lose it again."

"It was my doing that left you unable to sense the taig, Estil Halveric," the Lady said, as if continuing a conversation Kieri had interrupted. "Do not refuse my aid in rebuilding what my deeds caused to fall."

"Do not take on the responsibility of others," Estil said, in a tone she might have used to a child. "It was the malice of Achrya and Gitres, not you, that tore down those walls."

"I am well rebuked by a mortal," the Lady said. "And yet—may not a friend offer restoration even so?"

"I am well rebuked, to lecture one so far above me," Estil said, looking down. "My Lady, your kindness to us, all these years, has more than repaid any injury that might have resulted."

Kieri put one hand on Estil's shoulder and the other on his grandmother's. "Ladies, you are both more courteous than my stomach, which is empty of fine words and full of discourteous growling. Can you *please* end this competition of manners and let us find a place to sit down and eat? I dare not command either of you, and yet I am your king."

The Lady laughed, and after a moment Estil laughed, too. Each took an arm, and he walked them to the fire, where someone had contrived a table and benches. "Sit here," he said, handing them to seats on either side of the table, "and keep me company while I eat, remembering that I know nothing of the last part of the night."

One of Estil's daughters set in front of him a mug of sib, a jug of honey, a platter of bacon and flatbread, and a bowl of porridge.

Kieri's stomach took command, and he ate, as the two women talked, more easily with each passing moment. When he had wiped his porridge bowl clean with the last of the flatbread, he sat back. "So . . . it is gone forever, or gone for the moment, that menace?"

"Gone for a time," the Lady said. "Evil is never gone forever; the seeds of it are abroad in the world, and given the right conditions, it grows again. But for now—and I cannot say how long, perhaps a turn of the year, perhaps a lifetime—it is gone from *this* place."

"What made the fire and explosion?" Kieri asked. Sunlight now touched the ruins, and the smoke had thinned to a gray wisp. "It looked like it was in the stable cellar, but all that I remember being there was—oh." The wine, the brandy, the oil from southern berries. Barrels of the stuff, kept under the stable because no one lighted a flame in a stable and thus it would not catch fire.

"Gitres can bring fire from the sky," the Lady said. "Blowing open a cellar door would be no difficulty."

"That was southern wine, Andressat wine," Aliam said, coming to the table and sitting down beside Estil. He made a sad face, but his eyes were merry. "All that lovely red wine. All those juicy oilberries. And the oil for our lamps this winter."

"Be serious." Estil elbowed him; he laughed, and she poked him again. "You should be over there nailing the sticks together to make us a hut."

"Can't. Nails were in the stable cellar, too. They're scattered all over the meadow now." He made a face at her, then winked at Kieri.

"You can whittle pegs, then."

"Estil, my little bird, you are not going to pretend we have no help, and you are going to accept the help we're offered." His voice was sober now; he put his arm around her shoulders.

"It's—you built that wall, Aliam. *You* did. I remember—it's what you built and I cared for all these years, and it's gone . . ."

Kieri had never seen Estil cry; he looked to his grandmother, whose face at first showed only mild distaste but then warmed to compassion.

"Estil, Estil . . ." Aliam kissed her hair, murmuring. "It is never the same, one year to the next. We will build again; you will have more memories; the children will laugh in the halls and in the courtyard and in the fields. What more could we want than that? The same stones in the same place? The past to return? Brave one, dear heart, grieve awhile because you must, but then rejoice with me. The darkness has left my heart; do not let it invade yours." He kissed her again, hair, eyes, nose. "Or I will tickle you," he said.

Her eyes flew open. "In front of—you would not dare!"

"Oh, I would dare anything to see my love again in her own place, laughing and fierce all in one. Make peace with our friends, Estil, and take heart."

Estil dug her head into Aliam's shoulder, then sat up. "You're right, of course." She turned to the Lady, drying tears still streaking her face. "My Lady, I've been rude and silly, but now—whatever you wish to do, I accept with a grateful heart."

"You are most courteous always, Estil Halveric, and I say again I was well rebuked and bear no resentment. Day is here; the sunlight we need for a working of power is here. Tell me, Alyanya's own, what would you for your household?"

Estil looked confused.

"Is there not some part of your house you always wished were different? A chimney that did not draw well, a room with an ill-placed door?"

"The second pantry," Estil said, nodding. "Open the door and it bangs right into another one, so you have to leave the kitchen, shut that door, then open the pantry—"

"We will build better," the Lady said. She rose without appearing to move and reached out her hand. "Come with me, Estil, and we will look at that mess and consider how best to clear it."

Kieri set his elbows on the table, rested his chin on his hands, and looked at Aliam. "Well?"

"Very well, thank you. Gods, Kieri, I can't believe I was sunk so far I could think of nothing but death. Die? Leave Estil to grieve and my children . . . when so many love me? And leave you to rattle around on that throne surrounded by courtiers and not one man who knows war? Not that we want war to come here." Aliam nodded to the woman who offered him a mug of sib, and sipped from it. "I don't want a daskdraudigs either, but I'm glad to have some reason for my behavior other than simple idiocy."

"Father, should we let the horses into the field where that . . . thing . . . was?" Cal had come up; he smiled a little shyly at Kieri.

"Cal, I'm keeping your father away from his work; forgive me. Aliam—go on. I'll be there shortly."

By the time the sun was at noon, the Lady and other elves had cleared much of the tumbled stone away, setting the unbroken stones in neat rows, while the humans salvaged smaller, lighter items strewn across the meadow. Kieri, forbidden to work magic, picked up whatever he could find.

"Another bridle," Cal said. "I wish we'd find the rolls of strapping."

"I wish we'd find a whole saddle," Aliam said. "My backside's too old to ride bareback on that ridgepole backbone our horses have."

"You should buy Marrakai blood," Kieri said. It was an old argument. "They're double-backed and easy to sit on."

"And expensive," Aliam said. "Cheaper to buy new saddles. Gods above, what this is going to cost!"

"You'll have to take the Company south again, Father," Cal said.

"I might let you take it," Aliam said. "There'll be enough work here to keep me busy."

Cal glanced at him and went back to turning over rubble. "You feel up to it?"

"King's touch, Cal. I'm healed. And Kieri has no one in Lyonya who knows war the way I do. He should have someone here to depend on. Though he hasn't said yes yet." He looked at Kieri.

Kieri mopped the sweat off his brow. "If war comes, you are the commander I'd want in the field, Aliam. But I'm hoping it doesn't come. And it might be good for you to go back to Aarenis, recover—"

"I'm recovered enough to think clearly, Kieri. Look it in the face. Is the king of Pargun happy that his daughter did not return and is not your wife? Or the king of Kostandan?"

"It's not my job to send wild girls back to fathers who treated them badly."

Aliam put down the iron bar he'd been using to shift rocks. "Just what did their fathers do, but send them to the best man I know?"

"They didn't know that. Elis at least had sisters who wanted to come. I wouldn't have married them, either, but at least I would have felt better sending them home."

"What *did* you do with them?"

"Sent them to the Knights of Falk. Where Elis really belongs, I think, is with a Kuakgan. She reminds me a lot of Kolya Ministierra."

Aliam snorted. "The Lady would like that—I think not."

"Not like what?" the Lady asked, appearing beside them. "Your pardon, Sir King, but Estil asks for Aliam. She thinks they've found the token of the Halveric founder."

"The wardskull!" Aliam said, eyes alight.

"A head-bone, yes," the Lady said, with obvious distaste. Before Kieri could say anything, she spread her hands. "It is a human thing, I know, but it is alien to me. Kieri, grandson, let Aliam go and tell me what you were speaking of."

"He asked about the Pargunese and Kostandanyan princesses," Kieri said. "I did not want to marry them—"

"Wise," she said. "Neither one is right for you. And you sent them away, did you not?"

"Yes, but not home, since neither wished to return. I sent them to train as Knights of Falk."

"And you think one should be with a Kuakgan, and not with elves?"

"She is Pargunese," Kieri said. "She wants to live amid forests and breed horses, she says, but mostly she wants not to marry."

"There are other ways not to marry than cutting off an arm and grafting a tree onto your shoulder," the Lady said, her expression grim.

"*What?*"

"Did you not know that is what they do? Every Kuakgan, red blood with green, a tree with a limb once human, and the Kuakgan with an arm once tree. They thrive and die together."

"I did not. How—?"

"We know, because the trees tell us. If some men knew, they would cut down every tree, to kill the Kuakkgannir." She stalked off. Kieri looked after her; her abrupt changes of mood bothered him the same way her disappearances bothered him. All his experience told him rule required self-control, steadiness of purpose. He glanced around to see Amrothlin also watching the Lady, his expression guarded.

"Is she all right?" Kieri asked.

"She is . . . the Lady," Amrothlin said. "What were you speaking of?"

Kieri did not want to talk about tree-shepherds, or even princesses;

he went back to Aliam. "I have another good word. You must decide how good."

"Yes?"

"Andressat told me he met Arcolin in Aarenis, and Arcolin had recovered Cal's sword. He's sending it to me, to give to you. There should be no more relics of Cal's ordeal down there."

Aliam blinked. "I had almost forgotten. We never found it, and we searched. Where did Arcolin get it?"

"Andressat didn't say. Arcolin will tell us, I'm sure. The bad news is that Stammel's been blinded—I don't know how, as I've had no word from Arcolin since early in the summer."

"That's bad. He was a good man."

"He's still a good man, but . . . I know Arcolin will take care of him."

"Kieri, I want to take your offer—Estil would rather I stayed this side of the mountains, I can tell, and you already have a cohort of mine—but I can't leave here until we have a roof over our heads and at least beds to sleep on and a table to eat from."

"I know. Come when you can. The elves will help; it will not be as long as you think. I must get back—we'll leave in the morning, unless you need us."

"Do you never get tired?" Aliam asked.

"What did you tell me when I was a boy?" Kieri said. "Tired is a feeling, but duty is a fact, wasn't that it?"

"I knew from the moment I saw you, you would be nothing but trouble," Aliam said, rolling his eyes.

When Kieri reached Chaya again, more leaves had fallen and frosts had nipped the last roses in his mother's garden. The comfort of the palace had never seemed more welcoming: hot bath, soft carpets under his bare feet, soft clean clothes to put on. He came down to find a mug of sib steaming on his desk and Garris waiting for him with reports—and questions.

"It was a daskdraudigs," Kieri said. "And Aliam's fine now. The elves are there. I'll tell you the rest later—what about Andressat?"

"He rested two days, but would not stay longer. I couldn't tell if he was angry with you for leaving, or simply impatient to get on his way home. I sent him off with six Squires as escort. He won't have reached Verrakai's estate yet."

"The Pargunese?"

"They're definitely doing something, but we don't know what. You have letters from Arcolin. Apparently they were held up somewhere."

"I'll read them later," Kieri said. He took a swallow of sib. "Aliam's agreed to take command of our defenses, when they've rebuilt the house."

"Rebuilt—"

"I said it was a daskdraudigs. The house is mostly gone, the barns entirely."

"Holy Falk and Gird!"

"Yes. It was quite dramatic. Anyway, if the Pargunese are up to something, we'll have an experienced commander. With luck, they won't do anything until he gets here."

"With luck, they won't do anything at all," Garris said. "I should warn you, the Siers are trickling back in for full Council meetings, and they're all ready to remind you that you promised to marry."

"Will they never let up?"

"Not until you do. You know that. Is it because of Tammarion? Remembering her?"

"No," Kieri said. "I haven't found the right woman."

His Siers, the next morning, were as insistent as Garris had warned. He had run off without warning, into danger. The daskdraudigs could have killed him, and they needed an heir if they were to lose a king to rashness.

CHAPTER TWENTY-FIVE

Verrakai House, Tsaia

On her return from the Autumn Court, Dorrin planned to tell Selfer at once that Arcolin wanted that cohort to return to the Company. Instead, she found that the Count of Andressat had arrived the day before, accompanied by two King's Squires.

"He's not best pleased you weren't here," her steward murmured. "He's come from Lyonya, where he went to see the king, and he feels the king brushed him off, sent him here to get rid of him."

Andressat, touchy and proud—Dorrin was sure Kieri hadn't been disrespectful, but she could not imagine why he would have sent Andressat here. Not only had Andressat considered himself Kieri's superior in birth, he'd had a particular dislike of female soldiers, including Dorrin. Kieri must have had some good reason . . . but what? Dorrin braced herself for a difficult evening, when she'd hoped for a relaxing one, and asked where he was.

"He has the suite at the back of the house, my lord. I thought it best—"

"Excellent," Dorrin said. "I'll go at once. Send a servant to say I'm coming, and ask Cook to send up sib and cakes."

"My lord Count," Dorrin said, as she entered. "You are welcome here; my apologies for being from home and unable to greet you myself. My king bade me stay a few days after Autumn Court." Andressat had been reading, she saw; a litter of scrolls lay on the table.

"My lady—lord—Duke," Andressat said. "I—I took no offense; I have no right—"

He seemed older, much older, than he had when last she saw him, and it had been only those few years.

"I am but now arrived," Dorrin said, "and I have called for refreshment before changing for dinner." A timely knock came on the door; a kitchen maid entered with a tray. "You will join me?" Dorrin asked.

"Er . . . yes . . . thank you."

The girl poured sib into wide cups of delicate southern ware and set them on the table. Dorrin settled herself gingerly in the chair across from the one he'd been in. The last two days on the way, the weather had turned cold and wet; she was longing for a soft chair and a warm fire.

Andressat did not sit until she gestured to him, and then perched on the edge of his chair, obviously nervous. She had never seen him anything but confident, even arrogant; she could not believe that her own rank impressed him, having heard before his opinion of northern titles. Curiosity overcame her fatigue as the room's warmth and a few swallows of sib eased her bone-deep chill.

She waited until he, too, had drunk half his cup of sib and nibbled a pastry while she ate two. "My lord Count," she said then, "I am happy to have you here as my guest, but I do wonder that you have come so far, in this season. Surely it is some matter of importance that brings you here."

"Yes, my lady—lord—" He blinked, flushed, looked down. "I'm sorry; I'm not used to your form of address."

"No matter," Dorrin said. "Everyone stumbled over it at first. Tsaia has not had a woman duke for generations."

He took another gulp of sib, nearly choked, then put the cup down. "My lord Duke, what I have to say—what I wanted to say to the king—is a grave matter—a dangerous matter—but I must explain—"

"Go ahead," Dorrin said.

"It began when that man Alured—who now calls himself Visla Vaskronin—claimed the duchy of Immer," Andressat said.

Dorrin listened with growing interest—and alarm—as Andressat told her about Alured/Vaskronin's demands: that he be recognized as the legitimate heir of Immer from ancestry in Old Aare, that Andressat send his archives to Cortes Immer for Alured's scribes to examine.

"And that I would not," Andressat said, with some of the spirit she remembered. "My forefathers gathered all they could of old records—it is the greatest library in Aarenis. I would not lose it to that—person."

"How did he take your refusal?" Dorrin asked, though she was sure she knew.

"He threatened me," Andressat said. "Threatened me, and sent an envoy, with soldiers, to demand that I let his scribes examine every document in my archives. He was sure I had proof of his royal ancestry and was denying him out of my own ambition." Andressat met Dorrin's gaze. "I swear to you, Duke Verrakai, that I have no ambition of ruling Aarenis. It is enough for me to rule my own land well, even if . . ." He paused. Dorrin waited, but he seemed unlikely to continue, his gaze now fixed on his sib.

"This is certainly enough for me," Dorrin said, trying for common ground. "Though I had commanded a cohort, I had no idea how much work there is in a domain, even of this size."

"Yes," Andressat said. He sighed; Dorrin wondered if he longed for his much warmer homeland. "What you must know is . . . in my archives, I did find much of interest. Of interest to Alured, certainly, but also to everyone—everyone in Aarenis and also you folk in the north. I wanted to talk to the king about it, and apologize—"

"Apologize?"

"For my past rudeness." Andressat had flushed now, continuing to stare at the half-empty cup. "I—I always thought our claim to nobility was best, you see. The northern titles mongrel, born of nothing but ambitious pride. That we of Andressat, and the Duke of Fall, were the last and only to have direct descent from those who had ruled in Aare." He paused again, then gulped and went on. "I was wrong. I treated him—the king—and you yourself as if you were baseborn, persons of no lineage, when it is I who have no claim beyond that of . . . of convenience."

Dorrin stared; he looked up, and she saw his eyes glittering with tears he quickly blinked back.

"My pardon, my lord," he said, his voice a little thick. "It is still hard to admit."

She felt a rush of compassion for this old man, annoying as he had been before. "My lord Count," she said, "whatever you think of your lineage, you yourself have served your realm well. If my opinion counts for anything, you deserve your title."

"That may be," he said, "but the fact is that my ancestors who came to Aarenis from Aare were craftsmen, not nobles. The title was given because too few nobles escaped the final disaster to govern the land . . . Commoners were elevated, and my family, my lord, were one of them. I did not know this until this past summer." He went on, more fluently now that the worst of his shame had been told, to describe the flood that had caused his father and grandfather to reorder the archives and begin sorting and copying those damaged and how he himself had been trained as a scribe and scholar initially, before he came to rule.

By then it was dark, and despite the pastries and the fire, Dorrin was both stiff and hungry. She held up a hand when it seemed he was about to embark on another part of his tale.

"By your leave, my lord, I will go refresh myself before dinner, and after dinner we can resume."

He flushed again. "Of course. I'm sorry, my lord, I forget time . . . and you have journeyed today . . . perhaps tomorrow?"

"After dinner will be well enough," Dorrin said. "I am eager to hear more."

Dinner passed quickly; Dorrin and her squires were hungry and talked little. Andressat and the King's Squires who had accompanied him made their own inroads into the roast meats and other foods. The King's Squires asked leave to ready themselves for departure the next morning, now that Dorrin was in residence.

"I have an urgent message for your king," Dorrin said, "that I thought to send by one of my people—are you allowed to carry messages for others?"

"Certainly, my lord," the woman said. "If it will not delay us."

"No," Dorrin said. "My lord Count, if you will excuse me briefly, I will be back with you shortly in the sitting room." He bowed, and she led the King's Squires to her office. "I have a letter for the king from his former captain, Jandelir Arcolin, and a sword found in Aarenis, cleansed and blessed by a Captain of Falk, which the letter concerns."

She handed over the familiar message-case Arcolin had given her, the same kind they'd used for years in the Company, brown leather stamped with the fox-head and tied with maroon laces. "And here's the sword."

The man's eyes widened. "That's a Halveric sword! What was it doing in Aarenis? Halveric Company's been quartered in Lyonya the last two years."

"I know," Dorrin said. "It's a family sword; Arcolin thought Kieri—your king—should give it back to the Halverics rather than have Andressat take it, as it closely involved a matter of honor for both the king and the Halveric. Will you do this?"

"Of course," the man said. The others nodded.

"And give the king my heartiest good wishes," Dorrin said. "I will write him at length, with much that Arcolin told me, but tonight I must hear more from Andressat, and you want to leave early tomorrow, do you not?"

"Yes, my lord."

"Then order what you will, in hall and stable, and Falk's Honor go with you, if you leave before I rise."

"Thank you, my lord." They bowed and withdrew; Dorrin rejoined Andressat in the sitting room, where he had built up the fire.

He resumed without delay.

"It was a shock to find out we were not of pure blood," he said. "I did not want Alured to find out, lest he insist on removing my family from the rule of Andressat. We do not have the resources to resist him for long, should he invade—and yes, I think that a possibility. He is more like Siniava than any of us guessed. He wants to rule the south—all of it."

"Surely he doesn't think he can—" Dorrin began.

"Indeed he does," Andressat said. "Aarenis and more than Aarenis. He has heard rumors of a crown—of royal regalia that once belonged in Aare—"

Dorrin stiffened. "How—what made him think—"

"Rumors of such came through Valdaire after Midsummer," Andressat said. "I myself heard nothing of it until later, but apparently

Alured's spies in the north—yes, my lord, that is what I said, in the north—told him of some excitement at court when your king was crowned. I could not determine if this was the sight of the Tsaian crown, or something else. It is widely known that the northern rulers came from Aare to Aarenis, and then went over the mountains."

Dorrin felt her tongue cleaving to the roof of her now-dry mouth. Just as she and the king feared: Alured knew of the crown. Alured— ambitious and ruthless Alured—would want it.

Andressat went on. "He is more dangerous than Siniava . . . He wants it all: Aarenis, the Eight Kingdoms, and then—by what his scribe told me—he wants to mount an invasion of Old Aare and restore it to glory and himself to its rule."

"Does he know for certain that such a crown exists?" Dorrin asked.

"He believes so," Andressat said. "Were you at the coronation? Did you see anything to support his belief?"

"I was there." Dorrin tried to think how to proceed. Though too many people knew about the crown for it to remain a secret, King Mikeli had asked his peers to say only that it was held in the royal treasury. "Did you find out what Alured thinks the crown looks like? The Tsaian crown is mostly rubies."

"Was the Tsaian crown lost or hidden for a time?"

"No," Dorrin said. "I think it was made after the Girdish wars, as the old crown had been lost."

"Lost—its fate not known?" His eyes brightened. "That could be it—not a crown of Aare but of Tsaia's old king—"

"The royal treasury has several crowns," Dorrin said. "Rumors of a hidden crown before the coronation could have been spread by traitors among my own relatives. Alured's spies might have heard and believed such rumors."

"That could be," Andressat said. "But Alured believes in such a crown, and believes he has a right to it. He has gathered troops; I am convinced he is behind the counterfeiting of Guild League currency. He will have agents in the north, even now, seeking that crown. If he connects your name with it—"

"I doubt he will, but I take your warning," Dorrin said. "More important than my safety is the security of Tsaia. My king charged me with the organization of the kingdom's military—to assess the threat that disorder in Aarenis might spread north and to prepare. What you have told me makes it imperative that you go to Vérella and tell King Mikeli what you have told me. Tell me, what did Kieri—the king in Lyonya—say when you told him?"

Andressat scowled. "I cannot blame him—he, a king and royal-born, after the way I treated him in my own realm—but he scarcely listened. He was concerned about Aliam Halveric, whose lady had begged me to carry a message to the king—and when he read it he made haste to leave for Halveric Steading."

"What's wrong with Aliam?" Dorrin asked.

"I do not know," Andressat said. "He seemed older, and unhappy, but—" He shrugged. "I do not know why the king left in such haste, before I could explain my errand."

"Aliam took him in, when he was a starveling stray, and made him squire and then sponsored him to Falk's Hall," Dorrin said. "If Aliam needed him—if Estil thought Aliam needed him—of course Kieri would go at once."

"Yes, but—"

"My lord Count, I beg you not to think he left to slight you. His story is his to tell, not mine, but he has every reason to value Aliam Halveric highly, to consider his welfare important to that realm. Instead, let me urge you to go to Vérella and speak to King Mikeli. I will give you an introduction and an escort. If I were not needed here, I would go with you, so important do I think your warning. You must rest a few days, of course, but the king must know of the peril you mention before winter closes in and travel becomes difficult. You will wish to be back in the south, on your own land, by then."

The next morning, Dorrin talked to Selfer about the cohort's re-turn to the Company. "Arcolin will send some south early," she said. "He wants a full three cohorts in Aarenis next season, and will be sending at least a cohort as soon as he's made his dispositions in the north. From what Andressat tells me, he'll need every one of them, and there will be plenty of work."

Selfer nodded, trying not to look pleased at the prospect of returning to the Company. "When will you release us?"

"As soon as the Count is rested and can travel again," Dorrin said. "Andressat needs a strong escort to Vérella—the king must know what he told me, and it is not safe for him to travel alone. I presume you'll be staying on with Arcolin as a captain."

"I hope so," Selfer said. "Though I still want to complete my training as knight."

"I'm sure you will," Dorrin said. "I expect the Count will be ready to travel in a few days."

Andressat, when she asked, looked out the window at what was now a steady cold rain and asked if there was any chance the weather might clear later on. Dorrin thought of the high, dry hills near Cortes Andres and wished her magery could whisk him home. "It might clear," she said. "Not today or tomorrow, but perhaps the next day. Rain comes with the cold blowing down from the north this time of year."

"How many days to Vérella?" he asked.

"It depends on the roads," Dorrin said. "Right now they're muddy; this rain won't help. When they freeze, later in winter, before the snow's too deep, it's easier, but—" He was shivering at the thought. Dorrin looked more closely at his clothes. He wore southern style, she realized: cloth woven from the fibers of southern plants; her own shirts for campaigning were of the same stuff. His silk surcoat wasn't heavy enough for this cold spell.

How could she offer what he needed without offending him?

"After the Evener, people here wear wool," she said. "I daresay you brought no wool, thinking it too warm, is that not so?"

"Yes. At home we hardly feel a chill in air until half-winter and then it is but a chill."

"My lord Count, please honor me by accepting warmer clothes— plain but more suited to our climate—for the rest of your journey."

Andressat grimaced but then nodded, and she had warm winter clothes delivered to his suite. When he came back again, clothed in layers of wool, he looked much more cheerful and said he could be ready to travel in a day or two.

Dorrin took that opportunity to talk to the cohort herself. One or two, she thought, might want to stay with her rather than face a season of hard combat or retire to the harsher climate of the north. To her surprise, eight stepped forward at once.

"We never swore oath to Captain Arcolin," Vossik said. "Our oath was to Duke Phelan, only when he took the crown he released us, and then we came with you—we been with you all these years; we know you—"

"You know Arcolin, too," Dorrin said. "A fine captain he's always been and a fine count now. He'll be a duke in time, if that's what—"

"It's not." Vossik swallowed and looked at his companions.

"And there's Captain Selfer, who's your captain—he needs you—"

"Not as much as you do, my lord." Again that hasty look aside and back to meet her eyes. "We want to stay here. We want to serve *you*, give our oaths to *you*."

Dorrin looked at them: five men, three women, all veterans she'd known for years. All were Girdish, not too surprising, but— "Did the Marshal-General tell you to keep an eye on me?" she asked. "Is that why you want to stay?"

"No, my lord," Vossik said. "We wasn't even in Vérella with you, as you know."

"I know she's written Selfer," Dorrin said.

"Aye. He told us, too. And it's not that we don't respect him, but he's not you."

"I can't abide the thought of the stronghold without the Duke," Voln said. "It was him I swore fealty to, that first year, and now he's gone—"

"I can't go back," Natzlin said. She had been silent until then, as she had been since she returned from Lyonya, recovered from her physical wounds, but very different from before. "I can't go and see—think about—Barra—"

Dorrin felt more sympathy for Natzlin than the others; she had been so dependent on Barra, putting up with Barra's difficult personality and by that relationship isolated from others. But they were all correct: legally, these men and women had been oathbound to Phelan only so long as he was both their liege and Mikeli's vassal. Now it was as if he had broken his oath, and those who had sworn fealty to him were free until they swore to another.

"I'll talk to Captain Selfer," she said. "You're right: your oath to Phelan is void, and since you have not yet sworn to Arcolin, you're free to make your own choices. I will remind you that all your friends and companions of years past will be with the Company under Arcolin."

"But we were always in *your* cohort," Voln said.

Selfer, when she spoke to him, agreed that the eight could stay without argument from him. "The Company's still over strength. The Duke—the king—would not want his veterans forced into service, even if there were a legal way to do it, and there's not. They're veterans; they've the right to leave. In fact, I should probably ask them all openly—especially if you're willing to take those who want to stay with you. You know them; you can trust them."

"I'm worried about Natzlin," Dorrin said. "I know she's physically recovered from her wounds, but she's been so quiet . . . I don't know if she can recover from Barra."

"Better here with you than anywhere else," Selfer said. "And you wouldn't know this, but I've heard rumors about her and someone in a village near—not Kindle, but Oakmotte. Best thing for her, if it works out."

"You're right," Dorrin said. "And I could use as many as want to leave. They—and you—have accomplished a lot with the Verrakaien militia, but it takes more than a half-year or so to change a lifetime's habit."

Selfer's talk to the cohort resulted in seven more choosing to stay. He and Dorrin went over the accounts that afternoon as the cohort prepared to march—he insisting that the cohort had eaten enough at her table to wipe out the debts for which she'd signed and Dorrin determined not to take advantage. They shook hands on it at last. The next day a stiff north wind blew the rain clouds south, and the following morning Selfer mounted and led the cohort away, with Andressat, bundled to the nose, riding beside him. Dorrin watched her former cohort go with a lump in her throat. She'd thought she was past mourning for her old life, but that last glimpse of the fox-head pennant disappearing into the trees pierced her heart.

Enough. It was done, it was over, and she must waste no more time. She looked at the fifteen left behind, whose expressions showed what she felt, along with a determination to stick with the choice they'd made. "It's time to put on Verrakai uniforms," she said. "Change, and then come back and I'll take your oaths." They were back very shortly, bare legs now in gray wool trousers, blue tunics instead of maroon over them. Dorrin took their oaths using the same form she had used for the original Verrakai militia, with her squires as witnesses.

"You'll be the nucleus, the training cadre, for the force I'm supposed to keep ready for the Crown," Dorrin said. After what she'd heard from Andressat, she had no doubt the king would need it. "What I'm proposing now is that you'll be split into three hands, each hand having a sergeant and two corporals—though I expect you'll all be promoted within two years. You'll be paired with two or more hands of the existing militia, and I'm going to give each of the squires a chance to command one of these groups. I'll expect you to work with the new Girdish bartons and granges, to recruit suitable young people to the militia, and keep improving the skills and fitness of those already in."

"How much fighting do you think we'll see?"

"I don't know," Dorrin said. "I still don't know where all my relatives are, or when trouble might erupt elsewhere. But with you for a core, and the squires as trainee commanders, I can disperse the militia to cover more of the domain—and as you help the militia grow, that will improve even more. I'm thinking now of ten-day patrols, village to village with an overnight or two-night stay in each. One group will stay here, while the other two go out, and then rotate. You can model the proper way to move troops and treat civilians."

Next morning, Gwenno Marrakai headed east with her fifteen, under orders to patrol as far as the Lyonyan border, if possible, and then return. On the fifth day, Dorrin sent Dar Serrostin west. Beclan Mahieran, predictably, grumbled about being the last to leave on patrol.

"Why?" he asked.

Dorrin gave him her best quelling look. "The short answer is, because I ordered it. The longer answer—which you would have had without asking if you'd been patient—is that I wanted you for the south sector, which I consider the most difficult. You'll be going as far as Konhalt lands; as you know, they're also under attainder, and have a new count they don't know. It would not surprise me to find rebels lurking in the woods down there. You will have two full ten-squads, not just three hands of troops, and you have been given an

CHAPTER TWENTY-SIX

Lyonya

Kieri had just finished breakfast when he heard voices in the entrance, louder than usual. One of his Squires looked out. "Sir King, it's a courier."

"If you please," Kieri said to his breakfast companions, and they cleared the room at once as the courier hurried in. To the courier, Kieri said, "You are fatigued; will you have breakfast?"

"No, Sir King; the news is too urgent. I come from the Royal Archers, near the river."

"Invasion?"

"Not exactly . . ." The man handed him a scroll; Kieri broke the seal and unrolled it.

"You might as well have a hot drink while I read," Kieri said. "There's sib in the pot." He scanned the terse report. Someone had come across the river at night; a Royal Archers' patrol had taken him in custody. Though dressed like a fisherman, he claimed to be the king of Pargun. He had no proof of his claim; he might be crazy, the Royal Archer officer had written, but he carried himself like one used to command.

"Did you see the man?" Kieri asked the courier.

The man swallowed hastily. "Yes, Sir King. But I have never seen the king of Pargun, so I cannot say—"

"He swam, or came in a boat?"

"A boat."

It made no sense. Why would the king of Pargun—if it was he—sneak across the river at night? To spy? He must have spies; he would not need to spy himself. If he wanted to visit Lyonya—see his daughter, perhaps?—why not come openly, with an entourage?

"Did he say more?"

"I don't know, Sir King. The captain bade me ride with all speed; I left as soon as the captain had written that message."

"If he is the king—or the king's envoy—then I must know his purpose quickly."

"You cannot risk yourself—" one of his Squires said.

"He doesn't know my face any more than I know his," Kieri said. Surely he could ride north as fast as this messenger had come south, and surely the Pargunese—whoever he was—would not know how fast he could ride. "Aulin, tell Garris that I will need an escort of King's Squires, those well rested and able to ride at once for the river. Then tell the Master of Horse we will need remounts, as well as mounts saddled, and someone to care for them."

In less than a glass they were on their way, riding on a forest track Kieri had not seen before. Kieri wore hunting clothes without royal insignia; the King's Squires wore plain tunics in place of the royal tabards.

When he arrived at the Royal Archers' bivouac, a turn of the glass after sending in a Squire to warn the Archers he was incognito, their captain greeted him only as "my lord." Kieri nodded and looked around the camp until he spotted a burly man sitting against a tree, two Royal Archers nearby watching.

The prisoner wore a fisherman's rough smock, short trousers, and striped stockings; his boots were piled with his other possessions in the boat in which he'd come, now pulled up away from the water. His light hair—blond going gray—and pale blue eyes were common to many in the north, and his face and hands were sun-marked like those of men who worked outdoors all the time. The only indication of kingship was the gold ring with its seal, but his eyes reminded Kieri of Elis.

"He says if we kill him, there will be war and Lyonya will be burnt to ash," the captain said.

"I'm not planning to kill him," Kieri said. "Unless I have to. He might be a simple fisherman who's had river fever and merely thinks he's a king." Unlikely, but possible.

"With that ring?"

"Or a thief. Every realm has thieves, even Pargun." Kieri ignored the man, instead inspecting the boat and its contents. The boots had spur scuffs on the heels. He shook them. "Did you turn these out?"

"No, my lord. We saw the ring. The man's gabble sounded Pargunese; we thought you should see first."

Kieri upended the boots into the boat, shaking vigorously. Out fell a small knife in a sheath and four silver Tsaian coronets.

"He had eight coppers in his belt-pouch, my lord. Two with a Prealíth mark, one of ours, the rest from Tsaia."

Currencies mingled in river towns; that fit the character of a fisherman. Kieri felt inside the boots: nothing more. He pulled the knife from its sheath, watching the prisoner. The man's face showed no expression. The blade showed a dark stain, as if it had been dipped in some liquid, since dried. Poison, possibly. Kieri put it back in its sheath. The boot heels next—he twisted. One turned, revealing a small compartment. Inside was an oiled-leather packet marked with runes. Kieri tipped that out without touching it; poisons could be carried in such packets. Next he emptied the pack. In that were clothes more suited to a peddler than a fisherman, a box of trinkets—mostly small religious charms—and enough food for a few days' travel.

"When did you capture him?" he asked. He knew already, but the captive didn't know that.

"Three nights agone, my lord. We sent word to you—we thought the king should know."

"Word has been sent," Kieri said. He put down the box on top of the other things, picked up the small knife, and walked over to the captive. He could feel the man's anger and loathing as if it were visible waves of color. "He has been given food? You know the king's orders about that—?"

"Yes, my lord. Food, water, and a blanket at night, though we dared not unbind him in the dark."

Kieri squatted down in front of the captive. In Pargunese he said, "This is not a fisherman's knife. It is not the knife for gutting, or the knife for scaling, or the knife for filleting. With this knife, you would only poison a fish and make it unfit to eat. Why would a fisherman poison a fish?"

The man spat, but the gob of spit did not reach Kieri. Then the man looked away.

Still in Pargunese, Kieri said. "If I were minded to kill you, you would be dead already. If I were minded to hurt you, your flesh would already be torn. You claim to be a king in your own land—what are you doing here?"

The man looked at him again. In Pargunese he said, "Your king stole my daughter."

Kieri's brows went up. "Our king steals no women. And why would a king who believed such come himself and not send envoys or an army?"

"Envoys were with her; they came back without her. Stolen away, she was, sent to a brothel, a house of soldiers. That is not a matter for armies; that is a matter for a man of honor to meet her betrayer man to man. I must feel his blood hot on my hands myself; I must pull his guts from his living body myself." Fury flamed in those pale eyes.

"You intend to kill Lyonya's king," Kieri said. It scarcely seemed possible that an assassin would admit his intent so baldly. And the accusations—he could not take them in: they were unbelievable.

"And display his villainy for all to see," the man said. He seemed absolutely certain and, though angry, perfectly sane. "He debauched his own soldiers, and yet Tsaia would not denounce him. Even the Girdish, prigs that they are, made no complaints of him." He spat again, but this time more politely, to one side.

"I did not know this," Kieri said. He had never fully understood the Pargunese hatred for him personally; it had been a fact of his adult life, and nothing more.

The man nodded sharply. "None of you mageborn treat women with real respect," he said. Kieri heard a stir behind him and put up his hand; no one said anything. He nodded to the man, who after a look around shrugged and went on. "Your king," he said, squirming a little as if to settle into a more comfortable position for a long tale. "He held land in northern Tsaia; that you surely know." Kieri nodded. "He had a mercenary company before—perhaps you know that." Kieri nodded again. "Well, then. I know that in other lands, women train in weapons skills. So also a few of ours; it is not good, but it need not be an offense to the gods. Your king—*your king*—sent men out to find girls, young girls who knew nothing of weapons or war, and brought them to his stronghold. Far from their families, far from any protection of their kin, and there—there his soldiers took what pleasure they wanted."

Kieri fought down the urge to defend himself, explain. If this was what the Pargunese believed, then perhaps their enmity made sense of a sort.

"They became soldiers—they had to, to survive; they could not go home after such disgrace. Living among men not their families, alone—what else could they do but whore and fight?"

Kieri made an indeterminate sound, and as he hoped, the man went on.

"Never to marry, never to bear children for their family's honor, forever ruined—and yet, and *yet,* you gave him the crown. How you could endure such—"

"So how did he get your daughter?" Kieri asked.

The man grimaced. "He seduced her long ago, I fear. She was always rebellious; I blame her mother, who was from Kostandan, where women are allowed too much freedom. Her mother learned obedience before her death, but there is something in the blood. At any rate, my daughter would learn weapons lore from her brothers, and was happier on a horse than afoot."

"Pargun breeds good horses," Kieri said.

"Horses are well enough," the man said, "but ships are a man's wealth. It is by ships we know the most of your king's behavior. In far Aarenis, which no one else in the north regards, our captains visit every port, and there they have seen your king's soldiers, men and women alike, walking bare-legged in the marketplace. They bear themselves like harlots, those women—shameless and proud."

"Still . . ." Kieri said, letting his voice trail off.

"Your king is unmarried," the man said. "It is said he was married before, to one of his own soldiers, who bore his children. But he left her alone in the north, and she was killed because he did not protect her. Even so, as a king, I thought he must be surrounded by those who would keep him from such vileness. So, with due care, I sent my rebellious daughter to his court. If he married her, and proved honorable, it might bring peace to the north. She alone of my daughters might, I thought, be less apt for his abuse. If he insisted she ride and hunt . . . well, she would not mind so much."

Kieri stood up. "You must come to Chaya," he said, "and see the king."

"As a prisoner?" the man said. "To be killed like any common criminal? If that is your notion of honor, kill me here. Boast to your king of it, then. My brothers and sons wait across the river; they will avenge me and my daughter."

Kieri had not imagined this as his first meeting with the king of Pargun. "The king may not kill you," he said. "But you must make your accusations formally, in front of witnesses, and you will want to see your daughter—"

"I do not want to see her as she is now," the man said. "If I see her I must kill her, for her honor and mine." His eyes blurred with tears suddenly, the first emotion he'd shown other than anger. "You—if you do not have daughters, you cannot imagine what it is—those little soft faces, little flowers, we call them. Hers was as bright as any— she was willful as the early spring flowers that push through snow and will not droop or fold for frost or wind. We quarreled much as she grew older—but when she still had milk teeth and would climb into my lap . . ." The man shook his head.

"I, too, lost a daughter," Kieri said. He shut his eyes on the memory of Estil in his own lap.

"But not to such dishonor, I will guess," the man said. "My daughter's life is my pain, not her death."

"You must come to Chaya and meet our king," Kieri said again. "I thought at first you were a fisherman mind-mazed by fever or some demon, but now I think you may indeed be the king of Pargun. But since you came not openly in your own person, with proof of your identity, I am bound to send you thither a prisoner, though I will tell these men to treat you with respect."

"When I am dead, these trees will burn," the man said. "My army—"

"Do you wish to send word to them what happened and where you are going?"

"No. They have their orders. I have time enough to reach Chaya and your king, kill him, and return. If I do not, they will attack."

This was not what Kieri wanted to hear. He turned to the others and said in Common, "I now believe this man is indeed the king of Pargun." The king of Pargun undoubtedly knew more Common than he was comfortable speaking; he expected the man to understand. "He has a grievance against our king because of the matter of the princess. He must be taken to Chaya under close guard, but with all due respect. I will send horses, and send messages to Chaya, that the king's Council be prepared. Take all his things with him. One of you come with me."

Kieri mounted and rode off, meeting his Squires out of sight of the clearing. At a hand gallop, he rode for the reserve cohort, and explained that an attack might come at any time. "I need eight of your reserve horses: send them with this Archer, who will show the way. The king of Pargun must be conveyed safely—and swiftly—to Chaya. With not a word to him about me or his daughter, whatever you know or think you know."

"At once, Sir King." The cohort's captain had men and horses ready with commendable speed. "And?"

"Word to all near the river. The Royal Archers will inform the rangers. The Pargunese plan to fire the forest, burn Lyonya to the bare ground. They must come by boat; the Royal Archers and rangers should be able to cut their numbers, unless they come at night and cannot be seen . . . which is exactly what they'll do. I must go."

As he rode for Chaya, he tried to think what else to do. The Sagon of the west would be there of a certainty. Would they strip their eastern and northern borders as well? How many troops could they muster, and how fast? How many boats would they have ready? And how could he convince the king that he had not despoiled Elis? Without risking her life?

All this because he had let that wicked old woman Hanlin think he wanted peace. He did want peace—that was no lie—but he did not want the peace of defeat.

He changed horses at the first relay station, riding on through the night as Elis herself had, but with more awareness. If he had known the Pargunese thought women soldiers were all nothing more than whores for the men . . . if he had known the king would think an entry to Falk's Hall was a disgrace and not an honor . . . what else could he have done?

They were insane, the Pargunese. They had strong women and destroyed them, just for the men's pride . . . how was that honorable? He tried to imagine the king of Pargun and his grandmother talking . . . surely an elven lady could convince the man that strong women were not dishonorable. That imagined image dissolved as it came: the king of Pargun would believe he had been managed with elven magery, and he would never agree.

Another relay point—he chuckled as he remembered that he'd thought he wouldn't need so many personal mounts. Through the night, he found himself thinking of one mistake after another he'd made since he became king. Most, he knew, were trivial, and he'd corrected them, but this—this one could plunge his realm into war.

At the third relay point, near dawn, he stopped to eat; his Squires looked less tired than he felt, but not as alert as usual. He had explained to them, while riding, what the king of Pargun thought. They'd been shocked, first angry and then thoughtful, as he was. Now, after the meal, he shook his head when one of them stood. "We will rest until the sun is two hands higher," he said. He stretched out on the ground, feeling the healthy life beneath and around him, and fell asleep at once.

He woke before his Squires; the rangers at the relay station had more food ready, and he drank and ate before they were off again. Kieri thought about the taig, and what the Kuakgan had done the night of the battle. He had "roused the taig," Paks said, and the Pargunese had been afraid to enter the trees.

Could he do something like that along the river and inland? Make the forest impassable so the Pargunese could not reach it to burn it? Or did they have engines of war able to throw stones—or fire—the distance across the river? They traded all the way to Aarenis—he had not realized that—and so their captains would have seen such engines.

Back in Chaya, he collected his Council at once, adding several of the elves not usually part of it. He outlined the situation.

"They think you sent her to a *brothel*? Falk's Hall?"

"He has no conception of a woman choosing to be a soldier, and being one, other than coercion and rape," Kieri said. "He knows I've commanded units with men and women both, which in their terms means the women are being exploited by the men."

"That's—obscene."

"I agree. But he sees our behavior as obscene."

"But—he sent the girl to you—"

"To kill me. That poisoned knife she gave me, you recall? It was meant for me, on our wedding night."

"Gods! How can those people live?"

"I don't know," Kieri said. "But we must be ready to listen and try to understand if we do not want fires in our land. I'm sending to Halveric to come as soon as he can, house or no. I need whatever trained troops all of you have, as well. Untrained won't do: the Pargunese army is not a bunch of farm lads with sticks." He looked at the elves. "You must also help, if it comes to that. He has sworn to burn the forest to the mountains; I do not know enough yet about the taig to prevent it, without your aid."

"The Lady could convince him," one of the elves said.

Kieri shook his head. "I don't think so. His ideas are so fixed—he would believe it was all magery and not listen to her reasons."

"And you think he will listen to yours?" the elf asked.

"He may not," Kieri said. "I will do what I can to persuade him . . . I don't intend to let him kill me . . . and I do not know if he will return home if he doesn't."

"It seems incredible that he would come alone, in disguise."

"Yes. I don't know why he did that, either. Everything they've done—sending the old lady, sending Elis without warning, his appearance—makes no sense to me. Yet he is not a stupid man, or insane; we were enemies across a border, and everything he ordered there made sense, inconvenient as it often was."

"He's had an illness? He's had an injury?"

"Not that I could tell. It must be, as with this thing about women soldiers, that he thinks very differently . . . and he thinks we have the same ideas, just different values."

It did not escape Kieri's notice that he felt much more competent preparing for an invasion than he had in planning for peace. He set in order the movement of supplies, of reinforcements, pored over the maps . . . realizing that for the first time in his life he must trust distant field commanders rather than take the field himself.

Regular couriers brought word of the Pargunese king's progress toward Chaya. Orlith and other elves wanted more time to teach him more about the taig; he could spare very little. What he wanted was someone who could teach him more about the Pargunese, but Orlith knew little more than he'd said before.

"We left those eastern shores long ago," he said.

"To come here?"

"No. To Aare, most of those who had been east of the water. We did not like it. Too far from our people here in the west, and too full of rockfolk. Mountains come close to the sea there, north and south both, and they were not pleased if we did not stay on the coast. The Seafolk then were farther south and avoided us; we knew them little."

Interesting history, but what he needed now was some useful information, something that would help him persuade the Pargunese not to attack Lyonya.

On the third day, the Pargunese king and his escort arrived in Chaya. The king rode well, as Kieri expected. He watched from an upper window, and saw his people greet the king courteously. He would have delayed their meeting to give the king a night to recover himself from the journey, but he could not, with the Pargunese army poised to attack. The king would be fed, bathed, and dressed in what Kieri could only hope were acceptable clothes, and then they must meet.

Kieri chose to receive the king in the smaller reception room. When he went down to check the room, it was prepared as he had asked. No weapons in the room, no breakable carafes or goblets . . . and the guest's chair, massive and deep, would not make a throwing weapon.

"I still think you must bind him," Berne said. Arian nodded.

"It is gross discourtesy; he has been humiliated enough," Kieri said.

"He said he wants to feel your blood on his hands."

"I know. I was there. But he will not want it less for being bound. He talks of honor; let us see if he will give his word, and keep it."

"And if he does not?"

"He has no weapons, and no poison on him; he has been bathed and dressed in our garments. Aside from that, if he wants to fight me barehanded and is foolish enough to do so here—I am not incapable."

"I know, my lord king, but your life is our responsibility."

"You will be within call."

"We should be in the room with you. What if he calls up an evil demon?"

Kieri shook his head. "He could have done that to escape those who captured him. Let us not make up trouble for ourselves. Just outside the door will be well enough; he can't lock it against you."

He moved to the door himself, hearing approaching footsteps. The king, under close guard, was coming down the passage. He wore the garments he'd been offered, a velvet tunic over heavy wool trousers and low soft-soled boots. He stopped abruptly when he saw Kieri.

"You!" he said in Common. "*You* are the king? You lied to me."

"No more than you to me," Kieri said, "when you sent that old woman to spy at my coronation and she said you wanted peace. She should have described me better." The king said nothing. Kieri went on, this time in Pargunese. "You spoke to me of honor. If you give your word that you will not attack me while we talk, you will not be bound, and my Squires will leave us alone. Will you?"

"Why should I?"

"Because, if I wished it, you could be bound like a herdbeast and killed, or locked in a cell. If you are intent on killing me, you will have time. If there is a way of having peace between our people, yours and mine, I want to find it. And you will be more comfortable unbound."

"I cannot swear never to kill you."

"No one could swear that," Kieri said. "That is not what I ask. Swear not to attack me for one turn of the glass."

"And then you will kill me?"

"Not if I can avoid it," Kieri said. "Though I do not expect you to believe it."

The king looked at the King's Squires to either side of him, and shrugged. "It makes no difference, I suppose, one glass. You can lie, and I will listen, if that is what you want. But one of us will die, and if it is I, your land will suffer."

"If either of us dies, both lands will suffer," Kieri said. "My people would like to hear you say it in Common, if you will."

The king uttered an oath in Pargunese, then said in Common, "I have given my word not to attack your king for the full turn of a glass. I would see the glass."

"Here it is," one of the Squires said.

The king looked, and nodded. "Well, then. I am ready."

"Come in," Kieri said. "And be seated." He waved at the chair, and the king sat in it, gingerly at first, and then leaned back.

"It is too soft," he said. "A man would learn to slump in such a chair."

"My apologies," Kieri said, sitting in his own. "I was thinking of your long ride. I can have someone bring a hard one."

"No matter. Have your say; perhaps in this soft chair I can sleep and not listen to your lies."

"If you are trying to anger me," Kieri said, "and force me to fight you, that will not work."

"Will it not? I had heard you were a man easy to anger, quick to take offense."

"Perhaps I was once, but I am trying to learn better," Kieri said. When the king said nothing, he went on. "Until I came here, I knew nothing of where your people came from. I did not know you were Seafolk from over the eastern sea."

The king opened one eye. "Did you not? It is common knowledge with us. Where did you think we came from?"

"I suppose I thought you were mixed mageborn and old human, like most of those in the Eight Kingdoms."

"Mixed! We do not mix, and certainly not with magelords. You drove us out of our homes, and then, here, attacked us again." The king leaned forward. "And then, not content with attacking us, confining us to colder, less fertile land north of the river, you despoil my daughter."

"You sent her here," Kieri said. "Why?"

"My first wife's sister thought you might have changed, and of my daughters, Elis was the strongest . . . you had wed one of your soldiers before."

"She told me you had promised her a home far in the north, where she could live unmarried."

The king waved his hand. "It was a girl's fancy. And yet, I might have let her—she had frightened away several suitors—but when you came, I thought, if she and you wed, it might bring peace. Worth more than a girl's daydream, if that could be."

"Um." Kieri nodded at the pitcher on the table. "There's water, if you want it." The king shook his head. "Elis told me you gave her a knife—a poisoned knife—to kill me on our wedding night. That if she did so, and escaped, you promised to let her live as she pleased."

The king looked the way Kieri had felt when Elis told him. "She— she said *what*? I gave her no such knife!"

"She had such a knife. She told me where her escort kept it. I had their things searched, and it was there. She said she'd been forbidden all weapons but that, and that only after our wedding."

"I did tell them not to let her have weapons. She is a wildcat; she might have attacked her own escort." He scowled. "But I never gave her a poisoned knife to use on you, much as I wish you dead. And Elis . . . I cannot believe she would lie about that. Who told her?"

"She said her escorts told her it was your command. And it is her escorts, is it not, who reported to you that she had been dishon- ored?"

"Yes . . ." Now the king looked thoughtful.

"Tell me," Kieri said, "why you came alone, in disguise, instead of sending an envoy, or coming in person, openly. It is not a kingly act."

"It is *my* disgrace. *My* honor. My brothers—my sister-sons—all said so, and the challenge was given. It is our way."

"I do not understand," Kieri said, though he was beginning to guess. He needed better than a guess.

"A leader protects his people. If he cannot protect them, he is no better than a slave . . . someone will challenge for leadership, and ei- ther they fight for it or the others vote . . . it depends on the issue."

"And they challenged you because your daughter stayed here?"

"Because you sent her to that place of infamy."

"To us," Kieri said, "it is a place of honor, where Knights of Falk are trained."

"Falk!" the king said, and spat on the carpet. "A magelord! What could be honorable about Falk?"

"Do you even know the story?"

The king waved his hand again. "Something about working in a stable to free his brothers . . . that's not how to free prisoners. He should have fought . . ."

"That's what I told the Knight-Commander when I trained there," Kieri said. "He did not appreciate it."

"You trained in that place?"

"Yes." Kieri could feel the man's intense curiosity, and also his determination not to ask. "It is a place to learn more than just fighting skills. I did not grow up in this palace." As quickly as he could, he told the story: the fateful journey, the abduction, the years of torment.

"Scars do not lie, but men do," the king said. "If you have been so mistreated, surely you bear the marks of it on your body. Show me."

"I will," Kieri said. He felt suddenly cold, but not the same way he had as a boy. "I would ask that you allow one of my Squires to attend me."

"As you wish," the king said.

Kieri called Berne; he came in the door in a rush. "It is no emergency. The king has offered me no violence, but would see my scars; I want someone in the room while I disrobe."

"Disrobe? For this—"

"This *visitor*," Kieri said carefully, "has asked proof of my history. The proof lies in my scars."

"But . . . Sir King . . ."

Kieri shrugged. "If this ends our enmity, it will be worth any embarrassment." With Berne in the room, he felt safe enough to pull his tunic over his head; the momentary blindness always bothered him, but less this way. With the king's eyes on him, he unbuttoned his shirt, pulling it from his trousers and then taking it off. The scars had faded with age, as they did on most, but still made a raised pattern on his naturally pale skin. The newer scars, the ones from the wars he'd fought, were clearly made by weapons and overlaid the older, finer patterns laid on by his master in the years of captivity. He turned away from the king's eyes, raising his arms so they showed clearly, from neck to waist.

When he turned back, the king was staring, mouth a little open; his mouth snapped shut abruptly, then he said, "That was done when?"

"I was taken when I was four winters old, and did not escape for at least eight years. There are more scars, which you will *not* see unless you kill me and strip my body." Kieri said this as grimly as he felt; he saw understanding seep into the other king's face.

"You were only a child . . . and you say this was a magelord who did it? How do you know?"

"He had the magery to force people to stillness." Kieri put his arms back into the shirt Berne held for him, and buttoned it again. "He could force prisoners to silence even in great torment, or hold them motionless for the same."

"How did you ever escape? Eight years . . . no normal child could survive . . ."

"He had no intent to kill me. He wanted me alive, to suffer. But—" Kieri looked over at the glass, now quickly running out. "—you promised to listen for only one glass. I would not abuse your patience."

"Turn the glass again," the king said. "I am not convinced I will not have to kill you, but I must know how you escaped."

CHAPTER TWENTY-SEVEN

"I t is part mystery and part your own people," Kieri said. "How I was freed is the mystery; I do not understand it still, except as a gift of the gods. How I came back across the sea was a gift of the Seafolk, who, finding me hiding aboard and retching myself dry, did not throw me overboard to drown, but took pity on me for these same marks—some then still bleeding—and carried me across the sea to Bannerlíth and there set me ashore with a full belly, a few coins, and a shirt to my back. If not for the Seafolk I would not now be alive."

"You did not tell them who you were?"

"I did not know, by then. The baron told me a short version of my true name over and over, until it was all the name I knew. I was too young—I had a few memories, but no way to describe them to anyone and all I had learned told me it was dangerous to try."

The king chewed his lip for a long moment. "I heard a tale," he said finally. "I am a king; kings have spies; you will not despise me for that—"

Kieri shrugged. "Of course not. Any man of war must have spies."

"Good. Then—I heard a tale, brought by a spy from Tsaia, that you said something like this to that Council, and were believed."

"Some of them believed," Kieri said. "Some did not. But their belief or unbelief does not affect the truth of it."

"It is a tale someone might tell," the king said, "who perhaps had been orphaned and mistreated, and wanted to think himself a lost prince."

"Indeed," Kieri said. "But I had no thought of being a lost prince: not then, not later. I knew I had come from a good home, and had found myself in a bad one: that is all. When I came to Halveric—" It had been in this season, with the trees losing their leaves, the nights cold, the days crisp, and harvests gathered in. "—I came in autumn, having gone inland from Bannerlíth—something drew me; I knew not what. But having found scant employment, and none with winter drawing in, I came to Halveric Steading a starveling beggar. And they took me in, as your folk had done, and fed me and would have had me a house servant, as I had been trained and was neat in serving at table."

"From servant to squire is a long step," the king said.

"All praise to the Halverics for giving me every chance they could," Kieri said. "And that is a very long tale to tell. But it is due to the Halverics that, again, I lived—lived through that winter when I would otherwise have died, and lived years with them to relearn what a good home is, and then a good commander. You have spies in Aarenis, you said: they must have told you about Halveric Company."

"Yes. Good fighters, well-disciplined, and not such as we wanted to meet. Yours the same. But both of you use women badly, and do not protect them."

"Some women do not want to be protected," Kieri said.

The king snorted. "Oh, some girls are wild and think they want adventure; they little know what war is. They are brave enough, our women, but their blood should be shed only in the marriage bed, bearing strong sons."

"And daughters," Kieri said.

"And daughters, yes. We must have daughters for the people to have children and live on. That is why a brave woman's death in war is a waste." He paused, staring at his hands on his knees, a man clearly trying to think of something else. When he looked up, he said, "The tale I heard included a magic sword . . . made by elves, the spy told my advisor, but you might as well know we think elves are but magelords themselves."

Kieri nearly choked at that. "Elves magelords? No, they are not so!

They are Elders, like the rockfolk, older and wiser than men. But yes, that is my sword now—it always was, but it was lost when my mother was killed and I was taken."

"I would see this magic sword," the king said.

"As you will, if you trust me with a blade in your presence."

The king shrugged. "As you said, if you wanted to kill me, you could already have done it. I think a man bearing your scars is unlikely to kill an unarmed man sitting still and offering no insult."

"It is hanging just outside," Kieri said. He called again, and this time Arian answered. "Bring my sword, please, and then withdraw if the king of Pargun wishes it."

"I am as happy with a witness," the king said.

Arian brought in the sword and offered it formally to Kieri, laid over both hands. Kieri took it the same way.

"No one can draw it now but me," he said. "In proof of that, try it—" He held it out to the Pargunese, who stared a moment.

"You know I intend to kill you and you are giving me a magic sword? Are you indeed blind in the mind?"

"No," Kieri said. "But you are a man who wants proof, not words. You will find proof."

The king took the sword; Kieri ignored Arian's indrawn breath, and waited. A hand on the scabbard, a hand on the grip—the great green jewel of the pommel was dark and almost opaque. The king tugged. Nothing happened. He tried again; Kieri could see, under his sleeve, the bulge of his muscles. Again. The king looked up.

"So there is a trick to it?"

"Not a trick. Hold it so, and I will but touch the scabbard." The king kept his grip and Kieri put his hand on the scabbard, a light touch. The king's hand flew off the grip as if hit; he yelped. The sword swung toward Kieri, who put his own hand on the grip; the jewel burst into light, and he drew it singing from the scabbard, the blade glowing blue.

The king shrank back in his chair a moment, looking from the sword to his own hands. "I—it threw me off!"

"It did not harm you—"

"No—but I could not hold it when you touched it. And—" He eyed the blade again. "—and it is certainly magic, whoever made it." He kept looking, as Kieri sheathed the blade and handed it, on its belt, back to Arian, who withdrew with it. "If I had known this—known it, not heard vague tales—it would have suggested we might have a common enemy, but it still does not affect your treatment of my daughter."

"I treated her with all honor," Kieri said firmly, sitting down again. "She came uninvited, as you know; what you may not know is that she arrived before her baggage, having ridden away from her escort and tried to escape them. They followed at speed; they could not stop her, but were with her when she came to the palace in the dead of night."

"I was not told that."

"I presume they were ashamed at having lost her, even for a short while," Kieri said. "While I slept, my staff gave them rooms to suit their claims of royalty; I did not see your daughter until a day later, after she had rested and her baggage arrived. In the meantime, another uninvited princess had arrived, from Kostandan."

"From Kostandan? Who would they send, that half-cripple Ganlin?"

"Half-cripple?"

"Did she not limp along half-sideways? She fell from a horse as a child and could not walk at all for most of a year—she is some kind of relative of my wife's, so I heard things."

"She limps but little, and only when she is tired," Kieri said. "A pleasant girl, but another who did not wish to come. Her aunt is a formidable woman, and I wonder now if she told such tales when she returned home as your daughter's escort did."

"There can be no good tales told," the king said, his expression hardening.

"Can there not? Listen, then. Your daughter—and the Kostandanyan princess—had rooms in the guest wing of the palace. Their attendants were nearby, unless they were warded by female members of my household—King's Squires, in fact, well able to protect them should the need arise. They had the freedom of the rose garden, when their attendants permitted. When I met them at dinner, they and their escorts, they were both unhappy to be here—"

"And no wonder," interrupted the king. "Seeing what came of it."

"And each desired a private audience. I chose instead to speak to them only in company for some days. The couple escorting your daughter told me she was your pledge of desire for peace, a strong girl and perhaps willful, but certainly able to bear me strong sons. I asked if she was willing, and they shrugged—the woman shrugged—and said she might take some persuasion, but I was surely strong enough to master a mere girl." Kieri paused; the king said nothing. "I am not minded to 'master' the woman I marry and force a girl who does not want me. 'Court her but a little,' the woman said, 'and she will realize her good fortune.'" Kieri poured himself a mug of water and sipped. "It sickened me, but I did not yet know the girl was truly unwilling, and for courtesy I agreed to talk with her. We walked in the rose garden."

"Roses are a soft southern flower," the king said.

"My mother planted that garden," Kieri said. "I would not change it." He sipped again. "So we walked, and I asked her why she had come. She answered shortly at first, but finally said she had been drugged and carried away in the night. With my history, you can imagine, perhaps, how that affected me."

The king looked thoughtful. "I did not know," he said. "Now I see . . . it made you remember . . ."

"I always remember," Kieri said. "And I would not marry an un-willing woman, certainly not one who had been treated that way. I told her so; her first expression was relief, but then fear. I asked what frightened her, and she said your anger. You would punish her, she said, and she would never have the life she wanted." He paused again; the king's expression had softened slightly. "That is when she told me about the knife, and about what her guardians had told her were your orders."

The king's eyes flew open. "Orders I did not give. I will not say I never thought of that, because I did, but in the end I rejected it. No child of mine should play assassin; it is unworthy of royalty to do such deeds, and she, in particular, would feel that."

"But she thought you had. She begged my help. She begged me to contrive an escape for her. She would do anything, she said, be it never so hard or humble. She would cut her hair and dress as a boy; she would cut herself and scar her face; she would . . . she had a double-hand of ideas, most involving mutilation or death. She seemed in the mood I had been in, not caring if only I could escape."

"But I didn't—"

"She thought you had," Kieri said again. "She acted on what she had been told. Have you not done the same, and I as well? Do not all men, if they have been told plausible lies, believe them and act accordingly?"

"Perhaps . . . yes, I suppose so. But Elis . . ." His hands clenched and unclenched.

"She went on her knees to me, as if she were my subject, and would have clasped them, promising obedience to any orders I might give her—as long as they accorded with her desires, that is."

The king gave a harsh bark of laughter. "*That* is like Elis. Obedient to my will when my will ran with hers."

"I reminded her that might look ill, should her guardians be watching, and said I would think on it, but could promise no more for the time. I would, I said, keep secret our conversation and asked her to do the same. Then I took her back inside, and bowed over her hand, and had my interview with the other princess—with Ganlin."

"From what Hanlin says, she is far more biddable than Elis," the king said.

"Indeed she may seem so—she is younger by a few years, I think—but she was no more interested in marrying me than your daughter. Her injury and pain have taught her more patience, but her determination I judge not less. She first met your daughter a few years ago, in Kostandan—"

"My wife took Elis to visit her own parents. Apparently Elis behaved badly, and they came home early. She was found instructing Kostandanyan princes in the art of riding." The king's voice carried a mix of pride and ruefulness. "She wore trousers to do so, and her grandmother was scandalized and scolded my wife for her leniency."

"Ganlin admires Elis greatly; she is not as strong but has in some ways modeled herself on the Elis she saw in that visit. According to her, Elis is her best friend; they have written each other secretly—"

"What!"

"Using a courier between Pargun and Kostandan; I do not know who, because neither of them wants to get the fellow in trouble. At any rate, Ganlin knew of Elis's plans to have her own horse-farm, and planned to run off and join her there."

"Ridiculous!"

"On that I agree. Young people that age easily develop hero-worship of an older, more striking relative, and given time and freedom, out-grow it. Aliam Halveric's son Cal followed me around like a puppy when I was first a squire, but he had other models, and though we are friends now, it is no more than is proper. But still, when Ganlin also asked my help to escape the fate her father intended, and told me she, too, had been apprehended and forced to come to my court, I decided to help them."

"By sending them to . . ." the king did not quite say "brothel" this time, but his eyes said it for him.

"By sending them, at my expense, where they wanted to go—to a knights' training hall. I could have offered the choice of training with the Girdish, but Falk, I thought, would be more acceptable to you and to Ganlin's father. I was wrong, but did not know it."

"At your expense—you are not living off their pay?"

"Surely you have better spies than that!" Kieri let his anger show. "Falk's Hall is not some Girdish grange welcoming any farmer's brat who can pick up a hauk: the fees are high, and the students cared for as if they were the Knight-Commander's own . . . within the limits of the training, which is long and difficult."

"But they have both men and women there . . . it must be . . ."

"A place where well-born young men and women train to become honorable warriors, and some to become paladins."

"Oh, paladins!" The king sniffed. "Troublemakers, those are."

"Only for those desiring evil," Kieri said. "Look here—I am willing to admit that your ways are different from ours, and that you may not intend evil, yet do things I think are wrong. But to sneer at paladins—"

"*She* says they are troublemakers," the king said, making a hand-sign Kieri did not know.

"She?"

"You know. The Lady. The Weaver."

Kieri's blood ran cold. "You are not speaking of Alyanya the Lady of Peace or the Lady of the Ladysforest?"

The king looked blank. "I know neither of those ladies. I mean the true Lady, the Weaver, she who knows all secrets."

That could mean only one being: Achrya, Webmistress, who had attacked Kieri and those he loved so many times.

"You mean Achrya," he said.

The king made another gesture. "You must not say her name; she will be angry."

"I will be angrier," Kieri said. "Have you, then, been in league with her all these years? Was it *you* who connived at the death of my wife and my children, and yet you come complaining because I gave your daughter a chance at an *honorable* life?" Kieri felt his old rage rising within him, a white fire that yearned to consume the man who had killed Tammarion, their children, and yet would not have dirtied his own hands with the deed. "You made war on my children!" he said, knowing his voice hoarse with that rage.

"I—no!"

"When?" Kieri demanded. Some part of his mind told him to fight the rage, but he did not want to listen to it. Not with the memory of Tamar, of the children—

"Peace," said a voice. Kieri managed to turn away from the king, and realized only then he had grabbed the man's shoulders and held him down. "Peace," the voice said again, and calmness filled Kieri's mind even as the glow of elf-light filled the room. His grandmother stood in the doorway, watching him. He bowed.

"You have a strange way of seeking peace," she said. "I could feel the taig flinching from my own home and came to see what was afoot." She turned to the king in his chair, now rubbing his shoulders with both hands. "And you," she said. "You boasted of never having seen an elf, did you not?"

"Who are you?" he asked. And then, jerking his chin toward Kieri, "He hurt me."

She chuckled. "Hurt your pride, maybe, but not your body. Kieri, grandson, you will introduce me to this man."

Kieri realized then that he had never asked the king's name, and fell back on titles. "The king of Pargun, my lady. And this is the Lady of the Ladysforest, the ruler of that elvenhome kingdom."

The king stood and bowed. "My lady. I do not know the correct address—"

"No matter," the Lady said. "I suppose you are come chasing your wild daughter?"

"Er . . . yes."

"She will not go with you. She does not trust you."

"She must, or my people will come and burn the forest with scathefire that does not die."

The Lady seemed taller and brighter. "That will not happen," she said. She turned to Kieri. "Was it for this threat, and to save the taig, that you frightened the taig into retreat?"

"No," Kieri said. His anger felt cold and hard now, a cold ember of the fire before, but still solid in his mind. "He follows Achrya and I believe he planned the deaths of my wife and children years ago, with her help."

Her brows went up. "Well, king of Pargun? What say you?"

Before the king could speak, Kieri saw the thread of elf-light that coiled around him. The king would be compelled to speak truth.

It came out in Pargunese, in a rhythm that sounded more chant than speech. "When we came up the river, fleeing the magelords' slavers, the Earthfolk granted us landright from the river to the hills that lay between the forests and the horsefolk fields to winterwards. They said go not beyond the great falls, for there demons reign. But the slavers came and harried the river shore, and some of our people were taken. Beyond the falls the slavers could not go, and beyond the falls we went, only to be safe from harm. Then came the Lady, the Weaver, and gave us patterns of power for our women's looms, so the cloth of our sails never rots nor tears in the wind's grip. We could live there, She said, and worship what gods we would, as long as we did her bidding from time to time. It was her land first, she said." At first, he said, she had asked little, but king by king she had entered into the councils more and more . . . and yet she had brought peace and prosperity mostly, until the magelords came from the south. "And then was war, and blood like water, and bones like stones in the ploughed ground, and without Her aid, we would have perished. So are the words I learned from my father, and he from his, and he from his, all the way back to the beginning of our time."

"And did you connive at the deaths of my grandson's wife and children?" the Lady asked. Her voice was soft and sweet but held such menace as Kieri had never heard in it before.

"Never," the king said. "They were killed by orcs, I heard, and we have nothing to do with orcs. Nor was I glad to know them dead, for

I knew it would make the Fox angry, and he would find a way to blame us for it, as he finally has."

"And yet," she said, still sweetly, "you paid the man Venneristimon, who was his steward. What did you pay him for?"

"Venner?" The king looked startled. "For information on Phelan's movements, his plans for his army, that is all. I did not wish to find that army a day's ride into my kingdom; I needed a spy, and he was willing."

"It was Venner—" Kieri began, in a choked voice. She held up her hand. He stopped.

"It was that man," she told the king, "who planned the deaths of my grandson's wife and children. We know that. And you say you did not know?"

"I did not," the king said. His eyes were wide; he looked more like a man shocked at truths previously unknown than someone having the truth pulled from him unwillingly. "I bade him spy—so I would know if Phelan massed against me. Who—who told him to do that?"

"The same Weaver you worship," the Lady said. "Achrya the plotter, the secret weaver of tangled and poisoned webs, lover of plots . . . *she* told him."

Kieri glanced aside from the look on the king's face to the shelf where the glass stood, the last few grains to fall suspended, motionless, in his grandmother's trance of time.

"It . . . it cannot be," the king whispered; his eyes had filled with tears. "She said kill *children*? She—she has been good to *us*—"

"For her own purposes, possibly," the Lady said. "But she has wrapped you round in lies the way a spider wraps her prey, blinded you with that unyielding silk. You cannot see what is clear to see: not your daughter's true nature, not the ambitions of those at your court, not the character of my grandson. You are tangled in her web, nothing more than a morsel for her to devour at leisure, for she enjoys most fooling those who trust her." She waited a moment; he said nothing. "I would pity you," the Lady said, "if I could, for you have lost a child and a realm by choosing Achrya and evil. But it is not in my nature to pity those who harm my family, and you have done grievous hurt, though without knowing it."

"I'm . . . sorry," the king said. His tears had spilled over, wetting his cheeks.

"Grandson, what do you really want here? His death? Vengeance? Or peace?"

"I wanted peace," Kieri said. Slowly, slowly, that cold lump of anger shrank inside him. "I want peace now. But how can we have peace if he—if his people—do not? *You* can withdraw to elvenhome kingdoms where humans cannot come. We must stay in this world, and abide what evil comes—fight it or no, we have no safe havens."

"Your family—?" the Lady prompted.

"Died years ago. And I believe—" He did not want to believe, but the king's tears had convinced him. "—he did not really intend their deaths. Was he stupid to be fooled? Yes, but after all, *I* did not recognize that Venneristimon was one of her pawns until Paks exposed him." He looked at the king, who was staring at him as if he had sprouted feathers. "I was angry," Kieri said. "I am still angry that they died as they did. But we have killed enough of each other's people over the years; I will not kill you because of that."

"I am not so easily moved to forgiveness," the Lady said, her voice as cold as his heart had been. "But you are our king, and I must defer to your judgment." It was the first time she had ever said that or anything like it; Kieri wanted to ask why—but he could not, not then. She looked straight at the king of Pargun. "But you, mortal: whatever grievance you have against my grandson, give it up. Or it will become a matter between you and me, and thus to be settled in *my* realm, not his."

"Your . . . realm?"

"What humans call the elvenhome kingdom of Ladysforest. I do not choose to share its name with you." With that, she withdrew, the light folding in around her, and the last grains of sand falling at last.

"She . . . that . . . that is your *grandmother*?"

For some reason, after so much emotion, Kieri found this amusing. "Do you still think elves are but a variety of mageborn?"

The king drew a long breath and released it, half huff and half sigh. "No. No, she is . . . how old is she?"

"I have no idea, and I would not dare ask," Kieri said. "Thousands of years at least, I am sure. Certainly she was here—in her kingdom, which is not exactly the forests of Lyonya—when the first Seafolk came up the river seeking safety. She was here before the mageborn came over the mountains, and probably before they left Old Aare."

"She looks young . . . but not young."

"Yes," Kieri said. "But you and I, sir, are kings with a problem to solve. We do not, I assure you, want *her* to solve it for us."

That got him a sharp look, but the king relaxed. "I would have some water now, if you please."

"Indeed." Kieri poured him water. "And shall I now turn the glass again?"

The king shook his head sharply, swallowed, and said, "We are well beyond that. You are not my friend, and may never be, but I give my word not to attack you. I see no way to peace here, but perhaps together . . ." He drained the mug. "Is there any chance—*any* chance—that Elis would see me?"

"I do not know. I sent word to Falk's Hall that you had come and were concerned for her welfare. We may hear tomorrow if she chooses to reply. But she will have sworn an oath to obey the Knight-Commander and other officers while she is a student there. He would have to permit her to leave."

"She is imprisoned?"

"Only by her honor," Kieri said. "Should she wish to withdraw and return home, she would be provided an escort to the river. And the Knight-Commander, seeing it is a matter of royal concern, may well bring her here and order her to see you. If she does not obey, she will lose her place. Falk's Hall—like the other knightly training orders—is used to difficult sons and daughters of noble families."

"Then she might actually learn discipline?"

"She will, or she will not gain her ruby," Kieri said.

"And you?" The king seemed to be looking for that ruby.

"My ruby is still in the cabinet in the Knight-Commander's office, in a little box with my name on it, should I give my oath to Falk."

"You are strange," the king said. "You are not what I thought."

"Nor are you," Kieri said. "But it has grown late as we talked. Let us sup a little, and sleep, and in the morning consider what is best for both our kingdoms."

"And where shall I sleep?" the king asked, a little of his earlier suspicion returning.

"Not in *my* bed," Kieri said. "But if you will, in the same room where your daughter stayed when she was here."

"Locked in?"

"Watched, if you come out," Kieri said. "Have you no guards in your own palace in Rostvok?"

The king nodded.

The Knight-Commander, in Falk's red and white, sat with Elis at one end of the table; Kieri and the king of Pargun sat at the other. Kieri's sword lay athwart the table, a reminder whose domain it was, in case emotion overpowered reason. Elis, in the leaf-brown uniform of Falk's Hall for first-year students, sat bolt upright, pale, lips compressed. She was here by the Knight-Commander's orders, as Kieri knew, and she did not look at her father.

Her father scarce looked at anything else in the room but her.

Kieri tapped the table to get his attention. "We are met to discuss grave matters of state," he said. "Pargun is in disarray, and that disarray threatens to spill over its borders, the king tells me. Knight-Commander, I believe you have not met the king of Pargun: I present him to you. And to you, Sir King—" The title felt strange in his mouth, but it must be given. "—I present the Knight-Commander of Falk, he who commands in Falk's Hall, where Knights of Falk are trained."

The two men acknowledged each other with a seated bow. The Knight-Commander spoke. "I have brought Elis of Pargun as you requested, my lord king. As a student in Falk's Hall, she cannot travel alone, and she wishes to remain there until she has earned her ruby. As her guardian while she is under my command, I must ask if you intend to withdraw your support of her candidacy."

"No," Kieri said. "I support her still."

"Then it was not to send her home you had her brought here?"

"No," Kieri said. "I do not go back on my word. But her land and mine are at risk of war, and her father, Pargun's king, would have her know what is happening."

Elis opened her mouth, glanced at the Knight-Commander, and closed it again. Kieri turned to the king of Pargun.

"She is here," he said. "And, you can see, unharmed. Have speech with her, if you would." Down the table, he saw Elis pale even more; her eyes were wide.

"Daughter," the king of Pargun said. He cleared his throat. "Elis, the king knows . . . you must know . . . I did not, on my honor, want you to kill this king. What Countess Settik told you was a lie."

"Your *honor*!" she said, her voice edged with scorn. The Knight-Commander touched her arm; she folded her lips.

"I did break my word to you, that is true," the king said. "I did have you drugged and brought here—I thought your wish to live alone was but a willful girl's daydream, and you owed duty to serve Pargun in some way. Here, as a king's wife, you could do that, and this man—though as I thought a rough soldier—would neither fear you nor be disgusted by your own rough ways."

Elis said nothing, staring at Kieri's sword on the table with lips folded tight.

"I did not know, until this king told me of his talks with you, about the poisoned knife. I did not know that my brother planned to challenge me for the kingdom and so he told me—told all the court—that this king had not only refused to wed you, but had sold you to a brothel of soldiers."

Her head came up; her eyes flashed. "Einar?"

"Indeed. And before all he questioned my judgment and my fitness to rule. If I was so weak that for peace I would send my daughter to such dishonor, and not avenge her myself, with my own hands, then it was time for a better man, a stronger man, to rule Pargun or the whole kingdom would be sold like a slave." The king swallowed. "It was he who urged me on to send you in the first place."

"And now," Kieri said, "the Pargunese army waits across the river for their chance to attack and fire our forests and burn us all."

CHAPTER TWENTY-EIGHT

"Burn the forest?" the Knight-Commander said.

"Yes," the king of Pargun said. "It is what Einar said he would do to avenge both me, if I did not come back alive with proof that I had killed this king, and you, Elis. Our funeral pyre, to cleanse our honor and that of Pargun."

"You burn your own dead?" the Knight-Commander said, in a tone of horror.

"You do not?" the king said. "But—but how do you free their spirits, if you do not give them an honorable fire?"

Kieri spoke, before that got out of hand. "We can discuss later the ways of honoring the dead," he said. "But you must know, Sir King, that we burn only those whose evil threatens the land: orcs, other vile creatures, and the worst of criminals. Here is another difference between us that could be easily misunderstood."

The king chewed his mustache. The Knight-Commander had the expression of a man discovering half a worm in a fruit he has just bitten. Kieri went on.

"We must think and act quickly. The king, if he returns to Pargun without Elis and proof of my death, faces rebellion and death. If lucky, he tells me, he will be allowed to face his brother alone in mortal combat. He might prevail, if the fight is fair, but he might be killed through a chance of war or through treachery. Otherwise he will be killed, as soon as his army knows he has not avenged the presumed dishonor of his daughter, and his brother will take command—as it is clear from what the king has told me has been his brother's intention all along."

Kieri looked at the Knight-Commander. "Something we did not know—to these people, the Webmistress has appeared as a helper, even a savior, as she has enmeshed them in her plots without their awareness."

"That cannot be," the Knight-Commander said. "Every man and woman can sense evil and good—"

"Unless through long exposure they have been blinded and deafened," Kieri said. "They accepted her aid first in a time of great peril for them; they were new in the land and did not know one from another. But it is her influence that has kept them hostile so long, and she has kept them fearful with her lies and insinuations, and her punishments as well."

"You say they were new in the land—where did your people come from?" The Knight-Commander now looked at the king of Pargun.

"From across the eastern sea, from the land below the mountains," he said. "Those lords from Aare came and drove us out, enslaving us, tormenting us. We came here for refuge, for we had fished in these waters since time began."

"Ancestors of those who tormented me also tormented them," Kieri said. "And it was his people—the Seafolk—who brought me home again when I escaped my tormentor. We have that in common. It is not much, but it must be enough if we are not to see this land ablaze with war, and his as well. You know what the elves and some of the Council thought, when the sword proclaimed me. They were afraid I would bring war here, though I swore I had no such intent. A soldier, they said, could not bring peace."

"But you did—"

"No." Kieri shook his head. "I meant to; I wanted to. But I did not know enough—I did not know that in Pargun they believe all women soldiers—even women knights—are but playthings of the men they serve with. He believed all these years that the women who joined my Company and others were lured from home, from the protection of brothers and fathers, and then abused."

"Falk's Hall?" The Knight-Commander sounded as furious as Kieri had first felt.

"Yes. And his informants, her escorts—" He nodded at Elis. "—told him the same. So in my attempt to honor her wishes, and do her honor by sending her to you, where I knew she would be safe, I provoked this conflict. True, the king's brother had intended it, but I fell into his trap the same way the Pargunese as a whole fell into Achrya's."

"I must go back," Elis said in a small voice. "I must go back, mustn't I? To save the kingdoms. To save . . ." Her voice faltered. "To save the king's life."

"No," Kieri said. "If you went back, they would not believe what you said. Your father told me so. They want you back, but only to lock you up. That is a waste of any young life, let alone that of a princess of Pargun."

"But then he—"

"Be still, recruit," the Knight-Commander said, but not roughly. "You are not yet in command." Her cheeks flushed, but she said nothing. To Kieri, he said, "You have a plan?"

"I have a thought to lay before you," Kieri said. "Early this morning we two kings met and laid out every possibility we could think of. We may have missed something, but we think we have a way to have peace, with a king we know on the throne of Pargun, and Elis of Pargun safe and unmarried."

"A great ending, if such is possible," the Knight-Commander said.

"It will need your cooperation, and Elis's, if it is possible at all," Kieri said. "And Pargun may yet flare into war, for the king now understands that Achrya held her own aims, not the welfare of Pargun, uppermost. His brother, surely, is deep in her toils, committed to her service, and yet I believe these men—this king and many others—to be honorable at root, only mazed."

"You never thought that before," the Knight-Commander said, with a wry twist of the mouth.

"True, I did not," Kieri said. "I thought them bad men and enemies, as they thought me. A year ago—no, even last winter—I saw nothing but enemies to the east, where Pargun lay, and they, looking west, saw the same. And where did that get us all? Endless war, hot or cold. And all blinded by fear and anger, so evil—whether Achrya or another—could intrude."

"You sound like an elf," the Knight-Commander said.

"I am by half," Kieri said, shrugging. "But elf or human, I know that peace is better for the people and the land than constant war. It does not, as we have discussed before, mean unreadiness for war should it come."

"Well," the Knight-Commander said, leaning forward. "What is this thought?"

Together, Kieri and the king of Pargun laid out their idea, scarcely a plan as yet. Kieri made sure the Pargunese king spoke as much as he wished, that it was clear to Elis and the Knight-Commander that he was under no duress other than the reality of their mutual danger.

"Elis is of the royal house; she is nominally under the king's command at all times."

This time Elis merely looked at the Knight-Commander, not even opening her mouth; he shook his head.

"If we have peace, I need an ambassador at both this court and the court of Tsaia," the king said. "We have always used members of the royal family; as Elis knows, I sent my wife's sister here for the king's coronation. For the last coronation, one of my brothers; I have heard here that he made a fool of himself on southern wine."

"Brandy," the Knight-Commander said. "We thought you had strong drink at home."

"We do, but he was never allowed so much," the king said. "But he was a young man." He shrugged.

Kieri steered them back to the current matter. "As a member of the royal family, Elis could be an ambassador. She is young, and not yet skilled in the arts of diplomacy, but she is indubitably Pargunese."

"I could at least trust *her* to tell the truth," the king said. "She would always do so, even when it was inconvenient."

Elis chuckled; they all looked at her, and she blushed. "Go ahead," the Knight-Commander said.

"I'm sorry, sir—but the king—my father—is right. I hated courtly graces and pretense, and used to say the most appalling things . . . they were all true, but ill-timed."

"Falk's Knights must be courteous to all, in all difficulties," the Knight-Commander said. He glanced at the king of Pargun. "It is one of the Precepts," he said. "Our recruits must learn and practice courtesy, for Falk, even under humiliation, never stooped to rudeness."

"We value plain speaking," the king said.

"And we value the truth, but neither plain-speaking nor the truth need be rude," the Knight-Commander said.

"The day turns," Kieri said. "We have not much time, I think, from what the king said." The king nodded. "If we succeed, we will have more time to learn one another's ways, and discuss whether courtesy is lies or plain-speaking always truthful. But not now."

They all looked at him. He smiled at them, a smile he had used on his troops. It had the same effect, he saw.

"If the king appoints Elis as his ambassador, and can convince his nobles that she has been honored—and if he can convince them that my past torments across the sea create a common ground with his people—"

"But will they accept a woman so young as an ambassador?"

The king shrugged. "I do not know. I can hope. She is known to be strong-willed, and to have read more than any of our other children. And she is, for our people, over-age for marriage. As an ambassador, she would be serving our people, and be—at least formally—under my command. We have sent women before; she is just younger than the others."

"Her training at Falk's Hall?"

"On my orders," the king said, "now that I have met its commander, because I deem it the best way for her to learn about your people, and confirm or deny what we have long believed. All know she is awkward at court; at your court I would be fearful she might create an insult—" Elis looked furious, but said nothing, Kieri noticed. Only a short time in Falk's Hall and she was already learning self-control. "So I would tell my people," the king went on. Then, with a rueful look, "If they give me the chance."

"I have called a Council meeting," Kieri said. "They know, of course, about the Pargunese army across the river, and they know what forces we have, but I would refine this thought."

"It's sounding more and more like a plan to me," the Knight-Commander said. "It lacks only the way you will keep the king alive until he has told his tale. If his brother indeed intends to seize the throne, then he will surely be ready to silence and kill the man the moment he comes within reach." He looked at the Pargunese king. "Have you any trusted person to whom you can send a message? Any way to communicate other than by putting your skin at risk?"

"I thought I had brothers I could trust," the king said. "Until this." He scowled at the table.

"Iolin?" Elis asked.

"Perhaps," the king said. "One of my sons," he said to the others. "Elis's favorite brother."

"Why do you think him reliable?" Kieri asked Elis.

"He never liked my uncle Einar. He even thought—he thought Einar wanted my father's place. He had been friends with Einar's son Ailin, but they quarreled over that, last winter, and he said he dared not tell our father, for he thought Einar would hear and do worse."

"I will have to risk my skin somewhat," the king said, "because it is not kingly to risk others in my stead. My people think a king is like the captain of a ship—the king must care more for the others than himself. He must risk himself, when risk is inevitable." He smiled, a grim smile. "We do not have many aged kings."

"Iolin and my brothers will not live long if Einar is king," Elis said. "Indeed, he might contrive accidents for them now."

"We are able to think, Elis," the Knight-Commander said. "But you are right." He smiled at the king, and Kieri noticed it was a much friendlier smile. "Sir King, your daughter is more than just head-strong and hasty—she has a head apt for both diplomacy and command, should she submit to training." His smile widened. "Youngsters like these, once they start gaining their teeth, bite into life with gusto."

"So she did," the king said. "Had she been a boy—"

"We would not be sitting here trying to create a peace," Kieri said. " 'If only' will not serve us. She is what she is, what the gods made her. And we still need to get Pargun's king back to Pargun."

"I can see how you led a company all those years," the king said. "But I cannot see how I will have a chance to speak to my people."

"If you know someone trustworthy, to whom you could send a message, that one might arrange a meeting with you and some of your nobles. And Elis and the Knight-Commander, and me."

"In Pargun?"

"No, not in Pargun. I will not cross the river. But here, in one of the river towns."

A cold wind blew through the trees; the last leaves were falling fast, carpeting the track with crimson, scarlet, orange, and gold, the colors still brilliant even under the clouds.

Kieri and the king of Pargun rode side by side; ahead were half the King's Squires, and the rest behind. Though they had offered the king mail, he refused it, insisting his nobles would think he didn't trust them or had turned coward. He carried a sword as sharp as anyone's. The King's Squires had protested, but Kieri insisted. The king must be clothed and armed as a king, for this to have a chance at all.

Ahead Kieri saw the Halveric troop from the town's fort. He greeted Captain Talgan, then they went on into the wind's teeth; it seemed to sharpen with every stride.

"It's the river," Talgan said. "Looks like snow coming, too. There's already ice in the reeds along the shore."

Kieri had not visited Riverwash formally before; it lay surrounded by an arc of meadow, with a swampy area downstream before the trees closed in. A road forked off to the east, back into the trees to avoid the swamp. The river here looked like hammered pewter in the dull light, ripples chasing themselves across the surface. Across it, Pargun showed only as a dark mass of trees beneath low clouds furrowed by wind. A small crowd waited outside the town's wooden stockade and raised a shout as they came near.

Kieri waved to the crowd; so did the Pargunese king, somewhat stiffly. At the gate, two children wrapped in green cloaks and their anxious mothers waited to offer Kieri the only flowers left, pale asters in an untidy bundle, and a basket of fruit. Kieri dismounted and took them, touching each child on the forehead and then handing each a silver coin. Even the king paid toll to enter the town, but it was called "King's Grace."

At the fort on the riverbank, Kieri winced at the quality of the defenses. The Halverics had thrown up more earthworks, but it was more like a fortified camp than a true fort. It overlooked the landing stages that were stuck like fingers into the river; as a place to watch river shipping come in and out and back up the toll-keepers, that made sense, but he put it on his mental list of things to talk to the co-hort commander about.

On his orders, the cohort commander had reserved an entire inn, Sailors' Rest, for the meeting: Kieri sent two Squires to make sure it was ready, a fire lit and hot food and drink.

The cohort commander sent men to light the torches on the largest landing stage, a signal to those across the river, and two men strug-gled to hold a dark blanket behind them. The flames streamed in the wind; Kieri hoped they could be seen before it got much darker. Torches also lit the fort itself. He squinted into the wind. His old stronghold, days north of the river, would be even colder by now. He could imagine the bare branches of Kolya's apple orchard thrash-ing in this wind, the howl of it, the sentries up on the wall stamping their feet and hoping it was too cold for trouble to come in the dark.

There. A point of light flickered across the river. Someone had seen their signal. Now came the moment—would a boat come? Or would the king of Pargun's ambitious brother prevent it? He and the king, Elis and the Knight-Commander, went with the others to the landing stage. A boat was coming, rigged with a small sail.

"I can't see . . ." the king said.

Elis shivered; Kieri turned to her. "The cold?"

"No," she said, sounding sulky. "I'm afraid—afraid I'll do it wrong and ruin everything."

"We don't know what right is, so we don't know what wrong is," Kieri said. "You know the plan; you know the desired outcome. You know the people there and here both. Just think what you really want from this, and feel your way to it."

"Feel?" the king said, not quite scornfully.

"It is a situation for which none of us has a good set of rules," Kieri said. "Like a battle on unknown terrain, with new troops. She is your daughter; she is a fledgling Knight of Falk: she will do her best, and I suspect her best is very good."

"You honor me too much, Sir King," she said. She no longer sounded sulky.

"If this works," Kieri said, "no honor will be too much, for you or your father." He caught the king's eye. "And no, it is not southern flattery. Think what rests on it."

"I am thinking," the king said, "that it is time we moved to where the torches light our faces."

Flames whipped past them in the gathering dark. Kieri had found a tiara that a jeweler twisted into a half-crown for the Pargunese king. He himself wore his own. A risk, his Council had said. And he had said, "If I fall, you will have worse to worry about than a lost crown. Our only chance is for the Pargunese—enough Pargunese—to see two kings together, in council, saying the same things."

He hoped it would work.

The boat came nearer, driven by wind and steered across the river's current by a steersman standing erect on the high stern and plying his oar. The boat was half full: Kieri saw a boy or young man in rich garb, hard-faced Pargunese soldiers who must be his guard, and three other men, also richly dressed.

"That's Iolin," Elis said.

The boy made it up the steps of the landing stage first, light-footed and blown by anger as much as wind. "You!" he said to Elis, who had stepped forward to greet him. "I thought you wanted to raise horses, not go whoring among foreign soldiers! Do you even know what you have cost us?" He slapped her full in the face. Elis staggered and might have fallen if the Knight-Commander's shoulder had not braced her.

Someone just onto the landing stage from the boat yelled and ran toward them, but the king had already grabbed the boy about the body and, bellowing with rage, threw him off the landing stage into the river. The boy yelped, then came a splash and . . . nothing. Elis shrieked; the other men in the boat all yelled and came running at them; the Pargunese guards drew their swords.

Kieri ran to the downstream side in time to see the boy, encumbered by his heavy cloak, surface and go down again. "Rope!" Kieri yelled; one of the Halverics was already coming with a coil. "IOLIN!" Kieri shouted at the boy. "Rope!" The boy's face rose again, white and strained; Kieri threw the coil, and it landed near—the boy reached for it, but missed, and thrashed for it as the wind blew it toward shore, out of his reach. Then he floated into one of the pilings for the next landing stage downstream and grabbed on. "Get him!" Kieri yelled into the wind. "Down there—"

Two or three men came from a tavern near that landing, looked where Kieri pointed, and saw the boy. One dropped a rope to him; the others hauled a light skiff down the bank and pushed it out. As Kieri watched, they dragged the boy into the boat and got it back to shore, where they hauled him up the bank and then along it.

Kieri turned to find himself ringed by King's Squires, and the king of Pargun, Elis, and the Knight-Commander surrounded by Halverics, protecting them from the Pargunese guards, behind whom huddled the Pargunese lords, all but Elis with swords drawn. He wanted to knock all those heads together, but knew that as the natural irritation after a disaster narrowly averted.

"We are not here to fight," he said. "Put up those swords, and let us get this prince of Pargun somewhere warm, before he freezes or catches a river fever." No one moved for a moment but the three men pushing the sopping prince along the path. "Now," he said, putting more bite in his voice. One by one they looked at him, at one another. "We are going to that inn," he said, pointing, "where there is a warm fire, a hot meal, and dry clothes for this lad—" The dripping prince, now shivering, wet, and blue, had reached the top of the steps. "And warm dry beds," Kieri said. "For later."

The Knight-Commander obeyed first, took off his cloak, and put it around the shivering boy. "Come on, then," he said. The Pargunese king shoved his own sword back, and offered Elis his hand. The Halverics backed away; the Pargunese sheathed their swords raggedly and the Halverics in perfect order.

"Squires," Kieri said, and they finally sheathed theirs. "Come on now," he said, as if to a skittish colt or timid puppy. "It's far too cold to stand out here." Turning his back on them, he led them up and into the inn.

The innkeeper and his staff asked no questions but found clean, warm fishermen's clothes for the boy and wrapped him in a blanket in the inglenook. A long table had been laid, with not quite enough places—at Kieri's nod, the man quickly laid more. The room smelled of fresh bread just baked, roast meats, and spices. The men looked at one another, still clustered in their own kind. It was so like the way the elves and men had been—were still too often, if he was honest. Kieri ignored that for the time being, and let the servants bring them trays laden with hot sib and the herbal drink preferred in Pargun.

"Elis?" he said to her, as she stood near the Knight-Commander.

The mark on her face showed bright red against her pale skin. Her father was face to face with one of the Pargunese lords.

"I am all right," she said. "I should have expected that. I did, from my father's advisors, but not from Iolin; we were friends as late as . . . as when I came."

"And will be friends again, if you let him," Kieri said. "He is very young; he will be ashamed. Remember your duty; you are a princess of Pargun."

She nodded abruptly and looked over at the inglenook. The boy was not shivering anymore and had some color in his face; he looked utterly miserable.

"Your dinner, my lords," the innkeeper said; conversation stopped as two servants carried in a platter with a haunch of venison flanked by two suckling pigs, and another with a whole fish an armspan long. Behind came more servants with more platters: redroots, onions in cream sauce, cabbage sliced fine and steamed with vinegar and sugar—one of the favorite dishes in Pargun, the king had told Kieri. A casserole of steamed grain flavored with southern spices, breads rich with eggs and butter, hot from the oven.

Kieri and the Pargunese king moved to the seats reserved for them; Kieri looked over and saw that Elis had gone to the inglenook. She came out leading her brother by the hand. In a fisherman's smock and short breeches, he looked like a miniature and unbearded version of his father, sturdy and stubborn. Well, he had convinced their father; surely he could convince the boy . . . if Elis didn't. She sat at her father's right hand, and pulled Iolin into the seat beside her.

That said "We are family" as clearly as anything else; the other lords looked startled but did not argue. The king gave Iolin a sharp glance around Elis, but then nodded and said no more about what had happened. After that, the warmth and food had their way as Kieri had hoped. As the lords ate, the guards were served; most of Kieri's Squires ate with them; only two stood behind him. He did not protest; it was his kingdom.

When they had eaten the fish, the meats, the soup, the vegetables, the breads, and a dessert of apple tarts topped with heavy cream, one of the Pargunese lords belched loudly, leaned back in his chair, and smacked his hand on the table.

"You give a fine feast, Lyonya's king, but we are not here to feast.

You have our king tricked out in your clothes and a crown we have never seen. You are alive; that woman—" He pointed his elbow at Elis. "—is alive; what means this?" His Common was more accented than the king's.

Kieri answered him in Pargunese. "I but escort your king, who will speak to you. I will translate for the Knight-Commander of Falk, who does not speak your language."

The man turned to the Pargunese king. "Einar gave you challenge; you call us here to witness, and yet that king is alive and she is also, and I see no blood on your hands."

"Einar lied," the king said. "And not only Einar. Those I sent to escort Elis—"

"She is nameless!" the man said, thumping the table hard enough to make empty dishes dance.

"She is not," the king said. "Be still and listen!" Grumbling, the man sat back. "Those I sent to escort Elis," he repeated, "lied to her about my purpose. They told her she must kill Lyonya's king in the marriage bed."

A mutter of surprise. Kieri thought it genuine, from all of them.

"She is not an assassin," the king said. "And she had not had that word from me, myself. Elis will tell you her tale now." He gestured to her.

"I was angry when I woke and found myself in a boat on the river," Elis said. "But when they told me my father bade me kill Lyonya's king, I doubted it was his plot at all. We have all long hated and feared Duke Phelan, but my aunt Hanlin had brought back word he desired peace. I could imagine my father sending me to marry this king and then be an envoy of Pargun at his court . . ."

Kieri watched the reaction. She had schooled her voice perfectly; she sounded like herself, earnest and grave, angry here and confused there, describing how it had been, alone in a strange land, with her only countryfellows those she was sure had lied to her. One by one the lords gave up their slouches, their dismissive expressions, and leaned forward.

"So I thought, if I cannot marry this king, perhaps I can still speak for Pargun at his court. Only I did not know the language well enough, or the customs, and always my escorts were pressing me to seduce him. My lords, you have known me since childhood—I am not a girl apt at such arts." She smiled a little then, and two of the lords smiled and nodded. "So I asked the king to let me stay here, in Lyonya, but as an envoy of Pargun, and let me learn. And he suggested Falk's Hall, where I would be with other young women who, like me, loved riding and swordplay. It is a school, my lords, for those who would be knights."

Frowns now, but thoughtful ones.

The king took over in that pause. "My lords, if I had known what she was told, I could not have chosen her course better. To listen to her in Common now, she might have been born here—she knows more about Lyonya and its ways than any of us. She might have made a good horse-breeder, as she first wanted, but she is a far better envoy to Lyonya than we have ever had."

"But she has been—"

"Quite safe," the king said. "You know Elis—if she had been abused, she would say so." He turned to her. "Speak plainly, daughter of mine."

"I have been in no man's bed," Elis said. "And no man has been in mine. As I was when I left home, so I am now."

A moment of silence. Then one of the lords looked at the others. "Well. Well, that is not what Einar said. And you, Torfinn, you have never lied to me, even when I wished it. I do not see the black mark of a lie on your face now. Or on hers. And if that is so, then Einar has lied, and Einar's challenge is not valid. But how we are to convince the others I know not."

"I still do not know why we are sitting at the Fox's table and not tasting blood," the one who had first spoken said. "If he did not tup our king's daughter, he is still an enemy. We have no friends on this side the river."

"That's not true, Hafdan," the second lord said. "I have friends here, or at least men I trade with. *They* are not enemies."

"It is one thing to trade, and another to talk of peace with those who have swords all around us." His voice had risen; at the lower table, the Pargunese guards looked up abruptly.

"You are free to go," Kieri said mildly.

"I will, then," the man said. He shoved his chair back, scraping the floor, and stood.

"No," the Pargunese king said. "You will not, Hafdan. You will not go until all do, for I see the black mark on *your* face now. You were not asked; how, then, did you come?"

"I—" He looked at the other lords, who did not meet his gaze. "I wanted—"

The eldest lord looked at the king. "He came upon us as we traveled here, Sir King. We thought by mischance, but thought it best he come, lest by another mischance he carry word to Einar, which you did not wish."

The king pushed back his own chair and stood glaring at Hafdan. "You murderous traitor—you wanted me dead! You're Einar's man." He pulled off the gold circlet and tossed it on the table. Kieri had a moment to wonder whether it would be better or worse to stand; then Hafdan broke for the door, and the king rushed at him, grabbed him, and threw him down. The other Pargunese lords rose, shouting; Kieri was up without realizing it, and the Halverics had formed a line between the two on the floor and the Pargunese guards.

The innkeeper and servants hurried out and grabbed the goblets and crockery off the table; clearly they had seen dinners erupt into brawls before. Meanwhile, the two men on the floor, rolling over each other, struggled for mastery. The Pargunese lords stepped forward, back, hesitated, looked at Elis and at Kieri.

"What is going on?" Kieri asked Elis.

"Honor," she said. She had a hand clamped around her brother's arm, he noticed then, holding the boy back. "Hafdan insulted the king; the king insulted Hafdan by insinuating he was a traitor—he probably is, but it's still an insult."

"I should stop them," Kieri said. The two were both snarling like beasts, smashing each other with fists and head, kicking . . .

"No," Elis said. The Pargunese lords glanced at her, and took their hands off their swords. "It is the only way to settle it: man to man."

"They can kill each other if they want, but not on my land," Kieri said. "Dammit—I paid too much for a chance at peace to lose it for a brawl in a tavern!" The Pargunese king had the upper hand now and was throttling Hafdan; Kieri strode forward, putting a hand in the king's collar. "STOP THIS!" he roared, louder than the two men together. His voice startled even him; he had not expected that, or the light that now blazed from him.

The two combatants stared at him; the king's grip on Hafdan's throat loosened slightly, but he was not cowed. "It is an affair of honor! Let me alone—he is a traitor; I must prove it on his body—"

"Prove it somewhere else, then," Kieri said. "It is ill done to break guest-truce, and this landlord does not deserve to have a welter of blood on his floor. It is a Pargunese quarrel and none of mine. Get you across the river, and if you want to fight bare naked with teeth and nails, that is your business. You agreed to this parley, in hopes of a peace between our kingdoms. Bind this man, if you will, but let us not waste the time we have."

CHAPTER TWENTY-NINE

For a moment, the room was silent, everyone motionless, Kieri's light paling the firelight and lamps. Hafdan squinted against it.

"He's still a traitor," the king said. He jerked his head at the other lords. "Bind him like a thief." They came forward, one pulling a leather thong from his pocket. The king loosened his grip of Hafdan's throat, but still straddled him.

Hafdan's throat worked. "I thought—Einar was—right. You had—gone soft."

"Do you try to save your life?" the king asked.

"I only say—you are not soft."

"I am not, and Einar will find that soon enough." The king started to rise as the Pargunese lords leaned over Hafdan to grab his arms and bind them.

In that instant, Hafdan twisted, jerked out his dagger, and stabbed the king in the side, saying, "Not soft—but steel is harder." Before Kieri could do anything, one of the Pargunese had run a blade into Hafdan's throat.

The king put a hand to his side. "It will kill me," he said calmly. "But the traitor is dead." Then, with a groan, he slid off Hafdan's body and lay unmoving on the floor. "Tell Elis and Iolin . . ." But his voice trailed away.

Kieri had been stabbed so, by a poisoned blade . . . and Paks had healed him. But there was no paladin here, and he did not yet have the full royal magery . . . but what other chance was there? And the light had come, no longer flickering and uncertain, but still filling the room. Maybe . . .

He stepped over the traitor. "Knight-Commander," he said. "Come and help me."

"What you do?" asked one of the Pargunese lords in Common.

"Try to save him," Kieri said. The king's eyes were almost closed, but focusing on Kieri. "Breathe," Kieri said, as he would have to one of his soldiers. "Don't stop." He slit the king's doublet, the winter shirt, the undershirt, and cursed himself for not insisting the king wear mail. The wound in his side was clearly poisoned, already discolored; dark blood flowed out.

"Cannot. Is death wound," the Pargunese lord said.

"Be quiet and breathe," Kieri said, to the king. The Knight-Commander knelt at the king's head; he and Kieri locked eyes. "Knight-Commander, I ask Falk's aid for this brave man, a king, who has fought for honor—"

"Yes. I will pray—do whatever you plan—"

"I hope the gods will give me healing for him."

Kieri put his hand on the wound, as Paks had done for him. He had no idea what she had done or how; they had never talked about it. He had thought it beyond anything he would ever do or need to understand. He felt nothing at first but the hot blood, and the heart beating somewhere inside. Then, slowly, something nudged, pushed, urged him to—to what? He tried to understand, but it was not words or thoughts he could follow, just a feeling that this hand had to move, had to— He stared at the elven dagger he now held, his grandmother's coronation gift.

"No!" One of the Pargunese lords lunged at him, but two King's Squires stopped the man.

Kieri concentrated . . . lay the dagger so . . . let his desire flow down his arm into it . . . *Let him live. Let him live.* A shaft of white light shot up from the dagger's jeweled hilt, then reversed, glowing for an instant in the wound itself. The king cried out, jerked, and something dark flew out of the wound and landed clinking on the floor: the blade's tip. Bright blood flowed around the elven dagger, then stopped . . . and Kieri had a sickening view of the wound closing, the gaping flesh pulling together, layer by layer, the blood flow slowing . . . stopping . . . and the skin closing over it.

Kieri felt a great exhaustion settle on him, almost like that he had felt at Aliam's, and yet different. His vision darkened; he did not realize at first that his light had failed at last.

He looked around, blinking. The Pargunese lords huddled together; the one who had stabbed the traitor dropped his sword. It clattered on the inn's wooden floor. Elis still held her brother's arm. The Pargunese guards and Halverics still faced one another, tense and worried.

"You . . . saved me." The king lifted his arm and looked at his blood-streaked side. "How—?"

"Better gods than yours saved you," Kieri said. His head hurt; he felt dizzy. "And my grandmother's dagger."

"Elf-made?" The king looked scared.

"Yes." Kieri's head swam; he tried to push himself up and instead nearly fell over. Strong arms clasped him from behind.

"Sir King! Are you—"

"It's just . . . the healing," Kieri said. The stench of blood and death in the room sickened him. "Fresh air," he managed to say. Someone ran to the door and flung it open. In blew a gust of cold wet wind and a few snowflakes; he shivered, but the fresher air steadied him. Someone brought a chair and helped him into it. His vision cleared slowly. What a mess they had made of his carefully prepared meeting place. He took another breath, and another.

"You have it all," the Knight-Commander said to him, across the traitor's body and the blood.

"All?" Kieri said. His vision was clear now, but he still felt a strong desire to fall into a bed and sleep for a night and a day.

"Do you even know what you did?"

"Healed a wound, with the gods' aid." He bit down on a yawn. "I tried to do for him what Paksenarrion did for me."

"Did she tell you how?"

"No. We never spoke of it; I thought it paladins' mystery. It was a poisoned weapon, the same as this—the same poison, for all I know."

"Did she use a symbol of Gird?"

"I don't know . . . I was not in condition to notice."

"Light?"

"That, yes. She was the only light in the room for a time."

"As were you." The Knight-Commander sighed. "My lord king, what you have shown this night goes beyond our expectations. I heard about the daskdraudigs, but this—not for generations have we had a king with such powers. When did Orlith instruct you in healing magery?"

"He hasn't," Kieri said. "He said I still needed more training in other arts . . . I did manage to sprout a seed, though."

"It is more than a seed I witnessed," the Knight-Commander said. "It is a blackwood tree, grown to full height and flowering."

Kieri looked at the dead traitor; while he had rested, the Pargunese lords were stripping his body. One had a knife. He reached out, and Kieri understood. "No!" he said. They looked up, startled. The Knight-Commander glanced down and stared.

"No," he said, too. "You must not."

"But he needs," one of them said in halting Common, nodding at their king. "Einar said, he come back with man-pizzle, maybe prove honor. No pizzle, nobody listen."

Kieri switched to Pargunese. "I don't care what Einar said. You are not going to mutilate the body here, in Lyonya. This is my kingdom, and I forbid it." He glanced at his Squires. "Get a blanket from our gear and wrap him up well; take the body outside—the stableyard, maybe—and mount a guard over it. They can take it back to Pargun tomorrow. What they do there is their concern, not mine."

"You show honor to the traitor who would have killed me?" the king asked.

"It is not his honor that concerns me, but mine," Kieri said. "I have killed many men, but it is against my beliefs to treat their bodies as no more than that of a wolf or an ox, and take pieces. They were once men like me." He remembered having that argument with Aliam, the first time he went to Aarenis, and saw—with mingled horror and fascination—a belt decorated with human ears. *They're already dead,* he had said to Aliam, and Aliam had clouted him to the ground. *So will you be someday,* Aliam had said. *Should someone take your ears or scalp as a trophy, as if you were a wild animal?*

The king glared, then shrugged. "You saved my life," he said. "If that is your decree, in your own land, I will obey." He and the Pargunese lords moved away from the body. In Pargunese, the king spoke to the four Pargunese guards. "It is over—no more fun tonight. But if that king bids you do something, do it for me."

"We need to clean this room, and let the landlord finish clearing the table," Kieri said. "There is yet work to do; what we came for is not accomplished. I would see swords put aside and the floor cleaned."

By the time the body was gone, and the mess on the floor had been cleaned away, Kieri's headache had eased. With the door closed once more, the room warmed. Outside the storm beat at the town; wind shook the door and shutters in great gusts, and the chimney whistled and moaned. The landlord's servants having cleared the table—for a wonder, nothing had broken—the group settled around it once more. Kieri let the Pargunese king do most of the talking, speaking only when the king turned to him for confirmation.

The night dragged on. Twice the landlord came to ask if they needed anything, and finally Kieri told him to go on to bed. It was a full glass after that when the king finally got the Pargunese lords to agree that Elis was the only possible—and the best—envoy they could have to Lyonya, and the best chance of peace.

"Not that we fear war," one of them said, eyeing Kieri. "For the Lady promised us undying fire that would surely burn the forest to the roots and open the land for grain, if we had the courage to defend the king's honor."

"Undying fire?" Kieri suppressed another yawn and leaned forward.

"Yes," the lord said, turning to him. "The Lady, the Weaver, told us we would have with us scathefire that could not be quenched by anything, not even by the sea. Kindled from the bones of ancient dragons, she said."

"You know what the Earthfolk said about that, Knof," the other lord said. "We would be cursed forever if we set spade to that hill. They would withdraw their gift that they had long regretted."

"Yes, but *She*—"

"Einar told us what She said. He says She talks to him more than to the king."

"And Einar's a traitor, if the king's right. I understand that, Harn. But still—" The man looked at Kieri. "If we do want peace, it is not because we fear you, or fear war. You have hideous powers, that is clear, but so did those who drove us from our homelands." He spat, but politely, away from Kieri, toward the fire. "If you healed our king to impress us, know that I will not bend the knee to you without my king's orders."

They were prickly and proud as young boys in training, and yet, Kieri knew, they could not be treated as boys, not these men of the Pargunese king's Council. "I do not doubt your courage or your will," he said to them. Their wisdom, yes, but not their courage. "I do not want your submission; I do not want Pargun. But I do want my own land and people to flourish."

"Well." Suspicion in the tone, but agreement, too. "Well, I am not so fond of fighting I must pick quarrels out of the air. It will be as our king wishes."

As long as he was king. Kieri sent a prayer into the snow-blown night that this might be, and they sit someday eating and drinking again with no death at the end of it.

"To bed, then," the king said, slapping his knees. "We have far to go tomorrow, if we can even get across the river." Then he looked at Kieri and raised his brows.

"Upstairs or down, as it suits you," Kieri said. "I am going up." Despite the abundance of rooms, the Pargunese crowded into one on the ground floor; Kieri's Squires had brought his own bedding along, so he slid into familiar rose-scented sheets and was asleep at once. Outside his door, a King's Squire stood, and another at the head of the stairs.

In the morning, clouds and snow had blown past, and a pale blue sky scoured by wind opened over them. Kieri heard a noise in the stableyard below and pushed open a shutter, peering out to see the Pargunese king, stark naked, washing himself from a bucket of steaming water; two Pargunese lords, just as bare, were doing the same. Did they never stop proving how hardy they were? When the king had finished, he gave a shout and ran, bare as he was, around the yard, and the other two ran after him, all laughing like boys. Kieri eased the shutter closed, and shook his head.

He dressed and came down to breakfast to find the king and his lords dressed again, in clothes he had not seen, the king wearing mail and a different sword, this one with a richly jeweled hilt. On the table was a helm of the kind Kieri associated with Pargun.

"They brought my things," the king said. "If I proved worthy. You know, the only thing wrong with your kingdom, if you will forgive me, is the lack of proper baths. Those metal tubs you have in your palace—pfaugh. We have pools, with heated water, heated from underneath, hot channels. And the sweat-house, for cleansing from evil humors of the body. Your people should learn them from us."

"Perhaps we should," Kieri said. "And will, if time is given us."

"Elis can teach you," the king said. "If you learn about proper baths, perhaps you will know we are not merely wild men of the north running around naked in the cold." He gave Kieri a look that made it clear he'd noticed the shutter opening and closing.

Iolin, this morning back in his own clothes and sitting at his father's side, had a worn look, Kieri thought. If his father and the other Pargunese men had been after him all night . . . well, boys learned, or they didn't make men. Elis sat with the Knight-Commander, eating porridge so demurely Kieri wondered what she was up to. The Pargunese guards, at the other table, were eating like any experienced soldiers when hot food was available and a cold day of duty waited outside. Kieri sensed no real hostility there, and much less anxiety than the night before.

Before the glass turned again, they were ready to leave. The king grinned at Kieri and opened his arms. Kieri and the king embraced, pounding each others' backs.

"You saved me twice," the king said. "I will not forget that. If ever we must meet blade to blade, I will put nothing on mine but will."

"And I," Kieri said.

He and Elis and the Knight-Commander went with the Pargunese down to the landing stage. The Pargunese carried the wrapped body of the traitor, now frozen stiff. The boat they had come in was gone. "Back to Pargun," one of the lords said. "It is our own; we would not risk it." He took off his cloak and waved it three times. Across the river another wave—something that flashed. Kieri hoped it was not Einar's sword. A boat set out, skimming swiftly in the wind. When it tied up to the landing stage, Kieri saw long oars in it and seats for rowers. The two men crewing it lowered the sail. The guards lowered the traitor's body in, then the lords climbed down. The king embraced Elis and whispered something in her ear that made her blush; Iolin also hugged her, and then the king bowed to Kieri, who bowed in return. He and his son climbed down, and at the king's command everyone but the steersman took an oar—even the king. To Kieri's amazement, they all rowed—in perfect cadence called in the steersman's voice—out into the windswept river and the boat returned to Pargun almost as fast as it had come.

"Well," the Knight-Commander said. "That was . . . not at all what I expected."

"What we thought we knew was wrong," Kieri said. "Start to finish, the man surprised me again and again. I hope he lives and we have no invasion, but Elis—" He looked at her. "—I have been wrong about Pargun for a long time. You must help me learn."

"Of course, Sir King, though I have much to learn myself. Not only of your kingdom but—but everything a Knight of Falk must know." She glanced at the Knight-Commander.

Kieri spent the rest of that day conferring with the Halveric commander, the town mayor, and representatives of the rangers and Royal Archers who had ridden in to meet him. The town had records of past floods, freezes, and thaws in its archives; Kieri suspected that the Pargunese would rather attack over the ice, but after seeing the speed with which they could row across into the wind, he wasn't sure. To make up for the loss of business the night before, Kieri had arranged to hold a public reception in the same inn. He shook innumerable hands, accepted presents—more practical than had shown up at his coronation, for the local craft specialty was knitting the fine underfur of a wild animal that lived along the river, and every woman seemed determined to give him something she'd made. Soon he had enough mittens, socks, and caps for any three kings. That night, the inn was open for business downstairs; he and his party retired early, and the next morning started for Chaya. The wind had eased by then, though a skim of high clouds dimmed the sun.

Two days later, as the party neared Chaya, Kieri felt the now-familiar lift of heart as the tall trees of the King's Grove came into view. Though they had ridden through forests almost bare of leaves most of the way, the King's Grove held its leaves, now gold and orange, with touches of red here and there in the blackwoods, still mostly green. He felt an urge to leg his mount into a gallop, be home—his real home—as soon as possible, but made himself hold Oak to a quiet canter up the long slope from the bridge. Horns called; he'd been seen. He waved to acknowledge them, and had Oak at a walk before he reached the city.

The moment he was inside the palace, his staff descended on him. It was only midafternoon; he had been gone six days . . . he fended them off long enough to take a bath in the tub the king of Pargun had ridiculed, and change into more comfortable clothes. Then it was questions, complaints, disputes, and information someone thought he should know. He worked through a third of it before dinner. He had seen letters from both Arcolin and Dorrin in the piles of dispatches, and put them aside to read later.

After dinner, he had a meeting with the Council, attended by the Knight-Commander and, to the others' surprise, Elis. Kieri gave them a short version of the trip and its outcome, to the point where the traitor stabbed the Pargunese king.

"Didn't he have mail on? I know you found some to fit—"

"He wouldn't wear it. Said it would anger his lords; they'd think he didn't trust them."

"He shouldn't have, if one of them stabbed him."

"It wasn't one he'd invited. Someone who supposedly happened across them as they traveled, and they thought best to bring him along. He proved a traitor."

"Well, if he'd had the mail on—"

"'If only' mends no pots," Kieri said. He was tired, and also had no idea how to tell what had happened next.

"So the king died," Belvarin said, giving him the opening.

"No," Kieri said. "He's alive and back in Pargun, or I should say he was alive and his boat reached the Pargunese side of the river four days ago."

"So—it wasn't a serious wound?"

The Knight-Commander held up his hand. "You must tell them, Sir King." They had argued about this all the way back from Riverwash; Kieri felt it was boasting when he did not even know how he had done what he'd done, but the Knight-Commander insisted that was not the point: the Council needed to know what he was capable of whether he understood it or not.

"What? What?" Sier Tolmaric looked from side to side like a startled hen.

"I healed him," Kieri said. Best get it over. "I didn't know I could, but I was not going to watch him die of a poisoned blade—"

"Poisoned! You healed him of a *poisoned* wound?!"

"Yes," Kieri said. "Or rather, I believe the gods healed him at my request."

"The light," the Knight-Commander murmured.

Kieri sighed. "I would rather have told you after talking to my elven tutor. I am not sure how much of what happened was due to my elven blood and how much to the human powers I inherited. But . . . there was light."

The Knight-Commander snorted. "That is like saying 'There was blood' after cutting a pig's throat."

"You tell it, then," Kieri said. "Perhaps you saw more of it than I did."

The Knight-Commander's version went into details Kieri thought he could well have left unsaid. From their arrival in Riverwash to the Pargunese arrival, the king throwing his son in the river, all of it, including every detail of Kieri's own actions. "The light was not exactly the same as elf-light," the Knight-Commander said. "Not so . . . silvery. And no sense of being out of time or place, as when the Lady extends her realm. Commonplace things stayed commonplace. We were all startled into stillness, to be sure, but it was not the same as enchantment."

He went on to detail Kieri's appearance during the healing itself, the way the elf-made dagger flashed light, and the wound closing. "Then our king appeared unsteady; I expect it was the power he had used, drained from him." He went on, detail by detail, including the reactions of the Pargunese lords, the Pargunese soldiers, and what he had heard from the Halverics when he interviewed them later.

"You talked to the soldiers?" Kieri said. "I did not know that."

"You were exhausted," the Knight-Commander said. "I wanted to know what others had seen, to be sure I had not missed anything. You are as near as can be to a Knight of Falk, Sir King. Your deeds must be reported in our archives as well as those of the kingdom. I am of a mind that this is proof of Falk's favor, and you should have your ruby, vows or no."

The Council stared at him.

"If the Council needed proof that you were not just a soldier, not one to bring the waste of war here, this is more than enough," the Knight-Commander went on. "You risked everything to bring the king of Pargun here—to try to convince him of the need for peace between these two kingdoms—to give him a chance to make such peace—and spent your own strength to save his life." He looked directly at two elves, who for once seemed abashed. "I wish you had seen it. He is the king we hoped for."

"Now all he has to do is marry and get an heir," old Sier Hammarrin said, all too audibly. After a startled moment, a nervous chuckle spread around the table.

"As to that," Kieri said, "I have been, as you all know, busy learning this kingdom. I assure you, I have not forgotten its need for an heir."

"You're not going to marry that Pargunese girl just to keep the peace, are you?"

"No," Kieri said. "It is not fair to the young to marry old men. Though I am not yet old, and thanks to my mother's blood will live long, I have seen too much of life to be a good husband to a young girl. Young women should marry young men, and build their dreams together."

"That's a new idea," the old Sier said, shaking his head. "So you will marry an old woman, and by your magery she will bear children? Will she live to see them grown?"

His fellow Councilmen were trying to shush him, but once in full flow, nothing stopped Hammarrin.

"Or maybe you'll marry an elf and she'll outlive you. If she doesn't take it into her head to go get killed somewhere."

The elves around the table stirred and looked at Kieri.

"Whoever I marry," Kieri said, in a tone that silenced the old man for the moment, "it will be someone willing, someone old enough to know her own mind, someone who cares for this kingdom as much as I do. And," he said, looking around, "it will be my choice and hers. Not yours. Not yours to make, and not yours to criticize."

"Well said," Sier Halveric said. "Falk's blessings on your courting, Sir King, and I will keep my granddaughters home, then." He grinned; the others chuckled. Several daughters, Kieri thought, might be going home for Midwinter Feast.

CHAPTER THIRTY

When Kieri went up to his room that night and his attendants had left him alone, he went to the window, pushed aside the curtains, and leaned his head on the cold stone. Winter stars glittered in the cold sky. His memories of Tammarion rose, bright as ever, as clear as Torre's Necklace. He had never intended to cloud her memory with another woman in his bed, in his life.

"Tamar . . . help me," he said softly, to the night and the stars. "I'm sorry . . ."

As if she were in the room, he heard her laugh and the merest whisper of that loved voice—he had not heard it before, in all the years since her death. *You cannot dishonor me, love, by doing your duty—and your duty to your queen is love. Whom else could you love but a woman with a sword?* Light on his brow, the touch of her lips; faint in his nostrils, her scent. Then a curl of cold air took it away; and his eyes filled with hot tears. Silently, he wept, until the tears ended without his awareness and the cold air dried them.

A woman with a sword. His mind ranged over all the women he had known in a lifetime of war. He knew some of them had loved him, or thought they did. Aesil M'dierra would have fought Tammarion for him—and lost, he was convinced—but Tamar had not needed to fight, for he was hers already. Dorrin had loved him awhile, as juniors often did love seniors, and in Falk's Hall the young men and women thought and felt as young men and women, not seasoned warriors. But by the time she came to his Company, she had been over that, or so it had seemed.

He considered her now—a magelord born and bred, and now at least partly trained. But marrying a Tsaian noble would not serve his realm or Tsaia, and what he felt for her was admiration for someone else who had overcome childhood anguish to become better than anyone could have predicted.

Other women soldiers he had known—some nearly as good as Tammarion had been, and one now a paladin—had stirred his admiration of their skill and courage but nothing more.

After her one attempt at matchmaking, the Lady introduced him to no more elf-maids. Through Orlith, she sent her advice, suggesting he consider someone with at least some elven blood. "Your children will all have taig-sense, as you are half-elf," Orlith had said. "But their children and grandchildren might not, if you and they marry those without it. For the kingdom's sake, the Lady begs you, consider."

He had considered. Now he considered again, and fell asleep considering, to dream—not of marriage, as he half-expected—but of a woman no man could marry: Alyanya, Lady of Peace, crowned with flowers, holding a wreath of wheat and poppies in her hands. She held it out, and he felt the prickle of the wheat stems on his brow, the scent of poppies in his nostrils.

Kieri woke in the dark and thought about that. The Lady of Peace approved his attempt to make peace with Pargun . . . so he would expect. But wheat and poppies? By tradition, she carried those as signs of fertility.

He fell asleep again. This time he looked up—as if lying on the ground—and saw ranged around him shining figures that dimmed until he could recognize them. Only in a dream, he thought, would Alyanya—this time holding an armful of flowers—stand between a man in ruby-studded silver armor—Falk, that must be—and a broad-faced farmer in a blue shirt and gray trousers. Gird? Was he seeing Gird the way Paks did? And a black-haired, big-nosed young woman with a necklace of diamonds . . . Torre? And the other man in armor, his hand on the neck of a scaled creature . . . a dragon? Camwyn Dragonmaster?

Behind them all was light and music . . . music too beautiful to comprehend . . . and the light grew, once more absorbing their colors until he woke with a ring of silver brilliance still shimmering in his vision against the dark room. No doubt they wanted something of him, but what? He lay awake until dawn—not that far away, he could tell by the quality of the darkness—trying to understand.

He rose as usual, dressed as usual for weapons practice, and thus the first woman he saw was Arian, King's Squire, armed and—he had reason to know—capable. And attractive. A woman he could have loved, if only she were not so young. Half-elven, which would have pleased his grandmother. At the door of the salle, he met two more women with swords, King's Squire Lieth and Erris, Sier of Davonin, who had decided to take up swordplay for reasons no one but the Sier completely understood. A gray-haired widow with children and a first grandchild, she showed no interest in Kieri as other than king, but applied herself to her new interest with more enthusiasm than anyone expected. She took her bruises and strains with a shrug and did whatever the armsmaster told her.

Kieri hung up his sword on the King's Stand and glanced at Lieth. She had come with the others to Tsaia to find the king—to find him—and she had been captured with him. Even those few hours in the hands of enemies had been bad enough, but she had not flinched from that danger. They had that in common. Yet she, like Suriya and all the others who had also squired the former king, was human-bred, with only the barest hint of taig-sense. And he had never felt for her, as man for woman. The part-elven—Maelith, Esinya, Arian—

In that moment of musing, someone hooked a foot around his ankle and struck his back; he staggered, then fell. He was just able to roll to the side and up before Arian was on him, twisting away from his counter, and catching his arm in a way that forced him down again.

"Good work, Arian!" Carlion said. "Even a king should be watching his back, not daydreaming like a boy in love."

"You might have said 'begin,'" Kieri said, trying unsuccessfully to squirm out of Arian's grip.

"I did, twice. The other pairs were engaged, and you just stood there." Carlion walked over and looked down at them. "I'd yield, if I were you, Sir King. She has you well-pinned and could break bones if you didn't."

"Yield," Kieri said; Arian released him at once and stood. "I was thinking," he said to Carlion. "Affairs of state."

"An enemy won't care, except it makes you easier to take," Carlion said. Kieri noticed that Arian had moved out of his peripheral vision, and whirled just in time to see her begin another attack; she shifted at once to a new one, and they slid past each other, each evading the other's attempts. Again . . . again . . . and then Kieri managed to connect with one strike. Arian followed the line of the strike, rolling and coming up again.

"Too much time in the palace and too little time here, Sir King," Carlion said. "You must hand off some of the paperwork to clerks and add a session on unarmed combat alone. It may be mere stiffness from all those days on horseback, but it could kill you."

As he talked, Kieri and Arian went on sparring. When Kieri pinned her at last, Carlion nodded. "Enough of that now, but you, Sir King, would do well to add an afternoon session to your schedule until you regain your speed and the flexibility in your left arm."

"*I* did not heal someone of a poisoned dagger wound but a few days ago," Arian said. She glanced at Kieri, then back at Carlion. "If the king's grace is somewhat stiff after that, it is no wonder to me."

"Sa! And the gossip has not yet reached me?" Carlion scowled. "I will have a talk with my spies. And you, Sir King—you are supposed to tell me of any impediment to your training."

"I do not think it was that," Kieri said. "I think it is what you said, barring the lovesick part—I was thinking of other things, dreams I had last night that spoke of the realm, and I am well rebuked."

"If you are to be wed before I die of old age, you had better be thinking about the lovesick part," Carlion said. "Indeed, I do know that Pargunese princess is back here again—you called her back from Falk's Hall—"

"To convince her father I hadn't ravaged her, yes. She's returning to Falk's Hall. I'm not marrying her, or any princess. I will marry a woman of Lyonya—a woman, not a girl—a woman with a sword. If my Squires were not all too young . . ." He looked at Arian. The look he got back from her was challenging.

"You would consider marrying someone who pinned you more than once?" Carlion asked.

Kieri laughed. "My wife—my first wife—was a soldier, as you

know, and threw me more than once. And did so laughing, and laughed when I managed to outfence her. Aliam Halveric was the same with Estil, when they were younger, though she never fought in Aarenis. When I was a squire there, any time she was not big with child, she practiced, and I saw her throw Aliam into the dunghill once. None of us dared laugh, but they did."

After practice, Arian and Garris walked back to the main palace with him. Abruptly Garris said, "Will you be riding today?"

"No," Kieri said. "Carlion wants me for another session this afternoon, and that leaves no time for a ride."

"Well, then, with your permission, I'll take the mounts you rode on the trip out for exercise after lunch. I'll just tell the Master of Horse." Kieri nodded, and Garris strode off.

"If it is truly our ages," Arian said.

Kieri turned his head; she did not meet his eyes. "Sorry?"

"You said we Squires were all too young for you to . . . consider. We are not all as young as you may think. *I* am not as young as you may think. Half-elven . . . look younger." She looked up then. "I am not trying to ask anything of you. It is just that you should know."

Kieri stared. He had been so sure they were all decades younger; he had struggled so hard against what he felt. "How old—?" His voice stuck in his throat.

"Fifty winters," she said. She stopped, and he turned to face her. "My mother died two years ago; my father has gone back to the Ladysforest. He was glad to hear I had been chosen King's Squire. He said, 'So you're finally growing up.' Though he had not said so, I think he believed my time in the rangers was as much a girl's whim as Elis's horse farm."

Kieri felt his heart pounding suddenly, felt the heat of his blood racing. Arian? Could it be? And if so . . . what did *she* want?

"You sent Garris away," he said, hoping it was true.

"Yes. I said it might be a delicate conversation that no one should overhear." Arian looked across the wide courtyard to the stables.

"You have ambushed me again," Kieri said. "Hooked my ankle just as you did this morning—"

"I was hoping for your heart," she said. "But if it feels like an ambush, Sir King, I release you at once."

"I am all undone," Kieri said. "I had thought—among the rangers, the Squires, there might be women who desired me—"

"Might!" she said. She laughed at him, now, dark eyes alight with it. "My lord king, you little know what you inspire, if you think they only *might* desire you."

"And you?" He could scarcely breathe enough to say the words.

"From the day I first saw you," she said. "I knew it was unseemly, and knew I should, to save you embarrassment, turn right 'round and ride away. But you chose me for a Squire, chose me for those skills I admire in myself. The more I knew of you, the more . . . the more I respected, admired you. You have no idea . . . but my lord, if my interest does not please you, do not fear I will press it on you. I can stay, as your Squire, and say no word more, or go, if that is your pleasure, without complaint. I am not a girl of twenty or thirty, unable to manage my behavior, or a spoiled princess. What say you?"

Kieri stared, unable to look away. She was nothing like Tammarion to look at—dark hair instead of light, dark eyes instead of Tammarion's fire-blue, taller, a broader face—and yet— "I can scarcely say anything," he said. His voice came out gruff; he cleared his throat. "I never thought—" His voice betrayed him again. Her face changed expression, closing again to the mask of a Squire on duty. He reached for her hand. "No—no, do not go. Stay. Please—I must tell you—and I cannot tell you at this moment—but stay."

Her eyes lit up again; she had seen or heard something he did not know he had conveyed—but he meant it.

Garris, coming back from the stables, whistled a phrase of "Nutting in the Woods" and shook his head at them. "So that's how it is," he said. "And you have to stand out in the courtyard, like a—"

"Don't say it," Kieri said. He felt light as a bubble. "Do not say a word."

"I don't have to," Garris said, "with every window on this side of the palace full of faces."

Kieri glanced up; the faces disappeared in a rush; curtains fell. He looked at Arian; she was flushed but laughing, shaking her head.

"You are not embarrassed?" he asked her.

"Me? Oh, my lord—Sir King—I am too happy to be embarrassed by anything."

He laughed too, until a strong nudge by the taig broke into his laughter. "That's good because we must go somewhere. Now."

Her eyes widened. "Now?"

"The King's Grove. Or so the soles of my feet tell me—the taig is waiting."

"Oh— *Oh!* I feel it!"

"And possibly my grandmother."

Now she paled. "Now? The Lady?"

"I think so," Kieri said. The taig and his grandmother's command drew him. "Garris—we're going to the King's Grove—call another—" And he tugged gently at her hand. "Come, Arian, if this is what you want. If not, tell me now."

"It is . . . I'm just . . . I have no breath."

"Nor I."

By the time they reached the gate, Garris and Berne were also with them. Garris puffed a little, but Arian matched Kieri's stride effortlessly. At the entrance to the King's Grove, Kieri bade the others wait.

"We should—"

"I have a Squire with me," Kieri said. "And you know the Grove will not let harm come to me."

The light grew as they went deeper in; Kieri felt the elvenhome kingdom surge out to meet him. He looked at Arian; she said nothing, but nodded, her eyes bright. In the center, the mound rose as always, moss green as ever despite the depth of winter, and there the Lady waited, her expression more stern than Kieri expected. Slightly behind her was another elf, one Kieri had never met, clad in ice-blue and silver.

Arian knelt as Kieri bowed.

"Well," the Lady said, her head tilted slightly. "The taig brings tidings."

"Good tidings," Kieri said.

"We shall see," the Lady said. "This is the wife you would choose?" Her voice was cool, as when she had spoken to the Pargunese king.

"Yes," Kieri said.

"And when was this choice made, and how carefully did you consider it?"

Irritation prickled his neck. "I have thought of my future wife since I first learned I would have one," he said. "As for Arian, I have known her since spring—"

"I did not ask when you met her, but when you made your choice, grandson."

"I loved her before Midsummer, but thought her too young," he said. "Only today I learned her age, and then I knew." He took Arian's hand and pulled her close. "I do not choose lightly, grandmother."

The Lady's lips tightened. "She is half-elven, but not the half-elf I would have chosen—"

"And it is not you she will marry," Kieri said.

"For *you*, grandson. I would not have chosen her for you."

"She is brave, honest, generous—and she loves me."

"It is her heritage that I am concerned about."

"My mother was an honorable woman," Arian said. "You cannot say—"

"I do not speak against your mother," the Lady said. "But your father—" She gestured, and the other elf came forward. "Your father disobeyed my command when he made liaison with your mother; it was the third human woman he had made liaison with, in the short space of two centuries, and that is unseemly. Besides those he merely charmed for a night or two."

The elf raised an eyebrow at Kieri, spread his hands, and shrugged. "I am what I am, O Queen," he said. "I cannot help my nature. Humans fascinate me, and human women—" He shrugged again.

"So I have gathered," the Lady said. "And you have fathered too many children you did not stay to rear. You do not regard them as important—"

"I do," he protested. "But they grow so fast—"

"It is your father's character that concerns me," the Lady said to Arian. "You are his daughter; he is untrustworthy. How, then, can I trust you? Did you not seek to be a King's Squire because you wished liaison with my grandson?"

Arian was silent a long moment, then she spoke, her voice clear. "I first came to Chaya, seeking a place as King's Squire, because I had served long as a forest ranger, and hearing of the new king—the true king—wanted to see for myself. I did not think then of the man, only of the chance to make a change in my life at the time the kingdom was making a change. The taig sang to me, my Lady. I felt the spring rising in it, and in me. When I came there, like other rangers, other Knights of Falk, I helped where I could around the time of his coronation."

"As close to the palace as you could get," the Lady said.

"Yes," Arian said. "Because we all sought a chance to serve. I helped in the stables, and the Master of Horse assigned me to exercise those horses elves favor, the color of air and water."

"And had your chance then to make your plans—" the Lady said.

"I had none beyond applying for King's Squire," Arian said. "Like many others. The royal stables were full; the whole city was packed with visitors, as my Lady knows. All of us worked daylong and had no time for gawking. We knew the Master of Horse would keep account of our work, even had we been inclined to stray, and we were not."

Arian paused; the Lady said nothing this time, and she went on again. "I first saw the king on the day of his coronation. It was then as if the taig sang through me, but I thought it was the day, not the man, though the man was—" She glanced aside at Kieri. "—the king was magnificent, as my Lady knows." Another pause. "Then the Master of Horse asked among us for those unafraid of horses of air and water—to show the mounts he had picked for the king's pleasure. I went in the riding school at his command and there was the king with Lord Halveric and his lady and the Master of Horse. My Lady, my heart leapt in my chest; I saw him close and heard his voice and how he talked with his friends."

"And marked him as prey," the Lady said, "as your father did your mother."

Arian drew breath, but Kieri spoke first. "Grandmother, for more than a half-year Arian has served as King's Squire without once hinting she had any intentions, until I myself revealed an inclination."

"A half-year! That is a handful of breaths—"

"To you, who are immortal. To me, to my realm, it is more than long enough. You know they want me to marry and give them an heir. You said you wanted the same, back in the spring."

"I do, but—"

"Did you not have Orlith tell me I should marry part elven?"

"Yes, but—"

"And Arian is half-elven."

"Of the wrong heritage," the Lady said. "She will be faithless, like her father—"

"Why not faithful, like my mother, who never considered marrying anyone after my father left?" Arian asked. Anger edged her voice. "I was reared in her house; do you think I learned nothing there?"

"Not courtesy, that is certain," the Lady said.

Kieri stepped between them. "It is not your decision," he said to the Lady. "As for courtesy, I could trust Arian, like all my Squires, to remain courteous with Pargunese; if she is angry now, it is because you insult her."

"I do not—"

"You call us here, before you and her father, to berate her, accuse her of stalking me like prey, and tell her she is unworthy—and you think *she* is discourteous?"

"Grandson—!"

"I am ashamed of you," Kieri said. All his suspicions rose like ghosts around him, all his frustrations with her treatment of him. "I trusted that you would at least give us a fair hearing, and instead—"

The air shimmered; the ground trembled as the taig reacted to the anger of King and Lady. Arian and her father cried "No!" at the same moment; both knelt, hands on the ground.

"The taig cries," Arian said to Kieri. "I will not—I cannot—" Tears ran down her face. "I will not destroy the kingdom because of you—if it means that, then I will go away—"

Kieri heard her father speaking, but not what he said; he stared at Arian, then looked at his grandmother's angry face. The taig trembled around him; he reached to soothe it, as he had been taught. It shivered from the touch of his mind, then gradually relaxed; a glamour spread from the Lady, a spell of stillness and calm he could both see and feel.

"You see, grandson," she said, this time in a quieter voice. "You see what it would mean."

"Only because you are opposed," Kieri said, struggling for the same calm. "If you were not—"

"I will go," Arian said suddenly. "I will go far away and you will find someone else."

"No!"

"My lord—Sir King—I cannot be the reason this kingdom fails. *You* are what we need; you must be here, and king, and that means you and the Lady must sustain the taig."

The Lady nodded. "She is right, grandson. If we quarrel, the taig will fray."

"I did not start the quarrel," Kieri said. "You—"

"But I will end it," Arian said. "I told you truly, Sir King. If our marriage cannot be—if it would harm the kingdom—I will go and make a life for myself somewhere else."

"No," Kieri said again. "You must not—"

"*We* must," Arian said. "For duty. For the kingdom's sake."

"That cannot be right," Kieri said. He looked at the Lady. "Last night I had a—a vision."

She frowned a little. "Vision?"

"We had just come back from the north—it was a difficult trip—"

"The king of Pargun was stabbed by a traitor, and my lord king healed him," Arian said. Her voice too had steadied; Kieri felt hope.

"You *healed*?" the Lady said.

"Apparently," Kieri said. "But to last night—"

"But that—but Orlith has told me you are not yet trained—" The Lady sounded more worried than amazed.

"I had to try something," Kieri said, "or all my efforts would have failed and ensured a Pargunese attack."

"It was a poisoned dagger," Arian put in. "Nothing else but the king's magic would have saved him."

"How did you know—?" the Lady asked.

"I was stabbed much the same way," Kieri said, "and the paladin Paksenarrion saved me. I tried to do what she did. But that was days ago. Last night—I was thinking of Tammarion—thinking of the women I'd met so far this year—most of them too young, I thought, judging them by looks." He glanced aside at Arian. "And then she came to me. Came as she has never come before."

"Who? Arian?" the Lady asked.

"Tammarion," Arian breathed.

"Yes," Kieri said. "Tammarion. It was . . . it was not like I had ever imagined, the times I used to wish for it. Gentle. Calm. She bade me withhold nothing from my future wife. And she said whom else could I love but a woman with a sword."

"A soldier?" the Lady asked; she grimaced.

"A companion," Kieri said. "An equal, as Tamar was. A woman who could accept all my past—who would not be frightened or repelled by the scars on my body or in my mind, the violence in which I lived so long, the need a king has to defend, if need be with his own body, his realm. A woman of courage. And then I went to bed, and while asleep dreamed, a true dream. Alyanya came to me, and Torre of the Necklace, Falk, and Gird, and Camwyn . . . I woke refreshed and awed and then slept again. So when I went down to practice in the salle, I was still somewhat bemused."

"And there was Arian ready to snare you," the Lady said. "I blame you not, grandson, after a dream like that, but—"

"She did not *snare* me. Well, she did ambush me, in the salle, but that was at Carlion's command because I was not attentive. She dropped me like a stone. He also asked if I was thinking about a wife—everyone does, except perhaps you—and I said then I would wed a woman of Lyonya, a woman with a sword, and that if my Squires were not too young—and it was after that I learned they were not."

"And you chose the first at hand."

Kieri shook his head. "No, Grandmother. I told you. I had loved her before; I was pulled that way by the same force that pulled me to Tammarion."

"And yet," the Lady said, "the impediment remains. Her father had charms to entangle many women; I've no doubt she has charms to entangle men, whether she knows it or not. Tell me—" she said suddenly to Arian. "Have you had lovers?"

Kieri opened his mouth to protest, but Arian answered calmly. "Many years ago, I twice shared a bed with a young man. We were both, I believe, about twenty-four and had just won our rubies. He was killed by a daskdraudigs the next year."

"And would you have married him? Been faithful to him?"

"I do not know," Arian said. Her expression was thoughtful but remote. "That was half my lifetime ago, and he never asked. I doubt he would have; he had told me before that his family wanted him to marry in the old human lines, not half-elven. We celebrated our knighthood as many did—the king knows—" She looked at Kieri, who nodded.

"And that is all?" the Lady asked, with a glance at Arian's father.

"*Enough,*" Kieri said. "I do not see that these questions concern you, if I do not choose to ask them."

The Lady raised her brows. "She knows you had a wife; surely you should know if she had . . . liaisons."

"That is between her and me. And if she did, what matter?"

"If you truly cannot see what the matter is, then you do need my guidance and my questions," the Lady said.

"What I see is that you are using her to punish her father," Kieri said. "You are willing to risk the future of the realm to satisfy an old quarrel."

"You are wrong," the Lady said. "But you are not in a mood for reason. Will you at least delay until your blood cools?" Kieri felt another nudge from her glamour but resisted it.

"I have said I will leave," Arian said. "I meant it." She pulled her hand from Kieri's. "Sir King, you know the realm must come first. I will not be the cause of a quarrel that harms it. I cannot be. And it will be harder later." She looked at the Lady. "My Lady, you are wrong: I did not trap your grandson, and I am not like my father. It is indeed true love I bear for him. If you come to realize that, before he finds another, I am sure your taig-sense will find me."

Kieri reached for her, but she evaded him. "Arian, please—"

"No. War may be brewing with Pargun—we know that. The taig is in peril from without; it must not be in peril from within as well. Fix your mind on your kingdom, Kieri . . ." Her voice trembled on his name, the first time she had said it to him. "We have both been alone a long time; we are not children who must have their pleasures now or howl for them." With that she turned on her heel and ran down the hill's slope, vanishing into the path that led back to the palace.

"She is more a queen than you," Kieri said to the Lady. He could scarce keep his voice steady for the pain that pierced him like a blade, the anger below it that threatened to break loose again. "*She* thought first of the realm." He turned and ran down the hill, anger lending him speed. Where the other Squires waited, he ran past them without a word. He heard their voices, their footsteps, but ignored them.

CHAPTER THIRTY-ONE

When he reached the palace, Arian was nowhere to be found. Winded, Kieri checked the stables, in case she had taken a mount, and found her Squire's tabard hung neatly on the door of an empty stall. No other trace remained of her; she had taken her own mount and the travel pack all the Squires kept ready.

"We should follow her?" asked Kaelith.

"No," Kieri said. He could scarcely speak to anyone for the storm of emotions he felt. "It was her choice to leave; it will be her choice to return when she is ready." He could feel the taig's distress and struggled to calm himself. He didn't want to be calm; he wanted to smack his grandmother sideways, force her to accept his choice.

Orlith appeared in the forecourt. "Sir King, the taig—"

"Is not nearly as upset as I am," Kieri said. "I'm going to the rose garden."

"Do you want me to—"

"I want you to talk sense to the Lady," Kieri said. The year's frustrations edged his voice. "If you can."

Orlith's expression stiffened for a moment. "Oh," he said finally. "You have quarreled with her . . . about Arian?"

"Yes," Kieri said between clenched teeth.

"Where is Arian?"

"She left," Kieri said, "for the sake of the taig, she said."

"Oh," Orlith said again. "Oh . . . dear."

"If you can tell that . . . that *person* anything," Kieri said, "tell her—" But he could not say it, not to Orlith.

"May the First Singer grant you harmony," Orlith said.

"May the gods grant my grandmother sense," Kieri said, and stalked off. He knew his anger swirled around him like a cape; he knew it roiled the taig; for the moment he did not care. The taig *should* be upset; the taig should carry to his grandmother how he felt about her interference. All the year long she had failed him, refusing to help when he asked her, and now interfering when he needed only her acquiescence.

Doubt tickled his mind as he came into the rose garden, its bareness filled with the silvery chill light of winter. Not even a faint scent from the fallen petals this long after their bloom, nothing to soothe him but a quiet sadness. Was it really love he felt? Could he have come to love so soon?

He recognized the quality of light as enchantment and burst out, "Do not try that with me! I will not have it, I tell you!" The taig recoiled; the very rose stems seemed to twitch away from him. Kieri tried to reach out to the taig without encountering his grandmother's glamour; it was like reaching through water to take a pebble from the stream, but he felt the taig open to him a little. To the taig alone, he murmured. "I began to love her earlier, but tried not to, for her sake, for what I thought I knew. We are root and branch, fern and sapling, the moss and the bark . . . we have grown together all the seasons since I first saw her, that day in the riding hall, and for me that is time enough."

The glamour pushed doubt at him, but he pushed back, refusing. Finally it withdrew, but only a short distance. He thought he sensed his grandmother nearby, wrapped in the elvenhome kingdom, invisible but present.

"Sir King—?"

Garris. He didn't want to talk to Garris, or anyone, but Garris had to know something, to understand Arian's disappearance.

"Sit down," Kieri said, waving to the bench he sat on.

"What . . . happened?"

"The Lady did not approve. Arian left."

Garris stared. "You sent her—"

"No, not me." Kieri sighed. "I argued with my grandmother; the taig was upset. Arian left, she said for the good of the realm. It is not good for the realm, if I do not marry. And I will marry Arian, or no one."

"Oh." Garris locked his thumbs one way, then the other. "You're sure—"

"I'm sure that Arian has gone. I'm sure I will marry no one else. I'm sure my grandmother thinks I will change my mind. And I'm sure it's a complication none of us needed." He hoped the Lady was listening, but his sense of her presence had faded.

"Maybe she'll change her mind—"

"Who? Arian or my grandmother?"

"Either. Both. Maybe even you."

Kieri looked at him until Garris looked down and away. "Garris, you've known me how long?"

"Long enough to know you don't change your mind easily. All right. But—happy as I was to think of you and Arian—she's not the only—"

"She is for me."

"There are other half-elf Squires. And rangers."

"They aren't Arian." Kieri sighed again. "Garris, I'm not a youth. I've loved before; I've been married before. I know my own mind and heart. This is not some hasty infatuation, as my grandmother thinks. Nor some plot of Arian's. And I see no reason why I should not have the wife I want—the wife I already love. Her reasons—the Lady's reasons, I mean—amount to blaming Arian for her father's behavior. He sired her; he didn't infect her with whatever the Lady thinks is wrong with him."

"Um. People do inherit—"

"Garris, I don't want to be angry with you."

"And I don't want you angry with me. But as a friend, and as your subject, and as captain of your Squires: consider carefully. Maybe Arian has the right of it. If the Lady does not change her mind, and if your quarrel with the Lady imperils the taig, can you in good conscience continue that quarrel for the sake of a woman you have not yet married? As the king, healing and preserving the taig's health are your primary responsibilities."

Kieri shook his head. "If it were only convenience, or calculation, or mere affection, Garris, I could leave it—with regret, but I could. This is not the same. I know it must be Arian because—besides my own feeling—the taig itself told me. I felt it."

"You felt the taig more than the Lady did?"

"I don't know what the Lady felt, but I felt the taig rejoicing when Arian and I knew—"

"You were—very emotional—"

"I could not mistake one for the other, Garris, any more than I could mistake redroots for clotted cream."

"Well . . . what do you want me to do? Is there anything?"

"I would like to be alone for a while," Kieri said. "I don't— I can't—meet the Council right now. I need time to calm myself down, and try to calm the taig, just that."

"I will place Squires to guard your privacy, then," Garris said.

Kieri listened to his footsteps on the garden paths, then the gentle thump of a door, and stared at the falling water. He tried techniques Orlith had taught him, slipping his mind into the water. Cold water, winter water, ice-edged wherever it slowed down; he shivered, thinking of Arian off somewhere in the winter woods, alone.

"She would be very angry if she knew I had done this," a voice said. As beautiful as harp music, a gentle melancholy in it . . . Kieri looked aside and saw Arian's father sitting on the next bench.

"What—how did you—?"

The elf made a gesture with his hands, and a pattern of light formed. "The Lady's quarrel with me goes beyond my predilection for human women," he said. "We elves have gifts in different measure, as do you humans, and in my case—my sensing of the taig is greater than hers."

"How can that be?" Kieri asked. "She's the queen, isn't she?"

"She is the Lady of the Ladysforest," the elf said gravely. "She has great power—greater than mine, in many ways, but not in all. I honor her, but she resents that the taig tells me more than it tells her."

"If you know the taig so well, you know it rejoiced when Arian and I came together."

The elf said nothing.

"I do not know your name," Kieri said. "She did not introduce us."

"She did not intend us to know each other," the elf said. "My name is long and difficult in human speech, but Dameroth will do."

"Well, Dameroth, why have you come to me? And against the Lady's wishes?" Kieri had not known any elf to cross the Lady before.

"I want you to understand my daughter. Of all my children—and all are half-elven, as I sired no full elves—one of the Lady's complaints—Arian inherited most my sensitivity to the taig. It was her taig-sense, that and her mother—"

"Her mother?"

"Her mother had a strong sense of duty, and brought her up to the same. Put those together—" Dameroth placed his long-fingered hands palm to palm, then interlaced his fingers. "—the taig-sense and the duty, and she could do no other than leave."

"She could have trusted me—" The pain and humiliation he'd felt when Arian turned and ran down the hill stabbed him again.

"It was not lack of trust in *you*, Sir King," Dameroth said. "I know her well; I knew her as a child—and a stubborn little fireball she was, too. She befriended the taig early, and as a ranger bent her whole attention on the taig. She cannot ignore its distress any more than she could ignore a splinter in her eye. The taig and this realm have been her whole life. Her love for you has grown out of that, root and leaf and flower, and to live and flourish must remain so. She cannot sever that connection; the flower would wither and fade."

Kieri frowned. Of all the reasons he'd thought of, in his furious pursuit, this had not occurred to him.

"I have more experience of humans than the Lady," Dameroth said. "And in this matter, though I am partial, I am not blinded by anger. I saw true love in you, when you stood with her."

"Yes," Kieri said. "And I swear to you we felt the taig rejoice when we spoke together."

"Trust her," Dameroth said. "Her love for you is genuine; her sense of the taig is unerring; her loyalty to the realm is unbending. If she comes to feel that the taig truly rejoices in your marriage, she will come back. But for her, a half-elf, to place her taig-sense above that of the Lady whom we all revere and serve, to risk injury where she has been sworn to healing—that she could not do in an instant." Dameroth paused, but Kieri could think of nothing to say. Dameroth went on. "The Lady would tell you that I have no sense of duty, and I do not pretend that Arian inherited that from me—that is all her mother and her mother's teaching. But you should know that Arian will expect the king to do *his* duty, whether she is there or not."

"She is testing me?"

"No . . . not you. She is testing herself, her sense of the taig's need. But she will expect you to show the same diligence, the same loyalty, that she herself values and shows."

"You are not . . . putting a glamour on me . . ."

"No. I could, of course, but you are the king, and it would be discourteous." He paused, hummed, and then went on speaking. "That was to reset the boundary that let me come here without the Lady's knowledge. I hope. I want your kingship to succeed, and not only for Arian's sake. There are those who do not, even now. You are like a harrow that stirs the soil, bringing stones up . . . long-buried secrets will rise from the depths, and some will break on their hardness, elf and human, Earthfolk and folk of the air."

"Secrets?"

"Not mine to speak of. But you've already made changes in the relationship of elves and humans."

"They need to work together—"

"Of course. Most understand that, though they may not know how, or wish it were not necessary." He turned to look Kieri directly in the face. "I have said I want your kingship to succeed, and I do. I hope, as others hope, that it does not require too much of me. Can you understand that?"

"In a way," Kieri said.

"Your paladin—that yellow-haired girl—"

"Not *my* paladin," Kieri said firmly. "She's Gird's, or the High Lord's. And her name is Paksenarrion."

"I know. She meddled in forbidden things. Places. Unwitting, at the time, but she did. And it is in those things the great change began, both the change to this age and the change to come."

Kieri scowled. "I have no idea what you mean."

"No. And I do not know what, if anything, to tell you. If the gods are moving in this, it is not my place to interfere—something the Lady would agree with. But if they are asking me to speak, then I must. I dislike this uncertainty."

"I would prefer to know."

"I am sure you would, and yet knowledge given out of time can bring disaster."

"As can knowledge withheld," Kieri said. "In war, it is most commonly withholding knowledge that kills." Dameroth looked thoughtful but said nothing. Kieri went on. "Does Arian share your certainty about this change?"

"No. And I am not certain—it is the uncertainty that drives me to speak, but only partially. I will tell you this: what that paladin touched—in two places far apart—has begun the next great change. And I hear from elves in Tsaia that someone else you knew, your former Verrakai captain, has touched another, and the paladin with her."

"You can't leave it there," Kieri said. But Arian's father was already turning away; he vanished in a pulse of light. Another damned elf evading conflict, refusing to help . . . Kieri sat on the bench and stared at the water, thinking of everything Arian's father had said. Despite himself, he found his mind drifting to what hadn't been said. What had Paks done—or been involved in—that could bring about a great change—whatever that was? What places had she been? Kolobia? What else? It was easier, in a way, than thinking about Arian and why she had run away like that. Every time he thought of Arian, his anger rose again, and grief, and he could feel the taig react.

Where was Arian? Did even her father know? Was her father right about why she had left . . . and that she would return? What would the Lady do if she did?

He left the garden a little later, hardly noticing as the Squires on duty fell in behind him without speaking. He did not want to speak to anyone . . . he went down, and down again until he was in the chamber outside the ossuary. Sitting on the bench, taking off his boots and socks, he felt more numb and empty than he had before. Why had he come here? What could the dead tell him, that the living could not?

And yet . . . he went in and stood once more by his father, his father who had loved an elf and suffered her loss . . . suffered his son's loss.

"We both lost a loved wife," Kieri said, as if to that man. "We both lost a son, and I a daughter as well. I do not want to lose Arian. I don't know how—what to do—" He turned to his sister's bones and laid a hand on her skull. "As you were woman, sister, you may understand Arian better than I do. Help me understand, help me know what to do . . ."

Peace sifted down on him, flake by flake, it seemed. In the silence, in the freshness of the air, he felt calmer. Under his bare feet, the stone grew a little warmer; he felt moved to lie down, there in the aisle, having been invited. Under his back, the stone felt firm, warm through his clothes, almost as if shaped for him.

Rest. No outward voice, but an inward command. Why here? Why now? He closed his eyes, in spite of uncertainty. His thoughts wandered to the past, as far back as his arrival at Aliam's . . . as recent as the confrontation with the Lady . . . as distant as the coast of Aarenis and the king of Pargun . . .

And once again, his sister's presence, this time more clear than ever before. *They lie. She lies. She did not send the sword.*

Kieri tried to hold the same stillness, to listen only.

She called mother. She called you. She did not protect. The image he'd seen before: the Lady's face. Then another image: two elves talking behind the Lady. *They lie. They tell her lies. I saw. She bade me come. I refused. She hated me. A bad place. Evil.*

No image for the "bad place." Kieri struggled with himself, not to press for answers, to listen only, but he had to know, and the question burst from him. *Did she kill our mother?*

Silence. A sense of overwhelming grief, the grief of a child who does not understand the finality of death. Then: *Betrayal. Danger. Judgment.* And then, from more than one, unnamed and unnumbered: *Peace. Rest now.* He sank into that peace despite himself.

"Sir King?" The Seneschal's soft voice woke him.

Kieri opened his eyes. "I'm fine," he said. "They wanted to talk to me."

"Ah." The Seneschal's expression showed he understood who "they" were. "I can tell the others, if you like—if you need more time."

"No." He felt refreshed, though the ache of losing Arian—he

hoped for only a time—still hurt, and the warnings his sister had given him rang in his mind like trumpets. "It was time to wake. I don't understand it all, but it's something I needed to do." The Seneschal, he knew, would ask no more questions and might even understand more than he did himself.

"There have been things said," the Seneschal said. "About the king's choice and some disturbance . . ." It was not quite a question, but permitted an answer.

"What did you hear?" Kieri asked.

"I hear many things," the Seneschal said. "I repeat none of them." Then his expression softened. "Although, for the king, I will say that many rejoiced when it seemed the king had found a mate. And were shocked and alarmed when the King's Squire rode away, and the king returned in a passion. Only later did anyone hear, from the other Squires, something of what happened, though the details were uncertain. It was thought perhaps the taig had forbidden it—"

"The taig rejoiced with us," Kieri said. "The Lady my grand-mother objected. I was angry at the reasons she gave, and she was angry at my choice and my defense of Arian. That disturbed the taig, as you can well imagine. Arian—left."

"I have no dislike of the Lady," the Seneschal said, frowning, "but she is not beyond error. To go against the taig's joy . . . that is not wise. Arian will return."

"So I hope," Kieri said. "I trust her courage, but her sense of duty to the taig is as strong. She will not damage it."

"It is not she who damages it, if you and the Lady quarrel," the Seneschal said. "Arian was not angry, was she?"

"No," Kieri said.

"Then the taig's disturbance was not her fault."

"There is more," Kieri said. "You remember what I told you of the bones' messages?"

"Yes."

"And that I spoke to others?"

"Yes, that too."

"I was never able to ask the elves, or the Lady—they evaded me again and again—even Arian's father," Kieri said. "I still find it hard to believe, even after what the Lady has done this past year. She acts so—so strangely. Coming to my aid before I even arrived, cordial at

my coronation, then cold at Midsummer . . . refusing to come when I
asked . . . then coming to my aid and the Halverics' . . . then disappearing again, only to come and show anger to the Pargunese king. If
she were human and not elf, I would fear madness."

The Seneschal shook his head. "I do not know or understand
elves, Sir King. In my life, I have had few conversations with an elf;
they dislike the ossuary and do not make friends with palace staff. I
cannot judge the Lady's character. But she is said to be great in
power and wisdom. When she appears not to be, can we be sure we
understand?"

"I understand my mother and sister are dead, and I spent years as
a captive," Kieri said. He walked out of the ossuary and sat on the
bench to put his socks and boots back on. "Should she not have
known the taig's reaction?"

"That the taig rejoiced when you and Arian found each other?
She must have, if she summoned you—why else?"

"Could I have been mistaken? Could it have been only my own
joy?"

"No, Sir King. From all accounts your ability to read the taig is
more than adequate to tell joy from distress. And so is Arian's. The
Lady must have known, and yet she chose to ignore it . . . though
none of us know why, and I am not asking what you do not choose
to share."

"I will share it with you, who are guardian of the dead and can
keep secrets," Kieri said. "I will burst if I do not. The Lady likes not
Arian's father, a full elf, because she says he has fathered too many
half-elf children against her will. She thinks—she said—that Arian
must have inherited his irresponsible ways."

The Seneschal pursed his lips, then shook his head. "That is not
what I heard of Arian after she came here, Sir King. As you must
know, having had her as your Squire, by all accounts she is as bound
to duty as you yourself. Yet the Lady has power with those of elven
blood, even a little, and she may have planted doubt in Arian's heart
by enchantment."

"The Lady lies . . . that is what my sister's bones tell me. Could
she have lied to Arian?"

The Seneschal sighed, looking down. "It is not for me to say, Sir
King. I am of old human stock, as you know—not even much

magelord blood in me, and that is why I am guardian to the bones. We lived at peace with the elves long before the magelords came, and in our tales the Lady was always beauty and power combined. But not always what humans would call fair. It is that gift of enchantment, Sir King, by which they entangle our minds and hearts. Is that truth? Is it lies? We cannot tell."

Kieri had his socks and boots on by then; the Seneschal offered an arm, and he accepted it. "I thank you for your wisdom," he said. "I must go back to work now, but I will come again."

"And you are always welcome here, Sir King," the Seneschal said.

His Squires looked grave, but Kieri managed a smile. "It will be well," he said. "I cannot say what will happen, or exactly when, but it will be well in the end. I am certain of it."

He said the same to the Council.

"But will you marry her? And if not her, who?" Hammarrin again.

"You must trust me," Kieri said. "We have more than one thing to worry about—remember the Pargunese? One thing at a time, please." He looked at Orlith, sitting as usual in the far corner. "We must *all* consider the taig in our decisions." He saw from Orlith's face that the elf had taken that subtle warning.

With that, he insisted on the Council dealing with the other issues.

The day finally ended. Kieri lay long awake, staring into the darkness and wishing for some helpful vision, but none came. He was left to his own thoughts: his memory of joy, of anger, of grief . . . and where was Arian this night? Was she safe? Was she as unhappy as he was?

He finally slept, and woke with a headache that seemed to express all his frustration and confusion at once. In the salle that morning, no one referred to the day before, nor did Carlion say anything about his having missed an afternoon session. Kieri kept his attention firmly on the matter at hand, and no one withstood his blade.

CHAPTER THIRTY-TWO

Arian raced past Garris without even seeing him, running and leaping over roots and stones as if once more the girl she had been. She knew when Kieri turned to follow; she knew she had enough lead to get away if she did not stop for anything.

Her own horse, the mount she had brought with her back in the spring, had the end stall in the west-most wing of the stable, where the Squires' horses were kept. She slowed to a jog as she entered the stableyard, waved to the Master of Horse as she went by—a Squire on an errand, he would think. The tack room held travel packs as well as tack; she grabbed hers and went to her horse. As always, one mount was saddled for each Squire, in case of need; she laid her tabard over the stall door, lashed the travel pack to the saddle, tightened the girth, and bridled the long-legged bay, then led him through the yard to the narrow west gate, out of sight of the gate Kieri would enter.

The guard there waved. "Going far?" he asked.

"Later," Arian said. She mounted and legged the horse into a strong canter. Kieri would know which way she had gone, if he had her followed, but she hoped—she hoped he would not, and she hoped he would.

The bay, frisky in the cold weather after two days in the stall, kept her busy for the first half-glass—he shied at everything, buck-jumped twice, and tried to bolt. After that he settled, and Arian had all too much time to think as the forest closed around her.

Her father. The Lady. Kieri. Most of all, Kieri. *I am not a child. I am not an adolescent. The realm matters more.* Her father could be—had been, her mother always said—self-indulgent and irresponsible, but she was not. For the sake of the taig she had served as ranger, for the sake of the king she had served as Squire, for the honor of Falk . . . she reached out to the taig, as she had so often, but it did not answer. Well. It was still upset because the king and the Lady quarreled. They would get over it. The taig would get over it.

Blackwood, fireoak, pickoak and holm, yellowwood, holly, ash and hornbeam . . . she recognized every tree by its bark, its pattern of branches; she knew every leafless bush, every fern's brown fronds, now winter-marked. She rode one of the ranger trails, heading west, not thinking yet whether to turn south toward her home vill or north toward the river. For now it was enough to be back in the forest . . . she slowed, since her mount was willing, and opened herself to the taig once more. Nothing. She told herself winter had not yet turned; they were resting and not minded to bestir themselves without a good reason. One half-elf ranger was not reason enough.

Down at the root level, where tree touched tree, Arian tried to feel along them, back toward Chaya, but could reach nothing . . . only cold reluctance. That bad, then. She listened: a little wind, the rattle of a falling leaf here and there, no birds nearby. The ground lifted into one of the low ridges of western Lyonya. Up, up . . . rock outcrops, splashed with brilliant lichens. Through the bare trees she saw only sky, clouds moving in, one shelf above another.

She was hungry but did not want to stop for a meal; cold finally forced a stop so she could pull a heavy cloak from the travel pack. If only for the warmth, she wished she'd not left her tabard back in Chaya. And it would be stupid to ignore hunger; she took one of the wedges of travel bread to eat in the saddle and rode on.

As clouds thickened, the day darkened and visibility drew in. On this trail, she should reach a ranger camp by dark or shortly after. There might be no one there, but she could use the shelter and whatever food and fuel they'd left. She smelled the woodsmoke before she saw the flames, bright against the darkening forest, and rode in to find rangers she knew: Forlin, Mards, and Cuvis, all half-elves like herself, all former comrades.

"Arian! Well met, King's Squire. Perhaps you know what sent the taig into dismay this morning—is that why you are here?"

"I can tell only part of what I know," Arian said, "being King's Squire."

"I'll take care of your mount," Mards said. "I've done nothing much today but tend the fire."

"He was sick for two days," Forlin said. "We didn't want to have to carry him back."

"But I'm much better," Mards said. He was younger than the others, always eager to prove himself the equal of his elders. He took the bay's rein as Arian dismounted, stiffer than she wanted to be. "And I cooked today, so there's hot bread, soup—"

"And plenty for all," Forlin said. "You look like you could use a hot meal."

"That I can," Arian said. "Though something soft to sit on would be a mercy as well. I'm just back last night from a hard ride south from the river, and then—"

"Could they not find another to send?" Cuvis asked. He handed her a moss-stuffed cushion, the kind they used for sleeping, and she eased herself down onto it.

"No," Arian said. They asked no more; King's Squires were not required to account for themselves to anyone. "But if you have not heard about the king of Pargun and the situation in the north—"

"Nothing."

"Then I will tell you about that." While Mards unsaddled her horse and rubbed it down, Forlin handed her a mug of sib. Arian took a long swallow and said, "Had you heard about the king of Pargun coming across the river to kill our king?"

"That was true? I thought it was just a rumor."

"It was true. The Pargunese king was captured when he landed, and our king went to meet him and had him brought to Chaya. The Pargunese were told that our king had dishonored the princess Elis, and sent her to a brothel."

"What?!"

Arian explained as best she could, though Forlin, also a Knight of Falk, was outraged that anyone would suggest Falk's Hall was a brothel. She hurried through the rest: the conference in Chaya, finally convincing the Pargunese king he'd been lied to, manipulated by his brother and his brother's friends, the hasty plot to get him back to Pargun alive, the message sent to the king's friends in Pargun, and then the ride north, the confrontation, the traitor and his death.

As she talked, Cuvis served the meal, and they all ate. Despite the tale she told, Arian felt herself relaxing into the familiar setting— a ranger among rangers, eating together at the end of a winter's day. The tale slowed to that rhythm, until she came to the end.

"And then our king healed the king of Pargun, with magery—"

"Elven?" asked Forlin.

"I don't know," Arian said. "What he said was he tried to do what the paladin had done for him."

"But she's Girdish, isn't she? He can't have used Girdish paladin powers—"

"The dagger the Lady gave him at his coronation was involved," Arian said. "So I'd think it was elven magic alone except it had a different flavor."

"He is both magelord and old human on his father's side," Forlin said. "I suppose the others could have awakened. After all, the new Duke Verrakai's powers were."

"And how is the border with Verrakai now?" Arian asked. She did not want to add to her own story . . . not that night, at least. "Is it quieter, do you have fewer raiders?"

"It's been quieter since Midsummer," Mards said. "Right after our king came, we had a rush of refugees—some injured soldiers, some scared peasants. Then we had a little trouble, some kind of magic users or wizards, but we took care of those—"

"Shot them?" Arian asked.

Cuvis grinned. "They didn't think blackwood bows could reach that far."

"Six, altogether," Forlin said. "I'm guessing Verrakaien or half-bloods. All with Liart's symbols, when we searched the bodies." He stretched. "Not much since then, barring a little poaching right at the border. Nothing new in that. Sent 'em back with a lecture. What I hear is the new duke won't have any Bloodlord nonsense and she's making it stick."

"Did you send word to her about the six you killed?"

"No," Forlin said. "Why ask for trouble? If they're her relatives—"

"She was told to send them all in for trial—they're all under attainder."

"What's that?" Mards asked. Arian explained what Kieri had told her. The rangers looked shocked. "The entire family?"

"Yes. But this family has been trained to evil a long time, and they even killed their own children to transfer the spirits of elders—"

"Stop." Forlin held up his hand. "That is not something to talk about in the dark." His hand trembled. "Arian—if I did not know you for a truthful person—no, I cannot hear this. Not now."

Arian nodded. "You are right. And I am tired, so let me check my mount and then sleep."

Morning came with low gray clouds fat with snow.

"How far do you ride today?" Forlin asked, as they drank sib.

"I do not know," Arian said. "I was going west. Who is on duty at the border?"

"Brek, Taris, and Vorlas have this section, but they are forbidden to cross—we all are. You Squires, though, go where the king wills. If you are on your way to Tsaia, to the court, you would pass Verrakai lands near enough."

If she were on the way to Vérella, she would be on the road to Harway, and they must know that. Arian looked down. "I will think on it," she said. "It is true that the duke needs to know some of her relatives have been killed. Did you keep anything that might identify them?"

"We are not looters!" Mards said.

"I didn't mean that," Arian said.

"No," Forlin said, more calmly. "We did not think of needing to identify them, more than that they were Verrakai and attacking. We buried them with all their gear. I suppose, when the bones are clean and raised—though we had not planned to do that—some of their things might be found to name them. Others were there, though: Brek and Taris, but not Vorlas. Embres and Salzir, from the next border group south. I did not ask them."

"I will ask, if I see them as I pass," Arian said. "It would be more help to her if I had the names, or something from which she might infer the names. If not, it may be no use at all. Tell me all you remember—how many, what age they seemed—"

"Six. Two appeared to be in their forties or more, a few strands of gray in their hair, but still strong. One looked well grown but younger, perhaps late twenties or thirties. Three were younger again: perhaps twenty, a few years more or less. All male. They wore Verrakai blue under rough peasant clothes, and all bore Liart's symbol somewhere."

"It's snowing," Cuvis said, coming in with an armload of wood. "If you're not in a hurry, Arian, stay here with us another day."

She still could not feel the taig, she'd realized, and without that could scarce tell one direction from another without sun to guide her. "I will," she said. "And thank you."

"You can repay us by telling us what roiled the taig yesterday and why it's so reticent today."

"Yesterday—" She could think of no way to tell it that did not distort it. "The king and the Lady quarreled."

"Quarreled!" They looked as horrified as she felt. "Why? About what?"

"Me," Arian said. "The Lady is wroth with my father, an elf, and through him wroth with me. And the king is angry with her, for assuming I am like my father."

Forlin blinked. "That . . . does not seem enough to upset the taig . . ."

"You were not there," Arian said. "They were in the King's Grove, in the heart of it, and angry—"

"Ah. Well. But what had you done to anger the Lady?"

They were all looking at her now, appraising her as they would anyone. "It is a matter of the king's honor," she said. "And not something I should speak of, but to say his honor is unstained."

"And it affects the taig," Forlin said, not quite a question.

"It could, but it will not, hereafter," Arian said.

"Will you be back at court for Midwinter?" Cuvis asked, breaking the long silence that followed Arian's words.

"I don't know," Arian said. "It's unlikely, late as it is, and if snow comes. Perhaps I'll be in Vérella of the Bells or—if my mission takes me on—in Fin Panir. The paladin who came with our king told me about the High Lord's Hall there." They asked nothing more.

Snow fell all day, silencing everything but their talk, mostly rangers' gossip. Sometime that night the snow ceased, and the following morning, though not clear, showed the high clouds that meant no snow for a time.

Forlin sniffed the air. "You should have a fair day's travel, Arian. If you need provisions—"

"You have fed me a day and more," Arian said. "I have enough to make it to the next village, and they'll have supplies. I'll clean up for you—I have the horse, after all."

"Thank you," Forlin said. "Last time we had a horse here, we fed winterwards."

The rangers filled their packs and left, their footprints showing clearly on the snow-covered trail. Arian packed her own gear, tied her mount outside the lean-to horse shelter, and cleaned that, leaving a shovel of manure under each of the trees on the summerwards side of the clearing. The others had already raked the coals out and dumped snow on them. She scoured the pot they'd made porridge in, gathered more wood and stacked it with the rest in the hut, and brought in a bucket of water from the spring. By then the coals were cool; she ran her hand over the fire-pit and found no warmth that could kindle into dangerous flame.

With the camp tidy and ready for the next visitor, she had nothing more to do, but felt reluctant to leave. She leaned against a yellowwood tree, ungloved hands open on its broad-furrowed bark, hoping the taig would open to her. That tree responded, but when she tried to reach the larger taig, once more she could not. Tears filled her eyes; she thanked the tree, then stood back. No doubt now that she had been right to leave Chaya, if the taig still refused her.

She decided then to go to Tsaia, where she'd never been, and find Dorrin Verrakai. Dorrin had known Kieri for years . . . she would understand his actions, perhaps even his thoughts, as Arian could not yet. Though that would not matter, so long as the taig would not open for her and Kieri.

Two days later, she crossed the border on a trail Brek and Taris had told her of. "The Verrakaien use it to come here. No reason you can't use it the other way; you're a Squire, after all." The forest on the other side of the invisible line looked the same, smelled the same. It had a taig, of sorts—she could sense it, unlike the taig of Lyonya. She sensed damage in it, but recent healing. Even so much connection eased her heart, and strengthened her belief that she had been right to come this way.

She rode cautiously, aware that some in Tsaia might think her an invader. Once more she wished she had not left her Squire's tabard back in Chaya; it would have given her legitimacy. For most of a day she saw no sign of human habitation other than stumps of trees someone had cut—here five or six, there a single one. Toward evening, she smelled smoke and halted. Foresters? A farmstead tucked into the woods? Or—far more dangerous—brigands, even fugitive Verrakai?

Dismounting, she slipped the bit from her mount's mouth and tied on a nosebag with a few oats to occupy his mind while she went scouting. The low winter sun, this late, barely lighted the forest, though a few gleams picked out a lichen here, a tuft of moss there, far up on the tree trunks. Now she could hear voices—male voices—and she moved ever more carefully, alert to every hint the forest could provide. Smoke from an open fire: dried wood, not green. Oak and cedar, she thought. The breeze, moving toward her, brought a whiff of horse and some kind of meat cooking.

She reached out to the taig and felt its calm unconcern. She felt into the tree she hid behind, and received the same feeling, flavored with its own pick-oak resonances. Like all oaks, it had absolute certainty in its own rightness, stiff to its twigs. Through it, she felt up and down and sideways, to the root hairs that almost met the root hairs of the other trees nearby, to the twigs that touched now and then in the wind.

So those ahead had set sentries . . . that suggested something more dangerous than foresters cutting firewood. There—there—and there. A voice called, loud enough to break her concentration on the taig. Then a clanging: someone banging on a pot with a spoon, probably. Whoever it was feared no listening ears.

Arian went back for her horse. Mounting, she rode toward the camp sounds and smells, and when a horse somewhere ahead whickered, she let her own mount answer. Voices now louder . . . she rode on, following the obvious trail.

"Halt!" came a voice, and two blue-clad riders blocked her way. One was a young woman whose blue tabard had a knot of red and green on her heart-shoulder; the other was an older man who looked like a seasoned soldier. "Who are you, and what are you doing here?"

"I'm from Lyonya," Arian said. "I am seeking Duke Verrakai. Are you Verrakaien militia?"

"Are you from the king?" the young woman asked.

"No," Arian said. "But I have news, told me by forest rangers, I believe the duke will want to hear."

"You have not yet given your name," the young woman said.

"Nor have you answered my question," Arian said. "We know in Lyonya that Verrakaien were attainted and only the new duke's militia is legitimate. Are you Verrakaien militia, or fugitives?"

The man laughed. "You're bold to ask that question, coming alone as you are . . . but in fact we are the Duke Verrakai's militia. I served with her when she was your king's captain."

"And you might have known by my colors," the young woman said, flushing a little. "I'm a Marrakai, now squire to the duke."

Arian bowed slightly. "I'm Arian, a former forest ranger myself, which is why they trusted me with their message. I have no surname; we half-elves do not use them. And my pardon, squire; I do not know Tsaian colors."

"Be welcome in our camp, then," the young woman said. "We return to Verrakai House tomorrow; we can guide you."

"That suits me well," Arian said. "I have been in Tsaia before, but only in the south, as far as Brewersbridge twice and once to Thorngrove."

At the camp, Arian found men and women in Verrakai blue, most older than the squire. The veteran she'd first seen was their sergeant, and five of the troops were veterans of Phelan's Company. The others were native Verrakaien.

"Fifteen of us stayed behind when the rest of the duke's cohort went back to the north," the sergeant said. "We'd all been helping her get the locals trained and organized, so now she's split us up." He leaned closer. "It's partly to give these youngsters command experience, you know. This 'un is a Marrakai daughter; she'll make a decent captain someday. Still young, o'course. Younger than you."

Arian forebore to tell him how old she really was. The squire came back from checking on the sentries and sat down near Arian. "My name's Gwenno Marrakai," she said. "I expect he's been telling you

what a novice I am." She said that without any rancor. "I'm lucky to
have an experienced sergeant—my lord Duke made sure we each did."

"I don't know the correct courtesies," Arian said. "Your duke's a
woman, but you say 'my lord'?"

"For her, definitely," Gwenno said. "She's been a soldier all her
life, and in Phelan's Company they don't use different terms."

"It's much the same with our forest rangers," Arian said. "What
else should I know?"

"She's not as formal as some," Gwenno said. "I think it's mostly
military courtesy with her." She flushed again. "I like her. I know
that's not supposed to be important, but I do."

"Forgive my asking, if it's discourteous, but I always wondered—
I know Tsaians are mostly Girdish, and the Girdish train men and
women together in their granges. But I never saw a woman squire . . .
of course I saw only one noble household, and that briefly."

"It's unusual," Gwenno said. "Many households don't want the
responsibility. My father's a duke, too, and he was glad when Duke
Verrakai was named, because she's a woman. I had been begging him
to find me a place, and he'd kept saying there wasn't much hope."

"So . . . do noble-born girls not learn fighting skills?"

"We do, in the grange, just like our brothers. But beyond the
grange we have to beg lessons from our family armsmasters or relatives. Father sent my younger brother Aris off to Fintha to train with
the Girdish knights, but he wouldn't send me there." She paused.
"Is that a Falkian ruby? Are you a Knight, then?"

"Yes, I'm a Knight of Falk," Arian said.

"And you're not that much older than me," Gwenno said. "But at
least I'm a squire now . . . and my lord Duke has said she'll sponsor
me to the Knights of the Bells if I'm satisfactory. They don't take
girls—women—that often, but I'm sure she can convince them."

Arian looked at the unlined young face and kept her own counsel.
Through the evening, she saw evidence that the young woman, despite her age and inexperience, had the respect of her small troop.

The next day they rode off again. Arian was glad to ride in company that could distract her from her own thoughts. She sensed that
the taig here was recovering slowly from grievous wounds—evident
when they passed small areas of blight that made Arian shudder.
What had the old Verrakai done to cause trees to look like that?

CHAPTER THIRTY-THREE

When they came out of the woods and Arian saw across a river and its meadows the big stone house and its out-buildings, she felt a difference again—here was health only. One of the soldiers unfurled a pennant of Verrakai blue with a device like a many-pointed star; by the time they rode up to the house, a hand of riders had come to meet them.

In the center, a tall figure wore a chain of office—was that the duke herself? Arian reined back a little so that Gwenno Marrakai reached the other group first. Yes. That had to be the duke, from the courtesies exchanged. She had only moments to assess the woman she'd come to see. A face like a blade, but with laugh-lines as well. Erect in the saddle, broad-shouldered, weathered skin, dark eyes, steady gaze, intelligent and commanding. This was someone she could trust. And someone who knew things about Kieri she herself needed to know.

"This is Arian of Lyonya," Gwenno Marrakai was saying. "A former forest ranger, who brings news from Lyonya."

Arian met the Duke's gaze as Duke Verrakai turned to her.

"Are you one of Kieri's messengers?" she asked. "I thought he was using King's Squires now."

"The message is not from him, my lord. Forest rangers asked me to bring you this word—best given in private, I would judge."

"Very well," the Duke said. "Be welcome here, and I will hear your news when we are warm inside.

"Settle your troop," the Duke said to her squire. "Then eat dinner with us. Beclan left this morning for the south, so we will be a small group—Master Feddith has another of his headaches. You need not serve."

"Yes, my lord."

Arian followed the Duke to the house as Gwenno led her troop toward the stables.

"You're a Knight of Falk, too," the Duke observed, touching her own ruby. "Well met, Sister, and Falk's grace to you."

"And Falk's honor be upon this house," Arian said. She reached out, and they clasped hands in the Falkian greeting.

"You travel light for this season," the Duke said, glancing at the light pack Arian carried.

"It's my years as a ranger," Arian said.

"Enter, and welcome. If you've been traveling for days, I expect you'd like a bath."

"Yes, thank you, my lord," Arian said.

The Duke beckoned to a neatly dressed servant with a light blue tabard. "Bel will show you to a chamber and make sure you have what you need," she said.

Arian followed the servant upstairs and along a corridor to a room that looked out over a walled garden and orchard. She could hear shrill voices of children at play and looked out to see them scampering up and down paths at some game, their nursemaids standing by.

"The Duke's children?" she asked Bel, wondering how a woman soldier had borne so many.

"No, lady. These are the old . . . the former . . . they were too young to be attainted, I mean. The Duke's responsible for seeing they grow up good."

Arian saw one—a boy, she thought—throw a lump of frozen mud at another and thought the Duke had her work cut out for her.

"The bathing room's just along here, lady. I'll have the water hot in no time."

Soon Arian was bathed, dressed, and settled in a comfortable chair near the fire with a pot of sib and a plate of pastries; dinner, she'd been warned, would be some hours yet. "Someone will call me?"

"Oh, I'm sure my lord will come to you sooner," Bel said. She had gathered up Arian's clothes. "I'll just take these downstairs to wash, and they'll be ready for you in the morning."

"Thank you," Arian said. Shadows dimmed the garden and orchard below; she could hear shrill voices in the house now. She relaxed, muscle by muscle, letting her taig-sense reach out to the orchard. Fruit trees, some espaliered on the walls, answered her touch. A few, at one end of the orchard, were unhappy about something else . . . she concentrated. Bones? Children's bones? And something else—the roots were turning back from whatever it was.

A knock on her door; she pulled her attention. "Come in," she said. The door opened, and the Duke stood there without her chain of office.

"If you're rested, I thought you might give me what message you brought before dinner."

"Certainly," Arian said. The Duke sat down in the chair on the other side of the fireplace. This close, Arian could see silver strands in her black hair. The ruby in her ear flashed red in the firelight.

"You look part-elven," the Duke said.

"Half-elven, my lord," Arian said. "My father was elven; my mother old-human, a farmer in western Lyonya, only two days from the border."

"What news do you bring, then?"

"Six Verrakai trespassers attacked Lyonyan rangers; rangers killed them." Arian repeated the descriptions. "They were buried with all their belongings, including horned chains."

"That is good news," the Duke said, "though it may shock you to hear me say it. They were under attainder. If I could put a name to them, I could tell the king they are dead. I've worried they might come back and cause trouble here."

"Is that the last of them?"

"Almost certainly not." The Duke sighed. "My relatives could transfer their own minds and souls into another's body. The family rolls give some hint to the pretransfer identity of these, but I'm not sure they were ever all recorded. Most horribly, they killed children—sickened them to near death, and then forced themselves into the child's body, dislodging the original spirit."

"Falk's Oath!" Arian said. She thought of the orchard. "Did you— are any such children buried in the orchard out there?"

"Yes. The first I found. You cannot imagine—or perhaps you can—how horrible it was to realize that these children were not children at all, but ancient evil souls in children's bodies."

"*You* killed them."

"Yes." The Duke's eyes glittered with unshed tears. "I had to, to save the others. But it haunts me still." She took a deep breath. "Thank you for your news, Arian. At least there are six no longer a menace. Do you think I might gain permission to exhume the bodies and send proof to the king that they are dead, perhaps even identify them?"

"That I do not know," Arian said. "I know which rangers buried them, though I did not visit the grave site myself. It is our custom, as perhaps you do not know, to leave bodies in the ground until Alyanya has taken their flesh to replenish the earth, and then raise the bones. I think you do not have the same rites—"

Dorrin's brows had gone up. "No. We do not. We raise a mound, after a battle, or bury in permanent graves otherwise. What—" She looked worried. "What do you do with the bones?"

"Paint them with the life's story of the dead, and place them with honor," Arian said. "What else?"

"Old humans—you mean those whose people were here before the magelords?"

"Yes," Arian said. She could see that Dorrin was upset but could not imagine why. Surely a seasoned soldier would not be afraid of bones.

"My people were magelords," Dorrin said, her voice rough with emotion. "I think—I know—that magelords had a different use for bones, or some of them did. Nothing so benign as telling the stories of lives." She swallowed, then shook her head for a moment, and when she spoke, her voice had eased. "But tell me now—you say you were formerly a forest ranger—how do the rangers, or part-elves in general, regard your new king? You know, of course, that I served under him most of my life."

Arian shifted in her chair. "He is the king we hoped for," she said, trying to keep her voice steady. "He has already begun bringing elf and human closer together, and his taig-sense and magery—"

"Magery? I never knew him to have magery."

"Had he grown up in Lyonya, he would have received it from both parents, elven and human both: the royal magery was always joined."

"I wish I'd been able to attend his coronation," the Duke said. "I heard about it from Paks—the Girdish paladin you may have heard of."

"Yes," Arian said. "I met her once."

The Duke went on. "She changed his life for certain—she changed all of us, will or nil, when she returned to us as a paladin, and took Tammarion's sword off the wall—"

Arian said nothing, trying to gather her thoughts, and the Duke went on talking about Paks. The tale was long; the Duke had just worked her way up to Kieri's summons to the Tsaian court when a bell rang below.

"Good heavens, I've talked far too much," the Duke said. "Cook will be annoyed if we don't get downstairs at once." She grinned. "I may be a duke, but Cook is convinced dukes shouldn't be late to meals."

Downstairs they found Gwenno waiting in the small dining room. "All's settled, my lord," Gwenno said. "Troops have been fed, horses are all groomed and stalled, and no alarms."

"Excellent," the Duke said. As they ate, she asked her squire about the patrol; Arian listened without commenting. Gwenno's report was organized and concise, lightened with humor aimed mostly at herself. Afterward the Duke said, "We were talking about Paks before dinner, Gwenno. Arian here met her as well."

"Did you? Where?" Gwenno went on without waiting for an answer. "My father had met her at court, before Duke Phelan was found to be king. My brother Aris knew her in Fin Panir. And she was here when I arrived; she crossed swords with me—"

"And," the Duke said, interrupting this spate of enthusiasm, "she proved to all three of my squires that they still had somewhat to learn about swordplay."

"She gave me a huge bruise," Gwenno said, as if that were a reward. "And showed me how to improve my offside parries. And the next day I got a touch on her."

"Gwenno," the Duke said dryly, "is not deterred by mere bruises."

"I had brothers," Gwenno said, shrugging. "Bruises are just bruises."

"Until the blade's sharp," the Duke said. "Then they're wounds and blood and infection."

"Yes, my lord," Gwenno said, calming down.

"I'm not scolding," the Duke said. "But I'd prefer to send you back to your father in one piece." She turned back to Arian. "You said something about Kieri taking Paks as an example. You probably know she helped restore my own magery—did she help him recover his?"

"Not that I know of," Arian said. "I heard it was his elven tutor, Orlith." She felt breathless suddenly. She had hoped to find out more about Kieri's past before revealing anything about his present, or her relationship with him. But the challenging look the Duke gave her now, woman to woman, made it clear she suspected Arian was keeping something back.

The Duke would hold a secret given under Falk's Oath . . . but the girl? Arian turned to Gwenno. "I have things I need to say to your duke under an oath of secrecy, but I have no right or way to bind you to the same."

"Is this something for which another witness might later be desirable?" the Duke asked.

"I . . . don't know. I do know it's not something to be gossiped about widely."

"Gwenno's no gossip," the Duke said. "But she should not be burdened with unnecessary secrets. What involves the king of a neighboring realm may affect this. As a peer, I have a responsibility to my king—and think of that, Arian, before you divulge anything you do not wish Tsaia's king to know."

Arian held her peace until Gwenno had left the room. The Duke cocked her head.

"Well?"

"Some of what I say has to do with both realms, and some does not," Arian said. "First, what does: Pargun plans an invasion of Lyonya. Troops are gathering on the north shore of the Honnorgat."

The Duke's brows went up. "*That's* certainly dire news, and something I must report to King Mikeli. What's Kieri doing about it?"

"He's moved troops to the river: rangers, Royal Archers, and a cohort of Halveric troops."

"If so much is known to everyone, the Pargunese must know it, too," Dorrin said. "Where were you, that you know so much?"

"I said truly that I used to be a forest ranger," Arian said. "But like many others, I came to Chaya for the king's coronation, and was offered a position as King's Squire." She took a sip of water. "And I accepted. The king expanded both the number and the duties of King's Squires. We acted as couriers, and the women among us as squires to the foreign princesses who came in hopes of marrying the king."

"I met King's Squires," the Duke said. "Those who came to Tsaia with Paks, and some in Chaya as well. They wore his colors—you do not. Does this mean you have left his service?"

"In a manner of speaking," Arian said. "Let me tell the tale in order, if you will."

"Go ahead." The Duke's expression was grim.

"When princesses arrived from Pargun and Kostandan, all women King's Squires were assigned to guard them and learn what we could from them. Both princesses spoke Common well enough. Soon we realized that they knew each other." Arian went on to describe their demeanor, the messages they wanted passed secretly, and the reports the Squires made to Kieri.

"He wasn't interested in them as future queens?" the Duke asked.

"Not at all; he was adamant he would not wed any young girls, and not Pargunese, above all." Arian went on to tell the rest, including sending the girls to Falk's Hall.

"Their guardians agreed?"

"It seemed so at the time, but in the case of Pargun, that agreement was a ploy. That princess's guardians told Pargun's king that we'd sold his daughter to a brothel—"

"What?!"

"And a few tendays ago, Pargun's king came across the river alone, intent on assassinating King Kieri to revenge the insult."

"But that's ridiculous! Kieri would never—not even the Pargunese could believe—"

"They did, my lord. There's more—" Arian explained about the guardians' lies to the princess, the Pargunese king's visit to Chaya, and his return to the north, including the king's injury, and Kieri's healing of it.

"That's like what happened to *him*," the Duke said. "That's what you meant about Paks—she healed his poisoned wound."

"We were all amazed, you may imagine. Not in living memory of men has a Lyonyan king had such power."

The Duke frowned. "And yet you are not come as a King's Squire and his messenger. I do not understand. Nor why any of this should be held secret."

"So much is not—I agree your king needs to know it, and I expect the king has sent a courier direct to Vérella," Arian said.

"Why not you?"

"It is difficult." Arian took a breath and reached to the taig for support. "My lord, how old do you think I am?"

"Somewhere in your twenties—perhaps thirty."

"My lord, I am over fifty, and am like to live to near two hundred, as will the king. We are nearly of an age."

The Duke frowned. "You don't look it."

"No. It is my elven blood. I have lived all my life in Lyonya, where the taig nourished me. And that leads to the core of what I would have you hold close in Falk's Oath, Knight to Knight."

"If it does not harm those I love, I will hold it so," the Duke said, touching her ruby.

"The king chose many half-elves, men and women both, to be King's Squires," Arian said. "Because he himself is half-elven, and looks younger than his human years, we did not realize that he saw us all as younger than we are. Too young when he considered whom to marry."

The Duke's brows went up. "You love him."

"Yes. From the first, but he showed no sign that he cared for me. I am not a rash youngster to go chasing a man."

The Duke nodded. "I have trouble seeing you as my elder, looking so young, but I can believe a woman of fifty would not act like a girl of eighteen." She laughed a little. "I was a girl of eighteen when I thought he was the hero of *my* life. As he was, but differently than I'd imagined."

"All the spring, all the summer, into the fall," Arian said, "I respected him, as our king, and admired him for what he was doing, and my affections . . . grew. I said nothing; he showed nothing; I was careful not to hint. Then the morning after we came back from the north, I took him down in the salle."

"You took Kieri down?" This time the Duke looked startled. "I've sparred with him; I think I've taken him only four times in twenty years."

"He wasn't attending. Our armsmaster signaled me." Arian did not mention that she'd taken Kieri down before. "Everyone at the palace had been pressuring him to find a wife—even Armsmaster Carlion, that morning. So when he said he wanted to find a woman with a sword, my heart leapt, because he had smiled at me. And then he said, still looking at me, if only we Squires were not all so young, and left it unfinished. So . . . I told him I was not so young." Arian stopped. Her throat had closed; she could feel tears stinging her eyes. It had been so frightening to say that, to risk his scorn or his indifference, and then so wonderful . . . and then so terrible. The Duke said nothing. Arian managed to swallow at last.

"We saw each other, our hearts and our souls face-to-face. We felt the taig, and I was sure it rejoiced. And we were happy . . . but then . . ." She told the rest of it, knowing her voice was uneven, knowing that Dorrin could not possibly understand. When she was done, she stared at the grain of the tabletop in front of her.

The Duke sighed, a long noisy breath. "That is . . . incredible. I want to say stupid, but you're not stupid or Kieri wouldn't love you. But it's exactly what a youngster would do, balked in a first love affair; yet you say you're not a child. Why in Falk's name run away?"

Arian looked up to meet an expression both puzzled and amused. She had not expected that.

"The taig," Arian said. "It's the life of the land, more important than anything else. The king and the Lady, as joint rulers, must cooperate to keep it healthy. Their quarrel tore it, and I felt its pain. I cannot be the cause of that. If I'm not there, they won't quarrel, and if they make peace, the land may live."

"But . . . you want to marry him and he wants you." The Duke's voice was gentler; Arian did not look up.

"Only if it helps the taig. I can wait; the Lady may consent later."

"Can he?"

Arian said nothing. That question had pierced her every moment since she left. That he *could* wait, she was sure—but would he? Or would he think her faithless, for leaving? "That is the reason I came here," she said finally. Dorrin raised her brows; Arian went on. "You have known him for years; you know him better than I could in the short time he's been our king. I know it was necessary to care for the taig more than myself, but I do not know if he will understand. He was not brought up with the taig as I was; he discovered his taig-sense only this year."

"I do not understand how this—this tree-love, as it seems to me— would force you to leave. You said this taig rejoiced with you at first—"

"It has been my care my whole life," Arian said. "My happiness does not matter compared to the health of the taig. Think of Falk: He could have gone free and never ransomed his brothers."

The Duke shifted in her chair. "I am trying to understand, Arian, truly. Clearly you feel your duty to the taig strongly, but to my mind this calls for clear thinking. And you will excuse me, but you have not had my experience abroad in the world. Think back to Falk's Hall and those lectures on tactics and strategy."

Arian tried. "How will that help? I thought knowing more about him—"

"The problem is not Kieri," the Duke said. "He did nothing dishonorable in loving you, did he?"

"No."

"Nor, by your words, had you done anything wrong in loving him. The Lady accused you, but were you guilty of anything she accused?"

"No . . ."

"If the Lady's duty includes ministering to the taig, is it not *she* who should refrain from anger, put aside her own feelings for the health of the taig? It cannot be your duty alone."

"She's—she's the queen . . ."

"And what did we learn in Falk's Hall? High rank never excuses wrong behavior."

"No . . . of course . . . but . . ."

"Kieri is the king, her co-ruler: how has she performed her own duties, this past half-year?"

Arian felt a deep reluctance to reveal what she knew about that, but the Duke's dark gaze insisted. "The king has not been pleased," she admitted. "She has not come when he asked, when he wanted her counsel and aid. And yet other times she has come, as she did in that battle before he even arrived."

"Were you there?"

"No, my lord."

The Duke nodded. "I was. I saw her; I heard her. A being of great beauty and power—and yet, Arian, not flawless. She came late, and many died because she had not come earlier. Though we needed that help, she is not someone I would depend on. And now she's shown herself unreliable when the king needed her help, and hostile to you—creating a problem for the taig. If this were anyone else, what would you think? Imagine if it were another Squire or one of your Siers."

"It would be . . . wrong. Very wrong." Arian felt as if she had one foot hovering over a precipice.

"She seems inviolate to you because you are half-elven, I'll warrant," the Duke said. "Perhaps she has special power over you . . . elven mageries to cloud your mind? It is said the elves can maze humans with their glamours—can they maze one another?"

"I . . . I am not sure . . ." It was hard to think, hard even to hear what the Duke said. Could the Lady have cast a glamour on her? Or on the taig? Was that why it was closed to her in Lyonya but open here?

"If it was the Lady's anger that disturbed the taig—and if you and Kieri had done nothing wrong in loving each other, a love the taig recognized—then who is really responsible for the taig's distress?" Before Arian could answer, the Duke had gone on. "Remember what we were taught: though others thought Falk dishonored by the work he had to do, the gods did not agree. Your honor is your own: the Lady's honor is her own. She chose anger."

"You are saying it is her fault," Arian said.

"I am not part-elf," the Duke said. "So I have no loyalty of blood. I neither like nor dislike elves, except as they show themselves to me. Those I have met have been no more perfect than humans. The Lady, I will venture, may be mistaken, and moved by her own desires rather than wisdom."

Arian's father had hinted at this, but she had not believed him . . . could not, with what she now discerned in her own mind. As if a physical veil were ripped and blown away on a clean wind, Arian's mind cleared. "She put an enchantment on me," she said. "She locked my taig-sense—she wanted me to think it was my doing."

"Do you think she also enchanted Kieri?"

"I do not know," Arian said. "But he was angry with her—he did not act as if he believed her." Joy rose in her heart, along with shame that she had been fooled. If indeed the taig had not withdrawn from her—if it had been the Lady's doing—she could return, and pray that Kieri would understand.

"Will you return?" the Duke asked.

"Of course," Arian said.

"And if the Lady lays another enchantment on you? Because I think she will try. Have you the strength to hold her off?"

The joy faded. "I . . . I do not know."

"Do not go into battle without a plan," the Duke said. "Even though such plans are never perfect, it is better to have one. Tell me, how much experience have you had in battles?"

"Little," Arian said. "A few skirmishes with poachers, a daskdraudigs or two."

The Duke shook her head. "Forgive me for presumption, as I am younger in years than you—though not much—but I have experience you might find useful. Let's start again: call me Dorrin, Arian, and we will be sword-sisters, two Knights of Falk on campaign, shall we?"

"I . . . yes, my lord—Dorrin; I would be glad of your advice."

"As I see it, this is your situation. You and your king want to marry; his co-ruler opposes it for some reason—do you know the reason?"

"She doesn't like my father," Arian said. "She says he's disobedient to her and has fathered too many half-elf children."

The Duke—*no, Dorrin,* Arian thought—snorted. "That's not reason enough to oppose your marriage. Any intelligent being—let alone an immortal of such power—would know that. Either she has other reasons she has not told you, or . . . or something is wrong with her. Since she has been a problem for your king even before, you and Kieri must find out what it is. That's one goal." She held up one finger. "Then there's Pargun." She held up another. "If there's an invasion, how many troops has Kieri? The Pargunese? Do you know—does he know—whether the Pargunese king is still alive? And what are the elven resources?"

Arian answered as best she could as the questions went on and on. She had learned much from Kieri—all the Squires had—but she had also spent much time on the road, carrying messages, or with the princesses; she had only begun to learn how complex war and politics could be.

"I feel like a child," Arian said when Dorrin sat back and called for more sib. "Ignorant—"

"We know different things," Dorrin said. "I know nothing of your taig, or your elven relatives. When I was at the Hall, the part-elves would hardly speak to me. A foreigner, from a hated family . . ."

"Magelords."

"Yes. The kind of magelords who caused the Girdish Revolt with their cruelty." Dorrin gave her a lopsided grin. "But you, Arian . . . you are more like Tamar than I first thought. You think like her when you have the facts. And there are no cruel shadows in your past."

Arian thought about that. Her mother, strict though she had been, was not unkind, nor her elven father until—as she grew older—he went back into the elvenhome, emerging only rarely. "Like what happened to Kieri—the king," she said. "His captivity."

"That, and what happened to me, in this very house," Dorrin said. "You have none of that in you. Though I have no elven blood, and thus no taig-sense, I can sense old evil in humans well enough. Tammarion, like you, was all light, without shadows—Kieri had enough shadows for both. You will be good for him."

"If—"

Dorrin made a sound close to a growl. "Do not fall back into that, Arian. You want to be Kieri's queen—well, then, act like one."

CHAPTER THIRTY-FOUR

"I would like to do something for you, Dorrin," Arian said.

"No need," Dorrin began, but Arian held up her hand.

"You are a magelord; you are sensitive to good and evil in people. I believe you do have taig-sense or could develop it."

Dorrin looked as if she wanted to ask why, but instead said, "Do any pure humans have taig-sense?"

"Yes. And it is not just about trees; there is the water—"

"Water?" Now Dorrin looked a little frightened.

"All that live need water; to us springs are sacred. Taig-sense lets you find water and know if it is good."

"Magelords had water magery," Dorrin said. "When I first came here—"

"What?"

"There was a cursed well. I . . . the gods helped me take the curse off, and water came."

Arian waited, but Dorrin did not say more. "Let me show you," Arian said finally.

For a moment, Arian thought Dorrin would refuse, then she shrugged and pushed back her chair. "If you can do it and Kieri can do it, I suppose I can at least try," she said.

"We need to go outside," Arian said.

"At night? In this cold?" But Dorrin kept moving. "We'll go through the house to the garden," she said. "I want a wall to break this wind." She picked up a candle lantern on the way, and led Arian down a long straight passage that turned suddenly, went down three steps, then led to a door Arian thought might be under her own bedroom windows. "Here we go," Dorrin said. She pushed the door open and went out, waiting for Arian and then pulling the door closed.

Across the garden, in the lee of the wall, the wind bit less. Dorrin put the candle lantern on the ground.

"Now what?" she said.

Arian extended her own taig-sense, feeling for the tree with the strongest flavor of life. An apple tree, the oldest in the little orchard, gnarled but unafraid and still looking toward its next flowering. "Here," she said, laying her hand on one of the limbs. "Put your hand here, next to mine." Dorrin did so. "Do you feel the life in the tree at all?"

"I can tell it's alive," Dorrin said. "It feels different than a dead limb. Is that all it is?"

"No," Arian said. "Only the beginning. Now feel down the trunk, to the roots . . . there in the ground, the roots spread away into the soil . . . they are as alive as the tree. Can you feel them?" As she spoke, the taig spoke clearly to her, tree to tree all the way back to Lyonya. She pushed that aside for the moment.

"Something," Dorrin said. "I'm not sure . . . it's like a thread of . . . of light or warmth or something . . ."

"Follow it," Arian said. "There will be a spreading again; that is another tree."

"It feels—I can't say how it feels—oh!" Dorrin pulled her hand away.

"What?" Arian felt the tree's reaction, as sudden as Dorrin's.

"Something touched me!"

"Put your hand back," Arian said. "The taig wants to meet you."

Dorrin put her hand down and for a long moment was silent, still. Arian felt the taig reach again, and this time Dorrin did not pull away.

"It's all alive," Dorrin said. Her hand trembled. "All of it—I can feel it—"

"Can you feel anything of its mood?"

"Mood?"

"The taig is tender," Arian said, reciting her first lessons. "Like the freshest petal on a plum blossom. That is why it cannot be healthy around those who dwell in anger or hatred."

"How did it ever survive here?" Dorrin asked. "I would think my family's habits would've destroyed it."

"They needed this garden for food," Arian said. "They must have had a gardener who worked here at peace, as much as was allowed. They had to, for the trees to grow."

"Is the taig only about trees?" Dorrin asked.

"No," Arian said. "The taig is the life of all things that do not depend on cultivation. Trees, because they live longest, form the connection, year to year. The little things, that die back, partake of the taig while alive, but the trees persist." She wanted to say more, but Dorrin stood up just then, and pulled her hand back.

"I'm sorry," she said. "I felt it, I'm fairly sure, but I'm also tired and cold . . . it happens as we get older; I'm sure you could stay out here another turn of the glass."

"Then let's go in," Arian said. She gave the tree a gentle caress, and they went back inside. It felt almost too warm and stuffy to Arian, but Dorrin sighed with relief.

"I miss Aarenis," she said. "Others complained, but at least I was never cold down there." Then she laughed. "You'd think I'd just come from Old Aare's sand mountains. Tell me more about what I can do with this taig-sense."

"There are places in your domain," Arian said, "where the taig was sore wounded. I passed by some—deformed trees, barren ground. Using the taig-sense, you can find them."

"What can I do then?" Dorrin asked.

"Love them," Arian said. "Though that may sound too simple."

"No," Dorrin said. "I know better than that." She asked nothing more about the taig, however, and Arian said nothing more about Kieri. Instead, they talked of the Pargunese, Dorrin asking the questions she thought her king would ask. Arian answered as best she could. Soon Dorrin, yawning, suggested bed, and Arian went up to her room already thinking how soon she could return to Lyonya . . . to Chaya. The thought of the Lady's anger daunted her briefly—and what if she were bespelled again?—but even indoors she could feel the taig . . . weaker here, where it had been wounded and not nurtured, but connecting, root to root, with the taig she knew, that knew her. It called her, wanted her. She fell asleep easily, only to wake in the dark of night.

Taig—danger—a call almost panicky, as strong as she had ever felt. She reached out to the apple tree in the garden below, felt it strain to carry a message so far to one it barely knew, and soothed it. *I am here. I understand. Thank you. Rest now.* The tree relaxed into its winter doze, but she could not sleep, not without knowing what was wrong. Kieri? Something else?

Morning brought snow, fat flakes out of the sky with only a little wind. Arian startled the servant who was bringing up her clean clothes when she opened her door to carry her pack downstairs.

"You're not leaving, lady? Not so early? My lord will want to breakfast with you, at the least. And I have your things—"

"Thank you," Arian said. "When will breakfast be? I have far to go, and must start early—"

"Not long," the servant said. "My lord breaks fast early, and Cook's at work. Let me pack this for you—" She reached for Arian's pack.

"Well, then, if you'll bring it down when you're done, I'll just go see about my mount."

Downstairs, she heard voices in the kitchen. Dorrin had said the kitchen opened to the stableyard; Arian looked in. Cook—no doubt about which of the cooks working there bore the title—braced meaty fists in the pile of dough she was kneading and gave her a challenging stare.

"You're that ranger, I'll be bound. It's not ready yet—"

"Dorrin—my lord Duke—said this was the short way to the stableyard," Arian said. "I want to see my horse."

"Ah. Yes, it is. That side of the table, please, and out that door—" Cook pointed with her elbow and went back to kneading. Arian edged around the opposite side of the table, and out the door she found snow falling more heavily, covering the pave stones of the stableyard. Arian made her way across to where horses were stamping and whinnying for morning hay.

She found Gwenno and several of the militia inside, feeding and watering the horses, including her own. "I gave him only hay," Gwenno said. "I didn't know if you'd be leaving today or not, and—"

"Good thoughts, Squire Gwenno," Arian said. "But yes, I'm leaving;

he should have a bait of grain. I hope he behaved while you groomed. He's somewhat ticklish—"

"About that off hind. I noticed," Gwenno said. "But he stood at a word. He's a bit stiff in the back, too."

"I came with only one mount," Arian said. "Two would have been better, but—" She shook her head. "Thank you for grooming him," she said, laying a hand on the horse's haunch.

"It was nothing," Gwenno said, flushing. "I like horses. All the Marrakai do."

"Will you breakfast with us?"

"No, lady. I am on duty; I will breakfast with my squad." She looked down the stable aisle at the men. "My lord Duke says it is always good to see what the troops are eating and let them know you can eat the same."

"That's true," Arian said. "Good day to you, then. I don't know if I'll see you again before I leave, and if not, thank you for all your courtesy, both in the woods and on the way. Should you visit Lyonya, I will be pleased to greet you."

"Thank you!" Gwenno said. "Will you want your horse saddled? I can do that—"

"No, thank you," Arian said. "I am not sure how long I will be, since it would be discourteous to leave before speaking to the Duke. He should not stand saddled too long. He can have a bait of oats, however; he'll work that off today."

She made her way back across the stableyard. The snow would fall heavily for another glass or two, she thought, but then end . . . she should be able to make good progress. Inside, she found the kitchen crowded with children—the last thing she expected—all lined up along the table with cloths tied around their necks, Cook supervising as they kneaded little lumps of dough. Arian edged past them; Cook gave her a nod, and paused long enough to say, "Small dining room. My lord's down now."

The small dining room had a fire lit and a great covered tureen that smelled of porridge in the middle of the table. Dorrin looked up as Arian came in. Today she was dressed in dark woolen trousers, a gray woolen shirt, and a well-worn leather doublet, marked with obvious signs of a sword and dagger. "Your horse all right?" She pointed to a place set with plate, bowl, and eating utensils.

"Your squire Gwenno had already groomed him; he was eating hay. I must leave—"

"In this snow? Surely you can wait a day—I judge it will end later but be deep in places."

"I'm used to winter travel," Arian said. "The taig woke me; there's something wrong in Lyonya." She uncovered the tureen and served Dorrin a bowl of porridge, then one for herself. "Your cook is—"

"A tyrant in the kitchen. I know. Are the children in there yet?"

"Yes. I think she's teaching them to make bread."

"We all think—their tutor and I and the Marshal-General of Gird—that learning practical, useful things will be good for these children. I do not want to dwell on the life they had before. I'm trying to make it different in every way. How did they seem?"

"Energetic. Busy. I did see one of them throw a lump of frozen mud at another yesterday afternoon, from my window."

Dorrin shrugged. "We can't make them adult in a day—or even in a year, I suspect. A little mischief—it's much less than it was—doesn't worry me as much as cringing fear or sullenness. That's disappeared since about the Autumn Evener. We keep them busy, active, and learning. If you can believe it, there were eight-winters children who had never learned to read. Not even started."

Arian paused, spoon partway to her mouth. "Your taig-sense—it's not for the land as much as for the people—the children."

Dorrin looked surprised. "I suppose so. I never thought of that as taig-sense . . . but you and I were both trained in leadership." She went on eating.

Arian nodded. "Yes, leadership. What you're doing with the children—the way you talk about them—I can feel your attention to them, and it's much like mine to the taig. Did you never think of having children?"

"Never," Dorrin said, with emphasis. "This was a responsibility I never looked for. But the children deserve far better than what they had."

Arian ate the rest of her porridge before it chilled. One of the assistant cooks came in with a platter of sliced ham and another of eggs stirred with vegetables; she could see bits of green and red.

"Try that," Dorrin said. "It's a southern dish. I picked up the spices in Vérella when I was there. It's very warming."

"What are they?"

"The fruit pods of some plant; they come in green, yellow, orange, red. With eggs, we don't use the hottest."

Arian tasted carefully . . . the inside of her mouth warmed, but she liked the flavor.

"Kieri tried to grow them up at his stronghold, but the summers were too short and cool. They never set fruit. I think I can grow them here, if I give them some protection," Dorrin said. Then her expression changed. "You say the taig told you something was wrong in Lyonya—could you tell what?"

"Not exactly. I'm too far away, and your apple tree doesn't know me well. But it's serious."

"Serious enough for me to gather what militia I have and send a message to the king in Vérella?"

"I should wake the tree again," Arian said. "It might be, or it might be something . . . something with *our* king. Last night I couldn't tell exactly."

"Do you want me to come with you?"

"Thank you, yes."

They wrapped up in cloaks before venturing out into the snow. Arian felt something from the taig even before she got to the tree; as soon as she touched it, she felt the urgent call more clearly. Kieri wanted her—the taig wanted her. Something was wrong—something attacked the taig, in the north.

"The Pargunese," she said.

"Again?" Dorrin sounded more disgusted than alarmed. "They should've learned their lesson last time." She laid her hand on the tree. "Thank you," she said.

Arian felt the tree's response to Dorrin; she wanted to say something, but could not think what, the taig's call to her was so strong. She put her own thanks into the tree through her hand, along with the assurance that she was on her way home.

"I can't come with you," Dorrin said. "The king put me in charge of Tsaia's defense; I must mobilize what troops I can and warn other lords to ready theirs. It will be another day at least before I can start. But I will send an escort as far as the border, lest you run into a Pargunese patrol."

"I'll be fine," Arian began. Dorrin interrupted.

"You're a ranger, yes, and a King's Squire, and I do not doubt your skills or your courage. But you're also Kieri's future wife—and for that last, I will not let you go alone and unprotected into danger." She led the way inside, walking fast enough that Arian had to stretch her legs to keep up.

They found Gwenno in the kitchen. "There's danger," Dorrin said. "Gather your squad; you'll escort Arian to the border—will you go north toward Harway, Arian, or straight across?"

"I—hadn't thought of Harway. I was going back the way we came."

"If you choose to go by Harway—and I do not urge it if you need the other route and expect to meet rangers on your side—I can use Gwenno's squad to take word that can be passed by royal courier to Vérella. Otherwise I'll send another."

She felt the danger north and east, not south of east; if Kieri had gone to meet it, he might be there. "I'll go to Harway, then. On our side of the border, I'll find troops."

"Gwenno, have you eaten yet?"

"No, my lord, but I can eat in the saddle—"

"There will be time while your squad assembles, packs supplies. It won't be a long delay, Arian, but I judge a necessary one."

Arian was on fire to go at once, but in Dorrin she recognized someone with far more experience in war—if this was war. "I will wait," she said.

"Good," Dorrin said. "Then I won't have to knock you down." Her grin was friendly but firm. "Gwenno, tell your squad to get ready to leave but make sure they all eat first. You do the same. I'll be writing my message to King Mikeli."

By the time the group left, the snow had eased off, though the sky promised more to come. Arian worried a little about Dorrin, left with house staff and children, but the Duke said another squire would be arriving with his squad that day.

"The Duke worked on the road north to Harway," Gwenno said. "It's much better than it was."

"That may be," Arian said, "but snow hides any—" Her horse lurched as one hoof found a hole beneath the snow. "—problems." She looked over the group: Gwenno, one of the famous Marrakai family she'd heard of. Friends of Kieri's. Five soldiers who'd been in

Dorrin's cohort when she was Kieri's captain. Ten who were born and bred here, in Verrakai lands. The five former Phelani, though wearing Verrakai blue livery, were easy to pick out even though Arian had never seen mercenaries before. They looked harder than the others.

Near dark they stopped in a shelter Dorrin had ordered built: larger than the rangers' huts but on the same plan. Before they had even finished supper, they heard a horseman approaching; the rider hailed the camp. "Where's the Duke?" he asked. "I have a message—"

"If it's trouble with the Pargunese, she knows it," Gwenno said. "She's gathering her troops."

Again that night the taig woke Arian. She left the shelter to lay her hands on one of the trees; the taig-sense surged through her. More fire, more anger, to the northeast; the tree she touched, as part of a forest that ran from there east into Lyonya with few breaks, gave her much more information than the old apple back at Dorrin's garden. The taig recognized her as a ranger and called her to help. She felt cautiously through its fabric for the Lady—surely she would be active—but found no taste of her and little of elves. Kieri she did find, as a steadying influence, but he was too far away, and too immersed in the taig, for her to know exactly what he was doing.

By the next evening, they were near enough Harway to push on, arriving after dark.

CHAPTER THIRTY-FIVE

The Count of Andressat found the journey to Vérella, escorted by the Phelani cohort, safe enough but unpleasant: why would anyone choose to live so far north? Cold, wet, sunless country . . . but then the sky cleared on the last day, revealing the city ahead as if cut in crystal. At noon, they were close enough to hear the bells peal. Jeddrin felt his heart lift.

Duke Verrakai's letter gave him instant entrance to the palace, where he was assigned a comfortable guest room.

"The king will see you before dinner," a palace servant told him. The man was richly dressed, Andressat saw, an upper servant, surely, unless he was a nobleman. He wished he'd paid enough attention over the years to learn the colors and symbols of rank in this kingdom. In the interval he was offered a bath and refreshment, and by the time the summons came, he felt much better.

The king surprised him: so young a face, and yet so firm, and yet at the same time so welcoming. A young man of breeding, Andressat would have said, even without the crown he wore and the chain of office. Two armed guards stood either side of the king's chair. Andressat bowed low; the king waved him to a chair and invited him to sit.

"Duke Verrakai has written some of what you told her, but I would like to hear it all from you," the king said. "If it takes long enough, we can dine here, in my study, or break until after dinner. I normally dine with a few friends and my younger brother."

"As you wish, Sir King," Andressat said. He began as he had with the others, explaining about the family archives, about Alured's ambitions, about the rumors.

"What rank did your own family have in Old Aare?" the king asked. "Is there a chance you yourself are the heir?"

"No, Sir King." It was easier to admit to this young man, whom he had never insulted. "Though I long thought my family's descent came straight from Aarean nobility, in truth many lesser titles were created after the flight from Aare, and mine is one of those."

"It is what men do that matters," the king said. "By all accounts— what I have heard from Duke Phelan, who is now a king himself— you have governed well and bravely, as did your fathers before you. I merely asked to ascertain if you had a counterclaim to Alured's. As far as I am concerned, you are equal to any count of my realm."

Andressat blinked back the stinging in his eyes. The king could not realize his words were both reassurance and rebuke . . . for he himself had long considered northern counts as meaningless. He went on with his assessment of Alured's menace; the king asked pertinent questions about Alured's resources and the likelihood of war in the south spilling into the north.

"He believes there is an ancient crown in the north," Andressat said. "And he wants it."

"You think he would try to bring an army over the mountains?"

"He might—he was bold in Siniava's War and in a few years may have enough wealth and power in the south to do so—but my concern is that he will send agents to steal the crown he's heard of—and if they do not succeed, he will fabricate one and claim it is legitimate."

"My lord Count," the king said. "I would show you something except that it has withdrawn itself from our sight."

"Sir King?"

"It is true that Duke Verrakai found relics in her family estate that might indeed be from Old Aare. It is certain that they have magical powers. However, though they are housed here, only she can access them. An attempt to move them when she was not present proved . . . impossible." The king shook his head. "We do not know for certain where the items came from, and we know only a few of their powers: Duke Verrakai says they talk to her."

"She said nothing to me."

"I commanded those who knew to say nothing more. I myself have seen the crown—yes, there is a crown—rise from its housing and offer itself to her, but she did not take it."

"Why not?"

"She is my vassal; she knows it would be treason unless I commanded it—and I was not then crowned. Would I crown another in my stead? No. This land is mine, whatever land that crown belongs to, and whatever head it finally rests upon."

Andressat could not think what to say. After a pause the king went on.

"You say your archives gave you some description of items of royal regalia. Please tell me what they said."

"I brought a copy," Andressat said. "Copied into our modern trade language." He handed it over.

The king's brow furrowed as he read. "A crown . . . a goblet . . . rings . . . armbands . . . necklace . . ." He looked up. "What are 'jewels of sun and water'?"

"I don't know," Andressat said. "I dared not ask jewelers, on my way here, lest Vaskronin hear of it and know I was seeking them. If it simply means color, I would think pale jewels—blue or green, perhaps—"

"Blue," the king said. He gave Andressat a sharp look. "I know no more of you than I've heard from Kieri Phelan and his captains—they all thought highly of you as a man of honor. But if we discuss this more, you must give me your pledge to keep it to yourself."

"I—I—" Andressat struggled to express what he felt. This was not his king, but saying so would be rude. He had pledged fealty to no one but his own idea of who the real heirs of Aare might be, and still reeled from the discovery that they were not as he had imagined them.

"I'm not asking for an oath of fealty," the king said. "Merely that you pledge to keep secret what I may tell you or show you about what was found at Duke Verrakai's estate."

"That I can do," Andressat said. "I swear on Camwyn's Claw—" He saw the king's brows go up. "Camwyn Dragonmaster," he said. "Do you not acknowledge him as a saint?"

"Indeed we do," the King said. "Though here our patron is Gird, we recognize Falk and Camwyn as well—my younger brother, in fact, is named Camwyn in his honor; that's why it startled me."

Andressat relaxed a trifle. "I did not know that, Sir King. My pardon. But I swear on Camwyn's Claw to reveal nothing you tell or show me of this matter."

"Well, then," the king said. "Such regalia exist. Dorrin Verrakai found these things in her family's estate when she took it over, bound in different shapes by blood magery."

Andressat flicked his fingers.

"Yes, evil magery," the king went on. "And evil had already spread rumors of it, I believe in hopes that I would have Dorrin Verrakai killed as well, believing her a traitor. But she brought the regalia to me, gave them to me, of her own will." The king paused, moved a scroll on his desk back and forth. "But not, it seems, in accordance with their will."

"Their will?" Andressat felt the hairs rise on his arms and neck.

"Yes. I told you I saw the crown rise in the air. It is apparently some magery inherent in these objects—they wish to be hers—they wish her to take and use them."

"To overthrow you?"

"I do not know. Nor does she. But when the Marshal-General and a paladin of Gird tried to remove the box from our treasury, it became impossible to move and sealed itself—the wood joining as if all one piece—and now it opens only when Duke Verrakai herself commands it." The king sighed. "It has offered no injury to me, while so concealed, but from what you say its mere presence here could mean invasion from the south. When, do you think?"

"Not this year," Andressat said. He still wanted to know what the things looked like, but an assessment of the military situation was a far more comfortable topic. "Vaskronin has troops, yes, but only four or five hundred. He seeks to influence by stealth, at this time; Phelan's former captain Arcolin—"

"Now a count in my realm," the king said, "as I'm sure you know."

"Yes, my lord. Captain—Count—Arcolin says he is sure it's Vaskronin's men both making and passing false coinage to overturn the domination of the Guild League and give him free access to the Guild League roads in the south. I believe he has re-formed—or never gave up—his alliance with the pirates along the south coast. Certainly my attempt to ship wine and wool out of Confaer has been frustrated, both ashore and afloat, while thieves and pirates prosper."

"Kieri worried about that," the king said. "Before he learned his heritage, he warned us about the dangers of disturbance in Aarenis, but no one wanted to hear it. The mountains have always kept us safe from southern wars."

"Vaskronin controls the Immer from the coast up to Cortes Immer," Andressat said. "Beyond, on the east branch, where Fallo is, and possibly north and somewhat west as well. Count Arcolin is concerned about Vonja, and does not know the situation between Cortes Vonja and the cities downstream—Cortes Cilwan and below. He also is worried; he plans to take three full cohorts on any contract next season."

"Well . . ." The king considered. "He may be required to contribute to a force here, if we need to raise troops—but you think not this year or next season?"

"Not unless Vaskronin gains power faster than I expect he will," Andressat said. "Having an experienced force south of the pass, as advance warning, might be a very good idea."

"I will consider that," the king said, in a tone that made it clear he would not be commanded by an outsider.

Andressat thought what else to say—what would a young man with no actual war experience be willing to hear from a foreigner, an old man? He held his peace; Dorrin Verrakai had as much experience as he himself, and she was, she'd said, the king's new military advisor. She and Arcolin might convince him, where he himself could not.

"But you asked what the things were like," the king said, shifting in his chair. "The stones appear to be sapphires and diamonds, for the most part. The design is unlike that of the Tsaian crown, but ours—both this—" He gestured at the narrow circlet he wore. "—and the crown of state are scarce five hundred years old, made new after the Girdish wars. I would guess that the 'stones of water' are the sapphires, and the 'stones of sunfire' are diamonds, but there's another complication you might as well know. We asked both elven and dwarven ambassadors to comment on them—before the box closed itself, this was—and both said the items were neither made by their people nor were the stones from any source they knew. Dwarves, as I'm sure you know, can usually tell at once where a jewel came from, by its smell, they say."

"Would that mean the jewels came from Old Aare?" Andressat asked.

"It might, though the dwarf ambassador muttered something in dwarvish—which I can speak a little—that seemed to indicate they were not born of rock. That makes no sense to me, but he refused to say more. I do not understand all this that you transcribed, particularly this . . . is it a verse? 'Not a seed in the water, not dust in the air, not a thought in the mind, but that which breathed in emerges only in . . .' What is 'poilictu'?"

"That word I do not know," Andressat said. "So far we have not found that word again in any of the works in my archives, though I have my scribes alert to find it."

The king frowned. "It was a mystery before, and you but add mystery to it, and hazard as well." Then he shook his head. "No, I do not blame you, my lord Count. Rather, I thank you, for undertaking so long and arduous a journey to bring warning to us in the north. You would be welcome to spend the winter here, as your journey home, at least as far as the pass to Valdaire, will be unpleasant this time of year . . ."

"No, Sir King," Andressat said. "I must get home; I must see what is happening there, and prepare my domain for whatever that man does next. Indeed, I have been gone too long; I fear that he has already brought force against my people. My sons are experienced in war, having fought against Siniava, but it is my duty to be with my people at such a time."

"I understand," the king said. "And I commend your sense of duty . . . and also your wisdom in traveling mostly incognito. For that reason, I will not send an escort of Royal Guard with you—it did not save Kieri Phelan from attack, and it is impossible to hide the fact that whoever is so escorted is of particular importance to the Crown. Instead, I recommend that you remain here a few days while I organize a less conspicuous party for you to travel with, one that any single traveler might choose for safety from ordinary brigands. It's too late to pick up a trading caravan headed south. In the meantime, meet my nobles and speak before those of the Council about Vaskronin and the threat he poses."

"Thank you, Sir King," Andressat said. The king's plan made more sense than for him to set off alone on a road he had never traveled.

Less than a tenday later he was on the way south, once more riding with Selfer and his cohort, for Count Arcolin had sent orders for Selfer to take the cohort to Valdaire. The mounted troop traveled faster than any caravan; Selfer did not hesitate to cross winter-bare fields when necessary to bypass a muddy section of road, and only the foul weather—slightly less miserable for being at their backs—kept Andressat from seeing the first loom of the Dwarfmounts ahead.

When they turned to parallel the range and zigzag through the foothills, the weather lifted a little. "Can't we go straight?" Andressat asked Selfer.

"No, my lord," Selfer said. "This is the only road the gnomes allow across their domains. It's a very old agreement and they've no mind to enlarge upon it. It would be worth our lives to cut across even this—" He nodded to a bend in the road where it seemed an easy bound or two for a horse, though not a wheeled vehicle.

"We have no gnomes in the south," Andressat said. "I had not realized they were such fierce warriors."

"It was gnomes who taught Father Gird about military discipline," Selfer said. Without waiting for Andressat to show interest, he began describing the history of the Girdish rebellion.

Andressat recognized the enthusiasm of a true believer and tried to nod and keep an interested expression on his face, but the appearance at the roadside of six small gray-clad figures with pikes startled him into ignoring Selfer.

"What—who?"

Selfer stopped in midphrase. "Who—oh, rockbrothers. Gnome boundary watchers." He reined in and bowed from the saddle. "Rockbrothers, I greet you. Selfer of Phelan's Company."

"It is late to be traveling this road," one of them said, in a flat tone devoid of expression. "Caravans ceased." Dark beady eyes looked up and down the column. "It is that all are soldiers, is it not?"

"All but one," Selfer said, with a gesture to Andressat.

Andressat felt pierced by that cold dark gaze. He said nothing.

"It is that this one has a name?" the gnome said.

"This noble has reason to travel nameless," Selfer said.

"Nameless to men, mayhap, but not to us," the gnome said. "It is

the prince's wish to know all who travel here out of trading season."
At Andressat's hesitation, the gnome stepped into the road; the
others followed; they held their pikes as a bar across the road. Behind
Andressat, a horse stamped; he could feel the rising tension. "And
the truth, human, not some false name to befuddle fools."

"Jeddrin, Count of Andressat," he said. "Going home."

The gnome's brows rose. "Are you indeed?" He looked at Selfer.

"To my knowledge, and I have traveled with him from eastern
Tsaia, that is his real name," Selfer said.

"It is a pity you left home," the gnome said. "And a wise thing to
return. Far travel never profits." He gestured with his pike, and the
gnomes moved aside, three to each side of the road, pikes lifted. To
Selfer, he said, "You know the permitted campsites. Do not stray,
even if you see no more bound-wards."

"I will not," Selfer said. He pulled out his Girdish medallion. "I
abide the Law."

The gnome nodded, his expression softening for the first time.
"The Law abides. Go safely."

Andressat spoke up before he realized he would. "Sir gnome, my
respects, but I came north to warn of danger in the south. Your
friends here will no doubt warn you as well, but let me make that an
early warning. There is a bad man in the south who means to conquer
it all, and the north as well."

The gnome stared at him. "Did not Siniava die?"

"He did. This man's name was Alured, known as the Black, but
also as Duke of Immer and the new name he has chosen, Visla Vaskronin. It is my belief he will not abide any law."

"It is that you came north only to warn, and not to make profit?"
A hint of disbelief there.

"If it is profit to warn allies of danger, then it was both," Andressat
said. "I cannot stand alone against him."

"Ah. Exchange, then." The gnome thumped the butt of his pike on
the ground; the others followed. "By your leave, Captain of Phelan's
Company, this man might tell his story to our prince, and your troop
bide this night in our camp."

Selfer looked at Andressat and then at the gnome. "Sir gnome, I am
charged with this man's safety as far as Valdaire by my king. The
Law compels me to follow orders."

"It is not *his* safety at risk," the gnome said, putting fist to his breast and bowing. "Nor that of your troop. I deem his words of value, and value given must be for value received. If the prince deems my estimation of value wrong, then the debt will rest on me, as commander of this group of bound-wardens."

Selfer looked at Andressat. "It is acceptable?"

Andressat felt adrift; he could tell that the gnome was intent on this and Selfer felt no danger in it, but he had never met a "rock-brother" before. "I suppose . . ."

Very shortly the slope held fifty or more gnomes who seemed to rise out of the ground itself. They led the troop aside from the road, into the scrubby trees and then upward, until they came to an arched opening in the side of a grassy slope. Andressat, looking around, re-alized. that it would not be seen from any bend in the road.

"It is that you can make a camp?" the same gnome asked Selfer.

"Yes, we have tents," Selfer said.

"Then over there—" the gnome waved. "A stream for water. Vek-tran will show where to dig jacks. Andressat Count come with me."

Andressat shot a glance at Selfer.

"I will come, too," Selfer said. "I was not to leave his side. My ser-geant can organize the camp." He dismounted; Andressat followed. The soldiers followed the other gnome off to the side of the open area, and Andressat, Selfer, and the first gnomes approached the opening.

"How do I address your prince?" Andressat said. "I would not fail in courtesy."

"That is well thought of," their guide said. "For visitors of the young races, we find the full courtesies overfull for their memories. Let you greet him as most noble prince and law-warden, and that will be enough."

Andressat had caves enough—natural caves, uneven in their shape, cool in summer and most often used to store wine, though a few people built dwellings in them. He had thought of rockfolk as primitives who lived in such caves . . . what he now entered amazed him. Not a natural cave but a vast edifice hollowed out by masons of great skill. A level floor, neatly carved steps to change elevation, and a hall larger than any in Vérella or his own domain.

His guide had spoken only in gnomish to the wardens at the entrance and those along the way, one of whom had run ahead. And now they stood before a raised dais on which the gnome prince sat in his stone chair. He wore gray as plain as the others but for a silver chain and a great clear jewel like a drop of water, big as a hen's egg.

His guide spoke in gnomish for some minutes; Andressat wasn't sure what was being said or what he should do—staring at the prince seemed impolite. He let his gaze wander a little, to the other gnomes standing behind the prince, only two of them armed. He could read nothing in their faces; he could scarcely tell one from the other. All wore gray; all stood silent and motionless. Behind them was a pierced screen of stone through which he could not see; it had been carved into curves and twists that led his eye hither and thither.

A touch on his arm got his attention. "Do not look there," his guide said. "It will enchant you."

He did not know how long he had stood there; his guide was now making the introduction in Common.

"—the Count of Andressat, who rules in Andressat, a domain over the mountains. He gave warning of danger; I deemed it wise for him to speak in person to you. The other is known to us, a captain of Duke Phelan, who is now king in Lyonya."

Andressat bowed low. "Most noble prince and law-warden, it is a great honor to greet you."

"Rise up and show your eyes," the prince said. His Common was heavily accented but understandable. He stared Andressat in the face and then looked at Selfer, who also bowed and repeated Andressat's words.

"What warning?" the prince then asked.

Andressat repeated what he had told the bound-wardens.

"Is this man Girdish?" the prince asked; Andressat did not at once know whom he meant and hesitated. "Alured," the prince said.

"No, noble prince," Andressat said. "I do not know what gods, if any, he follows."

"Has he ever broken human law?" The emphasis on "human" was contemptuous.

"Yes, noble prince," Andressat said. "He was a pirate on the seas—attacked ships and killed and stole for profit."

"So also do war companies," the prince said, looking again at Selfer. "Is it not true of you, Captain, that you make war for money and not to uphold the Law?"

"Sometimes," Selfer said. "Not always. We may be hired to uphold the Law."

"Did you ever see this Alured?"

"Yes," Selfer said. "When I was a squire to Duke Phelan, I saw Alured the Black many times during the last year of Siniava's War."

"Was he a lawbreaker?"

"He had been," Selfer said. "And after Siniava was killed, he did things that were . . . if not against human law, against Girdish law."

"You are Girdish?"

"Yes."

"Do you not consider Girdish law human law?"

"Not entirely," Selfer said. "Gird learned about the giver of Law from gnomes, and what he learned he used in writing the Code of Gird—"

"Little enough," the prince said. "But the Code of Gird is not as corrupt as much human law." He turned and spoke in gnomish to one of the gnomes at his shoulder; that one hurried away. The prince looked back at Andressat.

"So: do you think this Alured most dangerous because he is a lawbreaker, or violent, or a strong leader?"

"I do not know," Andressat said. "He is all of those and cruel besides. Some things I know only by hearsay, but this captain may have seen."

"Captain?" the prince said.

"I saw him at Aliuna and other cities of the southern coast after Siniava's death," Selfer said. "He took pleasure in the fear and suffering of others. We had not seen that until then—it was a war, we were not always fighting on the same field, or nearby. It sickened me, and others, and even the Duke."

"Even the Duke? Was he, then, prone to cruelty?"

"No," Selfer said. "Not at all. But when angry, when Siniava had tortured his own troops, he swore vengeance."

"Vengeance is not justice; vengeance is not wise. So the Lawgiver said, and so the Law demands that justice be done, not vengeance taken. What does human law say?"

"My lord prince, human law varies. Here in Tsaia, in times of peace, private vengeance is unlawful: those accused must stand trial, and their deeds be shown to fall inside or outside the law. Across the pass, in Aarenis, the Guild League cities have one law, and others hold differently. But in time of war, against an enemy . . ." Selfer faltered.

"All are lawbreakers then," the prince said.

"Not so, my lord," Selfer said. "This Company, in which I am now captain and was then squire, and several others, had formed an agreement on law as related to war—"

The prince's brow rose a moment, then lowered again. "Those who fight to make the rules of fighting? That is strange indeed. And was any heed paid to the true Law?"

Selfer nodded. "My lord, our agreement with one another said that no matter what those who paid us wanted, we would not mistreat prisoners taken, but feed and house them, and tend their wounds. That care be taken, on the march, not to rob those a troop passed, nor harm those who did not seek to harm the troop. War always means killing, but it was our intent to limit it as much as possible to those whose business it was."

The prince drummed his fingers on the arm of his throne, then turned to Andressat. "And you, Count of Andressat?"

"We had a code of honor very like that of the mercenaries' code," he said. "No torture, no unnecessary killing, no attacks on those not armed. No destruction of orchards or fields, though a crop, in war, must be counted lost if an army came through. I will say, of Duke Phelan's Company, that they marched all through my domain and not a stray goat went missing because of it. No vines were harmed, no oilberry trees hacked. The same cannot be said," he said, "of Siniava's troops."

"It is a bad thing when a man formerly lawful falls into lawlessness through passion," said the prince. "It creates imbalance. Tell me, how did this Siniava die?"

"Aliam Halveric cut off his head," Selfer said.

"Without torment?"

"Yes."

"And how was he captured? In battle?"

"No . . . trying to escape through the lines disguised as a woman.

One of our soldiers, Paksenarrion, was on guard, and spotted him. She's now a paladin of Gird."

"Paksenarrion! One of our people owes a debt to her; if you see her again, tell her to bring the ring, that the debt may be paid." The prince tilted his head. "Or possibly the debt should be paid to the Girdish command, as she is now theirs." He looked back at Andressat. "As for your news, Count Andressat, we had heard of unrest in the south. None spoke of invasion across the pass, or anything that threatened us directly. But you think this is possible?"

"Yes, lord prince. As I told Tsaia's king, not this coming summer but later. The king assures me the other regalia are secure, but I believe this means Alured will come with force to take the crown, as soon as he has enough troops and control of the south."

"Foreign mercenaries stopped Siniava—why not Alured?" The prince turned to Selfer.

"My lord prince, I lack the experience of senior captains, but the south is still recovering from the former war, and if Alured has already suborned some of the Guild League cities, such an alliance as faced Siniava may not be possible."

"And yet you go south . . ."

"Under orders, lord prince. Nor do I know who might contract with us this coming year."

"Well." The prince turned to their guide and spoke a time in gnomish. Their guide bowed. He spoke again to them in Common. "It is that it was a good thing you brought this word of warning to me. Value was received; value will be given. If it please you, we will grant you and your companions swift travel to the pass, through our ways."

Andressat was not sure what this meant, but Selfer answered for them. "It is most gracious, lord prince, and if it suits Count Andressat, I accept."

"He rules you?"

"No, lord prince, but as I said, I am bound by my king's orders to accompany him as far as Valdaire."

"It is a boon rarely offered," the prince said; he looked at Andressat.

"I—I accept," Andressat said, hoping he was not making a mistake.

"Their companions have already made camp, lord prince," their guide said.

"In the outer day, then," the prince said. His companions on the dais picked up the throne—with him in it—and turned it around so he faced away from them.

"Come now," their guide said, and led them back outside into the raw dank wind that penetrated even the thick woolen clothes Dorrin had given Andressat. He shivered. As before, he shared the young captain's tent that night.

He woke at dawn; the camp was already astir, and Selfer gone from his pallet. Andressat hurried to ready himself for travel. All but the captain's tent had been struck and packed; as soon as he was out, that, too, came down.

As before, Andressat was impressed by how fast and completely these soldiers cleaned up the campsite, pushing sod back into the tent-peg holes, covering over the jacks after the last had used it. Selfer, he saw, was asking the gnomes who had come out to lead them away how they wanted the fire-pit cleaned.

To his surprise, these gnomes—not the same as the day before—led them away from the arched entrance he'd used before, more westward, along a narrow trail where they could ride only single file. Half the gnomes led; the other half followed. Andressat followed Selfer, chewing on a strip of dried meat that served instead of the hot sib and porridge he'd had so often on this trip. The trail trended upward and west, into rougher country than the trade road. Andressat caught but one glimpse of it between the tall rocks that now hedged them in, a little curve of beaten earth on the slope far below.

Sometime after midmorning, a cleft in the rock opened before them. "We go here," their guide said. "Big enough inside, but lead horses . . ."

Andressat shivered. The dark hole looked more like a natural cave, and he had no wish to spend days or weeks wandering in the dark. But Selfer had dismounted and followed their guides, and Andressat could not—in that narrow place, with the whole troop behind him—do anything else.

Once inside and around a knob of rock, he found himself on a smooth stone trail, here wide enough for three or four horses abreast, lit with a cool blue light. Here, as in the gnome prince's hall, the stone had been skillfully carved from the arched ceiling three times the height of a man to the floor crossed by grooves that would give purchase to the feet of horses or mules and also direct water off the trail. On this surface, they were now able to ride safely and quickly. The light was just enough to let them see the shape of the way ahead—sometimes curving, sometimes sloping a little uphill or down, but mostly straight and level. In that dimness, Andressat began to feel drowsy; his mind drifted to his own home, to the clear winter sunlight slanting across the vineyards, the long blue shadows. He did not think of the stops they must make to rest the horses, or food—the light never changed—he did not think of time.

"It is to dismount again," one of the gnomes said briskly, with a firm tap on Andressat's knee.

Andressat jerked awake—he felt mazed, stupid, as he swung a leg over and slid down to the stone. Ahead was a stone face with a gap much like the one they had entered. Outside was darkness.

Still dazed with sleep, Andressat followed Selfer and found they had come out on a slope that ran down before them. Mountains loomed behind them, black against a deep blue sky, lighter to the heart-side, eastward. A few stars still shone; the air was cold and smelled of snow, but gentler even so than the air of the north.

"That way—" Their guide said to Selfer. "—that way is the Val-daire road, down from the pass. The snow would have been deep there; here is only a little that will melt at sunrise.

"But—" Selfer sounded almost as dazed as Andressat felt. "But did we travel so far in just one day?"

"It was the prince's gift: to take you the way that is not measured with paces or furlongs or leagues or any human measurement. It was but one day's effort for you and your beasts, but without the prince's gift . . . it would be many days. Four or five at least, though the way is straight enough, compared to the trade road." A pause; Andressat was still trying to gather his scattered wits. "Not that any human will ever find it—or you remember it."

Andressat tried to fight off the wave of sleepiness that came over him but when his mind cleared again, he knew only that they were on the southern side of the pass with the Vale of Valdaire before them, and familiar smells came to him on a southern wind. Though he tried, he could not remember exactly how many days he'd been on the road since Vérella; everything was clear until they met some gnomes . . .

He shivered, though the day had warmed with the sun. He'd never seen gnomes before this trip and hoped never to see them again. For that matter, he never wanted to see the north again: too cold, too wet, and full of people he didn't know, not even counting the nonhumans.

When they reached Valdaire, Selfer saw him safe to a good inn, where his travel-worn clothing made his resumption of incognito as a merchant completely believable. "I could spare two men to travel with you to Andressat," Selfer said.

"What would it cost?" Andressat said. Despite the hospitality of those with whom he'd stayed, his purse was flatter than when he set out, the journey having been so much longer.

Selfer shook his head. "Nothing, my lord. Your safety matters to us, and in this season, traveling alone is not safe. Merchants frequently hire guards when not with a guarded caravan."

So it was that after a day's rest in a comfortable inn, Andressat rode up to the Duke's Company's winter quarters, where he met with Selfer and Burek, the two captains in residence. He recognized Burek at once, but tried to pretend he'd never seen his bastard grandson before. Burek, for his part, accepted the incognito without comment, but Andressat knew he'd been recognized.

"You are in more danger than I knew," Selfer said. "Our troops here have heard spies asking questions about anyone traveling alone or with a hired escort, other than merchants known to belong to one of the guilds. Someone—probably Alured—suspects that you are on the road, and it's clear you're being sought. Here's our plan, the best we could devise. Captain Burek's troops have been in the south this past campaign season and are more familiar with the current threats, besides being well rested. We think it better to use his for escort in this case. And he thinks you should have at least four; six would be better."

All he wanted was to ride for home the quickest way, but he would not ignore professional advice. "Thank you," he said. "But this is too large a gift—when I reach Cortes Andres, I must be allowed to provision all for the trip."

"Of course," Selfer said. "When would you like to leave?"

"As soon as possible. And should we travel the trade road, do you think, or cut across country?"

"How much would Alured like to capture you?"

Andressat's blood chilled. "I fear he would like it very much, and the scroll I have with me even more."

Burek looked at Selfer. "My troops are getting soft, sir, despite the exercises I put them to. I want them good and hard when Count Arcolin arrives. I think they need a good tramp on the road."

Selfer grinned. "How far?"

"As far as the borders of Vonja. It would be as well to check on that situation, too."

"I don't want—" Andressat began, then shame stopped him. If his was not the true pure blood of Old Aare, how could he so resent this young man for being born a bastard? What did bastard mean, after all? "I'm sorry," he said. "I'm sure you know best; it's only that I made the trip away alone for the most part."

"It is fortunate you chose to travel incognito," Selfer said. "We think it would be a good idea if you continued—but in another disguise."

Andressat had never expected to find himself in someone else's uniform, riding in the midst of the troop like any common soldier, while someone wearing his clothes rode south with a small escort of apparent Golden Company soldiers. He objected at first, thinking it was perhaps Burek's revenge for his own shabby treatment of him, but Burek explained with no hint of triumph.

"My lord, it is for your safety. If they have penetrated your disguise—if they have discovered that you are away from Cortes Andres—they will be watching for your return. You said yourself Alured wanted you and what you know; Alured has spies across Aarenis; he sent soldiers to your very doorstep."

"But that other group—are they not at risk?"

"Not much," Selfer said. "For one thing, they aren't Golden Company—we borrowed the uniforms. For another, we know Czardas and that part of Foss Council very well: they will have a long, frustrating chase and no profit from it."

Now Andressat jogged along with the Phelani cohort, listening to the gossip the troops passed among themselves. He heard about Sergeant Stammel, who had been stricken blind by a demon and yet learned to shoot a crossbow and take up the legend of the Blind Archer. He heard about wagers made, won, and lost, and what the troops thought about the change of leadership of the Company.

"Arcolin's fine," one said to another. "He's not the Duke, though. And it's too bad we never got to say goodbye to Kieri and give him the cheer he deserves."

"I could understand leaving the Company to stay with him," another answered. "But to stay with Captain Dorrin? Selfer's a fine captain; I wouldn't have chosen Dorrin."

"She was never your captain," someone else said. "Suppose it was Arcolin going away—would you stay with—" The man nodded to the front of the column.

"I would, unless Arcolin asked me particular. Lad's done well this past summer."

A grunt came in answer and a warning glance. Andressat saw that "the lad" had reined aside to watch the troop ride past. When it had, he rode to the front again. He did sit a horse well, Andressat had to admit, and his troops liked him.

On the border of Vonja, camped near one of the caravansaries where a few merchant groups were staying, Burek told them he was splitting the group in two. Andressat did not like the campsite; he worried that a spy might overhear Burek. But, as a common soldier, he could say nothing.

"Half will go north, make a half-circle, and half will go south, to do the same. Rendezvous at Foss, in ten days. You will live on field rations, camp in the open."

"But Captain, the Duke never had maneuvers like this in winter."

"The Duke's a king, and Arcolin's commanding now. He deems it good practice after two years of sitting on your arses in the north that you get more knowledge of lands where we might be hired next year."

"And I was just gettin' to know that redhead at the Dragon," said the man.

"The redhead!" That was another soldier, who punched the speaker in the shoulder. "It's not hard to get to know her—but that sergeant of Golden Company, Tamis Hardhand, would have somethin' to say about it."

Andressat realized that the banter was rehearsed when he saw one of the soldiers stare fixedly at another, who startled and then spoke up. "Captain, how far from the road must we go?"

"That's up to your field commanders—that'll be Sergeant Devlin and Corporal Arñe. I'll expect a rough map of your route, with hazards, trails, watercourses—"

"But sir . . . we aren't good—"

"You'll get better by doing. Arcolin wants more of you able to map. And a journal about each day's journey. I'll review those on the way back to Valdaire from Foss."

"You won't be with us?"

"I'll begin with the south group, but then I must go to Andressat. Selfer brought word: Tsaia's king wants a message taken."

"You'll want an escort—" This rather hopefully, from one of the oldest veterans.

"Yes, of course. Especially if the count refuses to see me, I must have someone who can hand over the message. It's probably just a formal announcement that he's been crowned, but—kings are kings."

Andressat squirmed; that had to be a dig at him. Yet he could see how it implied that he was there, in Cortes Andres, and not here, if anyone were listening. In that copse to one side of the camp, for instance.

"I should be at Foss in plenty of time to meet you," Burek said. "All I have to do is ride there and back. Now as to escort—" His eye roamed over the troop. He named four, and Andressat—presently under the name of Kerin—was of course one of them.

They started next morning as soon as it was light enough, a chill wet dawn. Winter in the south was never as sharp as in the north, but in this season what fell as snow in the Dwarfmounts fell as cold rain on the lands below.

"Takes somebody really interested to go stand in the rain this time of day," one of the others muttered when they were across the road and onto the fallow ground beyond.

"Maybe they thought we'd like breakfast with them," another said. A low chuckle ran through the troop. Andressat soon heard all about Cam's gambling, Selis's prodigious capacity for strong drink, Dort's intention to stay in the south when he retired. He felt isolated:

he did not want to talk to Burek even if, in his present guise, he could have done so. He had never listened to soldiers' banter; he had no way to join in. Besides, if any ears were listening, his accent would give him away as Andressat-born.

When Burek led his small group away from the others, it was still raining. If there were spies in the folds of land, behind rocks, in the trees or bushes, Andressat could not see them—he hoped any such were cold and miserable. The ground lifted away from the river, and soon they were riding inside the rain clouds themselves, hardly able to see a horse-length away, hearing only the clop and suck of hooves in mud, the creak of leather. Andressat tensed. Easy to get lost on these slopes; easy to stumble into a rough ravine; easy to be ambushed—five horses made enough noise for anyone to notice.

They made a wet cold camp that night, and Andressat woke when the wind changed and blew colder through his damp cloak.

Dawn broke with high rose-colored clouds and a peculiar clarity to the air below that meant, Andressat knew, western weather for a day or so. To the north, clouds still lay in the Honnorgat valley, but where they rode, they could see the shape of the land, now sparkling with wet in the thin sun. Water trickled musically into every depression, along every possible watercourse. Wide stretches of turf, inlaid with bands of trees . . . a flock of sheep, a mound of dirty wool, moved across a slope west of them.

They were almost to the border of Andressat, coming up through the bands of gray rock, when attack came. From behind a row of the rough gray stones, five men rose, two with bows in hand. Instinctively, Andressat slid off his horse on the off side; the animal squealed and plunged as an arrow struck its neck. Behind him, he heard arrows shattering on the rocks. Dort had been hit; he fell from his mount. Burek called commands Andressat did not know; the others were around him in moments, swords and shields out. He had the same, but he'd failed to grab his shield when he dismounted, and he'd never used a short sword in his life.

Someone else grabbed the shield from the fallen man's horse and handed it to him. "Heart-hand—hold it up like this," the man muttered. It was heavier than Andressat expected. "Sword's for stabbing. No fencing." An arrow clanged on his helmet; Andressat heard Burek say something else he didn't understand, and found himself shoved sideways by the others. They were now covering the body of their fallen comrade, who was not—Andressat was surprised to see—dead.

"Advance!"

That he understood. The attackers had come out into the trail now, leaving their bows behind. All but one carried medium-length swords, broad at the base. Burek held the right end of their own line; unlike the rest, he had an officer's long sword. Andressat glanced at the men on either side of him and tried to understand what he was supposed to do.

As the lines came together, instinct took over. Andressat had never fought in close formation, but he had seen Phelan's and Halveric's soldiers both drilling and in battle. That heavy shield gave not at all to blows by the enemy's swords, and his own short blade thrust forward as fast as those of his companions. One of the enemy fell, then two more. A thrown dagger zipped past and hit his helmet, stinging his arm as it fell away. Burek—he had no time to watch Burek. Then he heard the clash of blades behind him; he dared not turn and look, for the enemies in front. A blow in the back staggered him. He felt a body sliding down his.

Two of the three men in front of them continued to fight, but one turned away; Andressat recognized one of the archers. "Get him!" he said. "He's going for his bow . . ." Beside him, his two companions surged forward, and he moved with them; the two remaining enemy swordsmen fell. One of his companions ran over the dying and stabbed the enemy archer in the back. The man fell with a choked cry.

It seemed very quiet suddenly.

Andressat bent over, gasping; he had considered himself fit, but it had been many hands of years since he'd fought. Then he turned.

Behind him were Dort, now with his throat cut ear to ear; two enemies, both dead or near death; and Burek, a dent in his helmet and one arm bent the wrong way.

"Gird's gut," one of the soldiers said. "This is no good. Cam—get up on one of them rocks and see if there's any more trouble." He himself went to Burek. "Sir—?"

"Stupid of me," Burek muttered. "Blade caught in the neckbone—left me open—"

"Just stay still. Cam's high guard. Kerin—you stand watch there—"

"He can't—" Burek said, then bit back a cry as the soldier moved his arm.

"He did well enough," Selis said. He had Burek's glove off and the sleeve of his mailed shirt pushed up. Andressat glanced at the swollen dark bruise. "Bad break, this, sir. Needs a surgeon."

"Just . . . splint . . . it . . ."

"I've set bones," Andressat said. "Learned from a surgeon. We need something for splints." They were far from trees or even bushes, surrounded by turf and stones.

"Come hold his arm, then," Selis said. "I'll find those bows."

Andressat took hold of Burek's hand and looked him in the face. Pale, under its tan, but the eyes steady as they met his. He felt a rush of warmth for this man, blood of his blood. It wasn't Burek's fault he was a bastard; it wasn't his fault that he chose soldiering over horse-training. It was his own fault that he'd exiled the lad—lad then but man now—in a fit of temper.

"Sorry . . ." Burek said.

"It's a bad break," Andressat said. "But we should be able to save the arm. I'm sure at Cortes Andres they have a surgeon who can do more, but for now . . ."

Selis came back with two crossbows. "Just let me cut them apart," he said. His dagger slit the bindings, one cord at a time. He did so while standing, scanning the countryside. When he had the first bow apart, he said, "What about the front part?"

"The prod? Is it straight?"

"Seems so." Selis brought it over; Andressat looked at it.

"No—see that bend? We need straight—what about splitting the stock?"

Selis gave him a searching look, then nodded. Moving away, he set the stock down, bracing the butt with rocks, and brought the hatchet down firmly on the end; in two blows he'd created a small notch. He put in a wedge and began working his way down, wedge by wedge; on the third or fourth, the wood cracked the rest of the way; the roller nut flew out. Selis trimmed the rough edges of both pieces with the hatchet. "This do?"

"Good," Andressat said. "Now wrap them with cloth—and I'll need some cloth strips."

"You're sure you've done this before?"

Andressat nodded. "Something every—" He paused, glancing around. "—every soldier should know, my father said."

Selis cut away one of the dead brigands' clothes and ripped strips from the shirt. In minutes, he had padded both halves of the former stock and brought them to Andressat. "What do you want me to do?"

"Hold his upper arm here—yes, like that. I need to pull, to straighten this as much as possible." He glanced down at Burek's face, now beaded with sweat. "It will hurt, Captain, but if I can align the bones now, you have a better chance of regaining full use of the arm."

"Go ahead," Burek said.

Andressat took a firm hold. He had set many a broken wrist and forearm in the past, usually with good results, but those had not been the result of a sword blow that drove the mail into the flesh. At home, he would have bound fresh leaves of herbs against the swelling, to aid healing. Here . . . was nothing. Not even clean cloths. Nothing to do but set it anyway. He pulled firmly, feeling the bones grate; Burek made no noise. Finally, he felt what he had hoped for—larger pieces were end to end, at least—and he bound on the splints, with Selis's help. When that was done, Burek let out a long hiss of breath. Andressat touched his shoulder. "I'm sorry," he said. It meant more than one thing; he saw from Burek's expression that the young man took all that meaning.

"It's better," Burek said. That, too, might mean more than his arm. "We need to get moving."

"A sling," Andressat said. He fashioned a sling and helped Burek put the splinted arm into it. Selis helped Burek sit up.

"We'll get the horses, sir, and—I suppose we'll be taking Dort's body? There's no way to bury him up here."

"Yes. Kerin, you know this country—how far to a border fort?"

"We might make it today, Captain," Andressat said. "What about the enemy's arms?"

"We'll take those, too, if the horses can carry the load—wasn't yours hit?"

When Andressat stood again, he could see the horses not far away, nibbling the frostbitten turf. One—the one he'd been riding—still had an arrow sticking from its neck. "Mine still has the bolt in its neck," he said. "Could be a bad wound, could be nothing—won't know until we get it out."

It took another full glass or more to catch the horses, strip the enemy dead of weapons and money— "Sorellin coins—bet they're counterfeit," Burek remarked—and load Dort's body, wrapped in his own cloak, onto the pack horse. Andressat's horse carried a light pack; he rode Dort's, and they set off at a foot pace.

It was near dark when Andressat spotted the border fort tower. "Ride ahead—" he began, then looked at Burek. Burek's face was pale, taut with pain. "Sorry, Captain—"

"Good idea, though. Cam, go on and let them know we're coming . . ." He glanced at Andressat. "Should he—?"

"Yes," Andressat said. He reached into his belt-pouch and handed Cam a ring. "Show this, but only if you're sure it's Andressat troops."

Cam rode off at a hand gallop. Before they had covered half the distance—slower, now that it was dark—they saw torches approaching. Andressat's second son came with the party that met them.

"Sir, I was about ready to set out in search for you, though you had told us not to—I had no idea—"

"Nor I, Meddthal. I have traveled far indeed—but here we have a man injured—this is Burek, a captain in Phelan's Company."

"Burek—" Meddthal said; in the torchlight his expression was hard to read.

"Indeed," Andressat said. "And the reason I am alive to greet you. Is there a surgeon at the fort?"

"Yes—" Meddthal glanced again at Burek. "Captain, can you ride another glass, or—"

"I can ride," Burek said. "But not fast."

That night Andressat watched by Burek's bed. The surgeon had given him numbwine enough to put him to sleep, then unwrapped Andressat's splints and shook his head over the arm.

"It is not the broken bones—you know this yourself, my lord Count. It is the damage to muscle and sinew. And I understand you had no herbs, not there in the open."

Dark-bruised and twice its normal size, the arm looked grotesquely like that of a sun-swollen corpse. Andressat repressed a shudder. He had sent the lad away in anger . . . and now the man might lose his arm. "What can you do?"

"I gave him an infusion of cooling herbs with the numbwine; as you know, that is specific for wound swelling and also wound fever, but that was only a half-glass ago. I am cooling a paste of ganteh and lurz in tallow. If the swelling goes down, we may be able to save the arm. If not—"

"We must save it," Andressat said, surprised at the tone of his own voice. "I must talk with my son."

In the other room, Meddthal had a hot meal laid out. "Sir, isn't that the—"

"Yes," Andressat said. He sat down heavily. His sons knew he'd not liked Aesil M'dierra's junior officer, but not why.

"I thought he was with Golden Company."

"M'dierra sent him away. On my account, I learned." He swallowed a spoonful of hot spiced soup, then another. Meddthal dipped a slice of bread in oil, sprinkled it with salt, and nibbled on it as he waited. "So then he went to Phelan's Company—which isn't Phelan's anymore; it belongs to his former senior captain, Arcolin. Count Arcolin, now."

"Northern title . . ." Meddthal muttered.

"Don't, Medd," Andressat said. "But by the humor of the gods— and in this I can see the hand only of the Trickster—it was Burek who undertook to see me safe home, and Burek who saved my life." He drank more of the soup and sopped bread in the dregs. "I have many things to tell you all, but I am very tired. I was wrong about Captain Burek, though . . . wrong from the first . . ." He shook his head.

"Father—sir—"

"Not now. I must rest, but make sure he is not left alone, and wake me if there's a crisis."

In the morning, Burek's arm was no worse; the surgeon was guardedly hopeful. "His fingers are still warm; he roused once and drank more of the infusion."

"How long before he can travel?"

"You're not going to make him leave!"

"No, no, of course not. But he told his troops to expect him in Foss—if he cannot make that meeting, we need to send word."

"He won't be fit to move at all until I know whether the arm must go or not. A tenday, at the least, most likely longer. What are you going to do with that body?"

"I don't know what their customs are. And he is their captain; I should ask him."

"Not before noon, and he'll be groggy then. Ask one of the others."

Selis and Cam had made a neat Phelani corner of the fort barracks, all the gear stacked and covered with a cloak, but they were both in the stable, where Dort's body lay on a trestle. "How is Captain Burek?" Selis asked, and then—apparently noticing Andressat's change of clothing—added a belated "my lord."

"The surgeon hopes he might not lose the arm," Andressat said. "It seems no worse this morning, he told me. But now—I do not know your customs of respect for the dead."

"We bury them, of course," Selis said, as if that were obvious. "I was going to ask—"

"The soil here is thin," Andressat said. "Over solid rock. There's a dell a glass or so from here, where we've buried before, but it filled up during Siniava's War. We could raise a mound of stone—"

"It's winter," Selis said. "We can take him back to the others—it's only a few days. When can the Captain travel?"

"The surgeon says not for ten days or more," Andressat said. "That's if he doesn't lose the arm. The swelling must go down completely; the surgeon wants to be sure there's no pus forming."

"What's he doing?"

Andressat explained as best he could. "I know the rest of your cohort was expecting him to be at Foss when they arrived or shortly after. You will need to go and tell them he's not able to come. There are only two of you—I could send—"

"No, my lord." This time Selis remembered the courtesy. "We'll travel faster alone."

"Not with a body," Cam said.

They both looked at Andressat as if he might have some solution. He had none.

"We'll have to leave him," Cam said. "We have to let the others know about the Captain—get word to Captain Selfer. We'll need to ride fast, and we both have to go—you know that, Selis."

"I know, but—"

"Dort would say the same. So would the Captain, if he could."

Selfer watched the column coming up the track from Valdaire and wondered if Burek had stayed behind in the city for some reason. With or without a captain present, the cohort rode in perfect order and dipped the Company pennant crisply, as it should.

"What report?" he asked.

"Sir, Captain Burek was wounded; he's in Andressat, in the care of a surgeon."

Selfer listened to the rest of the story. Burek had been rash to take less than a hand of Phelani—two more would have changed the flow of battle—but he understood the reason: five could travel more quickly than seven, and he had already detached a hand for the decoy party that had approached Andressat from the west.

Burek had no memory of the previous days when he woke to find the surgeon rewrapping the splints.

"You'll do," the surgeon said. "Swelling's well down, and your hand's still warm. I expect it hurts some."

"Not that much," Burek said. His mouth felt furry and tasted horrible; the surgeon's assistant lifted his shoulders and held a cup to his lips. Burek swallowed: clean water with just a hint of mint.

"Wiggle your fingers," the surgeon said. Burek did so, and pain wrapped his arm. He clenched his jaw against the pain. "Um," the surgeon said, in a tone that meant something, though Burek didn't know what. "Still a lot of muscle damage. You'll need to continue with the infusion. And it's time you got yourself to the jacks, though you'll need some help. Get him up, Jens, but slowly—he might faint."

He was not going to faint. He told himself that, though his head spun when he first sat all the way up, his feet on the rug beside his bed. But with help, he did make it to the jacks and back to the bed, despite the sensation of falling sideways because of the weight of his splinted arm.

"Where are my men?" he asked, when he was back down.

"Gone to tell the others you won't be coming for a while," the surgeon said. "They left two days ago. The Count's offered you a place in Cortes Andres until you're fully recovered, once you can be moved. You're not going to risk that arm for six hands of days at least."

"I can't lie in bed six hands of days!"

"Of course not. But you must be down most of the time until I'm sure of that arm. You came close to losing it; I'm not letting your pride make it go bad again."

Burek tried to sit up again, but could not; the surgeon smiled.

"You'll be stronger each day if you do what I tell you. The herbal infusion is strengthening your blood; you must eat what I prescribe, and exercise exactly as I say, if you want the full use of that arm later—if it's possible, I mean." The surgeon paused. "It might not be, though the Count did a good job with that first splint. Do not blame him if it is not perfect."

"I wouldn't," Burek said. "Why would I?"

The surgeon pursed his lips. "I heard things—that he had once had a grudge against you. If so, you might think he took ill care on purpose."

"No," Burek said. "I had no quarrel with the Count and have none now. It is true he did not like me, but that's his business."

"He likes you now," the surgeon said. "It is not merely that he credits you with saving his life, but something else, which he has not shared with me—or anyone that I know of, though I could read it in his face and voice. It is almost as if he discovered a member of the family."

"I am not that," Burek said, looking away.

"I didn't suppose you were," the surgeon said. "But some men mellow in age, and others harden; I think now he's mellowed. Travel does that for some."

In another hand of days, Burek was able to come to the table for meals, where he found eating one-handed more difficult than he expected. Meddthal, the Count's second son and fort commander, was a lean, tough-looking man in his mid-forties. He treated Burek with courtesy, often eating his meals at the same time and asking intelligent questions about mercenary service without seeming to pry.

"My father said you'd served with Golden Company as well as the Duke's . . . did you like serving under a woman?

"Aesil M'dierra? It made no difference to me; by her reputation she's as skilled a commander—and as honorable—as Phelan or Halveric."

"I met Phelan, in Siniava's War," Meddthal said. "I'm not surprised he became a king, though my father was. I wonder how his successor will do with his lands."

"Very well, I think," Burek said. "Certainly the troops seem happy with him. And Captain Selfer—he was one of Phelan's squires."

"Glad to hear it," Meddthal said, "since it seems we're going to be seeing another miserable war. Damn these ambitious men! Why can't they be content to rule their own lands well? There's more than enough work for a lifetime in that, if you do it right." He shook his head. "Though it would be hard luck on you mercenaries, then. I suppose you like the life of the sword—"

"Not at the moment," Burek said, lifting his arm slightly in its sling. "But some of it, yes."

"I would rather go back to minding the wine production," Meddthal said. "But my father needs me here, so here I am."

"I don't want war," Burek said. "What little I saw of Siniava's War . . . no one sane wants that. But I do think wars come, want them or no—"

"Someone wants them, or they wouldn't—"

"True enough. Alured does, I think. Some demon drives men like him and Siniava. But there will always be brigands, even without a war, and someone must protect the farmers and merchants from them."

CHAPTER THIRTY-SIX

Chaya, Lyonya

Kieri woke with a start, as if someone had touched him with a coal. A vision of fire glittering on dark water, ships of fire . . . and the taig, roiled with fear.

He was out of bed before he knew it, sword in hand, feet planted firmly on the carpet. The sword steadied him, even as its jewel flared brightly in the dark room. Where? Where was the menace? It must be the Pargunese coming across the Honnorgat, but upstream or down?

And had the Pargunese king betrayed him? Or been overthrown? He reached out to the taig as he had done before, this time to steady it.

I am here. Your king is with you.

A knock on the door.

"Come," he said aloud.

"Sir King, I felt something—" It was Berne, one of the half-elven Squires.

"And I," Kieri said. "North—the Pargunese are across the river, bringing fire."

"What will you do?"

"Dress," Kieri said. "I can't do much like this—" He glanced down at his winter bed gown and his bare feet and gave Berne a rueful grin. As he'd hoped, Berne chuckled, a bit nervously. "It's not my first war," Kieri said. "Send to the kitchen—we'll need hot food as soon as possible—and to the stable—we'll need horses prepared for couriers.

Also Garris: he has the Squire roster. I'll be dressed and down by the time you're done."

As he lit the candles—by this time he had enough control of his powers to do that by magery alone—he wondered what prompted an attack now, at this moment. Had the Pargunese king turned against him? Unlikely, he thought. Had he been killed by his wicked brother? Possibly . . . though the reports he'd had regularly from the king had indicated he felt he was making some headway and wasn't in flight for his life.

Reports days old. Much could have happened, including the king's brother making an attack out of panic. Kieri reached out to the taig again, this time to call the Lady. She would have felt the disturbance, he was sure, and in this crisis he must ignore the anger he still felt against her. But he could feel nothing—had she, in her anger, locked herself away from him completely? Surely she would come, with the taig in danger.

He dressed quickly, mail under his outer garments, shirt, doublet, and capelet all in the royal colors, boots, and the day-crown he usually wore only for semiformal audiences. His people needed to see their king looking calm and regal . . . but martial, too. When he opened his door again, the Squires posted there looked worried. He smiled at them.

"Whoever ordered the attack cannot know how quickly word reached us," he said to them. "Remember, even the king of Pargun does not know about our taig-sense, or all the details of our deployments. I do not think this is his treachery, which means the attackers know almost nothing. They will think they can gain a foothold before we even hear about it."

"But what will we do?" Berne asked.

"Eat breakfast," Kieri said. "Never fight a war on an empty stomach."

Downstairs, servants scurried about; all seemed a confused bustle. Garris, his face blurry with sleep, at least had his uniform on straight as he came out of his office. "Is it war, Sir King?"

"I believe so, yes," Kieri said. "It seems someone in Pargun still seeks to burn us out."

"You'll want to send for Aliam Halveric, then—"

"Indeed. It is a shame to wrest him from a home still under repair, but I need him and his troops. And we'll need the rangers from the southern borders—and the west as well—but first, we eat."

Garris grinned, to the obvious surprise of the other Squires. "Aliam's rules, eh?"

"Right. It's near enough dawn; the kitchen may have already lit fires, so I suspect we'll be getting hot food soon."

"The Council?"

"I expect they'll arrive on their own while we eat. As will my elven relatives." Surely they would come, would appear any moment. "I am monitoring the taig now, but would like Orlith or another to do so as well."

"Is there any chance our river force can throw them back?"

"It might, depending on what force they sent and what their fire weapon is. The Pargunese king's mention of a 'forbidden hill' and 'dragons' fire' worries me. It may be nothing more than a scare-name, but if it's not—"

"Sir King—" That was the steward, looking both scared and determined. "Bread's not out yet, but there's porridge-cakes quick-fried and cold meats—hot sib in a few minutes."

"Excellent," Kieri said. "Come now—let's eat. Everyone needs to start this day with a good meal under their belts."

"My lord—" The steward bowed them into the small dining room.

Kieri and Garris ate heartily, and soon his Squires joined in. Kieri drank down a cup of hot sib in three swallows, finishing just as Orlith arrived.

"Sir King—I'm glad to see you're awake."

"The taig woke me, as I'm sure it did you. Have you eaten?"

"Yes," Orlith said. "Others are coming."

"The Lady?" Kieri asked. "I haven't been able to reach her through the taig."

"I expect so," Orlith said.

"Good," Kieri said, applying himself to another porridge-cake. "We will have a busy day. I would like you to monitor the taig, so that I can deal with other things from time to time. I'm staying in contact, but I don't want to miss anything it might tell us and yet I must attend to purely military matters as well."

"As you wish, Sir King," Orlith said, bowing.

"I'm sending couriers to bring in our reserves of rangers," Kieri said. "And the Halveric with his troops."

"I thought they were already here—"

"No." Had Orlith paid no attention earlier? "A cohort and a half are still south, with Aliam." Servants brought in a steaming basket of hot bread. Kieri broke off an end and slathered it with butter, then dripped honey on it. "Let this stand for the pastry," he said. "We're already talking business, and we must continue."

Garris pushed back his chair. "By your leave, Sir King, I'll get the couriers started on their way—and yes, I'll make sure they've breakfasted."

"Good. Whoever's at the river should already have sent to Tsaia to warn them, as well as to us. Send also to whatever domains you think might not be touched by couriers on their way to and from the river."

Garris bowed and left just as Sier Halveric arrived, more flustered than Kieri had ever seen him.

"Sir King!"

"Sit down," Kieri said. "Have some breakfast—"

"There's no time," Halveric said. "We must do something."

"We must prepare for a long and difficult day," Kieri said. "Eat, if you haven't. I'm sending couriers to Aliam and to steadings between here and the river."

"How long have you been awake?" Halveric asked, reaching for the bread.

"A turn of the glass, now. The taig woke me. When Aliam arrives, he will take command of all our forces, second only to me. I'd like you to see to provisioning, if you would."

"Of course, Sir King . . . you are so calm; are you not worried?"

"Worried? Of course. Panicked, no. This is not my first war."

He felt the northern edge of the taig flinch, as if from a blow; glancing at Orlith, he saw that the elf had felt it as clearly.

"Dry leaves and a wind from the north," the elf said. He did not need to say more. Kieri could almost feel his own skin crisping in a blaze, as dry leaves ignited and blew through the air, lighting the dry wood of fallen limbs . . . but deeper in the forest, the burning leaves fell on snowdrifts and went out. "They picked an ill time to use fire," the elf said. "Autumn before snow would be better . . ."

"That may have been their original plan," Kieri said, "which we delayed, by intervening in the matter of their king. Let us ask the gods for more snow—or freezing rain."

By dawn—a bitter, clear dawn, with north wind thrashing the trees—couriers were well on their way and Council members resident in Chaya were busy carrying out the tasks he had given them. Still he had heard nothing from the Lady, and Orlith, busy with the tasks Kieri had given him, merely shook his head when asked if she was aware of the taig.

"Will you take the field?" Sier Belvarin asked.

"Not now," Kieri said. "Captain Talgan is a competent field commander for the Halveric troops—I've seen him in action—and I must trust my ranger and Royal Archer commanders are the same, though they lack Talgan's experience. We should have couriers arriving this evening with reports."

The rest of the day, Kieri worked through the plans he'd made, nudging his Council into faster action by anticipating their questions and confusion. He spent an hour at midday, walking through the streets of Chaya, where rumors were already causing some disturbances, encouraging people to come to their local council if they wanted to know more. "I'm going now to talk to them," he said. "There's nothing you can't hear."

Men and women crowded into the meeting hall; Kieri told them what he knew, what he didn't know, and when he would know more.

"So far, the damage has not spread. It might—I do not know what this special fire is, that the Pargunese king told me about."

"Do the elves know? Does the Lady?"

"The elves have not told me, if they do, and since they love trees, I can't imagine they would keep it secret if they did. Here is what I want you to do: since we do not know yet how many they are, and exactly what they purpose, you must prepare yourselves for several possibilities." Kieri outlined these, and explained what preparations were needed for each. "You see there is much to be done, and you can accomplish this, if you start now, and do not panic."

"Are you going north?"

"Not yet." He saw relief on most faces; it surprised him. His own troops—his former troops, he reminded himself—were most confident when their commander took the field with them. These people seemed to want him near them . . . but then, it was the same impulse, just expressed differently.

Through the afternoon, his annoyance with the Lady's non-appearance grew; he tried to ignore it, lest it further disturb the taig. But where was she? Where could she go that he could not feel at least the touch of her power? He felt less keenly another fire blaze in the north; Orlith, he saw as he looked up, was monitoring it closely.

"I think the rangers are able to quench the fires," Orlith said. "It is nothing new."

"It is ordinary fire so far," Kieri said. "I do not trust that it will always be. If I had a weapon of unquenchable fire, I would not necessarily use it first."

"Why not?"

"I would see how well ordinary fire did . . . I would probe my enemy's defenses. An extraordinary weapon kept in reserve for the right moment has greater effect."

Orlith stared at him for a moment then shook his head. "I had not thought of that. Truly, your experience as a war leader may be more valuable than I thought."

"It usually is, if you're in a war," Kieri said. He finished the stack of orders before him. He felt stiff and stale—it would be turns of the glass yet before a courier would arrive. "I'm going to the salle for practice, and then a bath before dinner." He pushed himself to his feet. "Aulin, Sarol, have you had practice today?"

"No, Sir King. The others went earlier."

"Then come along; you can rotate in."

In practice garb, and with another mug of sib, he ran down the stairs, followed by his Squires, and found Carlion and Siger putting a group of lads in palace livery through elementary footwork drills.

"I wondered when you'd show up, m'lord," Siger said. "Knew you were busy."

"Busy, but not about to miss both my practices," Kieri said. "You'd never let me hear the end of it." He hung his sword up and began stretching, trying not to rush—it would not do to hurry through this, not in front of both senior armsmasters, one of whom knew him very well indeed.

Sure enough, Siger came over and watched critically. "Get that elbow right straight out, m'lord. You've another thumb width of reach that way . . . and your foot's not at the right angle."

Kieri moved his foot, straightened his elbow—a tight muscle in his forearm twinged—and finally Siger agreed he was stretched enough to begin practice.

"You lads, move aside," Carlion said. "By your leave, Sir King, I'd let them stay . . . Siger and I intend to work you hard this afternoon."

"I'd welcome it," Kieri said. He strapped on a banda, put on his gloves, and picked up a practice blade.

"The audience or the work?" Carlion asked.

"Both," Kieri said, with a quick grin for the audience.

"The middle range to warm up," Carlion said. The two armsmasters were already there; the moment Kieri stepped up to that division of the salle, they came at him from two sides. Kieri retreated along the line of the low ledge; they advanced, trying to press as he parried stroke after stroke—but as he neared the corner, they could not both find room to close.

Worries about the invasion disappeared, and he relaxed into the immediate moment, letting his years of practice take over, ignoring the gasps of the lads who were watching as his heel met one unstable stone that tipped beneath him. Along the side wall, then two quick strides—catching a flurry of blows on his blade—diagonally away from it. Carlion was caught behind Siger for a long moment, and could not reach him. Kieri tried to maneuver Siger so he kept blocking Carlion, but Carlion had too much space to move and too much sense to stay where he was. Still, he had a solid touch on Siger by the time Carlion was at him on the side again. Siger stood back, acknowledging a blow that would have put him out of the fight if it had been real. He would reenter the fray, Kieri knew, after a certain number of blows, as Carlion's reinforcement.

Best finish quickly, if he could. Kieri shortened his blade, coming in fast to parry Carlion's attack then make his own—a blow with the shortened blade, a leg-trap with one leg, and finally, when Carlion fell, a touch with the pommel to Carlion's neck.

"Yield," Carlion said.

"Accept," Kieri said. Instinct made him roll aside, just as Siger swung at his back from behind; the blow hit Carlion instead, though Siger pulled it.

"Hold," Carlion said, and Siger grounded his blade. Kieri and Carlion got up, both breathing heavily. Carlion grinned at him. "You are not so out of practice as I thought, Sir King. It's going to be annoying in a few years—you half-elves do not slow with age in your fifties or sixties or seventies, and we human armsmasters do. With you, I realize how much I'm relying on experience and tricks instead of bladework . . . and you have grown stronger and faster since you came."

"Indeed you have," Siger put in. "But then, though you worked daily last year back in Tsaia, you had no such salle nor as many to work with."

"Or the constant attention of two such armsmasters," Kieri said. "Now, sirs, if you're ready—"

"Sir King!" That from Sarol, at the door. "A courier's come!"

Kieri shook his head. "No, I must go. Damn the Pargunese!" He turned, leapt lightly over the low barrier between the middle and low sections, stripped off his banda, and handed it and the practice blade to one of the other Squires. He belted on his own sword and hurried into the palace.

Garris met him in the main passage. "He's in my office, with a pot of sib and some food. I thought you'd rather meet him in privacy—"

"Yes, indeed. Who is it?"

"Not a Squire—a Halveric soldier who rode straight through from Talgan. Says his name's Beldan."

Kieri felt a cold chill down his spine. "Garris, are you sure?"

"He's got a Halveric uniform on, Halveric-style sword. Why?"

"Stay close," Kieri said to his Squires. And to Garris, "Talgan knows that any message he sends will be taken on by a King's Squire at the first relay station. That's what we agreed."

"But he has the message pouch—and he said it was a special hand-to-hand only—"

When they came to Garris's office, the door was open and the office empty. On Garris's desk, the message pouch with the tooled Halveric insignia lay invitingly open, a scroll just showing; it looked wet on one side, as if the courier had ridden through a stream that splashed up onto it.

"He must have gone to the jacks," Garris said.

"I think not," Kieri said. "They tried assassination once; no reason they would not try it again—don't touch that!" he said sharply, as Garris reached for the message pouch. Garris stopped, hand out.

"Why?"

"Was it wet when you first saw it?"

Garris frowned. "No . . . I don't recall . . ." Then he paled. "Poison?"

"It might be." Kieri's mind raced. Where was the enemy? Would the man have fled, leaving the poisoned "message" behind? Or would he have stayed behind to accomplish more mischief? In the kitchens, poisoning the food? In the stables, poisoning the horses? "Are you wearing mail, Garris?"

"Me? No, I don't—oh." Garris's gaze sharpened. "Are you?"

"No—I changed for practice. I'll put it on—I want every Squire in mail, and that includes you. Everyone who has it—and send someone to the kitchens—to the stables—" He stopped and took a breath; it would not do to sound so worried. "We must be careful, but steady. I will go change."

Upstairs, Aulin and Sarol inspected his rooms before he went in. He decided to risk a quick bath: Joriam had it ready, herb-scented, with towels warming before the fire. The old man smiled at him, came to help him out of his clothes.

Pargunese hot baths might be better than this, but he found it hard to imagine. He eased into the hot scented water, and Joriam sluiced warm water from the ewer over him. He would have enjoyed a long soak but could not spare the time. Joriam said, "Soap, my lord—" Kieri turned just in time to see the old man's eyes go wide—and an arrow take him in the throat. Joriam slumped; the soap dropped into Kieri's hand.

Across the room, in the door to his bedchamber, stood a grinning stranger wearing a palace tabard; he held a short bow in one hand and an arrow in his teeth. Spitting the arrow into his hand, he said, "I do like it when they're naked and helpless."

Kieri hurled the soap at the man's face; the man put up his hand instinctively, dropping the arrow. As Kieri surged out of the tub and grabbed the ewer Joriam had set down, he saw the man fumble at the tabard, as if he expected to find an arrow there, and then dive for the one on the floor. Before he could reach it, Kieri was on him, smashing the heavy ewer in his face, a foot and then a knee in the man's belly, hitting him again with the ewer, and again . . . the anger he thought he'd worked off in the salle roared through him like the winter wind, even when the man lay still, blood running from his nose and ears. Kieri raised the ewer again . . . and stopped. He could hear his own harsh breathing and nothing else. The taig—he must think of the taig. The man was dead. He might not be the only assassin—and his people needed their king, not a wild man.

He looked for the fallen arrow, found it, and stood up carefully, watching where he stepped in case of any other hazard. As his pulse slowed, he felt chilled . . . Joriam, poor old Joriam . . . and who else? How had the assassin made it this far? How had he known where to go? Was it safe to call out?

His hands were blood-splashed; he dipped them in the still-warm bathwater, plucked a warmed towel off the rack by the fire and dried his hands, rubbed himself with it. Then he went back to the assassin, picked up the bow, put the arrow on the string, and walked into his bedchamber. He heard a cry from the corridor just as he saw the bodies of Aulin and Sarol and heard someone running toward him.

He had just presence of mind to drop the bow and grab his sword from the rack when two white-faced Squires, Edrin and Lieth, appeared. "Sir King!"

"An assassin," Kieri said. "I killed him, but not before he killed those Squires and Joriam, I'm sorry to say."

"He—you—you're alive!"

"As you see," Kieri said. They had both seen more than anyone here but Joriam; after a bath the old scars always showed clearly. "I need to dress," he said, laying his sword on the bed. Joriam, bless him, had set out clothes for the evening in the bathing room, but he was not going back in there, not immediately. "The bodies are in the bathing room," he said. "Joriam took an arrow in the throat. The Seneschal should be told, to honor our dead."

The bedroom felt cold after the bathing room; he went to his closet and began dressing, as the Squires called for more help.

"How many dead so far?" he asked.

"A groom, a bootboy, Aulin and Sarol, Joriam," Edrin said. "Garris told us all to put on mail. Most of us keep our mail with our travel packs, in the stable; I had just put on mine when someone found the groom's body and called out. Lieth and I ran for the palace. The other one—"

"Other one?"

"Claims he's a Halveric. Garris and the steward found him in the back passage; claimed he'd been to the jacks—"

"Is he alive?" Kieri asked, shrugging into a velvet tunic over his mail. He reached for the sword belt, snugged it, then sheathed the great sword.

"Yes, and bound to a chair in Garris's office. Sir King—how did you do it?"

"He flinched at the soap when I threw it," Kieri said. "Beyond that, the gods were on my side, I suspect." Dressed, armed once more, he felt better, though the anger simmered.

Now he heard more people coming, voices he knew: the steward, the Seneschal, Sier Halveric.

He started toward the door, but Edrin moved in front of him.

"Sir King—are you—you're not hurt!" That was Sier Halveric.

"No, I'm not hurt," Kieri said. To the Seneschal he said, "Aulin and Sarol died in my defense; Joriam also. And I understand an assassin also killed a groom and a bootboy. They should be treated with all reverence, and I am still unsure of the customs."

"Sir King, all will be done," the Seneschal said. "I have called for the burial guild; we will take the bodies and prepare them. By your leave, I will begin here." He knelt beside the Squires' bodies.

"Of course," Kieri said. "What shall I do to help?"

"Let us have a sheet from your bed—"

"Not the king's bed," the steward said. "Let me bring—"

"From my bed," Kieri said. "They died for me; they deserve far more than a sheet off my bed." He went to his bed, pulled back the covers, stripped off the sheets, and carried the bundle to the Seneschal.

"Half will do for each," the Seneschal said. "And as their deaths were violent, your sword may divide them."

The sword whispered through the sheets Edrin and Lieth held

taut, one after another; they helped the Seneschal straighten the bodies, ease them onto the sheets, and carry them to the passage. Kieri came to each, and knelt for a moment with a hand on each head.

"Falk honor your service, for which you have a king's thanks." Then he bent and kissed each forehead. "Fare well in your afterhome. You honor the gods you served."

He went with the Seneschal and the Squires into the bathing room, where they laid Joriam in a winding sheet; Kieri felt tears sting his eyes. The old man had been a comfort to so many—sweet, thoughtful, gentle—serving Lyonya's royal family all his life; he had been the one to recognize Kieri's sword when Paks arrived with it. To die like this—so violently, so unfairly—it was wrong.

The Seneschal finished with Joriam's body after Kieri had given his thanks and farewell blessing. By then the burial guild had arrived. Kieri and the Seneschal stood aside as they lifted Joriam's body onto a plank and carried it away. The Seneschal glanced around the room, then at the assassin's body. "And that one?"

"What do you with murderers' corpses?"

The Seneschal gave him a long look. "They were someone's get and sometimes someone's parent. We give their bodies back to the taig, but do not raise the bones."

"Do that, then, with this one."

"You broke his head," the Seneschal said. "How?"

"That ewer," Kieri said. "It was all I could reach as I came out of the tub."

"You were in the *tub* when he—?"

"Yes," Kieri said. The aftermath of the day hit him then and a mental image of himself—a naked, wet, redheaded man throwing soap and then charging an armed man with only a ewer for a weapon—almost had him break out into a laugh. He tamed it to a single snort and an internal chuckle. He must have looked ridiculous, as silly as . . . as the Pargunese king in the stableyard. He had better not, he thought, share that with anyone else.

When he came out into the passage, all the Squires in the palace were there, watching as the burial guild lifted the bodies of their comrades to carry them away. Some were weeping; some looked grim.

The guilt he had always felt at the death of any of his soldiers smote him; who was he that others should die because of him?

Because he was a king? Because he had been a duke? Because—

Peace, came a voice. *Because you honor them and they honor you. And you did not kill them. When you die, see that your death honors me.*

Kieri felt his knees loosen and stiffened them. That was clear enough, though he wasn't sure which of them it was, Falk or Gird or the High Lord.

Does it matter? asked a different voice.

No, it didn't matter. What mattered were his people and his land.

His Squires crowded around him as he followed the bodies downstairs. The lower hall was full of people: servants, other Council members, a half-dozen elves. Two other bodies were there, already wrapped.

"The usual place of initial rest is too small for so many," the Seneschal said.

"The dining room?" Kieri asked.

"No place where food is served," the Seneschal said. "What about the salle? It has a stone floor, for the washing, and could be consecrated for this use for the time needed."

"Take it, then," Kieri said. He followed with the rest as the burial guild carried the five bodies to the salle; the armsmasters bowed to the Seneschal and formally released the salle for his use.

Once the bodies were laid ready for the care before burial, Kieri went back to the main palace to see the other assassin.

The man bound to a chair in Garris's office wore Halveric uniform, and his skin bore evidence of time in the hot, sun-blazing south. His face seemed familiar. Kieri glanced at Garris. "What have you learned?"

"He keeps saying he's really a Halveric soldier and he doesn't know anything about the other one."

"I *am* a Halveric," the man said. "I mean, not a Halveric by family, but I've been in Halveric Company eleven years."

"I don't believe you," Kieri said. He hitched a hip onto Garris's desk and looked into the man's eyes. The man blinked, as most people did, and unlike the most egregious liars Kieri had known. "But let's begin. Why didn't you give your message to a courier at the relay station?"

"Because there *wasn't* a courier at the relay station," the man said. "Nobody was there. Just horses in the stable. I thought they'd probably already been sent, but Captain Talgan said his message had to get through. So I left my horse, and a note, and took one of the others."

"Why did you think others had gone if horses were there?"

The man's brow furrowed. "Well . . . I guess I thought those were the horses they'd left—but they were fresh. Maybe they left enough earlier the horses had rested up—"

"And maybe you're lying. What happened at the next relay post? More missing couriers?"

"No—but they let me have a horse when I told them I had to get through."

"You didn't think to hand it over and go back to your captain?"

"No, sir—my lord—because I was already too far to be back by when Captain Talgan said, and if I was going to be over my time, I thought it didn't matter how much—and they said fine, because they were a courier short anyway."

That sounded almost reasonable. Kieri tried to think of something to ask that a Pargunese spy couldn't have learned by lurking near the camp. "Did you come north with Talgan in the summer?"

"Yes, sir—my lord."

"Where was your closest camp to Chaya?"

The man stared, as if surprised. "Why, sir—my lord—*you* know—it was just down behind the palace, in the water meadows."

"And what did you eat—what were your trail rations?"

"Trail rations! We didn't eat trail rations. We had food sent out from the palace. Bread still hot from the oven, roast meat, even some of those funny little pastries with pointy tops—"

The man must have been with the Halverics, then.

"What's Captain Talgan's nickname among the troops?" Kieri asked. "The one you think he doesn't know?"

The man flushed. "It's . . . not polite . . . sir."

"I know that. Most nicknames aren't. Come now, tell me."

"You won't tell him I said it?"

"No," Kieri said.

The man knew the nickname and came out with it, still red in the face. "And it's only because that time old Sergeant Manka, that's been retired these five years, saw him in the—"

"I know," Kieri said. He sighed. "Beldan, I now believe you are in fact a Halveric soldier, but I am not certain you aren't also a traitor. Why is your pouch wet?"

"I told Sir Garris—it was the snow, falling off the trees and landing on the saddle. But the inside's not wet; I opened it to check before I went to the jacks."

"Well, Beldan, we have a problem. You're a Halveric veteran or someone who knows more about Halveric Company than anyone not in it should. You've got plausible answers to my questions. But I lost five men and women this evening to an assassin and was nearly killed myself, so you will understand why I am cautious."

"Yes, my lord, but—but can I have some water?"

"Certainly." Kieri glanced at Garris, who poured a mug of water. Kieri sniffed it carefully before holding it to Beldan's lips. The man sipped.

Sier Halveric came to the door. "Sir King—oh—Beldan!"

"You know him?" Kieri asked.

"Of course," Sier Halveric said. "Aliam uses him as a courier between Halveric Steading and Chaya. What has he done?"

"Perhaps nothing," Kieri said. "You can vouch that he's been with Aliam a long time?"

"Years," Sier Halveric said. "And honest." He beckoned Kieri nearer the door. "But not very smart," he murmured.

"Then it's his misfortune that he arrived the same evening as an assassin," Kieri said. He stood up. "Release him, Garris." To Sier Halveric he said, "I grant this man to you as armsman, Sier Halveric. Keep him close with you, if you will, until Aliam's troops arrive; he can accompany them to the north."

"Gladly, Sir King."

As Sier Halveric led the man away, Kieri heard him say, "That wasn't the king—that was Duke Phelan! I'd know the Duke anywhere!"

Kieri shook his head at Garris's expression. "It doesn't matter . . . if he'd seen me crowned, he wouldn't have understood. We had a man in my company who called his new sergeant by the first one's name for years." He stretched. "And now I'm hungry, and we still have to read that message."

Garris pulled it out, sniffed it. "Just water, as he said." He handed it to Kieri.

The report was clear enough: Pargunese troops had come across in boats, under cover of darkness, and set fires. Talgan's troops, rangers, and Royal Archers had fought them back to the river, but more were preparing to come over.

"The fire seems natural," Talgan wrote. "But the wind may not be. Prisoners speak of 'scathefire' that will burn all to the bare rock, but will not say what it is or when it will be used. In the dawn-light, as I write, I can see boats and fires along the far shore, but not how many soldiers the Pargunese have. One prisoner said the old king was disgraced and only fools followed him, that the weavers' Lady was with his king—" Talgan had included a sketch of the boats and his best guess at the line of defense, which wavered inland in multiple places.

"So the worst is yet to come," Kieri said. More Pargunese would be coming across the river, and his troops had not been able to clear the riverside. At least one courier was missing completely, probably killed by the assassin, who had been ahead of Talgan's messenger.

"Our people are holding, at least," Garris said.

"I want the Pargunese back in Pargun," Kieri said. "We can't just hold—we must push them out."

"Sir King, there's a meal ready—"

"Good."

The Council members looked frightened again. Kieri exerted himself to reassure them: he had not been harmed, he was fine, and though Talgan was undoubtedly facing a difficult night, with more Pargunese coming across the river, the situation was far from hopeless.

"But if they do break through—and this scathefire, whatever it is, can't be quenched—"

"And where is the Lady?" asked another; several nodded.

Kieri wished he knew the answer to that; she had promised the land would not burn, but where was she?

CHAPTER THIRTY-SEVEN

Harway, on the Tsaian-Lyonyan border

A patrol of Girdish yeomen challenged the party from Verrakai Steading before they reached Thornhedge Grange. "There's trouble in Lyonya," a yeoman said. "It's them Pargunese again. They're not sneaking through our fields this time!"

"I'm a Lyonyan ranger," Arian said, showing her blackwood bow. "I had taken word to Verrakai—the new duke—about some Verrakaien the rangers killed awhile back, and now I must get back. What's the best way?"

"The border crossing on the road," the man said. "Anywhere else you're liable to be killed as a spy."

"I need to give Duke Verrakai's message to the Marshal and the Royal Guard," Gwenno said. "There's a message to send to the king—"

"He'll have had word," the man said. "Commander already sent a courier. But that won't be the only one, I'll be bound."

Harway buzzed like a kicked beehive when they reached it. They passed patrols in the streets as Gwenno led the way; the grange doors were open, and the Marshal stood in the light, giving orders to groups of yeomen. Gwenno paused and gave him Dorrin's message, then rode on through the town. Torches edged the riverside.

"I must go on," Arian said, when Gwenno turned up a side street toward the inn Dorrin had specified.

"Tonight? But shouldn't you rest?"

"I can't rest now," Arian said. "The taig would wake me; I need to be in Lyonya, with rangers or—or wherever I'm told to go."

"We'll come with you to the border, then," Gwenno said, and signaled her troop.

Arian had no idea what the border crossing was usually like, but this night it was lit with torches, with troops of both kingdoms alert and determined to stop any spies. On the Tsaian side, only Gwenno's insistence that Arian had been the guest of Duke Verrakai—that Gwenno knew her personally—got her through to the Lyonyans. There, the guards recognized her part-elven blood and the black-wood bow.

"Yes, yes, you're one of ours, but why were you in Tsaia?"

"Ranger business," Arian said. It had been, in a way.

"But you're a King's Squire, aren't you? We have a list—"

"That, too, but this wasn't Squire business. Where should I go, do you think?"

"Riverwash. They have a regular courier service from Chaya, and someone there will know where you're most needed. But watch out for Pargunese on the river road."

"Can you spare a change of horse? I've ridden this one all day."

"Of course. Take your pick." He waved at the picket line in the wind shadow of a shed.

Arian moved her gear to a sturdy dark bay with no white markings to show at night, gave her horse a quick rubdown, and put him in the shed. Then she mounted and rode away eastward, letting the taig flow through her. Despite the taig's disturbance, it was a relief to have that connection back.

A chill wind blew from the north, stronger than it had been as they rode toward Harway. This close to the disturbance, she could easily tell what it was. Men setting fires in the dry leaves . . . men sneaking through the woods. She was a few sandglasses' ride from Riverwash.

She met one patrol at a little less than half the distance, rangers who knew her name from old times. All they asked was of Tsaia: did the Tsaian king know, would Tsaia come to their aid? Arian told them what little she knew and rode on.

Suddenly light bloomed in the sky ahead and riverward, first a yellow glow and then white. The north wind strengthened, as if in response. Arian's skin drew up; the taig's reaction was instant and violent—pain, terror, anger, all mixed. She legged her horse into a gallop and very soon heard the roar of flames that towered into the night sky. This was not ordinary fire . . . terrified deer ran toward her along the road; her horse swerved to avoid them.

She felt first warmth, then heat, and reined in as the road angled north to Riverwash: the entire town was ablaze. What had once been buildings glowed and fell in like coals in a fireplace, white at the center. The wind now blew toward the fire, pulled in by its heat, but then came a stronger blast from the north, and the fire bent over and moved south, toward the road . . . toward her.

Her horse squealed, jigged, tried to whirl. Arian held it firm long enough to be sure there was nothing she could do—the fire was coming fast and would cut her off from the east—she could not cross its path before it arrived. She turned back to the west, the horse in a panicky run.

The taig beat at her, its pain her pain, until she almost felt her own skin crisping in an instant. Grief, too, as she thought of the lives in that town, all gone in a few instants of agony. *Singer of worlds, help us. Adyan Namer* . . . she rode between cold and fire, and met the patrol she'd seen before riding cautiously toward her.

"What is that?"

"Scathefire," Arian said. She looked back. The fire was roaring away south; where they stood they could see the trees silhouetted against it. "The king of Pargun—when he came and King Falkieri met him—warned of a fire weapon he called scathefire. It cannot be quenched with water, he said."

"What *is* it?" They sounded as frightened as she felt.

"I don't know. Riverwash is gone—the whole town—burned in a few moments, I would guess. I couldn't—I can't imagine how to stop it—and the taig—" She was shaking, hardly able to talk.

"We must go across after it passes," the patrol leader said. "As soon as it's cool enough."

"But someone must warn Tsaia," another said. "They must know what this fire can do. Harway's built of wood as much as Riverwash."

"May it blow back upon those who set it," said another.

"It is aiming for our king," Arian said. She imagined the fire as alive, sniffing out the way she and Kieri and the Pargunese king had gone from Riverwash to Chaya.

"Fires do not aim," the patrol leader said.

"This one does," Arian said. She could feel it through the taig, the eager questing nose of flame, the long sinuous body of it, spreading but slowly to either side . . . like a daskdraudigs of flame, almost.

"Almost," said the man at her side. He was afoot; she had not seen him before, but now saw him more clearly than the darkness should allow. Her mount snorted and backed away so fast, it almost sat on its hocks. A faint odor of hot metal came from him.

"Who are you?" the patrol leader asked. "A Pargunese spy?" He drew his sword.

"Pargun is of no interest to me," the man said. "Nor is your sword a threat. That fire, however, is. Who set that fire?"

"The Pargunese," Arian said. "Or some of them. The King of Pargun would not, but his brother would."

The man looked at her; behind his eyes, flames danced.

"You are a fire-setter," she said. "Your eyes—"

"But reflect the true fire," he said. "See?" He moved so the flames were behind him, and his eyes merely glittered in the reflected light.

"I'm sorry," Arian muttered.

"It is well," the man said. "Now, I must follow the fire, for reasons that do not concern you, and I must also find who set it. I would have one of you, just one, as my guide and companion. The rest should ride to warn others, as you were planning."

The patrol leader opened his mouth, but the man's glance silenced him; the man looked at each in turn and then at Arian. "I choose you. Come." He walked away east down the road. Arian's horse shuddered, then took a step forward.

"Arian, you can't—" the patrol leader started.

"I must," she said. She wondered why she was so certain of that, but she had no doubt.

When they reached the place where the fire had crossed the road, the man paused, knelt, and put his face to the stones that stood blackened out of ashes. Arian, watching closely, thought she saw his tongue emerge, touch the stone, and glow slightly.

He stood up once more looking north to what had been Riverwash, where a few yellow fires burned to either side. "Fools," he said. "They have no idea what they have loosed, or what the cost will be."

"Do you know what this fire is?" Arian asked.

"Indeed, yes," the man said. "But it will do you no good to know; it will only frighten you."

"I am frightened now," Arian said.

"No," the man said. "Not truly. Not yet. Tell me what you know of this fire, what the Pargunese king told you."

"He said it was a weapon, a gift of the Weaver—the Pargunese think of the demon we call Achrya as their benefactor, for she gave them lands the rockfolk had barred to them."

"The rockfolk had reason," the man said.

"And there was a hill of some kind . . . with black rock, I think he said. The rockfolk told them to stay away from it, but Achrya told them they should enter and take what they found."

"And what did they find?"

"The king did not say, other than unquenchable fire."

"I wonder if he knew." The man stopped, turned to look toward the river. Along the fire's track marched a group of soldiers, pike tips gleaming in the light that the fire still gave. "You should dismount," he said to Arian. "Your horse will bolt; you might be injured. Take your horse over there—" He pointed some distance away.

Arian did as she was told, aware of a slight compulsion, but it also seemed sensible. If this were a magelord—she hoped not a renegade Verrakai—magic would certainly terrify her horse.

When she looked back, she saw no man but a large lump in the road, like a pile of rocks. Her first thought was daskdraudigs, but daskdraudigs did not have faceted sides . . . glittering . . .

Scales, she thought, an instant before the long snout lifted and the great eyes opened. Yellow as fire, bright as fire . . . the eye on her side of its head lowered a lid for an instant and then focused forward.

She could feel her horse trembling and laid her hand on its neck. "Be easy . . . it won't hurt you." She hoped. The horse quieted, lowering its nose to nudge her.

The soldiers marched nearer; she could hear the tramp of their feet, the jingle of their mail. The dragon shed light and heat, not as hot as the flame but steady; Arian could see back down the scathe-fire's track to the soldiers.

"Well, now," the dragon said to them. "I'm afraid you have done me an injury." Its voice now had no human overtones.

They halted, congealed into a compact mass, pikes askew. The smell of hot metal grew stronger; it was like being in a forge.

"What you want?" their leader said, in the same accent Arian had heard from the Pargunese lords. His shiny breastplate gleamed in the dragon's light, and a plume waved from his pointed helmet. Arian had to admire his courage, if not his sense.

"Recompense," the dragon said. "For your discourtesy and your abuse of my hospitality."

"What—"

"You stole my property. You used my property to call attention to me and my kindred, and our special places. Were you not warned away?"

"No," the man said. "The Lady Weaver said we could—"

"Your Lady Weaver," the dragon said, "is but a morsel to season my feast." Its snout lowered almost to the ground. "Did not the rock-folk forbid your going beyond the great falls?"

"Yes, but what of it? They little folk weren't using that land."

"And did they not specifically forbid you to touch any hill with black stone, with a spine in the shape of mine?"

The man laughed. "The shape of yours? Do you think I don't know you're a bunch of men in a dragon puppet, like those at winter fairs that come to scare the children? There are no dragons, not in these days. They died out ages ago, before the magelords came north." He turned to his men. "Come, now: this is no true dragon. Once we stick those pikes in it, you'll see it's naught but painted wood and canvas, lit from within by lamps—it will burn like their towns and trees—" He drew his sword and marched forward, followed by his troop.

The dragon did not move; the great eyes closed, its light flickered.

"And don't think you can escape by running out the tail," the officer yelled. The men moved more quickly, encouraged . . . ran up and rammed their pikes into its snout. And clanged on the scales without effect.

"You made a mistake," the dragon said, opening its eyes again. "Not for the first time." Tilting back its head, lower jaw still on the ground, the dragon let out a single spurt of flame, white as that burning in the forest, and the men—all of them—were gone in an instant. It tilted its head toward Arian. "I do not like cruelty," it said, "but I will not tolerate discourtesy, and I am not fond of stupidity."

Arian did not move.

"And are you truly frightened now, Half-Song? Or have you will to move and wit to speak?"

"Do you blame all for one's error?" she asked.

The dragon turned its head completely toward her, and both eyes blinked. "I perceive you are not frightened, for that question is indeed one of wit, from a creature of mixed blood. It would indeed be unjust to blame all for one's error, but these men came from a city burnt to ash by fire they raised—all its life turned to naught. So would you defend them?"

"For their invasion of this land, no. For their destruction of River-wash and its people, no. For their intent to burn and destroy, no. But only one was discourteous."

"Ah. And you thought it was that alone to which I responded?" Without waiting for an answer, the dragon went on. "I admit the possibility of confusion, but discourtesy was not all for which they were judged. Would you, then, save your land of forests? And that king I perceive you love?"

"I would," Arian said.

"At what cost?"

"At any cost," Arian said. "Life for life, if need be, though—as you dislike stupidity—I would prefer to spend it only to advantage."

The dragon's tongue lolled out, steam rising from it. "Come, then," said the dragon. "I know you to be valiant, Half-Song: touch your tongue to mine."

"My horse," Arian said.

"Quiet him with your taig," the dragon said.

Arian held her horse's head and murmured the foal chant; the horse relaxed, its head drooping, its lower lip sagging. Arian looked back at the dragon. "Whatever you do to me, do no harm to the horse."

One eye opened wider. "Valiant, indeed, to give orders to a dragon."

"The horse did you no harm," Arian said. "Let it be."

"Then remove your things from its body," the dragon said. "Then should . . . something . . . happen, it will have no hindrance in its flight."

Arian wanted to ask if something would happen but instead untacked the borrowed horse and stacked her gear neatly as if she were camping for the night.

The dragon waited, silent and motionless, its light almost withdrawn, only the tongue laid out on the ground glowing dull red, steaming.

The nearer she came, the hotter it felt; the tongue, close up, glowed like red iron. She looked up; the dragon's eyes stared beside its snout, straight into her face.

Then she bent and forced herself to put out her tongue and touch the dragon's, against all instinct and reason.

It felt cold and tasted of mint.

Startled, Arian pulled back; the dragon reeled in its tongue and said nothing for a moment. Then it sighed, a warm gusty breath that smelled less of hot metal and somewhat of summer.

"Half-Song, you have surprised me, and I am not often surprised. You have done well and you please me, but there is work to do. Will the horse I promised not to harm live if turned loose here?"

"Maybe," Arian said. "But it is winter; it needs shelter and feed, and the place I planned to spend the night is no more."

The dragon sighed again. "I do not break promises; the horse must be taken where it can live. And yet I need you, Half-Song. Can it live here through a day?"

"Yes, but not many days."

"I do not need many days. Pick up that bow and quiver, and stand on my tongue."

Arian picked up bow and quiver, and stepped onto the tongue: it felt solid as stone beneath her even as she realized she was being drawn into the dragon's mouth, past teeth more than half her height.

"Do not be surprised at anything," the dragon said. She realized it was not speaking with its mouth, but in her mind. "There will be strangeness, for one of your nature."

Then the dragon gulped, and Arian felt herself sliding, sliding . . . and landed in something soft and springy. So, she thought, I've been swallowed. She felt around—whatever the space, it was warm, dry, and surprisingly comfortable. She settled down, her back against a lump soft as a pillow, and laid her bow across her knees. She dozed off, waking some unguessable time later when the dragon spoke to her again.

"Stand up, and hold your bow close to your body."

She did so, and in the next moment the softness under her feet hardened; the sides of the container—stomach?—closed in, and she was back in the dragon's mouth, peering out between the teeth. Ahead was a fast-moving shape of white flame, but the dragon was faster.

"String your bow."

Arian strung it. Questions raced through her mind, but she said nothing. The dragon, she hoped, knew what it was doing and questions might distract it.

"Take out five arrows; put them point down in my tongue."

In the tongue? Arian took out the arrows and set them point down; they sank a little into the tongue that felt so solid under her feet. As she looked, the steel points changed, glowing first red, then white, without losing any of their elegant deadly shape.

"That fire below is my child. I cannot consume it; it is against all law. And your arrows alone would not touch it, but now they are tipped with dragon fire. Aim where I tell you."

In another instant, she was standing on the ground, with the raging flames coming toward her, their heat beating in her face, and beside her stood the man-shape she had seen before, the flames reflected in his eyes. He held out a handful of her arrows.

"Right in the middle—see the purplish ones?"

Arian set an arrow to the string and drew; the blackwood bent as sweetly as ever, and she sent that arrow straight and true into the purple-white flames. At once, those flames died, leaving a black hole in the wall of fire.

"There next!" He handed her another arrow. Arian shot again, and again the flames died; the others sank a little. He handed her another, and directed the next shot and the next. Each time the remaining flames lowered, and with the last shot, they all sank to nothing. The yellow fires to either side also wavered and died by themselves. The wind softened to nothing.

"Like daskin arrows for a daskdraudigs," Arian said.

The man murmured something she could not understand and

then sighed. "Yes," he said finally. "And also no. For a daskdraudigs pierced by daskin arrows returns to its true self, which is stone, freed of the evil that animated it. Dragonfire arrows kill the young and destroy their true nature."

"That was . . . a young dragon?"

"Our young are perilous, even for their fathers," the man said. "What they are, we all have been, but those of us suffered to live grow old and understand the consequences of actions, ours and others."

"Why do you call me Half-Song?" Arian asked. "Because I am half-Sinyi?"

"It might have been that, but no. You are half a song this land wants to sing. The other half of the song approaches, but the time is not yet."

"Kieri?"

"Your names have no meaning for me. Sorrow-King, I name him."

"He's coming here?"

The man looked at her, his eyes now glittering fire though the other fires were out.

"And we must go."

"No! I must see him; I must tell him—"

The man's shape vanished; the dragon returned, bulking huge in the darkness; only its eyes were alight. "This is not over; more fire will come before I find all my foolish sons. One who should be here is not; we must learn why, and fetch her hence."

"The Lady . . ." Arian breathed. "But she hates me."

The dragon's eyelids lifted. "What matter, when her realm is imperiled? I must have you, for the strength of your bow, and the land must have her, to command the taig—you cannot do that, can you?"

"No," Arian said. "I can sense it, and help it, but not command it."

"Then once more, come. There is no time to waste; by dark tomorrow we must have that immortal back, who should never have left."

Arian found the experience as strange as the first time and more disquieting. The Lady had laid glamour on her once—what if she did it again? What if the Lady bespelled her into thinking she did not love Kieri? Could she resist all the Lady's magery? If the Lady was so angry with Arian that she had stayed away, let the forest be burned—

but that was a violation of the taig. The Lady could be wrong; the Lady could be selfish . . .

But when the dragon once more let her see out, it was another fiery scene, and once more she thrust arrow tips into the dragon's tongue and took them out tipped with the dragon's fire . . . and once more the arrows stopped the scathefire. This time, others were close enough to hear: the shouts of terror as the flames towered over the trees, the shouts of relief when the flames fell.

They left quickly, and the next thing Arian saw out the dragon's mouth was a small, beautiful vale surrounded by mountains. She had no idea where it was, physically, but she knew what it was: the elfane taig, the holy center of the Ladysforest. Had the Lady come here to calm herself? Or sulk?

"It is a complicated matter," the dragon said. It had not changed back to a human form this time. "The history between us—the Sinyi and dragonkind—reflects certain fundamental differences in our natures. We are more comfortable, for the most part, with rockfolk, and of the rockfolk, with the kapristi, who are of the Law."

Arian had no idea how this bore on the problem of scathefire or her relationship to Kieri.

"I am very old," the dragon said. "And it is the nature of dragons to grow more wise as they age. It is not so for all." It rubbed its chin on the knuckles of one foot. "Sinyi . . . the Sinyi have beauty and wit and grace and share with the First Singer and Adyan the gift of making beauty. What they do not have is the clarity and logic of elder dragons: they are unable to think out the long consequences, and thus they make foolish mistakes."

"Are you saying . . . the Lady makes mistakes?"

"Flessinathlin Orienchayllin Belaforthsalth," the dragon said, drawing out the names. "If she were a dragon, and not Sinyi, the world would be different." One eye blinked. "I do not say perfect, but the problems would not be the same. And she would have been a most difficult dragonlet to bring to wise maturity, not only because of her sex."

"Female dragons are less wise?"

A huff of hot air answered that. "You have no need to know more of us, Half-Song, than pertains to the moment. I lay the foundation of your understanding where it is needed, and on it you must build a sound structure of your own." Arian said nothing; the dragon gave a short nod and went on. "The Lady of whom we speak is hasty for a Sinyi, and for a Sinyi more apt to risk conflict, though in both far less than humanfolk. It was her choice to center the elfane taig not only here, in a valley apt for such by its shape—a chalice to hold wonder— but to construct underground, in the rock, the physical center. She purchased stone-right of a dwarf king; she hired kapristi, gnomes, to carve the stone, though elven artists decorated it.

"You know what happened," the dragon went on. "Evil came— partly by other actions she took—and it became the banast taig, cursed. She had the courage to cut away that part of her power trapped there, accept diminishment, and she had the strength to still rule the Ladysforest. But when the evil was destroyed—and I have heard only that a paladin accomplished that—she yearned to rebuild the elfane taig as it had been, warding it more closely, and for that she sought once more the help of rockfolk."

"She's never liked rockfolk," Arian said, before she could stop the words.

"It is wise, when asking help of those one does not like, to con- sider well all consequences and treat one another with great care," the dragon said. "Words had been said, when the Lady first de- parted, words of blame to the kapristi as if the banastir were their fault, as if the evil entered through some flaw in the construction, which was not true. Perhaps the Lady had forgotten those words, but kapristi do not forget. The kapristi never thought stone-right should have been sold; that quarrel smoldered between kapristi and hakke- nen through times that would be long for you. And the dwarves, while always claiming their right to sell their own stone-mass if they wished, resented the Lady's decision to ask for kapristi workmen— not just once, but twice."

"She probably thought it would balance her favor to buy from dwarves but hire gnomes in the first place, and would be an insult to gnomes not to hire them the second time."

"A failure of foresight," the dragon said, "or understanding of the nature of the rockbrethren. As she failed to anticipate the results of her actions before."

She should not be listening to criticism of the Lady, even though she herself had reason to criticize. But she was Kieri's Squire, and Kieri's love, and nothing to the Lady but a problem to be tossed away. A confusion of feelings emerged in speech. "But why am I here? Is she?"

"She is below." The dragon tipped his snout to point at the ground. "Kapristi and elf together—as kapristi insisted—began cleaning out the debris left by the banastir the winter it was destroyed. There was much foulness, and some were sickened. Just lately, Flessinathlin arrived in haste, and in haste descended to view the progress made by those she hired." The dragon paused. "She was displeased, because work had scarce begun on rebuilding. Words were spoken by elf and kapristi, and none would share blame with the other."

"How do you know all this?" Arian said. "Where do you live?"

Another gust of hot, iron-smelling air. "I live where I please," the dragon said, "and where it does *not* please me for all to know. As for how I know what I know . . . I have a relationship with the hakkenen and kapristi, and so they speak to me."

Arian felt her brows rise. Before she could think how to ask, the dragon spoke again.

"It is not a matter that concerns you," it said. "What does concern you, Half-Song, is that the Lady of the Ladysforest is below, and cannot emerge without aid. The kapristi resented her words, and left, sealing the rock behind them."

"How did she get down there?"

"By a—" The dragon uttered a sound that had no meaning for Arian, but a picture built in her mind, a pattern similar to other elven patterns of power she had seen. "The kapristi thought it just to deny her the use of it to return outward. I disagree, though I also do not approve what she said, or her failure to foresee the results of her words and actions."

"But she has the taig—she can move with it anywhere, in an instant—"

"Not there, not now. She went under stone, into the realm of the rockfolk, and her power is with the living world, out here." The dragon looked at her. "But you are Half-Song; you have some strengths she does not. Especially when I lend you mine. Can you still see that pattern I drew in your heart?"

Arian reflected. It was there, clear and crisp as if graved in stone. Stone? She glanced at the dragon.

"Yes, stone. You need to go there, and repair the pattern the kapristi altered, so that she and her people can use it to return to the surface. If I go down, I will disrupt the work, possibly destroy it. It would be better, indeed, if she agreed to rebuild on the surface, and stay within her own realm, returning that below to the rockbrothers. But you are the one to tell her so."

"She hates me!" Arian said again. "She doesn't want Kieri to marry me! She could cast a glamour—"

"If you save her life and aid her to save the forest taig, she may change her mind," the dragon said. "But even if she does not, at least you will have saved the taig. If it concerns you."

"Of course it does!" Arian felt as if she were arguing with her mother. "But how can I go down, if she cannot come up?"

"Ah. Well, it will be another strange journey. Are you ready?"

CHAPTER THIRTY-EIGHT

C linging to the roof of the dragon's mouth while it pierced
earth and the rock ceiling of the great hall—carefully, to
cause the least damage—and then riding the dragon's tongue
down and down into the silvery elf-light to confront a very angry
elven queen—would not have been Arian's chosen activity for the
day, but she had no choice.

Arian caught only a few details of the glittering mosaic in the
upper part of the great hall, simulating the leaves of an early-summer
forest, or the great columns like tree trunks, before the dragon's
tongue set her down and withdrew. At one end of the long hall a dais
rose four steps from the smooth stone floor, and there the Lady stood,
surrounded by attendant elves.

"*You!*" said the Lady, as if everything were Arian's fault. Her
anger, thick with enchantment, pressed on Arian's mind. Everything
she could think of to say sounded ridiculous. The Lady's own escort
and the elves who had been working underground formed a solid
mass behind the Lady herself. All glowered at her. "You traitor," the
Lady said. "You figured out some way to trap us here—"

"No," Arian said. "You trapped yourself by your rudeness to the
rockfolk." She could hardly believe those words were coming out of
her mouth, or that she held off the Lady's enchantment so easily.

"How could you—?"

"We have little time," Arian said. "The taig needs you, Lady, and

I must repair the . . . the pattern." She could not make the sound the dragon made.

"You can't; it's broken. It was not of my making." The Lady drew herself up and folded her arms.

"I can repair it."

"You're only a half-elf, daughter of a—" The arms came down; the Lady scowled.

Arian kept her own voice level. "You have said you do not know the pattern: I do. Will you sulk here under stone and let your forest burn?"

"It will not burn—I would know if—"

"It is burning *now,*" Arian said. "The Pargunese brought scathefire from stolen dragon eggs."

The Lady swayed where she stood; Arian could see the shock on all the elves' faces. "I didn't know—how could I not *know*? I can't reach it—"

Arian felt a grim satisfaction: the Lady now felt what she had imposed on Arian. "Will you come, or no?"

"If you can repair the pattern—do so!" one of the other elves said.

The Lady moved aside, and Arian came forward. Once the dais had been inlaid with patterns done in mosaic, some purely elven in origin, but the most important—for the moment—the one the dragon had shown her. Now that pattern—and those within an arm's length of it—were gone, revealing rough gray stone. Heaps of colored stone chips, each heap a different shade of blue or red or green, filled the back of the dais.

"They left us these," the Lady said, gesturing at the piles. "Taunting us . . . for only rockfolk, they said, had the stone-wit to know how to place them and bind them in stone so they would stay if I stood on them. Can you repair what full-born elves cannot?"

"Yes," Arian said, once more surprising herself. Was she that sure? It must be the dragon's aid. "But Lady, you must be prepared to return this place to those who made it and those who gave you stone-right."

"I cannot!" the Lady said. "It is the elfane taig!"

"It is only elfane taig where the Lady can sense the taig and wear the elvenhome as a cloak," Arian said. "Here, under stone, is not your domain." She pointed to the ceiling. "There—where the taig longs for your return—is your domain and your duty."

Arian could feel the other elves' astonishment and dismay.

"You lecture *me* on my duty? You, whose father—"

"I have fought the fire you did not even know was burning," Arian said. "Where were you when the scathefire came, when the king needed your aid? Here, under stone—not in the real elfane taig. You did not even know the taig was in peril. Did not the First Singer charge the Sinyi with its protection?"

Shocked silence answered her. The Lady, after a long moment, bowed her head.

Arian said no more, but turned to the problem at hand. The scarred stone was no longer a circle but a rough oblong. Arian took one of her arrows and—fixing the pattern in her mind—set its point to the rock and began to trace the outline of the pattern. She paid no attention to the gasps of surprise as the arrow, its tip glowing, sank into the stone and behind its motion a groove opened. She concentrated on the pattern until she had completed it. As the dragon had first shown it to her, it had been only dark lines on gray stone, but now she felt an urge to give it color: she did not know why.

The others did not move or speak as she went back and forth, colored chips flowing through her hands, each to the place she knew was right. The light and dark blue, the bright and dark red, the single green, the rare touches of gold and silver. Moved by another impulse, she drew her sword and traced the now-colored lines in a different order than she had originally drawn the pattern. Now the colored chips flowed together, and the pattern lay fresh, unbroken.

When she looked again at the Lady, tears marked the queen's face. The Lady met Arian's gaze; Arian saw great sorrow there. Then the Lady turned to her entourage. "If a half-elf can do here what we full elves cannot, it is indeed not our place. We must give it up. The blame is mine; I wasted your time, brothers and sisters, long ago and once again, and offended those to whom the Singer gave the dominion of stone. I swear to you, I did so with good intent, but good intent does not excuse ill results. We must now return to the Ladysforest and do what we may for the taig, but afterward, if it is your will, another may challenge for my place."

"No, Lady!" Several elves protested, stepping forward. The Lady held up a hand to forestall them.

"It grieves me to say, but I was wrong; the taig is bearing the pain of my error, and the taig is—was—in my charge. Let us go quickly and spend ourselves in its defense." To Arian she said, "I am sorry you were hurt, child, by my anger. It was wrong of me to take, even for a moment, your taig-sense from you. I wanted only the best for my grandson, who had been so cruelly hurt so young." She stepped on the pattern Arian had made and offered Arian her hand. "Come with me, if you will, and I will do what I can to mend what I broke. Though I know you have another helper—" She glanced at the ceiling.

Go, said the dragon in Arian's mind.

Her resentment against the Lady was less important than the taig, than Kieri. She took the Lady's hand.

Once out of the stone, the Lady's connection with the elvenhome Forest moved them all to the edge of a long, straight ash-colored scar through the forest. Arian saw Kieri and a small group—Orlith among them, standing on the scathefire track—turn to the elvenhome light. And to one side, the dark man with flame-colored eyes.

CHAPTER THIRTY-NINE

By the third day of the attack Kieri felt that the situation had stabilized—though he still feared the magical fire the Pargunese king had mentioned, it had not yet been used. Someone had found the bodies of the couriers the assassin had killed, and another assassin—less skilled than the first—had been caught. Though Kieri's force was able to drive the Pargunese to the river in some places, the enemy still had a foothold on the south bank. Aliam and his remaining force would only now be hearing of the attack; it would be more than a hand of days before they could reach Chaya.

"Where is the Lady?" Kieri demanded of Orlith every day, and every day Orlith had no answer. "Why does she not come or send aid? Does she want the land burned to the bare rock as they've threatened? And where are the other elves?"

"I do not know," Orlith said. The elf looked almost as tired as Kieri felt, his usual bland expression strained. "I cannot sense her anywhere. I do not think she has been killed: the taig would surely react to that."

"The taig has enough anguish," Kieri said.

"I know. And before you ask again, I do not know where the other elves are: your uncle Amrothlin, for instance. It is as if the Ladysforest itself were withdrawn, though I can sense it, far off near the mountains. Even if she went below—"

"Below?"

"Into the elfane taig, the stronghold—even there I should be able to sense her, but I cannot."

For an instant, Kieri's mind threw up the memory of Arian's father, Dameroth, talking of Paks . . . of places no human should see . . . the elfane taig? Was that one of the places? He put that aside; it couldn't matter now.

"Without the Lady, or the guidance of another with her powers, the taig is defenseless," Orlith said. "If worse comes, neither of us can raise its full power."

"At the battle on my way here, a Kuakgan raised the taig—"

"We do not speak of Kuakkgani!" Orlith said.

"We speak of death and the destruction of the taig," Kieri said. "Surely you could cooperate long enough to save it."

"They are an abomination," Orlith said. "It cannot be."

"The taig doesn't think so," Kieri said. "And the Kuakgan I met was a healer; I saw him heal both man and horse."

"Oakhallow," Orlith said. "He is . . ." He paused and shook his head. "If the Lady is indeed gone, by her will or another's, then by the Singer's commands it is our charge, we remaining elves, to defend and uphold the taig by any means we can."

"So I believe," Kieri said. He felt a tiny trickle of hope. A Kuakgan might know what this mysterious scathefire was, might know how to heal what had already burned in more normal fires.

"You could command me," Orlith said. Kieri stared at him; Orlith, like the other elves, had made it clear that except for associating—unwillingly—with humans, he considered himself the Lady's subject, not Kieri's. "If the Lady lives, and returns, and I have accepted a Kuakgan into her realm, she will blame me."

"It is my decision," Kieri said. "And my realm, since she is not here." Nonetheless, he had no idea how to ask a Kuakgan for help. Master Oakhallow had come from Brewersbridge at Paks's request, but that was days away, even for a courier, and he had none to spare. That there were other Kuakkgani he knew, but not how to find one. Perhaps the Seneschal . . .

"Yes, Sir King," the Seneschal said. "There are a few kuakkgannir in Chaya, though their Kuakgan has her grove in Tsaia. But there may be a way . . . shall I ask?"

"Yes," Kieri said. "At the least, we must warn anyone with an interest in the taig of the danger . . . if that other weapon is worse than fire."

That night the first scathefire attack came. Faster than couriers could ride, the path of purple-white flame raced down from River-wash, near enough that the light of the flames could be seen to the north from the highest tower in the palace. Then—abruptly, just as the flickering of the flames replaced the glow, so close they were—they died. The dark returned, but the anguish of the wounded taig did not quiet. More than the trees had died.

By midday, Kieri knew that there had been two such fires, one halted farther away from Chaya but the nearer one, less than a day's ride. "I must see it," he said, over the objections of his Council. "If my magery can do anything to stop it, I need to know what it is before I can fight it."

Orlith and two of the remaining elves in Chaya rode with him, along with four Squires and—to his surprise—both senior armsmasters.

"It's not the first time I've been to battle with you," Siger said. "Magic fires I don't understand, but assassins in the bushes I do. And Carlion wants to see if my boasted ability to detect traps is real."

As the winter afternoon waned under a skim of high cloud, they rode north to find what the fire had done. An acrid stench met them as the breeze blew steadily out of the winter sky. The taig roiled below and around; their mounts jigged, snorting and switching their tails. Kieri tried to comfort the taig and knew Orlith and the elves were doing the same, but the wounds were too great.

Well before they reached the actual site, they could see a gap in the forest ahead—light pouring in where trees, even in winter, had scattered it. Then the extent of the damage spread before them, a wide swath heading north. All within it was consumed to soot and ash; trees on the margin were blackened, limbs on one side burnt away. Kieri shuddered. All the horses shied and refused to go nearer.

"It's like a great road leading north," Siger said. "Wider than the Guild League roads, even . . . but why didn't it spread to the side?"

"A weapon they could aim," Kieri said. "And halt here, as a warning of what they could do."

Carlion was off his horse, tossing his reins to a henchman, and walked ahead. "Sir King, there are tracks here. Two humans, both in boots, and some other marks I do not understand."

"They launched it there to burn back north?" Kieri asked.

"Not with the wind we had last night," Siger said. He, too, dismounted and looked at the ground. "Magical flames or not, it would move with the wind, not against it."

"Then—how did they get ahead of it to stop it?" Kieri asked. He dismounted; he wanted to see any tracks for himself.

"Someone already in place," Siger said. "But how they stopped it, once the flames were moving like that, I don't know."

"There's an arrow," Carlion said, pointing. He stepped forward.

"Hold!" Kieri said. Carlion stopped, looking back at him in surprise. "We don't know if the magic is exhausted: I don't want to risk you."

"Better me than you, Sir King. You have another good armsmaster, and the world has more of my kind than yours." Carlion walked out onto the ash some distance and bent to pick up something. Then he whirled to face Kieri.

"Sir King! It is a King's Squire's arrow! One of your Squires!" He looked around. "And there's another—and another—"

"How did the shafts survive?" Kieri asked. "It is not possible . . ."

"I'll bring them all," Carlion called. "Garris knows their marks."

Shortly he was back, showing the five arrow shafts. "I'd think the shafts would burn, leaving only the metal tips, at most," Kieri said. He picked up one of the shafts—scorched, indeed, but the pattern of rings that identified the archer still faintly visible on the blackened shaft. He turned it in the dimming light, trying to see . . . and his heart stopped, then thumped loudly before racing.

"Garris will know," Carlion said again.

"I know," Kieri said. It was hard to breathe. "Arian . . . she was coming back to . . . to warn . . ." Tears burned in his eyes; he could not blink them back before they ran down his cheeks into his beard. "She died bravely, as she would," he said, handing the shaft back to Carlion.

"My lord—" Carlion reached out, but Kieri shook his head.

"Just—let me—" He turned his face to the north wind, struggling against the white rage that he must not indulge. White rage had brought this fire—not his, but someone's. He had to breathe, he had to go on living, he had to be the king his people needed, and the man Arian had loved.

He looked at Orlith. "What can you tell about this fire—what is it?"

Orlith sniffed. "There's a scent—" He too dismounted and walked forward. "Iron . . . stone . . . blood. It has been long indeed since I smelled it—I should know it, but I cannot quite . . ." He bent to the tracks the armsmasters had found. "Here a half-elf . . . but this, that wears man's boots, does not smell like a man, nor does the taig regard it so."

"What about these marks?" Siger asked. "I can smell something, but I don't know what."

Orlith bent to those and then jerked upright. "Singer's grace! It cannot be . . . they never come to settled lands anymore—"

"What?" Kieri asked.

"A dragon," Orlith said. "A dragon was here."

"A dragon burned this? The Pargunese have a dragon on their side?"

"No! Never!" Orlith glanced at the other elves. "Dragons—adult dragons—are also creations of the First Singer, and they revere life and justice. They do not interfere in human affairs unless humans interfere in theirs, and we did not. But Pargun, it may be, did. Tell me, did you ever hear of dragons' eggs?"

"If you mean that old folktale where a fool finds a dragon's egg and tries to sell the jewels inside, yes. But that's just a story—parents use it to scare their children, but everyone knows there are no dragons anymore. Camwyn got rid of them."

"Not . . . quite." The speaker, barely visible in the gloom of the undergrowth to the side of the road, stepped out into it. Kieri's height, dressed like any winter traveler at first glance, leather cloak over leather jerkin, close-fitting shirt and trousers, tall boots. High cheekbones, long nose, slightly mottled dark skin, and surprisingly light tawny eyes gleaming from beneath the hood of his cloak.

Carlion, Siger, and two King's Squires had drawn blades all around Kieri before he could say anything. Kieri noticed the man wore no sword, not even a dagger.

"Dragon," Orlith said, hardly loud enough to hear.

The man tipped his head to Orlith, then looked back at Kieri. "You weep," he said. "Do you grieve for the land?"

"Yes," Kieri said. He did not believe the man was a dragon, though he was strange. Perhaps he was a Kuakgan. "I cannot heal this myself; I was hoping for a Kuakgan to help me."

The man looked hard at the elves then back at Kieri. "Do you consider the consequences of your acts?"

"Yes," Kieri said.

"And what did your Sinyi tell you about Kuakkgani?"

"They do not like them, for some quarrel I do not understand."

"I do," the man said.

"But the taig's need is greater than a quarrel," Kieri said.

"Quarrels are rarely just," the man said. He glanced back down the road. "Those horses should be farther away."

"Who are you?" Kieri asked.

"Who are *you*?" the man answered with a mocking smile. "Do you have authority to demand my name?"

"I am the king," Kieri said. "If you are human, and in this realm, then yes, I do."

"Well, king, I am not human, though I take this shape to cause less fear. My name belongs to me alone, but the Sinyin there was correct: I am a dragon. Over whom, I must inform you, you have no authority whatsoever."

"Did you burn this?"

"No. I stopped it, but not alone." The man tipped his head back and pulled something from his mouth—longer, impossibly longer. A blackwood bow. "The arrows you found came from this bow, and the woman who sent the arrows into the fire—"

"Died there," Kieri said. It came out half gasp, half cry.

"No," the man said. "She did not die."

"She is alive? Where is she?" Kieri's skin prickled up with a sudden chill.

"Coming," the man said. He looked Kieri straight in the face. "She is a very brave person, but she is only half the song. Are you the other half?"

Arian alive—could it be? Arian alive! Cold vanished in a rush of joy that warmed. "Yes," Kieri said. "I am."

"She is wiser," the man said. "But you are not unwise, and you know what she does not. Perhaps you are what the land needs . . . come near."

"My lord, no!" his Squires said as he took a step forward.

"I must," Kieri said.

"I will change, and offer you what I offered her," the man said. "But those horses—I do not wish anyone to be hurt."

"Dismount," Kieri said to the others, "and lead the horses back."

"You say you care for the taig," the man said, as the others did as commanded. "What would you give to save the taig?"

"Whatever is necessary," Kieri said.

"Have all your deeds been just?"

"No," Kieri said. "And though I regret those that were not, it does not change what came of my injustice."

"Perhaps indeed you are as wise as Half-Song. Abide there: I change."

The man's shape dissolved and then resolidified larger, larger still, darker, the faint smell of hot metal much stronger now. Then the dragon crouched before him, dark as old bronze, each scale distinct, the long snout, the great glowing eyes, the coils of tail.

"Come, now . . . touch your tongue to mine. Let me taste your justice, O king, and let you taste mine." Kieri stared a moment as a long red tongue slid out of the dragon's mouth. The air shimmered above it; the surface looked like red-hot iron, a few flakes of ash on its surface trembling from the heat.

What would you give for the taig? Arian, he was sure, would have risked this and more. He knelt, feeling the heat pouring off the dragon's tongue; it took all his courage to force his tongue from behind his teeth and touch it.

To his tongue it was hard, barely warm, and tasted of iron and spices. The tongue was withdrawn; as he lifted his head, the dragon winked at him. "You are a man of justice, whom anger no longer rules. Half-Song has chosen well. You will prosper."

Kieri had just stumbled to his feet when the dragon said, "They are come." Kieri turned and saw the silvery light of the elvenhome kingdom moving toward them down the road, within it the Lady and many other elves. The light washed out around him; he felt its effect on the taig where he stood, like cool salve on a burn.

Kieri wanted to demand of the Lady where she had been, but the look of grief on her face stopped him. She came and knelt to him, as she had not before. In a voice like liquid silver, she said, "Sir King, I am sorry. I should have been here, to know I was needed and be at your side. I am at your command."

She looked up then, the beauty of her face astonishing even in that crisis; from her violet eyes a few tears spilled. Despite his anger at her absence, despite the warnings of his sister's bones, Kieri felt pity for her, an immortal humbling herself before him. She too was a ruler; she was his elder in all things; whatever she had done, it was wrong for her to kneel like that. "Rise," he said. She stood, graceful as ever, but her shoulders drooped just a little, like a scolded child's.

She ignored, or did not see, the dragon still clear to Kieri's eyes in the road. Kieri glanced at the dragon—that eye of flame seemed to mock him—or the Lady. Confusion held him for a moment—what did she mean? He looked from her to the other elves and back at her—at the other elves—before speaking again.

"You know best how to help the taig, which sorely needs your aid," he said. "But I don't understand why you didn't come before." All the times before, he meant.

"I went beyond the taig's reach, and was trapped there," the Lady said. "I was wrong to do so." Was it really contrition in her voice, or a glamour? He wanted to believe her, but could such pride as he had seen her display before ever be truly humbled? "I would be there yet, ignorant of this attack, and helpless, if not for your betrothed."

"My betrothed—"

"Unless you regret your choice," Arian said, stepping out from between other elves. "For my flight that day—"

At the sight of her, Kieri forgot his concerns about the Lady. "Never," he said. "I regret only the hours we were not together. When I saw your arrows—I thought you had died—" His voice caught; he did not know which of them had moved, but she stood near enough now he caught the scent of her hair.

"When the taig woke me, that night in Dorrin Verrakai's steading—" Arian began.

"You went to *Dorrin*?"

"Time passes," said the dragon. "And enemies are not far to seek. I have business with them, but you, Sinyi and Sorrow-King and Half-

Song, have work to do as well." It lifted Arian's bow with its tongue and handed it to her. "You left this behind in the elfane valley."

"Thank you," Arian said. "Do you need me?"

"No, Half-Song. He does—" The dragon flicked its tongue toward Kieri.

"Lord dragon," the Lady said with another bow. She sounded more like her former self, regal and gracious. "Forgive me that I did not see you—"

The dragon cocked its head. "Seeing is not of the eyes only, Lady, as you surely know."

An expression touched the Lady's face that Kieri did not recognize. "Lord dragon, I accept your judgment."

The dragon huffed out a small breath with a hint of sulfur. "I have given no judgment yet, Lady, for the deeds are not yet completed. Have you healed your quarrel with the rockbrothers?"

"Not fully, but I renounce any claim to the rock-mass, as Arian said I must. For the rest, I will meet with dasksinyi when this crisis is over."

"Excellent. May you prosper, then, as Sinyi should prosper, in harmony and grace." The dragon vanished; a swirl of ash blew over them all and then settled.

"My lord king," the Lady said, "you have labored long on a task not entirely yours. I am here now, and many others: let us lift the burden, at least for a night and a day. Rest yourself, you and your betrothed."

Only elvenhome light gave guidance now, for dark had come, and Kieri could feel the taig reacting to something he thought might be invading troops. But now the Lady spread out her power, reaching to the edge of the forest, and the elves with her joined their power to hers.

"You can see and feel our work," the Lady said, when he hesitated. "Trust me now: I promise, when you are rested and seek me again, I will come to you, or bring you to me, as the taig needs and the Singer commands." She looked earnest enough; the other elves nodded. Could he really trust her, changeable as she was? Orlith nodded at him from behind the Lady's back, and he trusted Orlith now as much as he did any elf.

He had frightened subjects in Chaya who needed him; he had work to do and orders to give. Though he had healed a king and once raised the taig to save a friend, now he felt how much greater was the Lady's power, and that of the other elves. They could do what he could not. He looked at Arian and wanted nothing more than to reach Chaya in an instant, with her in his arms.

"I will come back," he said, hoping it was the right decision.

The elvenhome light strengthened, as the Lady turned from him, and he could feel the taig's anguish ease a little. He turned to Arian. "You have a long tale to tell," he said. "And we have a long ride this night, so I hope to hear it all."

O n the way back to Chaya, Arian rode double with another Squire until they reached a relay station; then she rode beside Kieri, and the others moved aside enough for them to talk. Arian told her story; Kieri winced at her description of taig-blindness, her realization that the Lady had imposed that taig-blindness, and listened fascinated to her analysis of Dorrin as duke, her introduction of Dorrin to the taig.

"So the Lady is more than fickle," he said. "She is cruel as well."

"I am not sure," Arian said.

"But she hurt you—"

"There is something—the dragon said she had made mistakes in the past, and that she had lost some power when she freed herself from the banast taig. But my feeling is that it is not all her own doing."

"You grew up here, among elves," Kieri said. "You are more easily entranced, perhaps."

"Perhaps," Arian said. "Certainly when I was younger, the very thought of the Lady of the Ladysforest . . . I was awed; we all were. But when she offered to give up her rule—"

"What?"

"There, underground. She did, and most protested, but I saw one or two who smiled before they protested. I had no time to think about it then, but now . . . It seems to me, Sir King—"

"Kieri. Always Kieri to you."

"It seems to me her mistakes might be, at least in part, arranged by another. Torfinn of Pargun had his traitors in the family: why not her?"

"You think she bears no responsibility for her deeds? For refusing my requests, for instance?"

"No. I do not condone her fickleness toward you, or her other mistakes, or her neglect of the taig's need. And she may indeed bear the whole guilt . . . but perhaps not."

"Do you believe her expressions of shame and contrition?" Kieri asked.

Arian looked thoughtful. "I believe she does not intend evil. I am not sure she knows what it is until its seed has sprouted and put out leaves."

"A dangerous ruler," Kieri said.

"Yes." Arian rode silently for a time, then said, "I find sorrow in my heart for her. Perhaps because we—I—thought her perfect, robed in elven light, so beautiful, so strong . . . we wanted her to be what she seemed."

Kieri, too, rode in silence awhile. "I felt pity only when she knelt to me," he said finally. "And wondered if she meant me to feel that, or if she felt what she seemed to feel. With elves, so much is seeming, illusions, glamours . . . I cannot completely trust her, not now." He glanced at Arian; even in dark night, he was sure of the expression on *her* face and that it showed exactly what she was. "I trust you," he said. "You are real."

It was midmorning the next day before Kieri and Arian rode into the palace courtyard, both stained with soot and ash, thirsty and hungry enough, as Kieri put it, to eat an ox, including the hooves and horns. Whatever the dragon had done when it left them, no more scathefire burned south of the Honnorgat. Low clouds had moved in, promising snow, moisture to ease the burnt ground.

Kieri went up to change; it hurt to know that Joriam was dead, but staying dirty was no honor to him. He relished his hot bath, his clean clothes, the—apparent, at least, however temporary—safety of his kingdom. Outside his window, the first fat flakes drifted down.

Dressed, and hungrier than ever, he went downstairs, flanked by Berne and Suriya. He could smell the roast meat, the new bread. Arian came in the front entrance, wearing her Squire's tabard again, as Garris emerged from his office.

"You're back," Garris said to Arian. "Put you back on the rotation?"

"No," Kieri said, before Arian could answer. He could feel himself grinning, and Arian, pink-cheeked, was grinning, too. "Arian has a special assignment."

Former Marine ELIZABETH MOON is the author of many novels, including *Victory Conditions, Command Decision, Engaging the Enemy, Marque and Reprisal, Trading in Danger,* the Nebula Award winner *The Speed of Dark,* and *Remnant Population,* a Hugo Award finalist. After earning a degree in history from Rice University, Moon went on to obtain a degree in biology from the University of Texas, Austin. She lives in Florence, Texas.

ABOUT THE TYPE

This book was set in Apollo, a typeface designed by Adrian Frutiger in 1962 for the founders Deberny & Peignot. Born in Interlaken, Switzerland, in 1928, Frutiger became one of the most important type designers since World War II. He attended the School of Fine Arts in Zurich between 1948 and 1951, where he studied calligraphy. He received the Gutenberg Prize in 1986 for technical and aesthetic achievement in type.